Candace Camp is a New ⟨⟩ S0-AFE-476 of over sixty novels of contemporary and historical romance. She grew up in Texas in a newspaper family, which explains her love of writing, but she earned a law degree and practiced law before making the decision to write full-time. She has received several writing awards, including the RT Book Reviews Lifetime Achievement Award for Western Romances. Visit her at www.candace-camp.com.

Also by Candace Camp

The Mad Morelands

Mesmerised
Beyond Compare
Winterset
An Unexpected Pleasure

The Aincourts

So Wild a Heart
The Hidden Heart
Secrets of the Heart

The Matchmaker Series

The Marriage Wager
The Bridal Quest
The Wedding Challenge
The Courtship Dance

An Independent Woman
A Dangerous Man

The Lost Heirs

A Stolen Heart
Promise Me Tomorrow
No Other Love

Suddenly
Scandalous
Impulse
Indiscreet
Impetuous
Swept Away

His Sinful
Touch

Candace Camp

MILLS & BOON

This edition published in Great Britain 2018
by Mills & Boon, an imprint of HarperCollins*Publishers*
1 London Bridge Street, London, SE1 9GF

His Sinful Touch © 2018 Candace Camp

ISBN: 9780263266689

09-0418

MIX
Paper from
responsible sources
FSC™ C007454

This book is produced from independently certified FSC™ paper
to ensure responsible forest management.

For more information visit: www.harpercollins.co.uk/green

Printed and bound in Spain
by CPI, Barcelona

PROLOGUE

HER EYES DRIFTED OPEN. It was shadowy and dark, the only light a small kerosene lamp on a chest across the room. But even in the dim light, she knew this wasn't home. Her eyes closed again, the lids heavy. She wanted to sleep again, but she knew she couldn't. Foggy and befuddled as she was, there was a sharp, insistent fear that prodded her to wake up.

She had to leave.

It was an effort to pull herself from the suction of sleep, but she had to. Something was terribly wrong. Vague, wavering images flittered through her brain— a dark carriage, a strange parlor, some man she didn't know talking, talking, his voice droning on. There was another man beside her, more familiar but still wrong somehow.

The only clear thing was an icy dread that was lying over everything. Something awful had happened. Was still happening.

That was why she must wake up. She had to get away. She swung a leg over the side of the bed. The next instant she found herself on the floor in a heap, her head rapping against the wood.

The surprise of the fall woke her up a bit more, and she pushed onto her hands and knees, then staggered up, grabbing at the mattress to steady her. Her stomach lurched and her head spun, and she was afraid that whatever she had eaten was going to come back up. She stood quite still, swallowing hard, and after a moment the dizziness receded.

She had to hurry. *He* would return. She started toward the door, driven by the need to escape this small, unfamiliar room, but finally her woozy brain reasserted itself. She must think before she acted. She should take something with her. She looked around but could not find her reticule. Where was it? She would need money.

And she mustn't look peculiar. Half her hair had come loose and tumbled down. Pulling out the pins, her fingers clumsy and slow, she wrapped the hank of hair in a tight knot and stuck the pins back in. She had the suspicion it looked quite off balance, but it would have to do.

She straightened her bodice and skirts, tugging at her sleeves. She wasn't dressed for traveling, but she was certain that she had, in fact, been in a carriage. There had been the noise of the wheels, the jingle of the harness. And this unfamiliar shabby room looked like an inn. But she was dressed in a frilly evening dress more suited for going down to supper.

Her stomach growled, and she realized she was hungry. There was nothing here to eat, but she saw glasses and a pitcher of water, and she was thirsty, too. She poured half a glass and gulped it down. That, too, threatened to make her stomach revolt, and again she waited it out.

Afterward, she felt faintly more alert and aware. She slid one hand into the pocket of her skirt and touched a folded piece of paper. She knew where to go.

She had spotted her small traveling case standing against the wall beside a masculine-looking piece of luggage. Grabbing her case, she hurried to the door. It wouldn't open. Numbly she rattled the handle and pulled in vain. She was locked in.

He had locked her in! She was swept by a sense of betrayal. How could he do this to her? She had *trusted* him. Panic swelled, threatening to overwhelm her. She was alone. All those she relied on had turned on her. Flight was impossible. She was trapped.

Fighting back the panic, she checked the chest and the small table beside the bed, but there was no sign of a key. Her steps wobbled as she went to the window and shoved it open. The room was on the second floor.

She steeled herself against despair. There was a drainpipe within arm's reach of the window…if she leaned very far out. But she had always been good at climbing and, better than that, there was a small roof below. If she fell, it wouldn't be nearly as far. The roof sloped slightly, so at the far end, it wouldn't be as long a drop, and there must be a supporting post to the ground that she could use. It wasn't impossible. All it took was courage.

She stood, leaning against the window frame, struggling to think. He would follow her. She had to be clever. A disguise! Opening the larger valise, she pulled out a set of clothes. There wasn't time to change—he might return at any moment—so she stuffed the clothes in her case. Shoes. She frowned down at her embroidered slippers, then grabbed the pair of shoes in his valise and added them, as well. Now it was too full to close, so she jerked out a dress in her case and rolled it up, stuffing it in the bottom drawer of the small chest.

As she started to close his valise, she spied a pouch tucked in the corner and pulled it out. It was filled with banknotes and coins. It would be wrong to steal it, of course. But how else was she to escape? She hadn't a farthing with her. In any case, it was her money really, wasn't it? She thrust the pouch into the pocket of her skirt and refastened the valise. Closing and picking up her own travel case, she hurried to the window.

The soft-sided carrying case went out first. It landed on the small roof below, rolled and slid off the sloping roof to the ground. She froze, her heart slamming in her chest. Suddenly a key rattled in the lock, spurring her into motion. She leaned out, stretching to reach the drainpipe. It was too far; she must crouch on the sill to extend far enough. She twisted, trying to pull her feet up under her, just as the door swung open and a man stepped in.

"No!" He slammed the door behind him and ran to grab her and yank her back inside.

She struggled wildly, kicking and clawing. "You monster! Traitor!"

"Ow!" He dropped her and stepped back, raising his hand to a long scratch blooming on his face.

She flew at him, shoving him back. He staggered, his face flaming with anger, and he slapped her. She reeled backward into the washstand, rattling the washbowl and pitcher. Her shock was almost as great as the pain in her cheek. No one had ever hit her. Bitter anger flooded her, overcoming all else, and she reached behind her, her hand closing around the handle of the pitcher. She threw herself at him, swinging the earthenware pitcher with all her might.

He managed to twist so that it didn't land full on his head as she'd intended, but the pitcher clipped the side of his jaw as it crashed into his shoulder, spilling water over him. He stumbled back, catching his foot on the rag rug, and fell.

Running to the window, feeling more clearheaded than she had since she awakened, she climbed up onto the sill. Crouching there and holding on to the window frame with one hand, she stretched out and wrapped the other around the drainpipe. She froze, her heart in her throat, but then the sound of him clambering to his feet gave her impetus to move.

Swinging out, she put her toe on the iron bracket securing the drainpipe to the wall and let go of the window, hastily grabbing the drainpipe just below her other hand. She clung there, shivering, feeling for a toehold beneath her. Blast these entangling skirts! She wished she'd had time to change.

The man shoved his head out the window and lunged for her, hooking his hand in the sash of her dress. She scrambled downward, her shoulders aching with the strain. He cursed, sliding farther out, and she jerked away with all her strength.

Suddenly he was tumbling out the window. His weight tore her from her desperate hold on the drainpipe even as it ripped the sash from her dress. She fell with him, one breathless flash of panic followed by slamming onto the roof below. Her breath left her and a sharp pain lanced through her head. Helplessly she rolled, her momentum carrying her down the slight slope of the roof. Then, once again, she was falling into emptiness.

After that, there was only darkness.

CHAPTER ONE

ALEX TROTTED DOWN the steps, business finished, but feeling vaguely dissatisfied. It wasn't only because he suspected that the man he had just left had chosen him to design his summer house less for his talent than for the opportunity to boast that the son of the Duke of Broughton had visited him this morning. The fact was, Alex had felt odd and uneasy from the moment he awakened this morning.

He glanced at his watch and decided to catch a hack to his office rather than walking. Con was leaving on one of his adventures this afternoon, and he wanted to be sure to catch him. Even though they had acquired other friends as they grew older, Con was, as always, his closest confidant.

His uneasiness wasn't worry over Con. He would know instantly if Con was in trouble, just as he had known his brother wasn't in the house when he awoke. Neither of them could explain their twin sense—it simply was—but likewise, they never doubted its accuracy.

Alex supposed that the odd wisp of alarm that had taken up residence in his chest was merely the residue from his nightmare. He didn't remember dreaming it, but he'd done so often enough lately to presume it had visited him again. The thing was…usually the nightmare awakened him, leaving him cold and sweating, but it had not caused him to feel this way the next day.

He stepped out of the carriage in front of the office building he and Con owned. It was a narrow stone structure, four floors high and sturdy. Alex might wish for a more attractive design, but it suited their purposes. The bottom floor housed a bookstore, and the floor above held his and Con's offices, with the upper two floors being the flat he and Con had established as their bachelors' quarters when they left school.

Even though they had moved back into the family home a year ago, they hadn't rented out the flat. One or the other of them sometimes bedded down there. Con used it more often, staying there sometimes when he was working on a case or had remained out on the town late.

Alex met Con's employee, Tom Quick, coming down the stairs. Tom, a few years older than Alex, had been plucked from the streets by their older brother, Reed, whose pocket he had unsuccessfully tried to pick. Instead of prosecuting the lad, Reed had clothed and fed him and sent him to school. Quick hadn't taken much to schooling, but he had been a loyal worker for the Moreland family ever since, at first running errands for Reed and then, ultimately, becoming the mainstay of their older sister Olivia's investigative agency. Con had acquired his services, along with the business, from Olivia a few years ago.

The blond man grinned in his cocky way, a distinct warning that something was up. Alex eyed him warily. "Is Con upstairs?"

"Oh, indeed," Tom answered with a chuckle. "He's there."

"What has he done?" Alex asked with some foreboding. Perhaps it *was* Con, after all, that had given him this feeling.

"You'll see," the other man said airily and trotted past him.

Alex took the stairs two at a time and walked past the closed door of his own office to the last door on the corridor. A discreet brass sign on the wall beside the door announced that it was Moreland Investigative Agency.

He opened the door and stopped short at the sight of his brother, his jaw dropping. Normally seeing Con was much like looking into a mirror. Con's black hair was a bit longer and shaggier, and he had taken to wearing a mustache. But, all in all, it was the same angular face with the same squarish chin and straight black brows, the same sharp green eyes, the same firm mouth always ready to break into a smile. Their height and build, the way they stood and walked, were all so alike that even their mother had been known to mistake one for the other from the back.

But today…Con's hair was pomaded and slicked back away from his face. His mustache had been waxed into long sharp points and twisted up at the ends into absurd curlicues. He was strangely larger through the chest and middle and even slightly taller, and his body was encased in a suit of eye-popping yellow-and-brown plaid. On the desk beside him were a bowler hat of matching brown and a shiny black cane with a lion's head for a knob.

Con laughed at his brother's stunned expression and struck a pose. "What do you think?"

"I think you've turned into a bloody Bedlamite, that's what I think." Alex laughed. "What in the world are you doing? I thought you were going to Cornwall to infiltrate that lot that says the world's going to end next month."

Olivia had opened an agency to investigate the wave of spiritualists and mediums in the past decade who had swindled gullible and grief-stricken people with tales of contacting their deceased loved ones in the afterlife. After she met her husband in the course of one of these investigations, her agency had had a rather sporadic existence, with Tom Quick doing most of the work. The agency had turned to a number of other investigative procedures, such as finding missing persons, uncovering financial frauds and investigating the backgrounds of possible employees or spouses.

When Con bought the agency from her, he continued the sort of detective work that Quick was justifiably known for, but he also delighted in returning to the investigation of otherworldly phenomena, going beyond Olivia's field of fraudulent mediums and their séances to reports of hauntings and mythical beasts and even, as in his newest case, a quasi-religious group proclaiming the end of the world.

"That is where I'm going," Con told him.

"I don't think you're apt to blend in very well in that costume."

"Ah, but you see—" Con wiggled his eyebrows "—I've found that looking outlandish is an excellent way to go unrecognized. All people will remember is this ridiculous mustache and obnoxious suit. When I get rid of them, no one will recognize me."

"How did you make yourself look so thick?" Alex poked his finger into his twin's chest and found it pillowy soft.

"Padded vest," Con told him proudly. "I have lifts in my shoes, as well. I would have liked to make myself shorter, but that's a trifle difficult."

"I daresay. I hope you realize you look like an utter fool."

"I know." Con grinned. "Watch this." He picked up his cane and, giving a sharp twist to the head, pulled the gold knob from the cane, revealing a slender knife extending from it.

"A hidden stiletto." Alex's eyes lit up. Alex might be somewhat more staid than Con, but he was not immune to the lure of secret daggers.

"Cunning, isn't it?" Con handed the weapon to his brother. "And though you wouldn't think so, it provides a good grip. I found it in the attic a couple of months ago."

"At Broughton House?" Alex turned it over in his hand, examining it.

"Yes, I was up there with the Littles."

Alex knew he referred to their sister Kyria's twins, Allison and Jason, who, since Constantine and Alexander had been given the nickname the Greats, were often referred to as the Littles.

"It was Jason who found it, but Allie discovered the secret to opening it—she's a bloodthirsty little thing, have you noticed? I had a devil of a time persuading her she couldn't keep it."

"Well, you know her father." Alex shrugged. "Next she'll be brandishing a pistol."

"Terrifying thought."

"Do you expect trouble at this place you're going? Will you need a dagger?"

"Not really." Con sighed. "I'm relatively sure he's swindling his believers—easy to persuade someone to hand over all their worldly goods when they think they'll be transported up to heaven in a few months. But I haven't seen any sign that he's gotten physical. Still, I like to be prepared."

Alex grinned as he handed back the knife. "Especially if it involves a clever trick."

"Of course." Con fitted the weapon back into its slot. "Care to come with me?"

Alex felt a twinge of longing. He and Con had shared many an adventure. It was only the past few years, when Alex had been studying at the Architectural Association and then practicing in his field, that Alex had stayed behind more and more, helping out only now and then with Con's investigations.

"No," he said reluctantly. "Better not. I have work to do on the plans for Blackburn's country house. And I have... I don't know, I just have a feeling I should be here."

"What do you mean?" Con set aside the cane and fixed his searching gaze on his twin. "Is something wrong?"

"No... Maybe. I don't know." Alex grimaced.

"You had a premonition?"

"Not exactly. I'm not like Anna. I don't see what's going to happen." Alex folded his arms. He never liked talking about his "gift," as Con saw it—or his "curse," as Alex was more likely to consider it. "I've been very out of sorts since I woke up. Restless. It's probably nothing, just some residue from a dream."

"You had another nightmare." Con was the only one whom Alex had ever told about his bad dreams.

"I suppose. I don't really remember it. I just woke up feeling…" He shrugged. Even with his twin, Alex hated to reveal the bone-deep fear that invaded him in these dreams, the paralyzing sensation of powerlessness. It was a form of weakness he hated in himself. "The thing was…it was something like the way you and I feel when the other is in trouble. But different somehow. I'm positive it wasn't about you. But I've never had that feeling about any of our other siblings."

"Do you think your ability is growing? Improving?" Con asked almost eagerly.

"I sincerely hope not," Alex retorted. "I'll go mad if I receive signals every time a Moreland gets into trouble."

"True. Theo's girls alone would be enough to keep you busy night and day."

Alex grinned but quickly turned serious again. "I wanted to ask if you had ever felt that way. If you sensed things about the others."

"No." Con looked vaguely wistful. "You know me—I haven't a smidgen of talent. I mean, other than twin speak." He looked thoughtful. "If you think something's wrong, perhaps I should postpone my trip."

"No. Don't be absurd." Alex shook his head. "I'm sure I'm staring at shadows."

"But these dreams…"

"You put more credence in my dreams than I do."

"We all know Morelands have significant dreams… except for me, of course. Think of Reed dreaming Anna was in danger, or the things Kyria saw in her dreams."

"I've never had a significant dream in my life. They're just nightmares. I've had them since we were thirteen."

"Yes, but those stopped years ago. It's only been recently that you've been dreaming about being locked up again. There must be a reason."

"Probably the squab I had for supper last night," Alex said lightly.

Con snorted, but he dropped the subject. That was one of the best things about being a twin—one didn't have to pretend, and the other knew without having to ask.

"I'd better be on my way," Con said, picking up his cane and the small traveling case on the floor beside the desk. "My train leaves at two, and I don't want to miss it."

With a grin and a twirl of his bowler, he popped the hat onto his head and left. Alex, a smile lingering on his lips, perched on the edge of Con's desk, long legs stretched out in front of him, and thought about his dreams.

He didn't recall the one last night, but he'd had enough of them the past few weeks to know what transpired in it. He was always lying on a narrow bed in a dark, cramped room, alone and not knowing where he was, and gripped by a cold, numbing fear.

The nightmares had started after the time he and Con had visited Winterset, their brother Reed's home in the country, when the two of them, out walking with Reed's future wife, Anna, had come across a farmer who had been killed. Both he and Con had been shaken by the sight, but Alex was the one who had lost his breakfast. Alex had returned to the house to bring Reed's help, while Con had stayed with Anna by the body. He had never admitted to anyone, even Con, how relieved he'd been to get away from the bloody remains.

Oddly, though, the nightmares that had disturbed him in the weeks afterward had not been of the dead farmer, but of the time almost two years earlier when Alex had been kidnapped and held prisoner in a small, dark room.

He had been scared at the time, of course, but he was used enough to getting in and out of scrapes—though it was more frightening, admittedly, when Con wasn't there to share the experience. Alex had kept his wits and managed to escape, and in the end, Kyria and Rafe and the others had come to his rescue. It had been an exciting story to tell and he'd basked in Con's envy of his adventure, but then, after his experience at Winterset, he had begun to dream about it again.

It had passed, of course. Indeed, it seemed to have marked the beginning of his odd ability. The Morelands were given to such oddities—significant dreams and strange connections to an unseen world, their habit of falling fiercely, immediately in love.

So it had not been a complete surprise when Alex started to experience flashes of emotions and actions when he gripped an object—though it had seemed most unfair that Con had not been burdened with a similar peculiarity. Con, naturally, would have been thrilled to have it.

Alex had learned to hide his ability from everyone outside his family, and he had also learned to control it so that he wasn't overwhelmed by, say, witnessing a murder that had happened years earlier when he happened to lean against a wall. As his control over the ability increased, the nightmares had lessened and finally ceased.

Until recently. The ones he had now were not exactly the same, for in the recent ones he was a man, not a half-grown lad, and the room where he lay in darkness seemed different—darker and colder and smaller. But the fear was the same. No, it was worse, for woven through it now was a soul-deep dread, an icy terror.

Impatiently Alex pushed himself up from the desk. What was he doing lounging about here? Over the years he had used his ability to help Con with some inquiries. It was one of the reasons that the agency had acquired an impressive reputation, particularly in finding missing persons. But his assistance was a carefully guarded secret. It was difficult enough making a reputation for oneself as an architect, given his aristocratic background and his family's eccentric reputation, without adding something as unusual as working for an agency that often dabbled in occult matters.

But with Con gone, there was no reason for him to be here now. He should go to his own office and work on his own business, as he had told Con he was about to do. Sitting here was not going to solve the mystery of his uneasy feelings or his disturbing dreams.

Alex had reached the open door when suddenly his lungs tightened in his chest. He was flooded with anxiety, even fear, but he knew it was not his own; he was feeling the backwash of someone else's emotions. He felt, moreover, a...presence. There was no other way to describe it. The sensation was so strong that he actually glanced around the empty office, as if he would find someone standing there. Of course, there was no one.

What if he turned out to be like his grandmother and started talking to ghosts? He tried to separate this sudden burst of emotion from his own, to analyze this new awareness. It was similar to the "twinness" he shared with Con—a knowledge that someone was nearby, an understanding that the person was in trouble. But he had never felt such a thing before, except with Con. And he was certain that this was not coming from his twin. It was...different.

He stepped out into the hall and looked over the railing to the lobby of the floor below. As he watched, the door opened and a short man entered. The newcomer crossed the entryway and climbed the stairs. And as he moved, the sensation moved with him. This man—or perhaps he was only a boy, for he was rather small—was the presence Alex felt.

The visitor reached the top of the stairs and started down the corridor toward him. The small man was dressed oddly—well, not oddly, really, for his suit was unremarkable. But he wore a workingman's cap with a gentleman's suit, and nothing seemed to fit him. His feet galumphed along, seeming too big for his body. His jacket was outsize, hanging loosely on him, the sleeves obscuring his hands, and his trousers were rolled up at the hem but still pooled around his ankles. He wore the cap pulled down almost to his eyes, hiding his forehead and shadowing the bottom part of his face.

He hesitated when he saw Alex, then started forward again determinedly. Alex watched him walk, and as he drew nearer, the whole sense of the man's wrongness coalesced into a thought.

"You're a girl!" Alex blurted out. He knew at once that he had made a misstep, for his visitor let out a little squeak and took a step backward. "No. No, wait, please don't go. May I help you?"

She pulled off the concealing cap, revealing a cloud of black curls that fell just below her ears. Without the cap, he could clearly see the delicate chin, the heart-shaped face, the big, deep blue eyes. And his entire insides dropped straight to the floor.

"I'm looking for the Moreland Investigative Agency."

"That's me. I mean, I'm Mr. Moreland. Alex, Alexander Moreland." He realized that he was babbling and he forced himself to stop before he started explaining about his brother and the agency and Olivia, who had started it, and everything else that came into his head.

The woman was beautiful. More than that, his feeling of connection and his uneasiness were both centered on her. How could he be so tied to a stranger, to someone not even in his own family? Oh, Lord, she wasn't a relative, surely?

He was certain of one thing—he could not let her slip away. So he pulled together the remnants of his aplomb and inclined his head, sweeping his arm out toward the open doorway in a courtly gesture as he said, "Please, won't you come in?"

Her smile was shy, and a faint flush rose in her cheeks; both things, he realized, were charming. She walked before him into the office and sat down in the chair facing Con's desk. Alex was careful to leave the door open, not wanting to alarm her, and took a seat behind Con's desk as if he belonged there.

He wasn't really lying to her, he told himself. He *was* Mr. Moreland, even if not the one she sought. "Now, please tell me how I may help you, Miss—?"

"I—I came here because…well, I asked the driver at the station where I should go. He said the Moreland Agency was the best in the city at finding someone," she said, twisting her cap in her hands and ignoring his implied question about her name.

"We will certainly do our utmost to help you." He opened the top drawer of the desk and was relieved to spot pencils and even a pad of paper. He set them on the desk and prepared to take notes, hoping that he looked like he knew what he was doing. "Now, who is it that you wish to find?"

She gazed back at him gravely and said, "Me."

CHAPTER TWO

"I BEG YOUR PARDON?" Surely he could not have heard her correctly.

"It's me I need you to find—not the location because obviously I'm here, but who I am." She sighed. "I don't know who I am."

Alex blinked. It occurred to him that perhaps this was an elaborate joke. This lovely girl was an actress, perhaps, and Con had… No, not Con. If Con had played a prank on him, he wouldn't have left. He'd still be here, laughing his head off. Alex glanced out the door. He had no feeling of Con's nearness. But who else would arrange a mad jest like this?

"I see," he said carefully and cleared his throat.

The girl jumped up. "I know. I know I sound as if I've escaped from Bedlam, but I promise you, I haven't. I mean, well, I don't feel insane…though I suppose I cannot really know, can I?"

She paused, looking so lost that Alex instinctively went around the desk to her, taking her arm and steering her back to the chair. He propped himself on the edge of the desk. "No, no, I'm sure you're not insane. It's just… I, um… Perhaps you could explain the situation further."

She drew a breath and folded her hands in her lap, looking every inch a proper English gentlewoman—

except, of course, that she was wearing an ill-fitting man's suit. "I don't know who I am. I cannot tell you my name because I have no idea what it is. I think…" Her fingers went up to her throat, touching something beneath her shirt. "I think it may be Sabrina because that is what is engraved on the locket I'm wearing."

"Sabrina it is, then." He liked the sound of it, the intimacy of calling her by her given name, as if he had known her for years. "If you will excuse the, um, the informality."

"Of course." Her cheeks colored again in that delightful way. "It's only reasonable, since I have no idea what my last name is." She added with a sigh, "Or where I'm from. Or why I'm dressed in this mad fashion."

"You know nothing about yourself?"

"No, nothing at all. It's the most awful sensation." Sabrina reached up a hand to push her luxuriant hair out of the way, and for the first time he saw a purple bruise on the side of her face. Two of them, in fact, one on her forehead and one on the cheekbone below, both at the edge of her hairline. He noted, too, that the hand she lifted was scraped.

"You've been hurt!" Anger rose in him so fiercely that he jumped to his feet again. "Who did this to you?"

He bent down to examine her bruises, gently lifting the curls aside. The soft hairs clung to his skin, sending a frisson of pleasure straight up his nerves. His gesture was far too intimate to be appropriate, he realized, and he pulled his hand back, forcing himself to return to his seat against the desk.

"I don't know who did it," she told him. "If anyone. Perhaps I fell. There's more."

"More?"

"Yes. There are bruises on my arm." She shrugged out of her coat and pushed up one sleeve almost to her elbow to expose her arm to him. There on the pale skin were small faint smudges of blue.

"Fingertips." Something clenched, cold and hard, in his chest. "Someone squeezed your arm tightly."

"I rather thought so. And look." She undid the top button of her shirt and pushed it down, revealing another long red scratch low on her throat. "And I think…" She frowned, reaching up toward the back of her head. "I think maybe I hit my head. There's a spot that's tender."

Quickly he rounded her chair and bent down to look where she pointed. Carefully he parted her hair, trying to ignore the way it felt beneath his fingers, the ribbons of excitement that stirred deep within him. He drew in a quick, hissing breath. "You're bleeding. I should have seen…"

He crossed the room to the washstand in the corner and wet a rag, returning to dab carefully at the wound. When she drew in a sharp breath, he said, "I'm sorry. I know this hurts, but I must clean it."

"I know. It was just that one spot that hurt. You're quite good at this."

Alex chuckled. "If there's one thing I know, it's cleaning cuts and scrapes."

"Your business is dangerous?"

"My childhood was." He smiled to show he didn't mean it. "My brother and I were constantly falling out of trees or rolling down the hillside or running into things." He paused, considering. "Come to think of it, we must have been clumsy little brutes."

When he finished cleaning the wound, he set the rag aside and took up his former seat on the edge of the desk. "Now, you remember nothing of your past?"

"No. Not who I am or what happened to cause these bruises or where I live. Nothing!" Tears glittered in her eyes.

"Very well." Alex pushed aside the thought of how much he would like to take the woman in his arms and hold her, comfort her. Crossing his arms across his chest, he said, "What is the first thing you *do* remember?"

"Waking up on a train. The conductor shook my shoulder and woke me up, said we had reached Paddington Station. I was quite groggy. I got off the train and started walking through the station. There were so many people, and it was terribly noisy. I was so confused and…and scared. My head ached. I was trying to remember where I was and why I was dressed this way. And I thought whoever was meeting me wouldn't recognize me. Then I realized that not only did I not know who I was meeting, I didn't even know who *I* was. It scared me, so I sat down on a bench for a while and tried to think." She shrugged. "It was useless."

"What did you do then?"

"I—I was hungry." She smiled faintly. "How very mundane at a time like that, but I was. So I bought some roasted chestnuts from a man with a cart. That's when I realized that I had some money—a good bit of money, or at least it seemed so to me." Her gaze sharpened. "So clearly I do remember some things—

I know a five-pound note from a shilling, and I knew that there would be hacks outside the station. I knew I was peculiarly dressed. I knew I was going to see… someone. It's just me that I know nothing about."

"Did you recognize Paddington?"

She looked thoughtful. "No. I just saw its name on the signs. I… Really, I don't remember much about the station. I was in a fog. But nothing looked familiar, and when I went outside, I didn't recognize anyplace—none of the streets or buildings. Perhaps I've never been here before. Or perhaps that's just something else I've forgotten."

"You said you had a locket. Let's start with that."

"Yes." Sabrina reached behind her neck and unfastened a clasp, pulling a chain from beneath her shirt.

Alex reached out his hand, and she laid it in his palm. It was warm from lying against her skin, and he found it unexpectedly arousing. He closed his hand around it and stood up, moving back to Con's chair behind the desk. It would be better if he were not so close to her. Besides, it gave him a little more time to hold the locket and focus his full concentration on it.

The longer he held an object, the more likely he was to feel something from it. Only very strong remnants of emotions or events leaped out to him immediately—which, fortunately, made it a good deal easier to live normally. The best way to use his skill was to hold the thing tightly and close his eyes, blocking out all other sensations, and home in on the target.

But that would look far too strange to do in front of a stranger. Especially in front of a beautiful girl whom he did not want to think he was insane. Fortunately, the sensation from the locket was strong. It was warm and loving and feminine. He had never noticed before that he had been particularly able to pick out a sense of gender, and he wondered for an instant how far his ability could go. He had never wanted to try.

The strongest thing he felt from the locket was the same sense of *her* that emanated from Sabrina. And love; the locket had been given and received with love. Unfortunately, none of that helped him to identify her.

Sitting down, he laid the necklace on the desk and studied it. It was quite small and in the shape of a heart, on a delicate golden chain. Inserting his thumbnail into an almost invisible crack, he sprang it open. On one side was written a date and on the other the name Sabrina, as she had told him.

He looked back up at her. "Do you think this is your birthday?" She would be twenty-one soon if so—four years younger than himself. It seemed the right age for her.

She shrugged helplessly. "I wish I knew. Then I'd know two things about me—my age and my first name."

"We also know that it's a nice little piece of jewelry, not extravagant, but I'd wager expensive enough. And given the way you speak and your manner, I would venture to say that you've been raised as a gentlewoman."

Sabrina grinned. "I fear that doesn't narrow it down much."

"No." Somewhat reluctantly, Alex handed the locket back to her.

"Maybe something else would help." She began

to dig in her pockets and pull out various items and set them on the desk: a pocket watch on a chain, a leather pouch that clinked when she set it down, a card, a dainty feminine handkerchief, a torn scrap of paper and, finally, a gold ring.

Alex felt as if his heart had flipped in his chest. "A wedding ring?" He reached out for the ring. "You're married?"

"I don't know." She frowned. "I don't think so. I don't feel as if I'm married. It was in my pocket. I wasn't wearing it."

He picked up the ring, set with a cluster of diamonds in the shape of a flower. "Perhaps you merely took it off to suit your disguise." He could sense some sort of strong emotion from the ring, but it was muddled, and the whisper of her presence was faint, not permeating it like the locket she'd worn. It could have come just from her carrying it in her pocket. Adding to the confusion was the sense of someone else. It wasn't necessarily *hers*.

"Maybe." She was looking at the thing with a certain disfavor, which Alex found made his chest feel lighter.

He set the ring aside and picked up the handkerchief. It was clearly expensive and feminine. In one corner was an embroidered monogram of a large *B* mingled with an *S* and an *A*. "This *S* would support your name being Sabrina. A last name beginning with a *B*."

Sabrina nodded. "Yes. But I've tried and tried to think of a name beginning with a *B* that might seem familiar, but none of them do. This is the bag of money." She opened the pouch to show him the contents.

Alex raised his eyebrows. "You're right. That is a good deal of money to be carrying about, especially for a young lady."

"It seems suspicious, doesn't it? A woman dressed as a man, traveling alone, no baggage, carrying a lot of money. I think I must be running away." She raised troubled eyes to him. "But from what?"

"Do you feel that you're running away or is it just the evidence?"

"Yes." She paused. "I don't know. I'm frightened. Coming over here, I felt that I must get here as fast as I could. But maybe that's because I don't remember anything about my life. That's rather terrifying, all on its own, and of course I'd want to find out who I am as quickly as I could."

"There are your bruises. Something happened to you." He was immediately sorry he'd mentioned it, for the fear in her eyes increased. Hastily, he added, "Of course it could have been that you were in a carriage accident."

He didn't believe that for a second. A carriage accident would have involved others, at least a driver. They wouldn't have let her just wander off, dazed and bruised. Nor did it explain the amount of money she carried or the fact that she had dressed up as a man. It seemed far more likely that someone had hurt her... and could right now be pursuing her. Thank heavens she had come here and wasn't out wandering around, lost and alone.

He turned his mind away from that picture and

reached for the piece of paper. It was torn across the top, and the rest of it was filled with elegant copper-plate handwriting:

> …do say you'll come. We shall have the most wonderful time. I am already planning a shopping expedition. My aunt has been so kind as to agree to accompany us.

This was followed by a detailed description of a hat that the writer had recently purchased, and it ended, as it had begun, in the midst of a sentence.

"Clearly it's a letter," Sabrina said. "But that's all there is of it. I've read it over and over, and I cannot glean anything from it. There's no salutation, no signature. She doesn't even say her aunt's name. I suppose it's from a friend or a relative, but why wouldn't I have brought more of it? And why is the page torn in two?"

Again, the letter held a trace of Sabrina, but he also sensed another person, perhaps more. It could have been handled by several people, for all they knew. What Alex could sense, quite distinctly, bothered him. As soon as he'd touched the paper, he'd felt a brush of anger, even rage…which would fit with the paper being ripped in half.

He turned to the pocket watch. There was no inscription inside or on the back. It was clearly a man's; both the style and the feeling that emanated from it told him that. There was also a whiff of emotion—sorrow? He wasn't sure. But with it, far more than with the ring, Sabrina's presence clung to it. He thought perhaps she had carried it for a long time.

A picture of a house flashed through his mind and was gone. Alex froze, his fingers closing around the watch. But across from him, Sabrina said, "What? Did you find something on the watch?"

"What? Oh, no." He smiled and shook his head, setting the watch back on the desk. Later, perhaps, when Sabrina was not there to see it, he could hold it longer, concentrate on it harder. There had been something there, he was certain.

"I don't think this will be any help," Sabrina said as she handed him the last item, a card. "A boy in the train station handed it to me. I think it must be some sort of advertisement, though I'm not sure for what. A milliner's, perhaps?"

Alex took one glance at the card, and his eyes widened. The piece of paper featured a photograph of two elegantly dressed young women in charming straw hats. They were facing away from the camera. On the other side was printed an address and the words "Come see us from the front."

"Uh…no, not a milliner's." He cleared his throat, aware that his face was turning red.

"Oh." She sounded a little disappointed. "I thought one of the hats was quite attractive." She peered at him. "What is it? Are you all right?"

"Yes, yes, of course." He had the feeling his smile was unnatural. It would certainly fit how he felt at the moment. He tried desperately to think of some way to turn the conversation, but his mind was a blank. Well, not a blank, really, but what was there was completely inappropriate.

She waited for a moment, then asked, "Then what sort of business is it? I don't understand."

"It's one that, um, well, isn't the sort of thing a lady usually receives. It's a…a man's sort of, um…"

Her eyes widened. "You mean it's a house of ill repute?"

"Well…yes."

"Oh, my." Her blush was even deeper than his as she snatched the card back and examined it. "They look so…ordinary." Again she sounded disappointed, so much so that he had to smile. "I thought they would wear something more, well, you know."

"Yes, I know." It was bizarrely titillating to be sitting here talking about bordellos with this girl, all the while remembering how her springing curls had felt beneath his fingertips. The fact that she was dressed as a man somehow only made it more tantalizing. His flush had started from embarrassment, but it was quickly turning into something else altogether. "I believe the intimation is that if one saw them from the other side, they would be more alluring."

"Oh. I see." From the way she was looking at the card, he suspected that she did not, but he refrained from saying so. Sabrina went on, "Have you gotten cards like this, too?"

"Well, yes, now and then." He cleared his throat. "Now, perhaps we might continue."

Her eyes glinted with amusement as she put the card back into her pocket. "Oh, here's the ticket." She pulled her hand out of the pocket, extending the piece of paper to him. "But all it says is Newbury to Paddington."

"Well, at least we know you came to London from Newbury."

"I suppose that is where I live," Sabrina said doubtfully. "It doesn't seem familiar…though, of course, nothing does."

"That gives us something to work with." He leaned back in his chair, thinking. "I know nothing about Newbury, other than it's west of Reading. I think. Wish Con was here—he's a wizard with geography."

"Who's Con?"

"My brother." Alex straightened suddenly, his eyes lighting. "That's it. I know where we should go." He turned and started for the door.

"Where? What are we doing?" she asked, following him.

"I'm taking you home."

CHAPTER THREE

"WHAT?" SABRINA STIFFENED, her eyes flying to his.
The nerves in her stomach had died down since she
had been here; she felt safe. Until this moment. Now
warnings about strangers and wild stories of white
slavers darted through her head—and, really, why
could she remember things like that and not have any
idea of her own name?

"No! I didn't mean that," he said hastily. "It's not
my home—well, I mean, it is, of course, but what I
meant is, it's my parents' home. My family's. My
mother and father will be there and…and lots of other
people. I promise you, it's perfectly respectable."

He looked so flustered she had to laugh. "I see.
Very well."

"I do beg your pardon," he went on as he ushered
her out the door. He offered his arm, and she automati-
cally reached to take it before both of them recalled
the attire she was wearing and they moved apart. He
continued, "I should have explained my reasoning
first. I realized that we could get help at the house.
Megan will know if there's been something about you
in the news or she can learn it. We'll call on my sister
Kyria—if you've gone to a party in London, she'll recognize you. And, of course, the most important thing
is that you need to be someplace safe."

"You think I'm in danger?" Alarm rose in Sabrina again.

"I don't know that you are." Alex hailed a passing cab, and once again they went through the confusion of his reaching to hand her up, then remembering she was dressed as a man. Inside the vehicle, he went on, "Perhaps there is some other explanation for your bruises and your loss of memory and your disguise, but I don't want to take the risk. Do you?"

"No, you're right. But, Mr. Moreland—"

"No, please, call me Alex. Or Alexander if you would like to be formal. It seems wrong that I should call you Sabrina and you call me Mr. Moreland."

"All right. Alex. But surely you don't want to bring danger into your parents' home." Sabrina looked up at him. He grinned, and it lit up the angular planes of his face in a way that made her stomach flutter.

"Don't worry. They wouldn't even notice." When she raised her eyebrows doubtfully, he laughed. "You'll see. Anyway, I'd back our butler to keep anyone out the door. He has a paralyzing stare." He raised his head, looking down his nose as if he had detected an offensive smell, and Sabrina had to laugh.

It was strange that she could feel so at ease with a man who was, really, a complete stranger. But when she met him, she had immediately thought she knew him. It had so startled her that she'd gasped and stopped. For a wild, hopeful instant, she had thought he would say her name and everything would fall into place. But it had quickly become clear that he didn't recognize her.

Still, she couldn't help but relax, and it had been easy to tell him everything. There was a strength in him, a competence that was immediately reassuring. He was just so…calm. He hadn't turned a hair at her peculiar attire, nor had he said that her even more peculiar story was ludicrous. No name, no memory, masquerading in men's clothes, bruises and a knock on the head—none of that had fazed him. He had simply listened and nodded, as if such things happened every day.

Having no knowledge or experience, she could rely on nothing but instinct. Instinct told her to trust Alex Moreland.

Still, she felt impelled to protest. "But that's too much of an imposition, surely. Your mother cannot like having some girl she doesn't know shoved into her life. Look at me." She glanced down ruefully at her attire. "I'm masquerading as a man, and she knows nothing about my family or what I've done. She's bound to be shocked."

To her astonishment, Alex let out a crack of laughter. "Trust me, it will take more than that to shock the duchess. Mother will be delighted. She'll want to question you on everything, of course."

"But I can't answer her questions. I don't know anything about myself."

"Oh, not things like that. She'll want to know where you stand on the vote for women and what you think about factory workers' conditions, foundling homes, that sort of thing—and if you don't know, she'll be delighted to tell you all about them."

"Oh." Sabrina gazed at him blankly, wondering if he was joking. And what had he called his mother— the duchess? Was this an affectionate nickname? Some sort of slang that was another thing she did

not remember? Surely the woman couldn't really be...
No, that was mad; Alex could not be a duke's son.

Sabrina found it hard to believe that his mother
would be quite so sanguine about her, as Alex
thought, but it seemed silly to keep insisting on her
own unsuitability. Besides, what else was she to do?
She had no place to stay, no idea where to be. If she
could only relax, take a little time, perhaps it might
all come back to her.

As the carriage rattled on, she studied Alex. He
was looking out the window, his face just as handsome in profile. Then he turned and smiled at her,
and she realized that, no, he could not possibly look
as good as he did straight on. She could not remember
what she considered an ideal appearance in a man,
but Sabrina had the feeling that Alex Moreland was
a perfect example.

He wasn't hirsute, as so many men were these
days—no mustache or beard, neatly trimmed sideburns, his thick dark hair cut short. But then, he had
no need to hide any feature. His face was perhaps a
little thin, but it suited the angular lines of his face.
He could have appeared somewhat severe, with those
sharp, high cheekbones and the slashes of straight
black brows, except that his green eyes were warm,
his mouth full and inviting.

Realizing she was staring rudely, Sabrina glanced
away. They were passing an elegant row of houses—
no, there was only one door, so it must be all one
house. Made of blocks of gray stone, it looked as if it
had stood there looming over the street for centuries.
She thought it must be some government building,

perhaps, but the carriage rolled to a stop, and Alex reached over to open the door.

Sabrina's jaw dropped, and her stomach fell to somewhere around her knees. Was this his house? She watched as Alex climbed out and turned to her expectantly. She followed him, filled with a dire suspicion as to why he had called his mother the duchess.

"Is this—" Her voice came out barely more than a whisper, and she cleared her throat. "Is this your home?"

"What?" Alex turned back from paying the driver. "Oh, the house. Yes. I know it looks a little…grim. But it's much nicer on the inside. You'll see."

Nicer? She wasn't sure what he meant by that. It certainly couldn't be grander. The door was opened by a footman; at least he was not dressed in livery, which she had half expected after seeing the size of the house.

"Good day, sir." The man took Alex's hat and turned to her expectantly. There was nothing to do but hand her cap to him, revealing the tumble of her hair. If the footman was surprised or confused by the odd picture she presented, he didn't show it.

"Hello, Ernest. Where's my mother?"

"I believe she's in the sultan room, sir. Her callers left shortly before you arrived."

"The sultan room?" Sabrina asked in a hushed voice as they crossed the floor of the large entryway, arranged checkerboard fashion in black and white marble tiles. She could not keep from staring around the huge hall, two stories in height and decorated with portraits and landscapes as tall as she was. A wide staircase, also in marble, dominated one side, splitting at the landing to go up in opposite directions. "There's a sultan here?"

He laughed. "No. Never been one as far as I know, though my grandfather knew some pretty odd sorts, I'm told, so perhaps there was a sultan in there somewhere. It's called that because my great-grandfather decorated it when he was in some sort of Arabic fever. It looks rather like the inside of a harem. Or perhaps it's a sheikh's tent. We were never sure. At any rate, it's rather ghastly, but we're all used to it, and it's more comfortable than the assembly room. Grandmother apparently tried to rename it the red salon— you'll see why—but that never stuck."

"Wait," Sabrina blurted, plucking at Alex's sleeve. "When you called your mother the duchess, you really meant it? She's a…a…"

"Duchess? Yes."

"Oh, my." She could feel the blood draining out of her face. "Then your father is…"

"A duke. Here, now." He grabbed her arm as she began to sag. "You're not going to faint on me, are you?"

"I'm not sure."

He whisked her over to a stone bench and went down on one knee in front of it, gently pushing her head down. "Just breathe. You'll be all right. I nearly fainted once, when I broke my arm, but it passed."

"You broke your arm?" She looked up at him. His face was only inches away, and the sight of him so near, his eyes warm with concern, was enough to steal her breath again. But this time the heat came flooding back into her face.

"Oh, yes." His worried gaze turned to a twinkle.

"I told you I was accustomed to dealing with bruises and cuts. Sprains and broken bones, as well. Now... feeling better?" When she nodded, he said, "I should have thought to ask. Have you eaten this morning? I'll bet you haven't."

"I don't think so. Not since I got off the train at least."

"We must remedy that. As soon as we've seen Mother, I'll ring for some food for you."

"Alex. Your mother—you can't introduce me looking like this." Her voice rose in alarm. She could picture his mother, an imposing woman, maybe something like the queen herself, stiff and haughty and looking at Sabrina as if she were a bug. "I didn't realize she was a... That your family was so...so grand."

"Oh, we're not grand at all. In fact, everyone says we're deplorably plebian." He grinned and hauled her to her feet. "Come, you'll see. She's not stuffy at all."

Sabrina found that hard to believe, but she had little choice but to follow, her cheeks already burning in anticipation of her coming humiliation. Alex took her arm—whether to support her or keep her from fleeing, she wasn't sure.

They walked down the hall and through a set of open double doors. As soon as they stepped inside, Sabrina understood both the names given to the room. The couches and chairs and a chaise longue were upholstered in a rich red damask, relieved only by the dark wood of various tables. The walls and even the ceiling were all hung with billowing folds of fabric so that it did, in fact, resemble the inside of a tent. A very luxurious tent.

"Alex, dear." A woman rose from a love seat. She

was tall and beautifully dressed, her hair a dark auburn almost overtaken by gray. She had clearly been a beauty when she was young—still was beautiful, in fact. It all added up to an imposing figure, though not the one Sabrina had imagined. But that image was dispelled by the warmth of her smile and the kindness in her gaze. "I see you've brought me a guest. Come, sit down, child. You look white as a sheet." Reaching out, she took Sabrina's hands in hers. "Goodness, your hands are cold as ice. Alex, ring for some tea."

As Alex turned to tug the bellpull, Sabrina said, "I beg your pardon for barging in on you like this, Your Grace. And I know the way I am dressed must seem, um…" Well, she really didn't have the words to sum up how wrong her appearance was.

"'Tis nothing." The duchess waved her words away and led Sabrina over to a sofa. "Now sit down here with me and tell me what has happened. I can see that you are in some distress. Is it an employer who beat you? Has your father turned you out of the house? Men! Taking their pleasure wherever, whenever they want, but woe betide the poor woman who's caught with the consequences—such hypocrites." She looked over at Alex with a smile. "Not my boys, of course. They're gentlemen just like their father. So I know it's not Alex who has gotten you into trouble."

Sabrina goggled. "What?"

"It's all right, dear." The older woman patted her hand. "You needn't be afraid here. No one is going to judge you. I don't allow that in any of my houses."

"Your houses!" What sort of house was she talking about—surely not one that handed out postcards at the train station? This was becoming madder by the moment.

"No, no, no…" Alex hastened to say. "It's not like that, Mother. Sabrina isn't one of your unfortunate young women. She's not, um…" He flashed Sabrina a distressed look. "Mother funds two houses for women who are in need, you see." He swung back to the duchess. "But this is different." He went on to tell her Sabrina's story.

To Sabrina's amazement, the duchess listened with a warm concern but no visible sign of alarm, despite the peculiarity of the tale. When Alex finished, she said only, "I see. Well, of course you're right, dear, she must stay here with us." She smiled at Sabrina. "Clearly you have been through an ordeal. I'll tell Phipps to make up a room for you."

"I hate to put you to so much bother," Sabrina began.

"Nonsense. No problem at all." The duchess gave her arm another pat. "I look forward to sitting down for a nice chat with you later." With that, she sailed out of the room, leaving Sabrina behind her in a daze.

"Don't worry," Alex said. "It truly will be no problem for Mother, as Phipps will take care of everything. He'll be delighted to have a crisis to deal with. It's rather boring these days with so few of us in the house. And while he is doing that, we need to get you something to eat." He led her from the room and down a hall into the back recesses of the house. "I hope you don't mind having a bite in the kitchen."

"No, of course not." It occurred to Sabrina that the kitchen staff might find it something of a problem to have them in their way.

But, as it turned out, the housekeeper, whom Alex affectionately called "Mrs. Bee," and the cook were as seemingly unruffled as everyone else in this household by the two of them sitting down to munch on cheese and bread at one end of the scarred worktable while the work of the kitchen went on all around them. It was clear from the way they smiled and worked around Alex that they were accustomed to him popping in and wheedling a bite from them this way.

Sabrina was not sure what life was like in her own home, but she had the strong suspicion that nothing in the Moreland household would be considered normal. The butler, Phipps, did his best to convey a sense of dignity and severity when he entered, but his presentation was sadly undercut by the loud voice of the cook scolding a potboy and the heavy *thwackthwacks* of the maid cutting up vegetables at the other end of the table.

"Pray permit me to show you to the Caroline chamber," he said to Sabrina, bowing.

"No need, I'll take her," Alex said, ignoring the butler's pained look. As he and Sabrina walked away, he leaned down and murmured, "Poor Phipps despairs of any of us ever showing the proper respect for our station. But his knees are getting arthritic and he oughtn't to be tromping up and down the stairs. Besides, he'd have nattered on at you about the grand history of the Morelands all the way up, which might very well have sent you running again."

Sabrina laughed. "I don't think I'm in danger of that. Frankly, all I want to do at the moment is sleep. I'm rather tired."

"I imagine you are. You must have been up before

dawn if you got into London as early as you did. Not to mention that whatever happened to you must have been an ordeal."

They climbed the staircase, which up close was every bit as wide and elegant as it looked from a distance. They turned to the left and were on the top step when a piercing noise, resembling the screech of a steam whistle, split the air.

Sabrina jumped and whirled. A large shaggy animal was bearing down on them at full speed.

"Steady on." Alex said, his hand going to Sabrina's elbow. "It's only Rufus. And my nieces."

The animal, she saw now, was a long-haired dog of some indeterminate origin. And hot on his heels was a red-haired moppet, hands outstretched and face gleeful. It was she who was emitting the ear-piercing noise. A little behind her came a slightly smaller girl of similar coloring, doing her best to keep up.

An attractive woman with hair the color of dark cinnamon hurried after the pair and called, "Athena! Brigid! Come here!"

Between the large dog, the madly running children and the wide marble staircase, it looked like a disaster in the making.

But then the woman called, "Rufus, stop!" She followed that with "Grab them, Alex, do—before they reach the stairs."

Before Sabrina's amazed eyes, the dog slid to a halt and ducked behind Alex, peering out around Alex's leg at his pursuers. Alex grinned and reached down to scoop up the girls, one in each arm, and place noisy kisses on the cheek of each. "Escaped again, have you?"

The little girls giggled, their quarry apparently no longer of interest, and chanted, "Uncle Alex, Uncle Alex!"

The smaller girl reached up to pat Alex's cheek, but the larger, faster one reached inside his jacket, searching. Alex laughed. "I haven't any peppermint sticks today, you little thief."

The children both began to chatter, rendering it almost impossible for Sabrina to understand anything either said. Then one of them turned and pointed at Sabrina and said clearly, "Who's she?"

"She's our guest," Alex told them. "Sabrina, I'd like you to meet my brother Theo's daughters. This little imp is Athena and this one is her sister, Brigid. Say hello to Sabrina, girls."

"Hello, Sabrina," they said as one.

Brigid turned her face into Alex's shoulder in an apparent attack of shyness, but Athena grinned at her with unabashed interest and said, "Are you a boy or a girl?"

"I'm a girl, but I'm wearing boys' clothes." Sabrina couldn't keep from smiling back at the girl.

"I want to wear boys' clothes," Athena decided.

Alex did his best to hide his own smile. "This poor beleaguered woman is their mother. Megan, allow me to introduce you to Sabrina. Sabrina, this is the Marchioness of Raine."

"Ma'am." Another title. But of course she would have one. Wasn't the heir to the dukedom often a marquess? Did that mean that Theo was the oldest? And was Alex actually a lord? Well, at least she could blame her lack of memory for not knowing the order of precedence.

"Call me Megan," the girls' mother declared.

"You're American," Sabrina blurted in surprise.

"Yes, I am. A stranger in a strange land." She reached out to shake Sabrina's hand in a firm, businesslike manner. "Pleased to meet you."

"Mama, I want to wear boys' clothes," Athena said, drawing the conversation back to the topic which most interested her. "Can I?"

"May I," Megan amended. "I don't know. I hadn't really thought about it."

"Me, too," Brigid announced. "I wanna wear boys' cloves."

"Clothes, silly, not cloves." Athena giggled.

"We'll discuss this later," Megan told them firmly. "Come here, you two." She reached out and took them, setting them down on the floor. Squatting down to their eye level, Megan went on, "Haven't I told you not to chase Rufus? You scare him. And it's not fair to run from Alice when you know she turned her ankle yesterday."

The girls nodded, the little one's lower lip beginning to tremble. "Yes, Mama."

"We won't do it anymore," Athena said gravely. "Promise."

"Good. Now you run back to Alice." Megan gave them a little push in the direction they had come from. Sabrina could see a harried-looking woman at the other end of the hallway hobbling valiantly toward them. "And apologize to Alice."

The girls took off at a run, and Megan rose, turning back to Alex and Sabrina. "Sorry for the interruption." Though her voice was friendly, her reddish-brown eyes studied Sabrina curiously. Sabrina suspected that the woman didn't miss much.

"I was just showing Sabrina to her room. She will be staying with us for a while," Alex explained. "She's in rather a spot. I was hoping you might be able to help us."

"Of course." Megan's gaze grew even shrewder. "What do you need?"

"For one thing, perhaps you could lend her something to wear? These are her only clothes." As she nodded, Alex went on, "I also wondered if you had heard anything about a young lady going missing. Or perhaps some sort of accident or even a crime where a young woman might have been injured."

"No…not yet. Why? Were you in an accident?" She leaned in a little, peering at Sabrina's bruises.

"I'm not sure," Sabrina replied, and Alex launched into another retelling of Sabrina's predicament.

Megan listened with interest, but the warm sympathy that had marked the duchess's face mingled with a certain skepticism in Megan's eyes. Her first words when Alex finished were "If it were Con telling me this instead of you, I would be certain this was a prank."

Alex chuckled. "No, no, I promise you, it's not. It's all true."

"I've heard of people losing their memory after being hit in the head, which you obviously were. I'll check with my contacts and see if they've heard anything."

"Megan is a newspaper reporter," Alex said in an aside to Sabrina.

"Really?" Sabrina looked at her in amazement.

"I was." Megan nodded. "Now I write mostly longer investigative pieces for magazines. I'll look into it and see what I can find."

"Especially Newbury. That's the departure point for her train ticket, so we're assuming that whatever happened would probably have taken place around there. But, of course, if it was that she had been kidnapped, that could have taken place anywhere and she merely happened to escape at Newbury."

"Kidnapped?" Sabrina gaped at him, but Megan seemed to find nothing odd in this idea and merely nodded.

"I don't know how much I can find out about something happening in Newbury unless it was really big news, but I will ask around," Megan told them. "And I'll look through my dresses for something you can wear, Sabrina. Some of my dresses would be too old for you, but I'm sure we'll come up with enough things. Anna may have left a few frocks here, as well—anything of Kyria's, of course, would be much too long." She whipped around and walked away in the same brisk manner with which she seemed to do everything.

"I don't think she believed me," Sabrina said.

"Megan has a journalist's nose for news. If there's anything there to find, she'll chase it down."

"I just hope… What if it's something awful?" Sabrina turned to him, brows drawing together anxiously. "I mean, what if I'm a terrible person or I've done something reprehensible? I could be anyone— I could have run amok and started chopping people into bits."

Alex smiled. "I think we can take the risk."

"Those names she mentioned—Anna, and Cara, was it? Do they live here, too?"

"No. Anna is married to my brother, and they live in Gloucestershire. But they often come to visit. And it's Kyria, not Cara. She's one of my sisters." He cast an amused sideways glance at her. "Odd name, I know, but my father is an antiquarian, and his particular field of interest is ancient Greece and Rome. Sadly, he insisted we all learn Greek and Latin growing up. The other thing he inflicted on us was our names. Mother put her foot down on some of the worst names, so Reed and Olivia managed to escape, and my name luckily was both normal and Greek. Poor Con, though, got stuck with Constantine. And Theo's full name is Theodosius. His twin is Thisbe."

"Oh, my. You have a great number of family."

"I suppose so. Theo and Thisbe are the oldest, then Reed. Next is Kyria, followed by Olivia, and Con and I bring up the rear."

"Two sets of twins!"

"Fortunately, we are on the opposite ends of the family, so we weren't all young at once. Kyria has a set of twins as well, Jason and Allison. But you don't want to hear the names of all my nieces and nephews. They're far too numerous." He stopped before an open door. "Here we are. This is the Caroline room."

"Why is it called that?" Sabrina asked as she walked past him into the room. Like every part of the house she'd seen, it was spacious and richly furnished but carried the patina of age and wear that spoke of comfortable use, not ostentation.

"Oh. It's named after some princess that spent the night here a long time ago."

Some princess, Sabrina thought with an inward smile. That was typical of the Morelands, she was beginning to realize. They were obviously a family of great station and wealth, but they seemed oblivious to it.

"Do you like it? I'm sure Phipps could move you to a different one." He glanced around the room, as if trying to judge whether it would do.

"Of course. It's very nice." It was, in fact, a little oppressive, with its heavy dark furniture and the looming tester of the bed, but there were two windows that opened on a large garden in the back—imagine that, a garden backed by an expanse of green grass and trees behind a house in London—and the bed looked wonderfully high and soft, as if one would sink into it like a cloud.

"And in a different wing from my chamber. Phipps does his best to keep us respectable despite ourselves."

"Really? You're a long way away?" That thought brought a little knot of nerves to her stomach.

"Not that far, really, just turn left down that hallway. But the 'bachelor wing,' as Phipps terms it, is suitably separate from the family and guest rooms. Mother never believed in shutting children away in a nursery, but neither did anyone want to have Con and me living too close by."

Sabrina laughed. "You make it sound as if you two were terrors."

"Well, we were also known as the Terrible Two, I'm afraid. Mother will tell you we were simply bright and inquisitive. But we did tend to be a little noisy. However, I think what made them want us at a distance was our boa."

"Boa? As in constrictor?" Sabrina's eyes widened, and she could not keep from casting a quick glance around the room.

"Yes. But don't worry. Augustus isn't here. After he got out and caused something of a riot in the streets, Mother made us leave him at the house in the country permanently. And we haven't any of the rabbits or guinea pigs or rats anymore. It's just Rufus and Wellie now."

"Wellie? Another dog?"

"No, not a dog." He shook his head, grinning. "I'll introduce you."

Sabrina began to smile. "You're a very odd man, Alex."

"Ah, but how do you know? Perhaps I'm quite usual, and you simply don't remember."

Her smile turned into a laugh.

At that moment, Megan swept into the room, carrying a stack of clothes, followed by a maid with an even larger armful of dresses, which she laid across the bed before leaving the room.

"Look," Megan said cheerfully. "Prudence found some things in Olivia's room as well as Anna's. They're not as simple as many I wear."

"I like your dress," Sabrina told the woman, meaning it. The lack of ruffles and bows let the elegant lines of the bodice and skirt shine.

"It's useful. People tend not to take a woman in lace seriously." Megan turned to Alex. "Time for you to leave, my boy."

"Oh." He looked startled, then embarrassed, his eyes flickering to the pile of white chemises and petticoats in his sister-in-law's hands. He cleared his throat. "Yes, of course." He started toward the door, then turned back. "Sabrina…I'd like to look at some of those items in your pockets again if I may."

"Of course." Sabrina slipped off the jacket and held it out to him. It was a relief to get rid of the encumbrance, but it felt somehow even odder to be standing here clad in trousers and a shirt, with only the vest over it. Her womanly figure was much more obvious without the concealing jacket.

Alex's eyes swept down her in a swift, encompassing look, confirming her opinion and making her flush with a heat that was only partially from embarrassment. She turned aside and found Megan watching her speculatively.

As soon as Alex closed the door behind him, Sabrina said, "You distrust me."

Megan laid the clothes in her arms out on the bed and turned to her. "The Morelands are a very friendly and open family. They believe in the basic goodness of people."

"But you don't," Sabrina ventured.

"I wasn't born a Moreland. I'm a hardheaded Irish girl from the Bronx." She came closer, and her brown eyes were no longer warm. "I won't let you hurt them. If you try to, I will make you pay. Ask anyone— Megan Mulcahey never gives up 'til she finds out the truth."

"I hope you *do* find the truth about me," Sabrina told her evenly, looking the other woman in the eyes. "My story sounds mad, I know. I probably wouldn't believe it, either, if it hadn't happened to me. But it's the truth. I have no idea who I am or why I came to London or where I belong. It scares me to death. I *want* to know who I am. Almost anything would be better than living in this void, even if it means finding out I'm a terrible person."

"Do you think you are? A terrible person, I mean."

"I don't know. I don't feel as if I am, but I suppose one wouldn't. People usually think they're right, don't they?"

"Generally, in my experience." Megan gave a little half smile and stepped back, her manner, if not warm, at least open-minded. "Come on, I'll help you try on these clothes while you tell me all this again. First, why do you think you might be a terrible person?"

"Look at my face. Something dreadful happened."

"You could have been the victim."

"Or someone could have been angry at me for a very good reason. Or I could have attacked someone and they fought me off. Any number of things, and they're all just speculation. But it doesn't denote a peaceful, ordinary life, does it?" Sabrina had shed her waistcoat as she talked and now started on the buttons of her shirt. "Why do men button their shirts up on the wrong side?"

"It's a wonder, isn't it?" Megan sat down on the stool in front of the vanity table.

"And then there are these clothes. Dressing up as a man isn't one's first thought, is it? If I was merely traveling, I would go as myself, surely. And why do I not have luggage?"

"To me, it speaks of a hasty flight from someplace or someone—in all probability, whatever caused the damage to your face," Megan agreed.

"Exactly. What ordinary young lady would do that?"

"One who was frightened. And clever."

"I'm certainly frightened. Not as much now. Alex—Mr. Moreland, I mean, or I guess it's Lord Alexander Moreland—he's very…calming, isn't he?"

"That's not the adjective usually used for one of the twins, but yes, I would say he's steady. It would take a good deal to alarm him."

"I think it would take a good deal to alarm any of you. His mother didn't turn a hair at my showing up like this—although she did take me for a loose woman!"

Megan chuckled. "That sounds like the duchess. She hired me even though she suspected I wasn't really a tutor. The Morelands are warmhearted, but it would be a mistake to think they aren't smart, as well."

"You mean you worked for them…under false pretenses?"

She nodded. "I passed myself off as a tutor for the twins. I had to get in, you see, because I was investigating my brother's death. I thought Theo had killed him."

"Your husband?" Sabrina stopped in the middle of stepping into a dress and stared at her.

"Well, he wasn't my husband at the time. And it didn't take me long to realize that he couldn't have done it."

"I must say, it seems to me you've little room to talk about deceiving the Morelands," Sabrina said with some heat.

"But you can see why I'm suspicious. Here, let me help you with the buttons." Megan came over and fastened the dress up the back. "This is one of Anna's.

It's a lovely color on you." She looked into the mirror over Sabrina's shoulder. "I've nothing against you, Sabrina. In fact, I like you. You're forthright. And, heaven help me, I'm inclined to think you're telling the truth. But that won't stop me from digging for information, and what I discover may not please you."

"I know. But I don't want to live in this limbo forever." Sabrina thought of the wedding ring, and something cold coiled inside her. "I must find out."

CHAPTER FOUR

SABRINA'S JACKET OVER his arm, Alex left the house, walking through the gardens and back into the almost sylvan piece of land beyond. A high stone wall blocked off the noise of the city streets, rendering it peaceful and quiet. Alex had discovered long ago that his "reading" of an object was far easier outside, away from the clutter that filled most buildings.

He sat down on a stone bench and took out Sabrina's possessions, laying them on the bench beside him. Closing his eyes, he held the cloth in both hands, trying to empty his mind of everything but the rustle of the leaves in the trees around him, the chirps of birds.

There was very little of Sabrina in this jacket. Very little of anything really, other than a vague masculinity and perhaps a sense of anger? No, too mild for that, more resentment perhaps. That told him nothing. He folded the jacket and laid it aside, then picked up the objects one by one.

The money pouch, like the jacket, held only a trace of Sabrina. There was that same masculine feel, along with a mingling of different feelings. That would be common for money, passing through the hands of many people, as it did. But what was interesting was the strong sense of another male presence besides the one from the jacket.

He had never really noticed this ability to pinpoint the presence of one person or another, just as he had not realized he could separate a feminine presence from a male one. Was it something new or had it always been there beneath the surface, something he'd ignored? He was inclined to think it was the latter.

What had always jumped out to him was the stark emotion attached to a piece, and he had not examined the subtleties. He had generally thought of the person who had held it as a man or woman, but that had been because he knew for whom he searched. Today when he met Sabrina had been the first time that he had sensed the identifiable presence of a certain person—apart from his twin.

That had made it easy to feel the same sensation in the objects. Her necklace, for instance, had been swimming with it. Picking up that thread had made it clearer that one of the other strands was also a lingering remnant of a different entity.

Suddenly he was discovering a whole new way to look at his ability—as a multitude of strands, some vivid, some dull, each one carrying its own distinct quality of emotion or place or person. The difficulty was in pulling out a particular thread from the tangled knot. It was an intriguing thing to explore. Unfortunately, it was of little use here as he could not form an image or identity for the person from the strands.

The one thing he had learned was that the money had probably been in the possession of the second man, the one who did not possess the jacket, for a longer time. Somehow this man's presence felt heavier—or

perhaps *fuller* was the better word. More developed—
that was it. He suspected the other man was older. It
was speculation, of course, but then everything about
his ability was merely his interpretation of a message.

There was little to be gained from the train ticket,
which had been handled by many people and in Sabrina's possession for only a short time. The handkerchief, too, had been handled by others, a servant
who had washed it in all likelihood. There was a
flicker of something when he touched the stitched
monogram, and he held that tightly between his fingers for a moment. Not Sabrina, but a woman—the
person who had embroidered it, perhaps? But again,
that could have been anyone from a seamstress to a
servant to a relative.

Finally, he picked up the thing he held the most
hope for—the man's pocket watch. He had gotten a
definite flash of a place from it. With some concentration, it might become clearer. He folded his hand
around the watch and focused.

A man, and again he had that sense of weight,
gravity, that made him think he was older. But he
was not one of the other two men he had sensed on
the jacket and money. There was a sense of satisfaction. A strong element of love. Alex concentrated on
separating that particular strand.

And there it was: a pleasant house, clearly the
property of someone of wealth, but not ostentatious.
Queen Anne style, white, with crisp black trim, carriage lamps on either side of the entry and a gold
knocker on the door—again, not grand or attention-
grabbing, just a plain gold knocker and plate.

It sat in a row of elegant town houses, and he was

almost certain it was located here in the city. He was even more certain that whoever the man who had carried this watch was, this house had been his home. Pride, love and security permeated Alex's sense of him.

Excitement rose in him. Now *this*, at last, was useful. Alex knew houses. He began to dig through his pockets. He had never quite given up his childhood habit of picking up odds and ends and stuffing them in one pocket or another; as a result, he always had a pencil or two and some scrap of paper.

He found a rolled-up flyer someone on the street had handed him the other day. Flattening it out on the bench beside him, he began to sketch the house on the blank back of a testament to the wonders of "Dr. Hinkley's Miracle Tonic—guaranteed to eradicate all one's aches and pains."

Alex worked as he always did, absorbed in the task, fingers moving quickly and surely over the page. He paused, studying it, then added a few more details. He spent another few minutes holding the watch and trying to summon up a fuller picture of the house, then added a bit of decoration at the corners and over the door. He would give the drawing to Tom Quick and set him looking for the place. Alex could make a pretty good guess as to what areas in the city it was most likely to be located.

He tucked away both drawing and pencil and turned to the final object. He had been curiously reluctant to examine it again. Foolish, of course. The small gold band set with diamonds wasn't necessarily a wedding ring. Even if it was, it wasn't necessarily Sabrina's. It didn't mean she was married.

Moreover, there was really no reason to be downcast at the idea. He barely knew the woman. He was not the romantic soul Con was, believing that all Morelands fell in love on sight. None of his sisters had; indeed, Olivia had had such an argument with her future husband when she first met him that both of them had been tossed out of the séance they were attending. And while Rafe had rescued Kyria from that tree, as Alex recalled she had been more irritated than bedazzled—of course, that could have had something to do with the fact that she had been trying to pull Alex and Con out of trouble. Thisbe had had a normal sort of courtship, if studying chemical concoctions could be considered a courtship.

No surprise that his vague, bookish father would have been smitten the moment he met the fiery-haired, forceful reformer who would become his wife. The duchess was, after all, something of a force of nature. Reed had pined for Anna for years, but Alex found it hard to believe that Reed, the most sensible of the Morelands, had really fallen head over heels the moment he saw her. And the whole account of Theo's seeing his wife in a dream as he lay dying was too bizarre to count as falling in love on sight.

What they had felt was attraction, just as he was attracted to Sabrina. It made sense. No Moreland could resist the lure of the unusual, and when it was accompanied by big blue eyes and a cloud of black curls and a mouth that invited kisses, of course he would be interested in her, even attracted. The connection between them was odd; he'd never felt it with any woman before, but that didn't mean it was love. He didn't know what it meant, but love had to be something more than sensing her presence.

It also had to be more than wanting to help her and protect her. Anyone would have felt a rush of sympathy at her plight, anger at the sign of bruises on her creamy skin. It wasn't the first time he had tried to help someone.

Which was exactly what he ought to be doing, instead of sitting here uselessly ruminating on his motives. Alex picked up the ring and closed his fist around it. Closing his eyes, he concentrated on the circle in his hand.

The aura it gave off was muddled, as if it had been handled by many people. There was less trace of Sabrina on it than on the handkerchief. If it was, indeed, a marriage ring, surely that meant it was not Sabrina's. Women rarely took off their wedding bands. Perhaps it was an heirloom, passed down through generations.

He had a suspicion that this line of reasoning was more wishful thinking than logic. The feeling of it was not murky and heavy, as old things often were, with generations of emotions darkening them, layer on layer. It was more…empty, almost, barely brushed with emotion.

That quality made it seem more likely that the ring was new, that it had sat in a jewelry store, looked at and held by many, but worn and cherished by no one. It made it seem likely that it was a recent acquisition, perhaps a present. Perhaps a wedding ring placed on Sabrina's finger only days ago.

Was she a newlywed? Had she run away from her husband? The bruises on her face would certainly indicate that she had good reason for leaving him—a frightening brute of a husband who sent her fleeing into the night. Alex realized his fist had tightened around the ring, and he forcibly relaxed it.

He surged to his feet. It was useless to sit here, trying to conjure up any more information from the objects Sabrina had with her. He had learned all he could from them, and he should get to tracking down the one lead he had obtained, the house. He would find Tom Quick while Sabrina was occupied trying on clothes.

That thought brought up a whole new set of images of Sabrina in frilly underthings, slipping dresses on and off, buttoning and unbuttoning. Better not to think about that, either. She was a guest in his home. Under his mother's roof. He knew nothing about her. He intended to help her, not seduce her.

Alex started to put the ring back in the outer pocket, but he decided it would be more secure in an inner pocket. He reached inside the jacket, finding the slit pocket in the silk lining. Shoving the ring down into the corner, his finger touched a piece of paper. Digging deeper, he caught the bit between two of his fingers and pulled it out.

Holding it up, he studied the small plain square of heavy stock paper. A slow smile spread across his face. Tucking the bit of paper into his own breast pocket, he turned and strolled back into the house.

SABRINA SAT ON the window seat, gazing out on the garden, as she waited for the maid to come measure the hems of her new treasure trove of dresses. Since the clothes had fit her well enough, she and Megan had been able to sort through them quickly.

Dealing with the Morelands was like being sucked into a whirlwind, she'd found, and this was the first time today that she had a few minutes to stop and think. As she watched, Alex appeared at the edge of the garden and walked toward the house, his head down. Apparently, like her, he had seized some time to consider the situation.

She wondered what his conclusions were. Heaven knew, she didn't have any herself. She felt as if she teetered on the edge of a deep abyss. How could she not know anything about herself? Absently, she reached up and rubbed her temples, hoping to soothe the ache that had been in residence there all morning.

It was easy enough to guess that she had received a blow—probably more than one—to the head and that it had caused her to lose her memory. It wouldn't be so frightening if only she could be certain that her memory would return. But what if it didn't? What if she never recalled who she was?

What if she was married? The thought made her blood run cold. It seemed peculiar; one would think her best hope would be to have a loved one who would be looking for her, who would be able to tell her everything about herself. Instead, she feared the idea. What if her husband showed up and he seemed a complete stranger to her? Or what if he showed up and she realized that she was frightened of him, even despised him, that she had in fact been running away from him?

She held her left hand up in front of her, scrutinizing the base of her third finger. There was no mark, no change of color in her skin, to indicate that she had worn a ring there. But of course, there would not be if she had not worn it long. She hadn't worn the ring but had carried it in her pocket. That would seem to indicate she wasn't married, but perhaps she had only done it because the ring looked too feminine for her masculine attire. Or maybe it had been merely wishful thinking.

Or maybe she was just grasping at straws, unwilling to believe she was married and yet felt so drawn to another man. Sighing, she let her head fall back against the wall. Closing her eyes, she thought about Alex. It was obvious that she was unfamiliar to him, yet she felt as if she knew him. The instant she saw him, elation had risen in her, as if she had found something important and exciting. Yes, she had been in a desperate state, scared and hoping for help, but what she had felt seemed much more than simply reaching a person who might be able to help her.

It wasn't relief that sent little sparks shooting down her nerves when he smiled at her. Nor was it safety that made her insides warm just now as she watched him walking toward the house, long-legged and lean. Everything about him—the thick black hair, the soaring cheekbones, the dark slashes of his eyebrows above clear green eyes—drew her. Even the sound of his voice was somehow stirring.

It was all disturbing…yet perversely delightful, as well. Even now, just thinking about him, she felt that same heat blossom deep inside her, aching and hungry. She wondered what it would feel like to kiss him, to have his arms slide around her in a way that wasn't about comfort or security at all. Her skin tingled at the thought of his touch.

Was this usual? Was this normal? It didn't feel

so. It felt strange and exciting. But perhaps it was quite familiar to her. How was she to know? Perhaps she was a woman of experience, and that was simply something else she'd forgotten. Perhaps she was a wanton.

She had no way of knowing, any more than she could be certain of anything about herself. She believed that she was a good person, that she had lived a pleasant, harmless life. But how could she be sure?

A quiet knock on the door interrupted her thoughts, and a maid came in. Sabrina stood up, and the maid came over to kneel at her feet, beginning to measure and pin along the bottom of the skirt.

"I'm sorry, I don't remember your name," Sabrina said.

"Prudence, miss," the girl said.

"I apologize for causing so much work."

"Oh, there's always something to do round the house," Prudence responded cheerfully. "I like the sewing better than some things. I'm hoping to be a ladies' maid one day." She sighed. "Though then I'd have to leave Broughton House. The duchess has Sadie already, and the marchioness don't use one."

"I take it you enjoy working here?"

"Oh, yes, miss. Mr. Phipps is a stickler—you have to do your work well. But he's fair. And the family is kind, even if they are a wee bit…different. There's some that think their ways are too odd. But the animals don't bother me, and even if I don't understand a lot of what she says, I don't mind when the duchess goes on about voting and sanitation and such. And it's not fair to say Lady Thisbe blows things up. There was just that one little fire in her workroom."

"I see." Sabrina pressed her lips firmly together to keep from laughing.

"You have to be careful not to touch the duke's old pots and such, of course. And Lord Bellard gets upset if you move his little men."

"His little men?"

"The toy soldiers he has set up—a terrible lot of them."

"Lord Bellard? There's another child living here?"

"Oh, no, miss, Lord B's old—he's the duke's uncle. He's sweet, really, even if he never remembers your name. For myself, I'm happy not to have to dust all those little things—or the duke's pieces of plates and cups. Some say the Morelands are too free and easy, but I like it that they don't have their noses in the air. Everyone here gets a day off every week, not just every other, and they pay more than anyone else. The duchess insists."

"They have been very kind to me."

Prudence looked up at Sabrina. "Is it true what they say, miss? That Lord Alex found you and you can't remember your name?"

"Well, I think I found him, but yes, I don't remember my name or anything else."

"My…" She let out a long sigh. "Isn't that a wonder?"

"A wonder?" Sabrina glanced at her in surprise. "What do you mean?"

"It'd be grand, wouldn't it, to be whoever you wanted? Choose your own name, where you lived, what you liked?" Prudence sat back on her heels, surveying her work with satisfaction. "There you go, miss. We can start on the next, if you'd like."

Sabrina stared at her, struck by the girl's words. Perhaps she was looking at her situation all wrong. Her slate was wiped clean. It didn't matter what kind of person she had been in the past. Starting today, she could be whoever she wanted. She and she alone could decide how she wanted to act, what she wanted to be, what she thought and felt and did. She could, in short, create herself.

She should be excited, not scared. What lay before her wasn't a deep abyss, but a limitless horizon. "Yes," she said, a smile curving her lips. "Let's begin."

CHAPTER FIVE

SABRINA SPENT MUCH of the afternoon trying on dress after dress while Prudence pinned the hems. However, she was sure the trouble was worth it when she saw Alex's expression as she walked down the stairs that evening dressed as a woman. She wore a lavender silk gown that belonged to Olivia and hadn't needed to be hemmed. Though it was largely devoid of ornamentation, it nipped in at the waist and flared to a small bustle in back, showing off her figure to perfection. The wide neckline bared her throat and much of her shoulders.

Alex's eyes widened, growing suddenly brighter, and he jumped up from the bench where he sat and went to her, reaching up a hand to her as she came down the final two steps. "Women's clothes become you."

He leaned in closer, his smile small and intimate, and Sabrina thought for an instant that he was going to kiss her. Fortunately, he did not try, for she had the deep suspicion that she would have kissed him back, and that thought was even more unnerving than the light in his eyes. Kissing, she realized, was not something she was accustomed to doing, no matter how licentious her thoughts had been this afternoon.

Dinner was a small affair, with only Alex and his

parents and his small, quiet uncle, Theo and Megan having a prior engagement. Sabrina was grateful. She had been nervous at the thought of meeting a duke, who surely would be more intimidating than a duchess.

However, as it turned out, the duke was a genial man—and very easy to engage in conversation. As long as she smiled and nodded now and then, he was happy to keep up a monologue about Roman and Greek architecture, artifacts, history—indeed, anything to do with ancient Greece and Rome. The fact that she understood only two-thirds of what he said was apparently not a drawback. Uncle Bellard gave her a shy smile and said nothing at all.

When the meal was over, they all lingered around the table, talking, which, memory-less as she was, Sabrina was quite sure was not the normal course of things. None of them even seemed to find it odd when the duchess had a glass of brandy along with the men.

She was grateful when Alex glanced across at her and smiled, then said, "Scintillating as I'm sure our conversation is, I suspect our guest is beginning to flag. It's been a very long, hard day."

Sabrina politely protested, but the duchess nodded. "Yes, of course. It's wicked of us to keep you up, child."

"I'll walk you back to your room," Alex offered.

"Perhaps you should. I got lost coming down to dinner, I'm afraid." She stood, taking the arm he offered.

"I hope you didn't get too lost," Alex said as they left the room and headed toward the stairs.

"No, I wound up in the nursery wing, apparently, and the little girls' nurse set me straight."

"Aside from that, I hope you've had no problems."

"None at all," Sabrina quickly assured him. "Everyone has been most kind." Even Megan had not been unpleasant about not trusting her. "I'm very grateful. I don't know what I'd have done if your mother hadn't taken me in. I've tried all afternoon to remember something, but my mind remains a blank." She looked up at him. "Will we be able to find out who I am? Is it hopeless?"

"Not at all. You mustn't think that. Megan already called on one of her reporter friends and set that in motion. If they hear anything pertinent, they'll let her know. And she has other contacts. I've set the agency's employee to checking out the train station, just in case someone has been there searching for you. He's also looking around in some other areas."

"Where? How does he know where to look?"

"Oh…well, he'll hang about where servants might congregate, the market or taverns or such, to pick up any gossip about a lady gone missing."

"I see." Sabrina had the oddest feeling he was holding something back. "What can I do? I want to help."

She expected him to tell her she could not, so she had marshaled her arguments in favor of it. But to her surprise, he merely nodded and said, "Of course. We can talk to Kyria tomorrow, see if she has any idea who you are. She and Mother and Megan are doing something, so she'll be here in the morning."

Sabrina realized that they were walking very slowly, dawdling as if they didn't want to reach her bedchamber. Which was, of course, the truth, at least for her. She sneaked a sideways glance up at Alex and found him watching her.

They reached the doorway to her chamber and turned to face each other. Sabrina was intensely aware of everything about Alex. She wished she could think of something to keep him here.

"Sabrina…"

"Yes?" Did she sound too eager? She could feel her cheeks begin to flush, and her breathing was shorter and faster. His eyes were dark in the low glow of the hallway sconces; she couldn't read them. But there was a softness to his features, a certain loosening of his mouth, that made her feel both twitchy and achy.

"I, um…" He reached out, but he only touched her shoulder and slid down her arm and away. He swallowed and took a step back. "If you need anything, I'm just down the hall."

Sabrina nodded, doing her best to hide her sag of disappointment. "Good night."

Impulsively he wrapped one hand around her arm and bent, pressing his lips to her forehead. "I'm glad you are here."

He turned without looking at her and walked away, disappearing around the corner.

HE WAS RUNNING, his feet flying, his heart pounding in a wild mix of excitement and fear. They were right behind him. Freedom beckoned just beyond the dark chasm. One leap and he'd be over. Safe. One leap.

His muscles bunched, and he flew across, but the emptiness beneath him was suddenly wide and fathomless. He grabbed for the other side, but there was nothing to hold on to. He plummeted into the darkness…

Alex shot straight up in bed, drawing in breath in a desperate gasp. He was suddenly starkly awake. His skin was slick with sweat, his lungs heaving as if he had indeed been running. Though it was from the same time—the escape, the mad dash across the roof and jumping across to the roof beyond—it was not the old familiar nightmare of being locked in a room. Nor the slightly different one he had been dreaming lately. But it was, he realized with a sudden vivid clarity, the dream that he had last night, the one he could not remember but that had haunted his morning.

Throwing back the covers, he jumped out of bed and hastily pulled on the trousers he'd thrown across the chair the night before. He grabbed a shirt as he went out the door, shrugging into it as he walked swiftly down the hall. Just as he turned the corner, Sabrina's door opened and she rushed out.

"Alex!" She flung herself across the feet between them, and he wrapped his arms around her, curling his head down over hers.

"Shh. It's all right," he murmured, one hand moving soothingly up and down her back. "You're safe."

Sabrina's body trembled, and her arms were tight around him, pressing herself flush against him. She was soft and lithe beneath his hand, her black curls tickling the naked strip of skin between the open sides of his shirt. He pressed his lips against her head, and the sweet perfume of her hair filled his nostrils.

Alex ached to comfort her, to protect her, and yet an entirely different ache was growing in him. She wore only a cotton nightgown, and his shirt was open, the top button of his trousers still unfastened. Their bodies were as close together as they could be and still be clad. He was acutely aware of the feel of her against him, the warmth of her body, her breasts pressing into his flesh, the length of her legs against his.

He should release her. Step back. Or at least stop caressing her.

Sabrina lifted her head to look up at him. Her soft dark curls tumbled entrancingly, her eyes were huge and dark in the dim light, her lips soft. And suddenly he was kissing her. Her mouth opened beneath his, her arms lifting to curl around his neck. She was pliant in his arms, her body melting into his in a way that stirred him even more. Nightmares, good intentions, notions of propriety—all fled before the heat and hunger welling up in him.

Changing the angle of their lips, he kissed her again, his hands gliding down over the soft swell of her buttocks, lifting her up and into him. She made a small noise of surprise deep in her throat, and the sound checked him.

In that instant, he recalled where they stood and the many doors along the hall. At any moment one or the other of his infernally curious family might take it into their heads to pop out. The duke slept like the dead, but his mother did not, and the thought of what his mother might say was enough to freeze his overheated blood. This was wrong on so many levels. Sabrina was here so that he could protect her, not seduce her. She was frightened and alone. He'd be a scoundrel to take advantage of that. And, however little he might want to admit it, she might be married.

He lifted his head, his arms relaxing around her. It took another moment, another steadying breath, to step back. "I—" His voice came out a croak and he started again. "I'm sorry. Forgive me. I shouldn't have…"

Alex shoved his hands back through his hair, fingertips pressing into his scalp as if to awaken his brain. He glanced around and was relieved to see that the corridor in either direction was still and empty.

Taking Sabrina's hand, he whisked her into her bedchamber, closing the door softly behind him. This, of course, was more dangerous territory, but he had to talk to her and he could not risk being seen with her dressed like this in the middle of the night. Even his tolerant relatives had their limits.

"Here, sit down." He led her to an overstuffed armchair, sitting down himself on the hassock in front of the chair. Taking both her hands in his, he said earnestly, "Deeply, sincerely, I do beg your pardon. I didn't intend— I wouldn't ever— You are just so beautiful. Not, of course, that it was in any way your fault," he added hastily. "It was entirely me."

"Not entirely." Her voice was soft but droll, as well.

Alex looked at her sharply and saw that her eyes were twinkling. She giggled, and he relaxed and sat back. "At any rate, it was wrong of me, and I do apologize. Now, as I should have asked you to begin with, what frightened you? A nightmare?"

"Yes." All amusement fled her face. "It was dreadful. I dreamed that I was falling."

"Falling?" he repeated, startled.

She nodded. "I know that doesn't sound so awful, but I was terrified. I was trying to get away from something, someone, I'm not sure what. It was all rather fuzzy. I climbed out a window, I think—it's already fading away. Someone was reaching for me, and I tumbled out into the darkness. I was falling. I couldn't breathe. I—" Sabrina stopped and drew a breath, her voice calmer but still shaky as she went on. "Then I woke up."

Alex stared at her, too astonished to speak. They had both just dreamed of falling? Yes, the Morelands tended to have strange dreams, but how could this happen? Had she somehow entered his dream, experiencing his climbing out the window and racing across the roof?

"Do you think that's what happened to me?" Sabrina lifted her hand up to the bruise on her forehead. "I fell out of a window and hit my head?"

It seemed logical. It occurred to him that perhaps his dream hadn't been about his escape years ago at all. Maybe he had just assumed it was, his mind making the logical connection to the time he had escaped as a child and that frightening leap between rooftops. Could he have somehow experienced Sabrina's dream? That must be utter nonsense. Yet...

"Alex?" Sabrina said tentatively.

"What? Oh." He realized that he had been so engrossed in his thoughts that he hadn't answered her. "Sorry. Just trying to reason all this out." He could hardly tell her his thoughts; she would be certain he was utterly mad. "Yes, to answer your question. It does seem possible, even likely, that you fell yesterday and hit your head. I would think one very well might dream about a frightening experience. I have done so myself."

"Really?"

He nodded, his thoughts once again going to his

dream. He had sensed Sabrina's presence this morning, but more than that, even before he saw her, he had felt her distress and confusion. If he could sense that something was wrong with her, as he was able to with his twin, perhaps tonight the terror of her dream had touched him, even in his sleep, causing him to dream something similar. Following that line of reasoning, his nightmare the night before might have been caused by Sabrina's actual fall. It made sense—in a very peculiar way.

"The thing is," Alex mused, "if you fell from a window and knocked yourself out, why didn't someone find you? If you were being chased, wouldn't the people chasing you take the opportunity to seize you? And if you were running away from your home and fell trying to climb down from your window, surely whoever was waiting for you would have seen it and come to your aid."

"Waiting for me? What do you… Oh, I see, you mean if I were eloping, then he would have been outside." She paused, thinking. "If that was the reason I left, it would explain that ring and why it was in my pocket instead of on my hand. I was secretly engaged, intending to get married. Maybe he wasn't there. I was going to meet him somewhere. Only, I fell, hit my head and lost my memory. Still, as you said, whoever was reaching for me would have seen it and taken the opportunity to catch me."

"True." He thought for a moment. "Maybe that person wasn't real but something your brain conjured up, a symbol of the pursuit you feared would follow."

"So perhaps everyone was still asleep, and I came

to before anyone was out of bed. Is that when I forgot who I was?"

"I don't know. All we're sure of is that you'd lost your memory by the time you reached London. But, whether you awoke from the fall not knowing who you were or it came to you later, when you awakened, you were aware that you must run. You sensed that someone was after you, so you took off. The same reasoning would apply whether you were eloping or a rebellious miss running off to visit her friend in London, or a schoolgirl escaping from some young ladies' academy." Another possibility, that she was a mistreated wife looking to escape her brute of a husband. He didn't want to think about that.

"True." Sabrina looked relieved. "It doesn't have to have been that I was eloping. But why didn't someone come after me? Wouldn't they have searched for me?"

"We don't know that they didn't." Alex wished he could call back the words when a new worry bloomed in Sabrina's eyes.

"Of course. You're right. They could have followed my trail. They could be here in London searching for me."

"No need to worry about that," he said hastily. "Even if they assumed you fled to London, how would they know where you went once you got here?"

"The driver?"

"Let's say they questioned the driver of every hack at Paddington, the most they could possibly learn is that you'd gone to the agency. Tom Quick won't reveal where you are, and Con isn't even here. No, if they think you've gone to London, then they're most likely to go to your friend who wrote the letter in your pocket. She will know nothing about you. Or if you come to London frequently, they'll go to the places you normally go."

"And I won't be there."

"Exactly."

She smiled and reached out to squeeze his hand. "Thank you."

His pulse leaped at her touch. It was mad that even so small a thing could stir him. He wanted to turn his hand over and clasp hers. Well, frankly, what he wanted to do was to pull her over into his lap and kiss her again.

"It's, uh…" he began before realizing he had no idea what he was going to say. "Very late. We should probably go to bed." His face warmed. "That is to say, we should sleep. I'm sure you're tired."

Sabrina was just looking at him, her eyes huge and serious. She was so lovely it took his breath away. And she was still wearing only a nightgown. He could see the soft rise of her breasts beneath the thin material, even the hint of the darker circle of her nipples. She had curled her legs up onto the chair, and the nightgown had fallen away a little, revealing her ankles. He could not keep from thinking about reaching out and sliding his hand up, pushing the material higher, her skin smooth beneath his fingertips.

Alex jumped to his feet. "There's no reason to be afraid."

"I'm not."

"It was just a dream—nothing will hurt you here. And I'll be right down the hall. You can call if you need me." Why couldn't he stop babbling?

He swung away and found himself facing her bed.

The covers were tossed aside invitingly, the sheets rumpled where she had lain. His mouth went dry as dust. He couldn't move, couldn't look away. He wanted to touch her so much the very skin of his palms tingled.

Sabrina rose to her feet, and Alex turned back to her. She was close to him; it would be only a matter of reaching out and taking her arm. Pulling her to him. He remembered in vivid detail each moment of that kiss earlier. Her taste. Her warmth. Her softness.

"Good night," he said hoarsely and hurried from the room.

CHAPTER SIX

SABRINA HUMMED TO herself as she fastened the buttons down the front of her shirtwaist. It was doubtless peculiar to feel so cheerful this morning after the bad dream last night, but that nightmare had been overwhelmed by the feel of Alex's arms around her afterward. Alex's kiss.

She smiled to herself. However little she might remember of her past, she was certain she had never felt anything as delightful. When she'd jerked awake and run from her room, she had acted instinctively, simply getting away. But when she saw Alex, she knew that what she was seeking was the safety and strength of his arms.

His embrace had provided that, warming and calming her, but as she stood pressed against him, she had become aware of much more than feeling safe. Her skin had tingled, and the feel of his body against hers, nothing but the thin cotton of her nightgown between them, had stirred her.

Lean and long, Alex was all bone and hard muscle. His shirt had hung open, unbuttoned, so her face had been pressed against his bare chest, his flesh on hers. She could smell the scent of his skin, subtle and slightly musky, and hear the rhythm of his heart. She'd felt his body suddenly flare with heat.

Sabrina had known what that flush meant, for she felt it racing through her own veins. Innately she understood the subtle signs—the almost infinitesimal alteration in his scent, the ragged draw of his breath, the way his muscles tightened. He desired her.

She had lifted her head, wanting to see his face. Wanting, if truth be known, for him to kiss her. And he had. Thinking about it, her lips curled up dreamily. His kiss had melted her, turned her quivering and mindless, for a moment a creature entirely devoid of thought or will, recognizing only the desire pouring through her. Looking back on it, it seemed a little alarming. At the time, it had been utterly right.

Perhaps she would come to regret it. It would be difficult to look at him today without blushing. If he counted her as less because of her response, she would rue it. But for those few moments, she had lived in a perfect world of pleasure. The truth was, right now she wanted nothing more than to return to it.

Sabrina pulled on her skirt and buttoned it up the side. One of the best attributes of Megan's clothes was the ease with which one could dress oneself—buttons where one could reach them easily, fewer petticoats and only the smallest amount of padding in the back to form a bustle. Best of all, she could wear them without having to tighten herself into a corset first.

She had goggled yesterday at Megan's breezy assurance that none of the Moreland women believed in wearing a corset. The duchess, she said, considered them a symbol of all that was wrong with women's current place in the world, designed to render them mere ornaments incapable of performing any useful task.

Sabrina studied herself in the mirror. Though the lack of a corset made her waist less waspish than was fashionable, there was a certain grace and fluidity that was lacking with a stiff corset. Best of all, she could breathe deeply. That had been one of the most pleasant aspects about wearing male clothing.

The lines of Megan's skirts were narrower, which, along with the smaller number of petticoats, made getting around much easier. Her clothes were also more versatile. Sabrina could wear the tailored skirt with only the cotton shirtwaist, or she could don a feminine version of a man's jacket, one that nipped in at the waist and puffed out on the sleeves. Either way, the ensemble looked crisp and modern and somehow professional, as if the woman who wore it was capable of doing things.

It was so much better than the frilly things young girls had to wear. Sabrina considered that thought and what it meant about the void of her past life. Clearly she liked this streamlined look, so that was another thing she now knew about herself. And, given the distinct tinge of resentment in her thought, Sabrina suspected she had had to wear the ruffles and bows she disliked.

That was a curious thing. She was a grown woman, nearly twenty-one if their guess about the date on her locket was correct. Surely she would have been in charge of her own wardrobe. Sabrina frowned. Had she been so under the dominance of a husband or parents? Or, not having met the Moreland women, had she simply been unaware that the difference existed? Neither, she thought, spoke very highly for her own strength of character.

Shrugging aside the thought, she headed downstairs. The dining room at first glance was such a blur of noise and people that for a panicked moment Sabrina thought of turning around and going back to her room. There seemed to be a veritable army of children, as well as several adults, some sitting, some standing, getting food from the sideboard, reaching down to grab up a running child, gesturing—and all of them talking at once.

Alex, standing at the sideboard chatting with another dark-haired man, saw her and exclaimed, "Sabrina."

At his word, all conversation ceased, and every eye in the place turned to Sabrina. She froze like a rabbit in the sight of a wolf. Alex set down his plate and came over to her, taking her arm and nudging her inside. "Kyria, this is Sabrina, whom I was telling you about."

A tall, red-haired woman who could only be the duchess's daughter kissed the child she was holding and set her down, smiling as she crossed the floor to Sabrina. Up close, Sabrina could see the faint lines beside her eyes, so Sabrina knew she must not be as young as she first appeared, but there was no gray in her vivid red hair and she was a stunning woman.

"Sabrina, this is my sister the Lady—"

"Just plain Kyria," the elegant woman said cheerfully, reaching out to shake Sabrina's hand. "As you can see, we don't stand on formality here." She waved a hand toward the table. "Don't be alarmed by all the children. It's mostly my brood. When they found out I was going out with Megan and Mother this morning, they insisted on coming over to 'look after Athena and Brigid'—though it's my opinion that they were seizing the opportunity to have a yard to play in."

Sabrina could see now that, aside from Megan's toddlers, there were actually only four young people, all of them with various shades of red or blond hair.

"Miss Davenport," Kyria addressed the plainly dressed woman sitting against the far wall. "I think it's probably time for the children to go back to the schoolroom."

The other woman curtsied and began to round up the children and shepherd them toward the door. As this took all the children bidding each of their relatives goodbye, as well as chasing down the elusive Brigid, it was a protracted process.

"Now, dear…" Kyria turned to Sabrina. "Alex told me about your problem. Such a curious thing. I do wish I could help." She studied Sabrina for a long moment, then sighed. "I'm sorry, but I don't recognize you at all." She turned toward her brother. "She's not one of the current crop of young girls making their come-out or any from the last several years." She held up a finger when Alex started to speak. "It's no use arguing. Trust me, Sabrina is far too lovely for me not to remember her."

"Then you think she's not from London?"

"I'm sure I wouldn't move in the same circle as Lady Kyria," Sabrina ventured.

"Oh, I have a very wide circle—or perhaps I should say a large number of them." Kyria smiled.

"Still, you're right, I can scarcely know every young gentlewoman in London. But you mustn't worry, dear. Alex will help you straighten it out."

"There are one or two avenues still to explore," Alex assured her. "Megan asked some fellow reporters yesterday, but she hasn't even started on her various contacts. If there's gossip in the taverns, Tom will find it."

Kyria linked her arm through Sabrina's and steered her toward the table. "Now, you must put it out of your mind. You know, when you stop thinking about where something is, you find it right off. Give it a little time. Have you met Theo yet?"

Theo, it turned out, was the black-haired man Sabrina had seen talking to Alex when she first walked in. It wasn't hard to see he was kin to Alex. Though obviously several years older than Alex and a little more fleshed out, his eyes were the same leaf green, and his hair was as thick and dark. There was about him a more rough-and-tumble look than she would have expected in a future duke.

"Come, let me introduce you to my husband, Rafe." Kyria led Sabrina toward a blond-haired man chatting with Uncle Bellard. Sabrina was surprised to see the diminutive, hunch-shouldered Bellard talking so volubly to anyone.

As if sensing her thoughts, Kyria said, "Rafe and Uncle Bellard are good friends. People are always surprised. They assume that Rafe's so handsome and charming that he's empty-headed, or that because he's an American, he's rather primitive—of course, that could also be because he has a sad tendency to settle things with his fists. But he and Uncle share a love of history." She smiled fondly. "Don't get caught in one of their conversations or you'll soon be struggling to keep your eyes open."

Both men stood as Kyria and Sabrina approached, Rafe's gaze resting on his wife with such warmth and love it was almost too intimate for company. It was easy to see why he was labeled handsome and charming. The sprinkling of gray in his hair mingled unobtrusively with the pale gold strands, and his eyes were a bright blue. A neatly trimmed Vandyke beard kept his even features from being too perfect.

When Kyria introduced him, McIntyre gave Sabrina a slow smile that lit his face, then he bowed gracefully over her hand and said, "Pleasure to meet you, ma'am."

His voice was rich and thick, like honey, with a faint slur that made it as lazy and warm as his smile. Sabrina imagined that a good number of women would not look past the charm to see the intelligence beneath. But Sabrina caught the shrewd expression in those vivid eyes, as wary as Megan's had been, and she knew that he, too, was suspicious of her.

"Sit down and eat," Kyria said, tugging Sabrina down into the seat beside her. "Alex, get the girl some breakfast."

"I can do it," Sabrina began, starting to rise.

"No, no, let Alex," Kyria said lightly, placing a hand on her arm, and though she smiled, Sabrina wondered if Kyria, too, held some suspicions about her. "I'm so eager to chat with you, and Mother and Megan and I must be leaving soon."

"You are going shopping?" Sabrina asked. Surely it was too early for making calls.

"Shopping?" Kyria laughed, exchanging a glance with Megan, who also seemed amused. "No. We're going to a gathering in Downing Street."

"Gathering?"

"Yes, it's a little impromptu demonstration that we've been planning for days." Kyria's eyes twinkled.

"What are you demonstrating?"

"Our support for women's suffrage," the duchess declared. "We want to show the prime minister that we will not be put off. No matter how long it takes, we will continue to fight."

"Mother is hoping we'll get arrested."

"Arrested?" Rafe turned to his wife with alarm. "You're going to jail? Kyria... No. You can't."

"I can't?" Kyria cocked an eyebrow at him.

He changed tactics, his voice turning to a wheedling tone. "Be reasonable, darling. I can't let you rot in a cell. I'd have to break you out, and then I'd wind up there myself. What are our children going to do with two prisoners for parents?"

Kyria chuckled and patted his arm. "Don't worry, they won't arrest us."

"The prime minister is terrified of the duchess," Megan explained.

"Salisbury," the duchess said, her mouth turning down in disgust. "That dreadful man. His beard is bigger than his brain. And his spirit is smaller than either."

"You'll never sway Salisbury," Uncle Bellard told her, shaking his head. "He didn't even want to give workingmen the vote."

"No, of course not." She sighed. "Still, one has

to forge ahead. Someday we'll manage to get their attention."

"Don't fret, Emmeline." The duke smiled benignly at his wife and reached over to pat her hand. "I'm certain you'll get arrested one of these days."

The duchess laid her hand on his. "Thank you, dear."

The conversation continued in the way Sabrina soon learned was the normal course in the Moreland household—the room was lively and noisy and filled with laughter, as there was talking across the table and down it, multiple conversations with the participants switching from one conversation to another and topics wandering all about.

At one point, Megan, across the table from Sabrina, leaned forward and said confidingly, "Yes, it's always like this. You'll get used to it after a while. The first few days I was here, I was surprised. It was more like my family's mealtimes, not what I expected from the British aristocracy."

"It's quite…wonderful, I think." Sabrina grinned. "I have the feeling, though, that it's not what I'm accustomed to."

"Still no glimmer of memory?"

"No." Sabrina went on to tell her of her dream the night before, carefully expurgating what followed afterward with Alex. "So I wonder if I might have fallen." She shrugged. "That seemed important information last night. Now I don't know if that's really any help."

"It's a new bit of knowledge—it's bound to help. I promise, as soon as we're done at the Women's Franchise League, I'll start making the rounds of my contacts."

The meal wore down and the women left, with Rafe and Theo offering to escort them to their destination. Alex rose and turned to Sabrina. "Ready to investigate?"

"Yes, of course." She popped to her feet.

"Good. Then let's be off."

"What are we doing? Where are we going?"

"It's a surprise." There was a twinkle in his eyes, and Sabrina was reminded of her feeling the evening before that Alex was holding something back.

"You've found out something!"

"Perhaps." He smiled.

Sabrina stopped, putting her hands on her hips. "Alexander Moreland, you tell me what it is right now."

He laughed. "You're as easy to tease as my sisters." He held up his hands as she started to take him to task. "No, wait, don't ring a peal over me. I'll tell you." He reached inside his jacket. "Yesterday I found something in the jacket you were wearing."

"What? How? I looked all through the pockets."

"This was quite small and caught in the corner of an inside pocket." He reached into his pocket, drew forth a small square of paper and held it up. It was a plain sheet of stiff paper, rather like a ticket, but only half the size of the train tickets. A set of four numbers was written across the top.

"What is it?" It didn't look like anything that would bring that look of suppressed excitement to Alex's face. "A ticket? To what?"

"It's a baggage claim. You have luggage waiting for you. And we are going to Paddington Station to retrieve it." Taking her arm, he swept her off down the hall.

CHAPTER SEVEN

IT WOULD HAVE been a more satisfyingly grand exit, Alex thought, if they had not had to first collect their hats and gloves and Phipps had not insisted they take the Moreland town coach. But when the butler looked at him in that pained way and said, "But, sir, the ducal carriage is the appropriate transportation for a genteel female guest, not a common hansom," Alex had no choice but to give in.

"Sorry," he said to Sabrina as they waited on a bench in the hallway for the carriage to be brought round. "Poor Phipps is very grieved by our family's lack of decorum. And no one except Reed or I will throw him a sop of grandiosity now and then."

Sabrina laughed. "I don't mind. Besides, it gives me a chance to take you to task."

"That's what I feared." Alex smiled, belying his words. He enjoyed looking at her, her cheeks flushed, her blue eyes sparkling with excitement. How lovely she was; he wasn't sure whether it was her eyes or her heart-shaped face or her thick black hair that drew him more. He never would have guessed that a woman could look so enticing with short hair. Despite Sabrina's best efforts to pin the mass of curls up into something resembling the sort of upswept hairstyle women wore, strands of hair kept escaping, framing her face with curls.

"Why didn't you tell me last night that you'd found this ticket for my luggage?"

"I wanted to surprise you. Besides, we couldn't go until this morning anyway. I could have gone yesterday afternoon before supper, but you were busy, and I assumed you would wish to go, too..." He trailed off, his tone questioning.

"You're quite right about that." Sabrina turned the chit of paper around in her hand, studying it as if it might give up some vital secret. "I'm not sure I've seen one of these before. Have I just forgotten?"

"You've probably never dealt with checking in your luggage. A young lady wouldn't, as a rule—a maid or escort would have done it for you. Or perhaps you never traveled much."

"No. Perhaps not." She looked thoughtful. "Maybe I lived an unremarkable life in the country."

"Mmm. Until you decided to dress up like a man and take off for London."

She giggled. "That doesn't sound unremarkable, no. Perhaps I am someone wild and uncontrollable, and my family has to keep me locked away."

"Then good for you for escaping. Hopefully you did them some damage in doing so." He reached out to brush his fingertips across her bruised forehead. It made his chest tighten with fury to think of anyone hurting her. "When we find who did this, I'll make him regret it."

"I think you would." She smiled up at him.

"Of course." He held her gaze, thinking how easy

it would be to drown in those eyes, how much—how very much—he would like to kiss her right now.

Sabrina turned away, ducking her head as if she had sensed what he was thinking, and when she spoke again, she went back to the subject of the claim ticket. "I must have checked my bag this time or why else would I have this?"

"I don't know. Perhaps one of the train attendants did it for you. I think any of them would have seen that you were a young lady of quality."

"And apparently incapable of doing anything?"

He chuckled. "Sheltered, let's say. Though my mother would be happy to lecture you on the idea that young ladies are fettered with the shackles of ignorance and inexperience by the very people who claim to be protecting them." He paused, then added, "Don't, I pray, bring it up unless you are prepared to spend several hours listening to her."

She smiled. "I won't."

"The carriage, sir," Phipps intoned and swung open the front door in a grand gesture. The butler fussed about, holding an umbrella to shelter them from the drizzle as they walked the few feet to the carriage and opening.

When they finally pulled away, Alex let out a sigh. "I understand why Mother hates to take the coach. We could have been halfway there by now if I'd hailed a hack."

"Yes, but we wouldn't have gotten to ride in this lovely carriage," Sabrina pointed out.

The coupe-style carriage was elegantly appointed, with stuffed leather seats, silver-plated hardware and walls lined with quilted burgundy satin. Even the ceiling was covered in the padded material. As a finishing touch, a silver calling-card case was attached to one wall.

The windows in the door were large, and Sabrina spent most of the trip staring out at the buildings and people. Alex, sitting beside her, was free to look at her all he wanted, which, he decided, made for a very pleasant trip. Maybe taking the coach was a good idea, after all.

He was a young man who enjoyed the company of women, and he had not lived a celibate life, but he could not remember any woman who had ever made him feel as this one did. Not the cheerful tavern girl who had introduced him to the pleasures of the flesh, nor the sophisticated widow, several years his senior, who had taken him in hand when he and Con had entered Society in London after college. Nor any of the handful of women after her with whom he had conducted discreet affairs.

Sabrina turned and smiled at him, and he felt as if the sun had risen, casting its glow over him. What was it about her that made her so much more desirable than the young ladies with whom he'd danced at parties? The thought made him go cold as he realized that she might belong to another man.

"I'm sure I must not have lived here," she said. "It's all so strange—the people, the traffic, the street after street of buildings." She turned back to the window. "Yesterday it seemed frightening. But today...I find it fascinating."

Once inside Paddington Station, she craned her neck to stare up at the vast glazed roof. "It's huge.

And look at that ceiling. It's like three gigantic glass barrels cut in half and laid side by side."

"Yes." Alex glanced at her, smiling a little at her awestruck expression. "You saw it yesterday."

"Yes, I know, but I was groggy, and all I wanted was to get out, and I didn't really *look* at it. It's magnificent."

Alex joined her in contemplation of the arched roofs, supported by iron ribs, that covered the tracks. "It is rather splendid. Brunel was a master at engineering and design."

"Who?"

"Isambard Kingdom Brunel." Alex rolled the name out grandly. "He designed it—as well as a number of bridges, tunnels and the Great Western main line itself. Although Matthew Digby Wyatt did some of the minor work, as well."

"You know a great deal about buildings."

"Yes, well." Alex shifted somewhat guiltily. "You see…I wasn't entirely clear yesterday." Why hadn't he just explained it all then; now he felt as if he'd been lying to her. Worse, he was afraid she might think the same. "The investigative agency actually belongs to my twin brother, Con."

"But you said—" Sabrina paused. "Actually, no, I guess you didn't say you worked there. You said you were Mr. Moreland. Then you don't investigate things?"

"I help Con out from time to time," he quickly assured her. "With, um, various aspects of the business." And there was another pitfall; he couldn't let her know exactly how he helped. "I didn't mean to mislead you. It was just that Con is out of town and you needed help. I knew Con would agree, and so I... Well, it was the easiest way. It didn't seem important at the time to explain it fully. I wasn't trying to deceive you."

She looked at him with those clear blue eyes and said simply, "I know."

Alex relaxed into a grin. "I am actually an architect."

"You design buildings?" She swept her hand in a vague gesture at their surroundings. "Like this?"

"Well, not like this. But yes, I design buildings. Houses. Sadly, my services are not in great demand."

"Really? I would have thought many people would want to hire you. If nothing else, they could boast about knowing the son of a duke."

"There is that. I fear some of my custom probably does stem from that motive. But in general, I think people assume I'm probably not very good, that I've gotten by on my family's name. A number of the people I trained with resented my taking up space at the institute—it was their opinion that I was merely dabbling. On the other side, the peerage is aghast at my taking up a career. It would be all right if I were one of those nobles like Carnarvon and Bess Hardwick, who were mad about building and hired people to design houses, then oversaw and bullied the poor chaps while they built them. But to go to school and learn design myself and, even worse, actually hire myself out, well, that's 'just not done.'"

Sabrina smiled. "I would think you might already be accustomed to that attitude."

Alex shrugged. "You're right. It's the sort of thing

people say about all of us. We are 'the Mad Morelands.'"

"What?"

"That's what they call us. My family." He shrugged.
"I suppose we are a trifle odd."

"But in a very nice way," Sabrina said. "I like your
family. They're so…"

"Bizarre? Flamboyant?"

"I was going to say warm and welcoming." She
gave him a severe look. "Surely you don't disapprove
of your family."

"No!" He looked startled. "Of course not. I love
them all. Well, my immediate family. There are some
outlying relatives I would gladly do without." The
sound of her sparkling laughter made him wish he
could think of something else amusing. Instead, he
went on, "In truth, I fear I don't live up to my family's standards."

Now, why had he said that? No woman wanted to
hear how a man had failed. As if he could escape his
words, he turned and steered her toward the baggage
room across the way.

Unfortunately, Sabrina didn't drop the subject.
"Why do you say that? I'm sure it's not true. I would
think you're an exemplary son."

"Thank you for that." Foolish to feel so warmed
by her polite statement. "What would be exemplary
in most families is the opposite of the standard in
mine. I'm not the sort to shock society or to plunge
into anything with single-minded devotion or to defy
the world. I'm just not…I don't know, exceptional."

"That's silly. You are exceptionally kind. You took

me in and are going out of your way to help me. Not everyone would have done the same."

"For you? How could they not?" She glanced at him, startled, and he realized that perhaps he had given too much away. He cleared his throat and walked a little faster.

"You know," Sabrina said, "I think it might prove rather tiring to be around someone who was always defying the world or shocking people."

Alex chuckled. "You're right about that."

"You shouldn't discount yourself."

He lifted his brows. "That's the first time I've been accused of that. According to my tutors, I thought I was too smart for my own good."

"I must say, they don't sound like very good tutors."

"That was what Con and I thought. Ah, here we are." They reached the counter, and Alex handed over the claim ticket.

Beside him, Sabrina fairly vibrated with anticipation. Alex had to admit that, when the clerk handed over the smallish, soft-sided bag, he, too, was seized with a desire to sit down right there in the station and paw through it. It would, however, be imprudent to do so. Case in hand, they walked swiftly back through the crowd and out to their waiting carriage.

As soon as they were seated, Alex offered Sabrina the bag. Setting it on her lap and taking a deep breath, as if she were about to plunge into a lake, she unfastened the clasp and opened it. The inside was seemingly filled with white cotton and lace. Sabrina pulled out a pile of material and handed it to him. Alex saw that she had pulled out feminine undergarments—embroidered, frilly white chemises and pantalets, a

petticoat, nightgowns, stockings. He was taken unaware and instantly aroused, so much so that it would
have been embarrassing if he hadn't had a pile of cotton in his lap.

He could not resist taking a chemise between his
fingers, smoothing his thumb over the embroidered
flowers across the neckline. It fastened with slender
ribbons of satin. They were all modest garments, but
the mere fact that they had lain against Sabrina's skin,
the intimacy of holding them, was seductive.

"Shoes!" Sabrina said with delight and pulled out a
pair of slippers. "Oh, this is wonderful. Megan's feet
are smaller than mine, and my toes are so pinched.
Here's a frock." She pulled out a dress, crumpled
from being rolled up and stuffed in the bag, and
shook it out. It was the sort of garment young ladies
often wore, white cotton with a pink flowery print
and decorated with ruffles around the hem, neckline
and sleeves. Another set of ruffles marched down the
front on either side of a row of small decorative buttons. Sabrina frowned. "It certainly doesn't look like
the kind of dress one travels in, but I guess she—I
mean, I… Isn't it peculiar? I feel as if I'm looking at
something that belongs to a stranger." She turned to
him. "I like Megan's clothes much better than this."

He determinedly focused on the dress. "It does
look a trifle…schoolgirlish."

"You mean fussy." She turned back to the bag.
"Gloves. A brush and so on." She held up a silver-
backed hairbrush and matching hand mirror and
comb.

"It's a very nice set. Clearly you don't live in pov-
erty." Alex reached out and took the mirror from her,

turning it over to look at the filigreed silver back. "Another monogram. *SB* again."

"That's all. Nothing else but a toothbrush and a tin of tooth powder and some more handkerchiefs. Oh, and a pair of gloves." Sabrina heaved a disgusted sigh. "You'd think I could have packed one thing that helped. The rest of that letter, for instance. Calling cards."

"I must remember that from now on—always pack a card with one's name and address on it."

She rolled her eyes at his attempt at a witticism and began to roll up the dress to stuff it back in the bag. Something crackled, and she stopped. "Wait. What's that?" She moved her fingers over the cloth. "I think there's something in the pocket of this skirt."

Digging her hand into the pocket, she pulled out two pieces of paper and held them up to him. "Look at this. More train tickets!"

"The devil?" Alex leaned forward, peering at the two tickets. "This one is from someplace named Baddesly Commons to Newbury. That makes sense. You traveled from some smaller town to reach the main line at Newbury. But this one…" He plucked the ticket from her hand, rubbing his thumb over it. The faintest trace of excitement and fear clung to it. "This one is from Newbury to Bath. The opposite direction of London. It's not been marked. See? It wasn't used."

"What does that mean? Why would I buy two tickets?"

"It means you were creating a false trail. Someone is chasing you."

CHAPTER EIGHT

SABRINA'S HEART HAMMERED in her chest. She *had* fled from someone. She had known that was what the tickets meant even as she asked the question. Her hope had been that she was wrong. "But why? Who?"

"I've no idea. But why else would you have bought this other ticket? It might be possible that you bought it intending to return to Newbury and take this train from there, but if so, why isn't there a return passage to Newbury from London? And why wouldn't you just have bought the ticket from London to Bath instead of returning to Newbury first? It fits with everything else. You have only one bag, something you can carry without needing help. It was packed in haste—there is only the bare minimum of things here. You wouldn't have packed this way for a pleasure trip. You dressed up in disguise. You bought a ticket to two different places so that someone following you wouldn't know which way you'd gone."

"I knew he—they, whoever—would follow me." Sabrina made herself think coolly and clearly. This was no time to panic. "If he went to the ticket master and asked if a young lady of my descript—" She stopped, eyes widening. "I have it! What if I packed and escaped whoever it was in this town of Baddesly Commons? Took the train to Newbury and bought a ticket to Bath. Then I could have gone into the lavatory and changed into men's clothing—say I bought some there or was clever enough to bring them in the bag with me. I roll up my dress and stick it in the bag; I cut off my hair and I go back out to buy a ticket to London, but this time as a man."

"And when they came looking, asking for a young lady who might have bought a ticket, the ticket agent would remember you and tell them you went to Bath, not think of the boy who later bought a ticket to London." Alex grinned. "How devious—I like that."

"Unfortunately, I know as little about who's chasing me as I do about myself." Sabrina began to sweep up all the articles she had pulled out and return them to the suitcase. She realized that in her eagerness to discover what was in the bag that she had simply tossed the first pile of clothing in Alex's lap. All her underthings. Personal, intimate pieces of clothing. She flushed with embarrassment. What must he think of her? And she could scarcely reach over there and pick them up.

Sabrina glanced up at his face and was suddenly certain that Alex knew exactly what she was thinking. Her cheeks heated even more. His gaze dropped to her mouth, then hastily back, and she thought, her chest knotting with anticipation, that he was about to kiss her again.

But then he looked away, breaking the moment. He took the bag from her and began putting the clothes back into the case, carefully not looking at her. Sabrina looked down at her hands, folded in her lap. She must stop all these crazy, wayward thoughts. Alex Moreland, son of a duke, was not for her—even if she knew who she was or what she was running from. Even if she was not already married, which she was beginning to be more and more frightened that she was.

"Why do you think I ran away?" she asked, wanting to pierce the awkward silence. "It wasn't a carriage accident or someone abducting me—not with this much evidence of planning."

"Probably not. Though I suppose an abductor could have grabbed the bag of clothes, as well." Sabrina fixed him with a skeptical gaze, and he said, "Yes, well, I'll agree it's not very likely."

"Do you think I am married to him?" she asked in a soft voice, keeping her eyes steadily on her hands. She didn't want him to see the tears she feared might come. "It seems logical. I have a wedding ring. My face is bruised. How likely is it that my husband hit me and I ran away from him?"

"We don't know that," Alex told her firmly. "Sabrina, look at me." He reached out and took her chin, tilting up her face so that their eyes met. "There are several other possibilities, as well. That ring might be just a ring, or it could be some family heirloom, your grandmother's wedding ring, say. We know that you have bruises, but they could have been caused some other way. And if someone did hit you, we have no way of knowing whether he attacked you, so you ran away, or he hit you *because* he discovered you were running away. It could have been a stranger, a thief or even some other relative—a father, for instance."

"You think my father beat me?"

"I don't know. I certainly hope not. I hate to think that anyone would have done such a thing to you. But my point is that we have no way of knowing until we find out who you are and what happened to you."

"Why would anyone but a father or husband be chasing me? Why would it be important to make me return?"

"I don't know. Perhaps you have something of his."

Sabrina gaped at him. "You're saying I stole something? That I'm a thief?"

"No. Sometimes people have disputes over things—heirlooms, for instance. So one might take something that was in another's possession and not consider it stealing. Or maybe he stole something from you, and you got it back—that ring, say."

"You think the ring is that valuable?" Sabrina asked doubtfully.

He shrugged. "It could be an heirloom. Or maybe it was the other way around—he wants something from you, and you're afraid he'll force you to give it to him. Not necessarily something you have on you at the moment. Something at home or…or in a safe, perhaps."

Sabrina sighed. "Whatever it is, what are we to do now? How can we find out what's going on?"

"There are still some other avenues to explore. Tom Quick is investigating; Megan might hear from one of her sources."

"But it seems unlikely that anyone in London would know anything about me. I came from this Baddesly place. It might be the key to all this."

"True. And that is why I suggest we talk to Uncle Bellard."

"Uncle Bellard? But why?"

"If there's anything to know about Baddesly Commons, he'll know it. He's wild about history, and he never forgets anything. Well, except things like coming down to supper or taking off his nightcap. But when it comes to names and events, he's spot-on."

"But how will that help us?"

"It may not," Alex admitted. "But he might know the names of people who've lived there—perhaps some family whose surname begins with the letter *B*. Or something about the place that might jog your memory. A house. A famous ancestor. Some obscure battle."

When the carriage rolled up in front of Broughton House, they went immediately up the stairs. After dropping off the bag in Sabrina's room, they turned the corner into the hall where Alex's chamber lay.

"Phipps calls this the bachelor suite," Alex told her and flashed a grin. "My room and Con's are on this side, with our sitting room in between, and Uncle Bellard's rooms are across the corridor at the end of the hall."

As they started down the corridor, one of the doors flew open and a maid bolted out, cap hanging over one ear and her hair in disarray. She turned and shouted into the room behind her, "I will not stay in this madhouse another minute!" She slammed the door and took off at a run for the back stairs.

"Bloody hell," Alex muttered and strode down the hall.

Sabrina hurried after him. As Alex opened the door, a maniacal cackle sounded in the room and a woman exclaimed, "Give that back, you thieving devil!"

Alex strode into the room. "Wellie!"

Sabrina, right on his heels, took in the room at a glance. It appeared to be a sitting room, with over-stuffed chairs and a standing lamp beside the fire and a gaming table, flanked by a liquor cabinet. A tall bookcase, packed full of volumes, was against the wall closest to her. A few more books were stacked beside one chair, and the small table between the chairs held an empty whiskey glass. An old cricket bat was propped in one corner.

It was, all in all, a very comfortable, masculine sort of place. The only oddity was a very large mesh cage standing before a broad set of windows. Inside the cage were three branches at different heights. The door to the cage stood open.

A maid stood in front of the bookcase, glaring up at the top, her hands on her hips. When Alex entered, she turned to him and said in an aggrieved voice, "He stole me duster again, Master Alex."

"I do apologize, Nancy. I forgot to put him in his cage before I went down to breakfast. I hope the new girl wasn't too frightened."

"Her," Nancy sniffed. "She's like to jump out of her skin over the skull in Master Con's room. She's another one gone."

Skull?

"I daresay." Alex turned to address the top of the bookcase. "Wellington. Give that back. You know you're not supposed to frighten the household."

Sabrina followed his gaze to the top of a tall cabinet and her mouth dropped open. A large bird stood on the edge of the bookcase, black talons curled over it. It was bright red all over its head and upper body, with a rich purplish-blue belly. Its beak was black and curved down sharply, and from it dangled a small feather duster. The parrot tilted his head to look at Alex with one bright eye for a moment, then dropped the cleaning tool. The maid rushed forward to pick it up and disappeared into the adjoining room, fussing with the feathers and muttering as she went.

"I tell myself Wellie thinks the feather duster is another bird invading his territory," Alex told Sabrina. "But I'm afraid it's just that he loves to send people into hysterics."

From the bookcase, the parrot squawked, "Nevermore."

Alex sighed. "I do wish Kyria's brood hadn't taught you that so thoroughly. You are not a raven, Wellie."

The bird shifted back and forth and in a singsong voice said, "Wellie, good Wellie."

"Yes, well, I wish you would be. You know how the duchess hates it when you frighten off servants."

"Did she say *skull*?" Sabrina asked.

"What? Oh, yes, Con has a skull on a chest in his bedchamber. Something from one of his cases. Not real, of course," he quickly added.

Wellie let out a squawk that sounded like the cackle Sabrina had heard earlier, and he swooped off across the room, ducking through an open doorway on the opposite side from the one the maid had exited through. Sabrina could hear the parrot calling out something in his rough voice. It sounded like "Con."

"It's looking for my brother," Alex explained, then he called to the bird, "Con's not here. Come here, Wellie. If you're good, I'll take you to Uncle Bellard's." He turned to Sabrina and explained, "He's very fond of my uncle's rooms. There's a particular bust he likes to perch on."

An instant later the parrot was back, settling down on Alex's shoulder. "Wellie, good Wellie."

"Yes, yes." Alex reached inside the cage and picked a nut from the cup attached to the side, holding it up to the bird. Wellington cracked and ate it, all the while regarding Sabrina with his beady black eyes. "Wellie, this is Sabrina. Can you say *Sabrina*?"

He twisted his head a different way and squawked.

"Sorry." Alex grinned at her. "I shouldn't try to teach him your name. He'll be a dead nuisance if he learns it."

"He's beautiful. He's so big...and red."

"Red Wellie," the bird offered, and Sabrina laughed. "He's gorgeous." She stretched out a tentative hand. "May I touch him?"

"Yes. He won't bite. He'll just take off if he doesn't want to be petted."

But the bird stayed put as Sabrina stroked a gentle finger over his head. Spreading his wings a little, Wellie preened, then folded them back down.

"Shall we go?" Alex opened the door, stepping back with a grand sweep of his arm to usher Sabrina out. He made an odd picture, so handsome, so elegant...and sporting a vivid red-and-blue parrot on his shoulder.

Sabrina smiled to herself and started down the hall, wondering what oddity awaited her next in the Moreland household.

CHAPTER NINE

SHE SOON FOUND OUT. The door to Uncle Bellard's sitting room stood open. Sabrina stopped in the doorway, gazing around her in wonder. The chamber was less a sitting room than a display area. Scattered all about the room, among a few chairs and an occasional stool, was a hodgepodge of tables of various sizes and heights. Whether they were scarred and pitted, or shiny and new, or gilt-edged Louis XVs, round, square or rectangular, all of them were filled with toy soldiers.

"Uncle Bellard reconstructs famous battles," Alex explained, his hand on her elbow urging her into the room. "That's Agincourt. Waterloo. Something or other at Sedgemoor." He waved his hand around. "The rest of the collection's at the estate house."

"It's very impressive."

"It usually leaves one speechless." Alex cast her a grin, turned and said, "Uncle Bellard?"

Distracted as she had been by the displays, Sabrina had not seen the small man standing in front of a large bookcase, perusing its shelves. His uncle had apparently not noticed their entrance, either, for he turned now at Alex's words, looking pleased, his head tilted inquiringly. With his beaked nose, bright eyes and hair sticking out in odd clumps, he reminded her forcibly of Wellie.

"Ah, Alex." He beamed at his nephew. "I didn't expect you. And Miss, um…"

"Sabrina."

"Yes, of course." He felt for the spectacles that were sitting on his head and pulled them into place. "You're the young lady with the amnesia. Most fascinating." His gaze moved to Alex's shoulder. "Hello, General. Haven't seen you since you stole Henry."

"Henry the Fifth," Alex said, apparently interpreting as he pointed toward one of the tables. "Agincourt." The parrot left Alex's shoulder to perch on a bust atop a cabinet, where he could survey the room and the street outside. "Don't pick up anything, Wellie, or it's back to your cage."

"Good Wellie," the bird squawked.

Sabrina looked around the room with interest. Every wall was lined with bookcases, and several more tomes sat stacked on chairs, tables and the floor in a seemingly haphazard manner. It was not only a display room, but also a library.

She moved closer to one of the tables, where an elaborate replica was laid out, including a painted papier-mâché landscape with figures of trees and shrubbery and even a small house, as well as two lines of armies, one wearing Scottish tartans.

"Culloden," Bellard told her helpfully. "There's Trafalgar." He pointed to another layout, where tiny boats sailed on a mirror sea.

"Did you build these?" Sabrina leaned closer, fascinated.

"What? Oh, yes, I laid out the armies. Alex and

Con made the hills and valleys when they were younger—well, mostly Alex. He was always interested in building things. Con liked to map out the terrain." He beamed at her, then at Alex. "Now, what can I help you with?"

"What makes you think I came here for help?" Alex protested. "Perhaps we only wanted to chat."

"I may be old, boy, but I'm not senile yet." The old man's eyes twinkled. "I don't think you're squiring a young lady around to show her some musty old books and battles."

Alex grinned. "What do you know about Baddesly Commons?"

"Baddesly Commons." He considered the matter. "It's a village, isn't it? What happened there?"

"Nothing that I know of. I just thought if something had, you would be familiar with it. And if you did, you might know what families were in the area."

Bellard frowned. "Hmm. Well, let's take a look at the map." He led them over to a wall that faced onto the street, where four long, narrow windows were interspersed with maps. The centerpiece was a very large map of England set on corkboard. Pins of various colors were stuck in it haphazardly. "You have any idea what part of the country?"

"We think it's not terribly far from Newbury, though I don't know in what direction. I would guess north or south of it. Sabrina took a train from there to Newbury to catch the line to London. She wouldn't have had to if it lay east or west of the town. Actually... Of course! It has to be south. The railway runs down to Winchester, not north from Newbury."

Bellard slid his finger slowly down in a line.

"Aha!" He tapped the map, twice. "Here we are. Baddesly Commons. Hmm." He furrowed his brow. "I can't think of anything significant about this area. Actually, Wellington built a country house not far from here." He paused as the parrot let out a screech and repeated his name. "Yes, Wellie, quite right. But I believe it's east of there a bit."

"Stratfield Saye," Alex agreed. "Highclere is in that area, too, I believe."

"Highclere? What's that?" Sabrina asked.

"Lord Carnarvon's house. Family name is, um…"

"I believe they're a minor line of the Herberts," his uncle offered.

Well, that certainly didn't start with a *B*, Sabrina thought—*not* that she was likely to be related to a lord.

Alex looked to Sabrina, and she shook her head. "None of this sounds familiar to me."

"Well, no, it wouldn't to most people," Bellard agreed.

"I hoped that if we learned a little about the places, the people, something might spark a memory for Sabrina," Alex explained to his uncle.

"I can look into the local histories and find names of the local families," Uncle Bellard suggested.

"That's too much work," Sabrina protested.

"I don't mind." Bellard smiled. "I quite enjoy reading about history, even when I don't know the people. There are so many interesting things that crop up. I just need to find the right books." He waved his hand vaguely toward the shelves he had been perusing when they entered.

"What about Bath?"

"Bath. Oh, well, yes, there's quite a bit of history there, all the way back to the Romans. But what does Bath have to do with it?"

"I'm not sure," Alex admitted. "It appears she bought a ticket to Bath as well as one to London. We believe it was probably done to confuse her pursuers."

"Someone is pursuing you? Oh, my." Uncle Bellard frowned. "Do you know why? No, of course you don't, silly of me. My dear girl, it's a very good thing you came here. We have a bit of experience with these sorts of things."

Since this was the last thing Sabrina had expected him to say about her situation, she could only stare at him.

"It's possible," Alex went on, "that there was no reason to buy a ticket for Bath other than that it lay in the opposite direction from London." He turned toward Sabrina. "But I thought that perhaps it had some significance, some reason why your pursuer would think you were more likely to go there than London."

"If there is, I don't know it. I don't know much of anything about the place, really, aside from the waters. And there's a cathedral there, isn't there?"

"Yes, indeed, a lovely cathedral. It's a very charming town, not as fashionable as it once was, of course. The Romans called it Aquae Sulis, as the Celts had called the sacred spring Sulis after one of their goddesses. Easy for the Romans to change the goddess to their Minerva. There were… But, no, I'm wandering afield." Uncle Bellard gave Sabrina a shy smile that won her heart. "I fear history will not be much aid in this situation. The thing is, Alexander, Bath wouldn't necessarily be the destination. From Bath, one can travel to several different places. Anyone pursuing Miss, um, Sabrina would have to know that she could go north into the Cotswalds or down to Taunton or Exeter, even into Cornwall. One could continue west to Bristol, and from there, to Wales or, well, almost anywhere, if one took a ship. So someone who knew her might have a reason for thinking she was traveling to any one of those other places. Bath might be enough to send him haring off there."

"You're right. It's a clever place to choose, especially if, as Sabrina thinks, she doesn't know London well."

"Unfortunately, it doesn't tell us anything about who I might be," Sabrina said.

"Mmm. That's true. Well, I shall see what I can find out about Baddesly Commons in my books. Perhaps that will give you somewhere to start." Bellard nodded to them and shuffled off toward the opposite wall, lined with bookcases.

Sabrina looked after the old man in concern. "Isn't this too hard for him? Should he do all that standing?"

"Uncle Bellard isn't nearly as fragile as he looks—just as he's not really so vague, either. I think they're both a bit of protective coloring, like a chameleon, so that people will leave him alone to putter about, doing what he likes. I've seen him stand in here for hours, placing his replicas just so."

Sabrina glanced around at the numerous tables. "They're really remarkable. It's all so painstaking and meticulous. It must take a great deal of research."

"It does. But as he said, delving into history is what he loves."

"What are we to do while he is searching?" Sabrina asked. "It's all very well that your uncle and Megan and your employee are looking for information, but I cannot bear to just sit about waiting. I should be *doing* something." She frowned. "Perhaps I should simply go back to Baddesly Commons. Maybe I would remember everything if I saw it again, and if not, at least someone might recognize me."

"No!" Alex looked alarmed. "We've no idea who might be pursuing you or why. You'd likely walk right back into whatever you escaped from. If you want to see if anyone recognizes you, you should do it here in London, where you have my family and the safety of this house."

"But—" Sabrina began.

"Yes, yes, I know, it's unlikely you live here in London, and obviously, you ran away from whoever it is in another town. But you came to London for a reason. Maybe you don't live here, but you might visit sometimes. You might have a relative or friend who lives here who you believe would help you. The person who wrote you the letter, perhaps."

Sabrina considered the idea. "That does make some sense. But walking all around hoping someone will spot me seems a bit…haphazard."

"I was thinking more of accompanying Kyria to some parties or the theater, something like that."

"But your sister didn't recognize me."

"No. But Kyria doesn't know everyone in Society. And if you haven't been here before or only infrequently visited, then she wouldn't know you. But that doesn't mean she might not know your friend or relative."

"There's really no reason to think my friend or

relative, even if they exist, would move in the same circles as an aristocrat."

"She might not. That's why we would go to the theater or opera as well, get an ice at Gunter's, visit some of Kyria's favorite stores. It would cast a wider net. It *is* haphazard. I'll admit that. I am flailing about a bit, hoping to hit something. But the thing is, those would all be enjoyable things to do. Wouldn't you like to go to a ball or to see a play? Spend some of that large amount of money you carried? If no one recognizes you, it's not a complete loss—you will still have an enjoyable time." He smiled. "And so will I. I would very much like to show you the city." He held out his hand to her.

Sabrina hesitated, then slipped her hand into his. "That is what I would like, too."

CHAPTER TEN

ALEX SAT AT his drafting table, staring out the window. He had come to his office to work, but so far he'd spent most of the day brooding. For the past two weeks, they had followed his plan to see and be seen around London. They went to a play with Megan and Theo. They attended the opera, visited museums, went to a small soiree. When Alex had to work at his office, Kyria took Sabrina shopping for a hat and gloves and all the sundry little things one needed when all of one's possessions consisted of a brush-and-comb set and some underthings.

Alex and Sabrina volunteered to accompany the youngest members of the household to Hyde Park, since their nanny was still hobbled by her sprained ankle—frankly, after they'd chased the two little girls about all afternoon, Alex wondered how in the world their nanny managed to do it by herself normally. They took Kyria's brood to Gunter's one day for ice creams and wound up back at Kyria's house playing games, where "the Littles" and their older sister Emily invented more and more outlandish histories for Sabrina and her arrival on a train in London, until they all dissolved into laughter.

Sabrina had clearly enjoyed the time, but they had discovered nothing regarding her identity. What Alex had learned was how very much he hoped Sabrina was not married. He went to bed every night thinking about her, and every morning he woke up eager to see her. Even his nightmare of being locked in a room, which had visited him again twice, did not linger, for thoughts of Sabrina soon filled his mind.

It was dangerous being around her so much. It would be sheer folly to fall in love with a woman in her situation—even Theo, the least likely member of his family to warn against danger, had taken him aside yesterday and reminded him of all the reasons Alex should guard against losing his heart to Sabrina.

Yet he could not seem to be reasonable. Every time he saw her, he wanted her more. Last night, when she had come to dinner in that lavender gown with the wide, off-the-shoulder neckline, it had been all he could do not to take her in his arms and kiss her. It was worse, he thought, having kissed her that one night. If he had not, he wouldn't have known how she tasted, how she felt in his arms, how her soft body fitted against his.

Her hair enticed him; her wide blue eyes entranced him. Her voice, her quick light laugh and her smile all teased at his nerves. He had to remind himself several times a day that it would be the act of a cad to take advantage of her. Perhaps if it had just been lust he felt, he could have managed to stay away from the house, spend less time with her. But the truth was, he simply enjoyed her company. He liked to talk to her, to make her laugh, to watch her enjoyment of every new thing she found. The time he spent away from her, the minutes seemed to crawl by. He would imagine what she was doing and envy whoever was with her, and he could not keep to any task for longer than a few minutes.

He wished Con were here. He wanted to talk with him about all the crazy new feelings that tumbled around in his chest. And for some reason he could not define, he wanted Con to meet her. He wanted the two of them to get along. He wanted—

His unconstructive thoughts were interrupted by the sound of Tom Quick whistling as he walked up the stairs. Seizing on the opportunity to leave his worktable, Alex sprang to his feet and went to the door.

Tom grinned. "Hello, guv. You must have read my mind. I was just coming to see you."

Excitement rose in Alex. "What is it? You've found out something, haven't you?"

"No word anywhere on any young lady missing," Quick told him, coming inside and shutting the door. "But I think I've found your house. There's the address." He set a piece of paper on the drafting table, then flopped down in a chair as if exhausted. "I tell you straight, it was a piece of work, that. I've walked up and down every swanky street in London. There were a couple of others that looked close, but this one fit down to the knocker on the door."

Alex studied the address. It wasn't far. "Did you discover anything about it?"

"Haven't looked at any records. I asked next door, and the servants said nobody lives there. That's all they knew. T'other side said the chap that lived there died some years ago—six or seven or more, they thought. They agreed it's been empty these past few months, but before that, it was leased out for the Season every year."

Alex nodded. It was the custom of many who lived on their estates to rent a home in the city for the months of the social season. A house in this area would have been easy to market. It gave him a bit of a pause; perhaps the watch was connected to someone who had lived in the house for only a few months. In that case, it probably wouldn't provide them with any clues.

But no, the feeling in the watch had been deep and fond. It was much more likely to have belonged to someone who owned the house for at least a few years—perhaps the man who the neighbors said had died a few years ago. It could have been Sabrina's father or grandfather. If he had died some time ago, that would explain Sabrina's finding London unfamiliar.

"What about across the street?"

"The servants there were too proud to talk to some passing stranger. Big place, went all the way to the corner—not as grand as Broughton House, but still… I decided to give up and not ask any farther down the street. I was hoping to catch you before you went home."

"Yes, that's good. Tom, I want you to find out whatever you can about the place—who it belongs to now and so on. I'm especially interested in this chap who died. What was his name? Did he leave it to someone? Sold it?"

"Will do, guv."

"Would you stop calling me that?" Alex said in exasperation. "I'm five years younger than you."

"Ooh, I can't do that, sir. Wouldn't be respectful." Tom grinned cheekily.

"Wouldn't be irritating, you mean."

Tom's chuckle as he went out the door was agreement enough. Alex, shaking his head, began to put away his materials. He'd done enough on the plans for the moment. He needed to let it settle in his mind before he made any changes. Besides, he was too eager to go by this address.

He had the hansom drop him off a block before they reached the house, then walked past it. His heart picked up its beat when he saw it. Tom was right. This was the place he'd seen. There were some low bushes missing along the foundation, and the shutters and front door were black. Changes, he thought, since the man who owned the watch had seen it last. Somehow, seeing it, he felt even more sure the home had belonged to the owner of that watch.

It was a graceful house. Alex would have liked to linger for a moment in front of the house and examine it, but he didn't want to draw any attention to his interest. One set of the neighbors, at least, were a gossipy lot. He contented himself with a quick glance that encompassed the area, including the narrow walkway along the house to the less elegant side door.

He walked the rest of the way home. It served to eat up some of his energy. He was eager to tell her his news. Eager to finally get to *do* something for Sabrina.

Alex's vision of a dramatic announcement was rather diminished by the fact that Sabrina was not in the cozy sitting room upstairs, nor even the sultan room, so that he had to prosaically hunt through the house for her, finally stopping one of the footmen to ask where she was. Denby told him she had gone for a walk in the back, so he headed into the garden.

He spotted her on the other side of the formal flower beds, strolling across the grass toward the high back wall. She was wearing one of Megan's dresses, striped in white and a deep vivid blue, with a practical narrow skirt, devoid of ornamentation except for a wide sash that turned Sabrina's waist into nothing. The sash tied in the back in a huge, saucy bow that made a man's hands fairly itch to reach out and untie it.

She must have heard his footsteps on the gravel path of the garden, for she turned and saw him, her mouth widening into a smile. Her pace quickened as she came forward to meet him, and he thought she must have seen something in his face, for she called out, "What is it? Have you found something?"

"That I have. Or, rather, Tom did. It's the house that—" He paused, realizing he was suddenly on shaky ground. "Uh, it's a house that I think may be connected to you."

"A house! But how did he know? How did he find it? Is it my home?"

Why hadn't he thought to have a story prepared? He needed a plausible reason why Tom had been searching for a certain house, one that did not involve himself getting "emanations" from some inanimate object. But at the moment he could not come up with one, so Alex sidestepped the issue and said, "No, I'm sure you don't reside there, at least not recently. It has no one living in it right now, but for the past few years it has been let to various people."

"It's a rental house? But what does it have to do with me?"

"I'm not really sure. That's why I thought I'd go there this evening."

"But how can you find out anything? You said there was no one living there."

"That's the best time to search a house."

"Alex!" Her eyes widened. "Do you mean you intend to…to break into the place?"

"I'm not going to break a window or anything." Alex grinned, inwardly congratulating himself on successfully diverting her attention.

"But you haven't a key," she pointed out. Her eyes narrowed. "Are you going to pick the lock? Where did a duke's son learn how to pick a lock?"

"From Tom Quick. Con and I often hung around him when we were young. He was actually more a pickpocket when he was a lad, but he'd also learned a number of other useful ways of availing himself of money."

"Your employee is a thief?" She stared.

"Not any longer. The last wallet he took belonged to my brother Reed."

"He stole your brother's money? Then Reed hired him?"

"Well, first he sent him to school. He saw better qualities in Tom than a number of others had."

"Clearly." She came closer. "Alex, I insist on going with you. It is my future—well, my past, really—and I should be there, too."

"Of course. Why wouldn't you?"

"Because…well, I thought you'd object. I thought you'd say it wasn't the sort of thing for a lady, that it was too dangerous or 'just not done' or something of that sort."

"Oh." Alex paused. "I suppose it could be danger-ous. I hadn't thought about that. It's just that Kyria would probably have boxed my ears if I'd said some-thing like that to her. Olivia and Thisbe, too. And I shudder to think what Megan would do to me." He frowned. "But perhaps you shouldn't go. I don't think anything untoward will happen, but it *is* breaking and entering."

"Don't you dare have second thoughts about it," Sabrina warned, fixing him with as stubborn a look as any of his sisters. "I'll do worse to you than they would."

Alex laughed. "I know better than to forbid you, believe me."

"When do we go? Now?"

"No, it's still daylight, and this is something bet-ter performed under the cover of darkness. Tonight after supper—and wear something dark."

Sabrina's eyes sparkled. "Megan lent me a cloak the other day. It's midnight blue and has a hood."

"Perfect. And the most sensible shoes and skirt you have—just in case we need to run."

It was his own wardrobe that was the most difficult to blend in with the darkness, given his plethora of starched white shirts. He solved the problem by raid-ing Con's closet. Con was bound to have something for the occasional breaking and entering. In fact, Con turned out to have an astonishing array of disguises; deep down, Alex suspected, Con would have liked to be on the stage.

Under the curious gazes of both his dog and the parrot, Alex dressed in a dark, collarless working-man's shirt and rough coat, adding a pair of his own supple black leather gloves. There was nothing he could do to hide the paleness of his face, but the flat black corduroy cap pulled low on his forehead helped somewhat.

Rufus padded after Alex as he went down the hall and knocked softly on Sabrina's door. She popped out as if she had been waiting. He saw, approvingly, that she wore a simple dark blue bodice and skirt with no bustle and few petticoats beneath, as well as serviceable black leather half boots. Over her arm she carried a cloak.

"Excellent." He could not keep his mind from going to the thought of her lack of petticoats beneath her skirt, but he pulled it firmly back. "Let's go down the back way. I'd just as soon not have to explain what we're doing to anyone in my family—not, of course, that they wouldn't do the same sort of thing themselves."

"Won't the servants wonder?"

He shrugged. "Perhaps. But they're accustomed to our odd fits and starts, as Mrs. Bee says."

Sabrina cast a doubtful look over at the dog as they walked quietly to the back stairs. "You're taking Rufus? Isn't he rather noticeable?"

"He is unfortunately light-colored," Alex agreed, looking down at the nearly white dog with splotches of dark fur. "Still, who's going to think someone's taking a dog with them to break into a house? And he can stand watch for us to make sure no one catches us by surprise. Besides, he knows something is up, and he'd raise such a ruckus when I left there'd be no hope of getting out quietly. I was lucky to get out without Wellington, as well."

As he expected, the servants cleaning up the kitchen spared barely a glance at them as they passed through. From force of long habit, he filched a scrap of meat from the platter and slipped it to Rufus.

"Stop encouraging that mangy hound, Master Alex," the cook said without turning around.

"Careful, Gert, Rufus will think you don't like him," Alex responded.

The woman snorted, glancing over at them and taking in their appearance. "Looks like you're the one needs to be careful, Master Alex."

"I will." Alex opened the door to usher Sabrina out.

"And don't toss that poor girl into one of your fracases now."

"Gert!" He turned back with a mock gasp, placing his hand against his heart in a dramatic way. "You wound me."

"Get on with you." Gert waved him away, unable to hold back her grin.

Outside, he turned to find Sabrina watching him. "They're all very fond of you."

"They all think I'm still twelve years old." He reached out and took her cloak from her to drape around her shoulders. Gazing down into her face, he tied the ribbons at the neck. His hands fell away, but he was reluctant to step back. "There, you look suitably stealthy."

"Oh, I have more," Sabrina said with a saucy little grin and pulled something from her pocket. "I have a mask!" She lifted the black half mask to her eyes and tied it behind her head.

There was a subtle seduction to the mask, dark and

satiny against her creamy white skin, concealing her even as it exposed the curve of her mouth beneath it. She appeared faintly mysterious and utterly desirable, and, with the lilt of her teasing laugh running through him like a fingernail sliding down his spine, all he wanted to do was kiss her.

Fortunately for his willpower, Sabrina stepped back and pulled up her hood. Truth was, this guise only increased the throbbing inside him more, for she looked like a woman bent on a secret tryst. But at least her movement had broken his momentary trance, enabling him to pull together his scattered thoughts.

"Well…" Alex cleared his throat. "Let's be off. We've a crime to commit."

CHAPTER ELEVEN

THEY STROLLED ALONG the street, Rufus trotting happily beside them. Aside from his first impulsive dash down the block when they left Broughton House, the dog stuck close to Alex's side, only occasionally stopping to examine some particularly appealing scent.

The evening darkness wrapped around them like velvet, hushed and foggy, with streetlights creating warm pools of golden light along the way. In the distance, he could hear the clip-clop of horses' hooves and the rumble of wheels as some carriage rolled down the street, but here he and Sabrina were alone together in this strangely intimate atmosphere.

She had her hand tucked in his elbow, and he matched his longer stride to hers, separated by mere inches. She was close enough that her perfume tickled at his senses, making it difficult to think. The thought of her dabbing on perfume to go break into a house was absurd, but he was glad she had done so, even as distracting as it was.

It was not far from Broughton House to their goal, and he saw it now in the block ahead. "There it is." He kept his voice low. "It's in the next block, the second house on the opposite side of the street to us."

"The white house with black shutters?"

"Yes, that's it." He waited for some sign of recognition from Sabrina, but there was nothing, even in the emotional presence of her that lay quietly in the back of his brain. He had sensed a hum of excitement in her from the moment they left the house—it was beginning to feel normal to be so aware of her—but it heightened only slightly in anticipation when she saw the house. He had the disappointing suspicion it was not her home.

They walked past the house and turned up the small walkway between it and the next home. Alex had picked up a lantern from the gardener's shed in back of their house, but he had not lit it, the glow from the streetlights being adequate. But as they walked into the inky passageway, he stopped to light the lantern, shutting down all the sides except one, which he kept only partly up. It was just enough to cast a glow in front of their feet and keep them from stumbling.

"What if someone sees us?" Sabrina whispered.

Alex glanced over at the neighboring house. "I doubt they will. No lights in the rooms upstairs. I imagine the servants are too busy to look out here. But if they do, well, we'll just have to brazen it out."

"You can brazen out forcing a lock?"

"I imagine so. If not, I suppose we'll have to run for it." The prospect of excitement was beginning to fizz in his blood like champagne. It had been a good while, he reflected, since he'd had an adventure. He grinned down at her upturned face. "Don't worry. If it comes to that, I'll just have to knock him out."

"Oh." Her eyes widened a little. Alex had to fight an urge to lean down and kiss her.

They reached the door at the far end of the house and Alex set down the lantern, lifting the shield a little to cast more light on the lock. Reaching inside his jacket, he pulled out a small leather case and took a couple of slender metal tools. He went down on one knee and slipped the wires into the keyhole. Sabrina stood behind him, her skirts hopefully blocking the dim light from the street.

He had just heard the sweet click of the lock turning when Rufus, patiently waiting, suddenly made a low noise deep in his throat. Alex dropped the shield on the lantern, concealing the light, and at the same time stuffed the tools into a pocket. He sprang to his feet, turning to look down the walkway.

A sturdy figure came into view, the hat on his head identifying him as a bobby. He was strolling along with an air of unconcern, no doubt walking his nightly route. Still, at any moment, he might look this way. Quickly Alex wrapped his arms around Sabrina, pulling her in close against him and burying his face in her neck to conceal the telltale paleness. "Shh. A bobby."

They waited, listening to the sounds of the man's footsteps. Alex was intensely aware of Sabrina's body in his arms, her heat and softness, the tantalizing scent of her perfume filling his nostrils. Her breathing was rapid, her breasts pressed against him. The danger of their position seemingly only added to the enticement, heightening every sensation, every emotion.

As the bobby's footsteps faded into the distance, they remained as they were, arms still clamped around each other. Alex lifted his head and looked down into her face. She was gazing back at him, the hood falling back a little on her head to frame her face perfectly. Her eyes were soft and dark, unreadable in the dim light. Alex stood for a long moment, thinking of all the obstacles and cautions that separated them, the many reasons he should let her go.

He bent and kissed her.

Her lips yielded to him, more than yielded—she answered back, her mouth hot and eager. Her arms went around his neck, and she pressed up against him, her lips clinging as hungrily as his. Her kiss was heady, intoxicating, shattering his composure and sending all his careful thoughts into oblivion. All he could think was how much he wanted her, how good it was to taste her, how much more he could feel.

He slid a hand beneath her cloak, finding and caressing the soft mounds of her breasts. She made a soft noise of surprise against his mouth, followed by a far more sensual moan. When his mouth left hers to explore her throat, she sagged against his arm, turning her head to expose her throat to his kisses.

"Here, now, what's going on?" A man's loud voice cut through the haze of their passion, and they sprang apart, turning toward the man standing a few feet from them in the open doorway of the house next door. Light spilled out of the room behind him, silhouetting him and making it impossible to read his face, but his voice marked him as a servant of the house rather than the master. "Who are you, and what are you doing here?"

"Stay here," Alex murmured and strolled forward, pitching his voice toward the other man. "I don't see that it's any of *your* concern." His voice fairly dripped with hauteur. Carefully he stopped outside the light from the doorway; it would not do his pose of aristocrat any good if the man saw Alex's attire.

"It is if you're robbing that house," the other man retorted, though his voice lacked a good deal of its former conviction.

"Well, it is *my* house now, so I'll thank you to go back inside and let me get on with viewing it. What is your name? Who is your employer?" Alex disdainfully looked the smaller man up and down. "Is he aware that you have the habit of accosting his neighbors?"

"I... Uh, what?" The man goggled at him, his face now filled with uncertainty, and he slid back a step. "No! I mean, beg your pardon, sir, but I thought you was, you know, a thief. No one lives there."

"Well, as you can see, I am not. And my friend..." His voice changed on the word, infusing it with a smug innuendo, as he glanced back at Sabrina's obviously feminine shape. "Mrs. Blackwell will be living here now. You will doubtless find she is a most... retiring neighbor, and I am sure you will treat her with the utmost respect." His voice hardened on the last statement and, giving the man a short, sharp nod, he swung around and walked back to Sabrina. In a softer voice, yet one that still carried clearly to the man behind them, he said to her, "Don't worry, luv, he won't bother you. No one crosses the Viscount Chumley. Now...where is that blasted lantern?"

Ignoring her astonished expression, he bent down and raised the shield on the lantern so that it shed more light on the situation without really illuminating their faces. Hoping he hadn't been wrong about hearing the lock turn earlier, he reached out and turned the doorknob, breathing a silent sigh of relief when it opened easily. Stepping back, he ushered Sabrina into the room before him, and Rufus trotted right after them. Alex turned to close the door and saw the other man's back as he went into his house.

Alex snapped the lock closed and turned to lean back against the door, letting out an explosive breath.

"Alex!" Sabrina was staring at him, her fists on her hips. "I can't believe you said that to him. You made it sound as if I...as if I was—"

"A woman of dubious reputation being set up as a lord's mistress?" he asked, quirking a brow.

"Yes!" She began to laugh. "I don't know whether to be offended or impressed."

"No need to be offended. I did make you an *important* woman of dubious reputation—Chumley's a viscount."

Her laughter increased. "Is there a real Chumley?"

"I've no idea. I just imitated a chap I knew at Oxford."

"How did you know to do that? I was sure we were caught. I had visions of the duke having to come bail us out of jail."

"Now, there would have been a sight." He smiled. "I suspected the fellow would back down if I was haughty enough. He couldn't know, you see, if the house had just been let or sold. What footman's going to want to get into an argument with a viscount? The trick was not to answer his questions, as if I was in the wrong, but to turn it back on him. Arrogance and disdain will usually carry the day."

"That's wicked."

"Well, yes," he agreed. "But it does come in handy. Now we won't have to worry about someone next door seeing our light through the drapes—they know we're exploring our new abode."

"*My* new abode, you mean," Sabrina amended with a grin. "You, obviously, will remain living with your wife, like the cad you are, all the while keeping your mistress in style."

"My dear girl, you wrong poor Chumley. Doubtless Chum had to marry a cold, haughty heiress to save the family estate from ruin, dooming him to a loveless life."

"Chum?"

"That's what his mates call him." He grinned, enjoying the sound of her laughter.

"You're incorrigible." Sabrina turned away, casting her gaze all around. "Well, nothing seems familiar here."

"I wouldn't think the kitchen would. Let's explore further." He raised the shield on the lantern a little and poked his head into the small rooms attached to the kitchen. "Storeroom. Scullery. Ah, here's the butler's pantry leading through to the dining room. Rufus, sit. Guard."

The dog whined but sat down, ears pricked alertly. They made their way through the lower floor of the house. The furniture was mostly concealed under dustcovers, giving it the vaguely eerie atmosphere of a house long unoccupied. There were few decorative items to be seen, aside from the paintings on the walls, to give it a feeling of people living there. One wouldn't leave any personal items, he supposed, in a house that was rented out to strangers, but it was discouraging to his hopes of gaining information from the place.

To Alex's senses, it had the bland, muddled feel common to public places. Alex tried to lay his hands unobtrusively on as many items of furniture as he could, but he picked up no sense of the people who had lived here or the events that had happened. It was his experience that only the most recent or sharpest, most impactful of emotions were absorbed into objects. Something dear and personal, such as the man's pocket watch, was most likely to retain some feeling of him; he had probably carried it near to his heart for years on end. But with unimportant items, especially those used by many people, there was little to work with. Still, Alex walked through all the rooms, doing his best to open his mind to any stray sensation that might come through.

Sabrina trailed after him. "Who owns this house? Why is it empty?"

"I've no idea. All I know is what the neighbors told Tom—its owner is gone and it has been leased the last few years to different families."

"Gone? He died?"

"Or moved away. Or sold it. Tom is going to look into the records tomorrow."

She glanced all around. "It seems rather sad, doesn't it?"

"A bit," he agreed, walking down the hall to the next room. It was large, a formal drawing room, he supposed. Sabrina, coming in behind him, let out a gasp. Alex whirled to face her. "What? Did you see something? Remember something?"

"No, not exactly." She was gazing at the large painting that hung over the mantel. In it, a lovely woman with dark hair was seated on a bench in a garden. "I just… I don't know. It startled me. I'm not sure exactly why. But I—I can't put a name to her. I can't even say that I feel I know her. It's just… I felt something." She frowned, then made a dismissive gesture. "I can't really explain." She sighed. "I'm afraid I'm not much use."

"No, that's fine. We'll figure it out." He squeezed her hand reassuringly. It seemed only natural to keep her hand in his as they made their way down the hall.

The next room contained empty bookshelves and a desk that proved to be equally empty. A comfortable leather chair sat behind the desk. Alex rested his hands on the back of the chair, and here he felt something faint and indefinable. But it was the same presence that he had felt holding the pocket watch. Here, at least, the man still lingered, confirming Alex's belief that he had been the master of this household. But who was he? It was maddening to find the place cleared of papers or possessions that might identify him.

Sabrina, letting go of his hand, walked around the perimeter of the room, peering at the artwork. He joined her, holding up the lantern to illuminate the paintings more clearly. On one wall was a map, reminding him of his uncle, but there were no useful pins or markings on this one. Next was a pen-and-ink drawing of an impressive church.

He bent closer to peer at it. "I don't recognize this church. Do you think—"

"Oh, that's Wells Cathedral." Sabrina moved on, then stopped and swung back to him, her eyes wide. "How did I know that?"

"The same way you know any number of things.

It's general knowledge you acquired sometime in your life."

"Do you think I'm right? That is Wells Cathedral?"

"I don't know. I've never seen the place. We can look it up when we get home. But why would you say that if you didn't recognize it? The thing is, if you recognize this, it's familiar to you for some reason."

"Did I live in Wells?" she asked, her voice rising in excitement. "Did whoever owned this house? Is that why he had the drawing?"

"I don't know. But I think the artwork on the walls, like the furniture, probably belonged to the original owner and is left here for the tenants."

"Do you think I knew whoever owned this house? That woman in the painting?"

"I hate to jump to conclusions, but it certainly is possible. Even likely. I don't remember if Uncle Bellard mentioned it, but Wells is one of those towns that one could go to from Bath."

She nodded, her face lighting with eagerness. "Come, let's look upstairs."

The staircase was a graceful spiral curving up from the foyer. Whoever had owned this house, Alex thought, he liked it. Clean, simple lines and elegant touches. It was the sort of house a man might want to buy…if he was considering buying a house. What might he discover if he were to pose as a possible buyer?

Sabrina went lightly up the steps, Alex following her. The first room was entirely empty, the second held several pieces of furniture, all covered except for the bed. Alex found his eyes straying to the bed. He glanced at Sabrina and found her gazing at him;

she turned quickly away. The very air was suddenly fraught with tension.

All he could think of was that moment outside, when he had taken her in his arms and kissed her. The memory of it was enough to send a shiver through him. But he could not repeat it...no matter how much he might want to. He turned abruptly and left the room.

All the rest of the rooms were bedchambers. Alex went through them quickly, the tension in him rising with every room. The chamber at the rear of the house was the largest. It would be the quietest, too, far removed from the street's traffic, so it was likely the master's bedroom.

If nothing else, he would have realized that from the size and grandeur of the bed centered on the opposite wall. Rounded posts, carved with spirals, speared upward, capped at the top with a tester covered in dark green velvet. Curtains of the same color hung at each of the posts, so that the occupants of the bed could close them and create a cozy, warm, intimate refuge. The thought of it turned his mouth dry.

He turned and saw Sabrina standing in the doorway, gazing at him. His heart clenched in his chest. She had pushed back her hood after they had come inside, and the dark blue material made a soft backdrop for her wealth of black curls. Alex remembered how those curls had felt in his fingers, and he ached to touch them again. To caress her face. To rediscover the gentle curves of her body. Kissing her earlier had been a grave mistake; it only made him want her more.

"Sabrina…" Alex had no idea what he was going to say.

"Outside, earlier," she said, coming forward a step. "When you—"

"I shouldn't have," he said quickly. "It was wrong of me. I took advantage of the, um, moment."

A faint smile curved her lips. "It was a moment worth taking advantage of, I think."

He wondered if she realized how seductive she looked, how much she affected him. He rather thought she did. The thought that she meant to tease him only spurred his hunger more. "Sabrina, you mustn't… It would be wicked of me to…"

His voice trailed off. The gentlemanly thing for him to do was to walk away. The right thing. He reached out a hand to touch her hair, taking a curl between his fingers. Unable to help himself, he sank his fingers into her hair, tilting her face up. He looked at her for a moment, feeling as if he were teetering on the brink. Sabrina ended his indecision by going up on her tiptoes and kissing him.

Alex was lost after that. He had no idea how long they spent locked together, only that he was drowning in the heat, reveling in the taste of her mouth, the softness of her skin. Boldly his hands roamed her body, pressing her into him, curving around her breasts, sinking his fingertips into the fleshy curve of her buttocks, separated from him by so few clothes.

He kissed her lips, her face, her throat, then shakily unbuttoned the top few buttons of her dress to make his way down to the soft curve of her breast. Slipping his hand inside her chemise, he lifted her breast, cupped it as his mouth closed over her nipple.

He felt the trembling in her flesh, but more than that, he felt, deep inside him, her thrumming excitement.

Her fingers slid into his hair, pressing against his skull, and she let out a soft seeking noise, her hips moving against him. Alex felt Sabrina's desire surge within her, her heat flooding into him. Her passion heightened his own, so that the two of them burned with an ever-brighter flame, until he thought the fire must consume him.

"Sabrina, Sabrina," he murmured, his lips coming back to hers. He ached to be with her, in her, to lose himself in her. And he knew, with a fierce certainty, that if he let himself go further, he would not be able to stop.

With a low noise of frustration, he broke away. Gripping one of the towering bedposts so hard that his knuckles were white, he waited for the tumult inside him to subside.

"We cannot," he said in a hoarse voice. "You know we cannot."

"Alex…"

"No. Sabrina, do not tempt me, please. I am discovering how weak I am. And it would be wrong of me, of us. I will not put you in this position. We don't know your circumstances. You could be married. Once you recover your memory, you might regret this, regret me, forever." He drew a shaky breath, surprised at how sharply it pierced him to think of her regretting being with him.

"I know." Her voice was subdued. "I don't…want that, either." She cleared her throat, and he heard the rustle of her skirts as she moved away. "We should finish here and go home—I mean, go to your home."

He glanced over at her. She was walking around the room, looking at the pictures, hoping for another clue to her identity. He went to the opposite wall, struggling to tamp down his emotions. He'd never felt this way in his life—so driven by need, so frustrated and, yes, even fearful of what he might find.

Sabrina continued to talk as she searched, her voice nervous and light, filling the uneasy silence. He heard her without really listening, too wrapped up in his own roiling thoughts, until suddenly her words stopped.

"Alex?" she said then, her tone odd. "Come look at this."

He crossed the room in a few quick strides, alarmed. She was staring fixedly at a picture on the wall, a photograph this time. Alex stopped behind her, looking over her shoulder at the group portrait. A man—a little portly, hair graying—stood behind a seated woman. It was the same woman who was in the portrait downstairs, though clearly several years older. Next to her stood a girl, perhaps eleven or twelve years old. Her face was heart-shaped, her eyes large and light-colored, and her hair, held back by a ribbon, was a mass of tumbling black curls.

"Good Lord," Alex breathed. "That's you."

CHAPTER TWELVE

"THAT *WAS* ME, wasn't it?" Sabrina asked. Too stunned to speak, she had been silent as they left the house and started back to the duke's mansion. But as they walked, her mind began to churn, filling with questions. "Who was that man? That woman? Are they my parents? And what happened to them?"

"I don't know who they are," Alex answered, his brow furrowed with concern. "But that child—she looked so much like you. I cannot help but think that it's you."

"They must be my parents. Why did they leave? Where did they go? Do you think I ran away from them?"

"I don't know their names. I told Tom to check into the property records tomorrow, and that will give us a name. Once we have that, we can hopefully locate them."

"They looked pleasant, don't you think? Surely it wasn't he who—" She gestured vaguely to the bruises on her face.

"I hope not. We'll find out, Sabrina. I am much more hopeful about it now. It was something of a shock, seeing your picture, but that was the clearest evidence we've had."

"But how—" She frowned in thought. "I still don't understand. How did you know to go to that house?"

"Oh. Well." He shrugged, glancing away. "I didn't *know*. It was just, um, something that Tom discovered."

"What? Something he overheard in a tavern? A document he found? He must have had some evidence."

"Yes, of course, I'm sure he did. I'm just not sure…"

Sabrina stopped. He was acting as he had the other day—not meeting her gaze, shifting about. "Alex. You're lying to me."

He had walked on a step or two before he realized she'd stopped, and he turned back to her, his face wary. "Sabrina…I'm not lying. It's just… There are things that…" He shrugged.

"That what? That I shouldn't know? Why? Because I am a woman? Because they are so horrid?"

"No, no, it's nothing like that."

"I thought you were truthful with me." Sabrina's stomach was suddenly icy. "What else haven't you told me? What else do you know?"

"Sabrina! I am… There's nothing— Oh, blast!" He swung away, then turned back, his face pained. "It's nothing to do with you. It's just… It's me."

"What do you mean, it's you? What about you? I don't understand. What does that house have to do with you?"

"Nothing. I know nothing about that house, except what I've told you. It's more, um, the way I found out."

"You don't want me to know how you found the house? Why? Alex, was it…criminal?"

"No! I assure you, it was not criminal or wrong. I just didn't want you to think I'm mad as a hatter. I didn't want you to pull back from me."

"What?" She stared at him, nonplussed. "Why would I think that? I wouldn't."

"Don't be too sure. Most people would." He sighed, then, looking like a man swallowing a bitter draft, he said, "I can sense things sometimes by touching an object."

Sabrina stared at him blankly. "I don't understand."

"It doesn't happen with everything. But if there's enough emotion attached to it, enough importance, enough horror or love or violence, I can sense it. Sometimes I can put a face to it or I know what happened there. I… Once, when I was about fourteen, I leaned against a mantel in a room, and suddenly I knew someone had been killed there. I felt the rage and saw the blood spilling from someone's head."

Sabrina drew in her breath sharply at his words. "No! What did you do?"

"Well, it scared the devil out of me, I'll tell you. It was at an inn. Fortunately, I was with Reed and Anna. They believed me. You see, it's not just me. My whole family is…" He shrugged. "The Morelands aren't just eccentric. Uncle Bellard is eccentric—he loves history, especially military history, and he has the time and money to indulge that interest. But my grandfather was given to peculiar notions about health and was always chasing some cure or other, although in fact, I don't think there was anything to indicate that he was actually unhealthy at all. Until he managed to kill himself following some quack regimen of wrapping wet sheets around himself in the middle of winter."

"Many people are obsessed with their health and always looking for some miracle cure. That's not that odd."

"What about talking to one's deceased friends and relatives?" Alex asked drily. "My grandmother did that. She claimed to have regular conversations with my grandfather after he died, which is probably more than she had when he was alive. Also, she talked to her dead mother and one of her cousins."

"Well, no, I don't suppose that's very common."

"My sister Olivia used to expose spiritualist charlatans. She's the one who opened the agency years ago. She caught them at their tricks and debunked them. But then, one time when she was in the midst of one of her investigations, she herself saw a ghost. Not one, but two. Saw what had happened to them—in the Middle Ages, mind you—and, to top it off, had a struggle with some evil power that had lingered there."

"Is your sister given to delusions?"

"No! Not at all. Normally she's the most skeptical of persons. I think she really did see them. Then my sister Kyria came into possession of a huge black diamond that had supposedly belonged to some ancient goddess. She had strange dreams about someone who died long ago in a temple, a worshipper of that goddess. She saw things, knew things that there was no reason for her to know. My brother Reed had dreams that his future wife, Anna, was in danger. Anna herself has visions of the future. My brother Theo saw *his* future wife in a dream ten years before they met. Not only that, she gave him a medallion, an actual physical object, in that vision. The thing is, I believe them. I know it all happened. Which I suppose means I'm as mad as everyone else in my family." He stopped, letting out a deep sigh.

Sabrina looked at him for a long moment, then said, "Or perhaps it means that all those things happened."

"You mean, you believe me?"

"Were you lying to me?"

"No!"

"Then I believe you." Sabrina had to smile at the astonished look on his face. "Alex." She stepped forward, taking his hand. "I remember nothing of my life. My world is a blank slate. I have no evidence that such events can't occur. You, on the other hand, have evidence that they do. I trust you."

"I can scarcely believe it." He smiled faintly and moved closer, taking her other hand as well, his fingers interlacing with hers. "I feared you would run from me screaming."

The look in his eyes warmed her all through. "No more than you ran screaming from the woman who came into your office, dressed up as a man, and told you she had no idea who she was." He smiled at her words, and she went on, "Many people would have labeled me mad, but you did not. What you've told me is astonishing. Amazing. But it's not insane."

He leaned down and pressed his lips softly against hers. "*You* are astonishing. Amazing."

"Now I will not feel so odd when I tell you that, even though we've never met and I can't remember anyone, when I first saw you standing there in the hallway, I thought I knew you."

His hands tightened on hers. "Knew me?"

"Yes. As if you were a friend, a... I don't know, someone I knew and trusted. Until I saw it was obvious that you had no idea who I was."

"I felt it, too."

"Really?"

He nodded. "I knew we hadn't met. I could never have forgotten your face. But I felt somehow that we are connected. Before you came into the building, I...sensed you."

"What do you mean? I don't understand."

"I don't, either, really. But I knew someone near the office was in trouble, frightened. The next instant, you walked in the front door, and I was certain it was you whom I had sensed."

"Has that happened to you before?"

"No. Never. I have always had a certain link, I guess you'd call it, with my twin brother."

"I had heard that twins do."

"I don't know what he's thinking or feeling or doing, but I know if he's nearby, and I know if he's in trouble. It was like that...only different."

Sabrina chuckled. "Well, that's clear." The thought that he had never had this connection with anyone else—with another woman—probably should not warm her, but it did. She looked intently into his eyes. "Tonight, when we... Did you..."

"Sense what you felt?" Heat flared in his eyes. "Yes. Did you?"

"Yes." Sabrina nodded, uncomfortably aware of how much she had felt—her own desire burgeoning in her, fed, it seemed, by the passion flooding from him.

She looked away, unable to keep his gaze. "Alex...I fear that what we feel is dangerous."

"I know." He sighed, released her hands and turned away. "For all the reasons I said earlier in the house, we should not act on what we feel."

Sabrina fell in beside him, and they walked on. She didn't want to think about what they should not do—or what they felt. "So how exactly did you find that house? Did you see it lurking about in my mind?"

"No. I can't read anyone's mind, for which I am eternally grateful. I got it from holding the things that you had with you."

"You mean, when you touched that ring or...or something, you knew the address?"

"If only I could! No, I didn't know where it was located or even what role it played in your life. When I held the pocket watch, I saw that house. So I drew it and gave the drawing to Tom to find."

Sabrina's eyes widened. "No wonder it took days."

"Well, from the look of it, I had some idea the areas where he might find it, but yes, it was quite an undertaking for poor Tom."

"Is that man in the picture the owner of the watch?"

"I don't know, but it seems likely. I couldn't tell much about him from the watch. I could sense love and pride. It's hard to explain, but there was a certain sense of him, his being. And in the study there, I felt traces of that same presence. I think he must have lived there."

Sabrina nodded, sorrow settling in her chest. "He must be dead, I think. Don't you? Why else would I be in possession of his watch? And you told me the neighbors said he'd been gone from there for years."

"I rather think he is, yes." Alex's gaze was kind. "I'm sorry."

"Thank you." She half smiled. "It's odd. I didn't recognize him—I have no feelings for him. But it makes me sad. Perhaps he was my father. But whatever he was to me, I'll never know him now." After a moment, she added, "If he is dead, that means he couldn't have been the one who hit me, so I'm glad for that."

"We will find out who he is and what happened to him," Alex said firmly. "I promise you. Soon you'll know everything about yourself."

Knowing how badly Alex wanted to reassure her, Sabrina smiled at him. But it had been so long…in her heart she was beginning to wonder if she would ever know herself.

The next morning, Alex and Sabrina went to Uncle Bellard's room as soon as breakfast was over. He hadn't come down to eat, so Alex grabbed a plate of food and Sabrina a cup of tea for Alex's uncle, and they carried them up to him. Sabrina was worried that perhaps the fragile-looking man was ill, but Alex assured her that despite his appearance, his great-uncle was as strong as an ox and had no doubt merely lost track of the time.

When they opened his door, she saw that Alex was right. Bellard was sitting at one of the tables, hunched over an open book on the only surface not covered with models of battles. He was dressed in the evening clothes he had worn the night before at supper, indicating that he had never gone to bed, and his wispy white hair stuck out all over his head in all directions, as if he had been tugging it with his fingers. This surmise was strengthened by the fact that his hands were plunged into his hair right now, holding his head, as he read.

He did not look up at the sound of their entrance, and Alex had to call his name twice before the old man glanced up. "Oh, Alex, dear boy. I thought you were out on one of your adventures."

"We were...last night. It's past breakfast now."

"Is it?" Bellard looked toward the windows, where light shone from beneath the edges of the drapes. "Excellent. I *thought* I was getting rather peckish."

"That's good, because we brought you up some food."

"I was reading about the Battle of Thermopylae. I'm not as much a scholar of ancient Greece and Rome as your father, of course, but I found it fascinating. Hopelessly outnumbered, standing firm at the pass—it's the perfect example of courage, but also a textbook use of the terrain to counter one's lack of numbers."

"Indeed," Alex agreed. Sabrina wondered if he knew what Uncle Bellard was talking about; she certainly didn't. However, she had found that ignorance was no obstacle to a conversation with the historian. Alex set the plate down on the table beside his uncle's book. "Here you are. May I move your book?"

"Oh, yes." The old man glanced around at the jumble of soldiers emptied out on one end of the table and the floor beside him already stacked with books. Finally he carried the large book to his chair by the fire, laying it out open on the seat. "There now. This looks delicious. And tea! Thank you, dear girl."

Bellard set aside his reading glasses and tucked

into his food. Dispelling all notion of the lack of mental acuity his vague manner implied, he said, "Did you find anything at the house you visited last night?"

"We did, indeed." Alex pulled up a stool for Sabrina to sit on, then perched on the edge of the table, bracing himself with one leg on the floor. "We found a photograph of a family—we think the child in the picture was Sabrina."

"Really?" He looked at her with bright interest. "But you did not, I take it, find any indication of a name."

"No. Only the furniture and wall decorations were left there. All personal items had been cleaned out. It's obviously been occupied only by tenants."

"I wonder why they left the paintings," Bellard mused.

"Gave it a homier look, I imagine. People living there just for the Season wouldn't want to be hauling all their paintings about, but bare walls make it so obviously leased. Tom will look into the records today, but there was one other thing we discovered that might help. We're assuming that all the paintings were left there by Sabrina's family—certainly the photograph and a large portrait were. There was another pen-and-ink drawing in the study. Sabrina recognized the subject as Wells Cathedral."

"Wells, eh?" Bellard was quick to catch the significance. "So you think that perhaps you are familiar with Wells. That you perhaps lived there at some point. Or at least visited often."

"Exactly," Alex agreed.

"Of course, I'm not sure I was correct," Sabrina added. "It might not have been Wells."

"That's easy enough to check," Uncle Bellard told her cheerfully, setting aside his half-finished plate and popping up to go to his book cabinets. He slid his fingers along the spines of one shelf, pulled one out and flipped through it, then did the same for another. "Ha! I knew there was a drawing in one of these books, just couldn't remember which." He brought it back to the table and laid it down, open to a drawing of a cathedral.

"That's it," Alex said. "It's from a different angle, but that's the same cathedral."

Sabrina nodded. Strangely, the more she learned about herself, the more uncomfortable she felt. "I suppose I could have recognized it from books or something."

Alex gave her a skeptical glance. "Do you know what Durham Cathedral looks like? Or Winchester?"

"No. I agree—I must have some sort of familiarity with the place."

"I'll start looking into Wells." Uncle Bellard sounded pleased with the idea. "Wells is very old. It had a Roman encampment, you know—natural place to build because of the three wells it contained. In the civil war it was besieged by parliamentarian forces, and they damaged the cathedral. Stabled their horses in it." Uncle Bellard sighed. "Used the statuary for target practice, too. One wonders why these religious warriors are so intent on destroying things. The last of the Bloody Assizes were held in Wells, as well."

"I've heard of the Bloody Assizes," Alex said. "But I don't know what they were about."

"They were after the Battle of Sedgemoor in the Levels, when the Monmouth Rebellion collapsed."

"The Levels?" Alex asked.

"The lowlands in northern Somerset," his uncle explained.

"Glastonbury Tor is there," Sabrina added, and both men turned to look at her. She shrugged. "Apparently I know Glastonbury Tor, as well. It stands in the midst of the Levels, just this one single hill, with nothing but flat land all around it. It's eerie when you see it in the distance rising up out of a mist."

"They say the Levels were once part of the sea and Glastonbury Tor was an island in it," Bellard said. "Some people also think it was the island of Avalon of Arthurian legend. Miss Sabrina, I think it's more and more likely that you have lived in that area. I have a number of books…" He trailed off, moving toward the bookcases.

"Perhaps Wells is where you moved when your family left the house we were in last night," Alex suggested.

"But why did I start out in Baddesly Commons? And why would I have gone to London? Why wouldn't I have gone to Wells if it was my home?"

"Perhaps just to throw off your pursuer." Alex shrugged. "It would make that ticket to Bath even more reasonable, as if you were running for home. The thing is, you must have lived in London as well, even though it didn't seem familiar. Those pictures in that house, you being in possession of the owner's pocket watch…"

She nodded. "Yes. No doubt you're right. It's so disappointing that the house didn't waken my memory."

"Well, it's been six years since the owner left. You would have been young, and memories fade. Still, when you were getting that ticket to Wells and to London, you would have known about the house and thought you could stay there. Or perhaps you have a relative or friend here—the letter writer seems likely—whom you believed would shelter you. Hopefully Tom will find out something from the records, but while he is looking, I think it's more important than ever to find someone who recognizes you."

"You mean go to another party?"

He nodded. "After seeing that house and the portrait of that woman, I think it's very likely you know someone who moves in Society. We've gone only to small sort of gatherings before now. But tonight Mrs. Roger Dalhousie is hosting a gala. It's always a crush—Mrs. Dalhousie casts a very wide net. Kyria is going, and I think Theo and Megan could be persuaded to, as well. With all six of us, our entrance will be noticed. Even if it's not, the odds are Megan will trigger some sort of contretemps before the evening is over."

Sabrina giggled. "Does she always?"

"Almost without fail—well, being American and Irish and a reporter, not to mention a reformer like my mother, she's bound to offend someone sooner or later." He grinned. "We'll go up and down the grand staircase several times just to make sure everyone sees you."

"Very well. But it seems an awfully haphazard method."

"It is. But it's better than doing nothing."

That evening, as Alex had predicted, they made a grand entrance, arriving with Kyria's usual lateness, so that the family group walked down the wide stairs into the ballroom alone. Since Kyria wore a peacock blue gown, with a pin of jeweled stones resembling a peacock itself in her vivid red hair, it would have been difficult for anyone not to notice them.

Hard as it was to shine with Kyria in the party, Megan managed it, wearing a flame-red dress that picked up the reddish highlights in her hair. Kyria had chosen a pale pink satin gown for Sabrina, assuring her that it was the perfect foil for her dramatic black hair and strawberries-and-cream complexion. And, of course, when Sabrina tried it on, she saw immediately that Kyria was right. The ruche of the skirt's lush material combined with the delicate color of the gown managed to make it look both luscious and demure at the same time.

Walking down the stairs on Alex's arm, Sabrina felt like a queen making a state entrance. Her nerves quivered at the thought of being the object of so many people's gazes, but with Alex beside her, she could ignore the stares.

The party was, as Alex had predicted, a crush. They wove their way through the crowd of people. Kyria greeted people right and left, skillfully managed to slide out of entangling conversations and avoid outright introductions of Sabrina, having no last name to give. Sabrina met a veritable sea of faces without recognizing a single one. It was a relief, after a long tour of the room, when Alex declared that they had done enough for the moment.

As the others wandered off, Alex snagged a couple of glasses of punch for Sabrina and himself. There was another smaller staircase at the opposite end of the huge room, and he steered her over to it, carefully maneuvering it so that they stood a couple of steps up on the staircase as they chatted, still in full view of the party.

At first Sabrina was uncomfortably conscious of being an object of attention, but after a few moments, she forgot about everyone else, as she was caught up in her conversation with Alex. So she did not notice the woman approaching them until the woman, only feet away, exclaimed, "Sabrina? Sabrina Blair? Whatever are you doing in London?"

CHAPTER THIRTEEN

SABRINA WHIRLED AND stared at the woman, shocked. She was taller than Sabrina and demurely dressed in a white dress accented with rows of lace ruffles around the bottom of the overskirt, sleeves and neckline. Pale blue bows decorated each point where the overskirt was raised to reveal the froth of lacy underskirt. Wearing pristine white gloves and a strand of modest pearls around her neck, she looked every inch a proper young lady—corseted, straight, her neckline not too high to be unfashionable, nor too low to be indiscreet. Her eyes were a quiet gray blue, and the only flamboyant thing about her was her wealth of hair, a vibrant reddish gold, which she had tamed into a conservatively upswept style.

She smiled as she walked forward and said, "I didn't realize you were here. Peter said nothing about it." As Sabrina gazed at her blankly, her steps faltered and she stopped. "Sabrina?" The smile dropped from her face, surprised puzzlement turning to hurt. "Sabrina? What—" Her gaze flickered toward Alex and she stiffened a little. "I didn't realize you knew Lord Cons—" Her eyes narrowed. "No, wait, I'm sorry, you are not Lord Constantine, are you? You must be—"

"Alexander. Yes, you're right." Alex smiled and bowed to her. "You know Con?"

"We are acquaintances, nothing more." She offered him a tight smile. "Pray forgive me. I did not mean to intrude on you and Miss Blair." She nodded politely toward Sabrina and started to turn away.

"No, wait!" Sabrina finally broke from her paralysis.

"Yes, please," Alex agreed, smoothly drawing the woman aside to the relative seclusion of a potted palm against the wall. "We would very much like to talk to you."

"I'm sorry," Sabrina told her earnestly, reaching out as if to take her arm, then dropping her hand. Hope and fear churned in her chest. "Please. I... Obviously I should recognize you."

"Recognize me!" Their visitor goggled at her, red rising in her cheeks. "I should think so—we've been friends since we could walk!"

"Miss—" Alex began. "I'm sorry, but I don't know your name."

She quirked an eyebrow but said tersely, "I am Miss Holcutt."

"Did you by any chance write Miss Blair a letter, inviting her to visit you?"

Miss Holcutt gaped at him. "Yes, of course I did. I always do—" She swung toward Sabrina. "Sabrina, I don't understand. What is going on? Why are you—"

"Miss Holcutt." Sabrina took a deep breath. "I know how bizarre this must seem, but the thing is, I don't remember you. I don't remember anything. I had no idea what my last name was until you just called me Sabrina Blair. The only reason I knew *Sabrina* was from my locket." Her fingers went instinctively to touch the gold locket at her throat.

"Your mother's locket?"

Tears sprang into Sabrina's eyes. "Is it? It belongs to my mother?"

"Yes. Mr. Blair gave it to her when you were born."

"Then that *is* my birthdate."

Miss Holcutt gazed at her for a long moment. "This is real? It's not…some sort of jest?" Her eyes went to Alex.

"No, it's not a joke," he told her. "I promise. Whatever you may have heard about Con and me, neither of us would play such a prank. And to what purpose?"

"I—I see." It was clear she did not. "But how… Why—"

"I don't know," Sabrina said. "I don't know anything. We think I hit my head somehow. Whatever the reason, I remember nothing before a fortnight ago."

"But this is so…"

"Preposterous?" Sabrina offered with a wry smile. She had no recollection of Miss Holcutt, but she instinctively liked her and felt at ease with her. It was not difficult to believe that the woman was her friend. "I know. It's even more preposterous to be living it, believe me."

Miss Holcutt smiled, visibly relaxing, and Sabrina thought that she had, finally, completely believed the story. "My name is Lilah—that's what you usually call me."

"Lilah." Impulsively Sabrina took the other woman's hand. "Oh, Lilah, this is wonderful! I have a million questions to ask you."

"Of course. But I don't understand. Why did Peter

not tell me? I just spoke to him and his father as they came in, and he said nothing about you being here." She paused, her forehead wrinkling. "And how could you not know your last name when Mr. Dearborn and Peter are with you?"

"Who is Mr. Dearborn? Who's Peter?" Sabrina asked. An icy fear began in the pit of her stomach, and beside her she felt Alex stiffen.

"Why, your guardian, of course. Mr. Dearborn is your guardian. And Peter—"

"Sabrina!" A man's voice cut through the noise of the party. "Oh, my God, Sabrina! Thank heavens you're all right."

They all turned to see a young man plowing through the crowd toward them, an older man in his wake. Sabrina did not recognize either of them, but the ice in her stomach grew, and she took an instinctive step back. She saw Lilah glance at her in surprise, and Alex moved forward, placing himself between Sabrina and the approaching men.

The young man stopped, casting an assessing glance at Alex before turning back to Sabrina. His eyes were intent on her face as he said, "Sabrina... Father and I have been looking for you all over."

"Who are you?" Sabrina asked bluntly. His intensity bothered her, as did the way he looked at her, his eyes lit with significance, as if he were conveying some secret message.

"What?" His jaw dropped. "What do you mean?"

"I don't know who you are."

The older man had joined them and he looked equally astounded by Sabrina's words. "What the devil! Sabrina, stop this nonsense and come home at once."

"Miss Blair isn't going anywhere, sir," Alex told him firmly. "I'll repeat her question. Who are you?"

"She doesn't remember anything," Lilah said, joining the conversation. "I don't understand why you didn't tell me about this, Peter."

"I—I didn't know." He glanced at her, then back at Sabrina. "You don't remember anything?"

"No." She shook her head.

"Good God," the older man blurted. "This is—" He stopped, apparently unable to come up with a word to encompass the situation.

"But, Sabrina," the younger man went on, watching her carefully, "I'm Peter. I'm your husband."

All the air went out of Sabrina's lungs. She thought she was about to faint, but Lilah grabbed her arm and held her upright. Sabrina leaned against her gratefully.

"Odd, then, isn't it, that she's never mentioned you?" Alex said in a cool voice, crossing his arms. "I'll ask you once again, sir. Who are you?"

"I am Niles Dearborn, not that it's any business of yours," the older man snapped. "I am Miss Blair's guardian. This is Peter, my son, and as he just told you, Sabrina's husband."

"Yet you just called her *Miss* Blair."

Color rose in Dearborn's face. He clenched his hands at his sides. "A natural mistake, as they were only recently wed. I don't know who you are, but this is no concern of yours. Come, Sabrina." He reached out an imperious hand toward her.

Sabrina shook her head. "No."

"What?" Dearborn stared at her in amazement, as did Peter and Lilah.

"She said, 'No.'" Alex raised his voice, and the other man glanced at him in irritation.

"Who the devil are you?"

"I am Lord Alexander Moreland." There was an imperious tone to Alex's voice that Sabrina had never heard before. "Miss Blair doesn't wish to go anywhere with you, and her wishes *are* my concern."

Mr. Dearborn's gaze turned wary, and beside him his son murmured, "The Duke of Broughton's son, I believe, Father."

"Yes, well." Dearborn cleared his throat and began in a more conciliatory voice, "As you can see, Mi— Mrs. Dearborn is unwell. Her memory is faulty."

"It strikes me as peculiar," drawled an American voice, "that a woman's husband wouldn't have noticed before now that she had lost her memory."

Sabrina glanced over, surprised to see that Rafe had taken up a place on the other side of Alex, his relaxed posture and faint smile somehow conveying a threat. Kyria was next to him, her sharp eyes going from Alex to the Dearborns, then to Lilah. A quick glance to Sabrina's other side showed Theo and Megan walking up, as well. She realized that the Morelands were drawing around her to protect her, and the thought warmed her, melting away the cold core of fear.

"Or that she was missing for two weeks," Alex added drily.

Mr. Dearborn glanced at Rafe, then Theo and Megan. "That is easily explained. Sabrina and Peter were in a carriage accident. Peter was knocked out, and when he came back to consciousness, Sabrina was gone. We had no idea what had happened to her."

"I see. So naturally you decided to go to a party," Alex said.

Anger flashed in Dearborn's eyes, and Peter jumped in and said, "It wasn't like that. We've been looking for her all over. We only just got to London. We thought perhaps Sabrina had come to see Miss Holcutt. Her butler said Miss Holcutt was here."

"So you were not in London when you mislaid Miss Blair?"

"Her name is *Mrs.* Dearborn." Peter's jaw clenched.

"She belongs at home," Peter's father said gravely. "Doubtless Sabrina cracked her head in the accident— that's why she doesn't remember who she is. I've no idea how she wound up here with you, but she is not your responsibility. She clearly needs medical attention, and I intend to take her home and get a doctor for her."

"I don't want to go home with you." Much as she appreciated Alex and the other Morelands coming to her defense, Sabrina decided it was time for her to speak up herself. "Whatever you say, I don't know you, and I don't want to leave with you."

"Sabrina…dear girl." Dearborn's voice turned avuncular. "You're not yourself. You must be reasonable. I only want to help you."

"No." She turned toward Alex, feeling a little panicked. Dearborn sounded so rational and she suspected that she sounded more like a recalcitrant child. What if the Morelands agreed with him? "Alex, I don't want to live with them."

"Don't worry. You shan't. I'm sure Mr. Dearborn

doesn't want to cause you any further distress." He turned to the other man, his eyes hard. "Do you, sir?"

"Of course not." His smile was more a baring of teeth. "But she will feel much better when she is at home, where she is among familiar things, people she knows."

"She is familiar with us," Alex told him flatly. "I am sure you would not wish to force her to do something she doesn't want to. Something that would cause her further distress. We all want what's best for Sabrina, don't we?"

"Of course. Of course. But what is best for Sabrina is a matter that should be decided by her husband," Dearborn insisted.

Alex's fists clenched at his sides, and Sabrina laid a hand on his arm. Kyria swept forward, moving between Alex and Mr. Dearborn. She gave him a brilliant smile and, raising her voice, gushed, "My dear Mr. Dearborn, you simply must let Sabrina continue her visit at Broughton House. The duke and duchess have grown so fond of her. Why, just the other day, my father was telling Lord St. Leger that she brightens up the day for him. And, of course, she has become just like a sister to the marchioness."

Kyria paused, then turned toward Megan, who gazed back at her blankly and said, "Who… Oh! Yes. Yes, indeed, just like a sister. Isn't that right, Theo?"

"Indeed. I say, sir, I believe we haven't been properly introduced. I am the Marquess of Raine." Theo stepped forward to shake Dearborn's hand. "Please allow me to introduce my wife, the marchioness, and my sister the Lady Kyria. And this is Lady Kyria's husband, Mr. McIntyre."

"No title." Rafe flashed his charming grin and stepped forward to pump the man's hand, as well.

"Ah, but in America, you're the silver king, aren't you?" Theo said jovially. He and Rafe were now flanking Alex, and Kyria dropped back to loop an arm around Sabrina's waist.

"Rafe, dearest, I believe it's time we took Sabrina home. She's looking a trifle peaked, I'm afraid." She flashed another smile at the Dearborns. "It was a pleasure to meet you, gentlemen."

"Of course, darlin'." Her husband moved to Sabrina's other side, and they started away, the other Morelands falling in behind them.

"Wait!" Peter snapped, moving to intercept them. "You can't do this. Sabrina is my wife—she belongs to me. You cannot keep her from me."

"She belongs to you?" Kyria said with an ice that was worthy of the duchess. She drew herself up to her full height, which was a good inch taller than Peter Dearborn, and stalked toward the man.

"You mean, like your hat or your horse?" Megan asked.

"Oh, dear," Rafe murmured in an amused voice.

"Yes, I fear the man is in for it now," Theo agreed.

Alex turned to his brother and brother-in-law. "I'm going to take Sabrina home now, while the Dearborns are under direct fire from Kyria and Megan. You'll stay to support the ladies?"

"I don't imagine they'll need any support," Rafe replied, grinning. "But we'll enjoy the show."

"I'll send the carriage back."

"No need to hurry, son, I suspect we'll be here awhile."

Alex offered Sabrina his arm, but she held up her hand. "Just a moment." She looked around and found Lilah Holcutt standing at the edge of the rapidly growing audience of partygoers. Sabrina slipped over to her.

"Sabrina, I don't understand," Lilah said. "What is happening?"

"I'm not sure. But, please, will you call on me tomorrow? I'm at Broughton House. Do you know it?"

"Yes, yes, of course."

Sabrina smiled and turned back to take Alex's arm. They wound their way through the knot of people as the voices rose behind them until Megan's American voice rang out above the hubbub. "A woman is not property, Mr. Dearborn! Just because *you* hold antiquated, inhuman notions—"

Alex grinned at Sabrina, and they ran up the steps and out the door.

CHAPTER FOURTEEN

ALEX CHUCKLED AS he handed Sabrina up into the Moreland carriage. "I'm sure Mr. Dearborn had no idea what he was getting into." He climbed in after her. The carriages were all jumbled in together, as was common at a large party. It would take some time before they were able to get away. Alex didn't mind; a quick glance around assured him no one had followed them, and the thought of spending extra time in the carriage alone with Sabrina appealed.

"I'm so sorry. I ruined that poor woman's party and landed Kyria and Megan right in the middle of this mess."

"Believe me, Kyria and Megan are thoroughly enjoying themselves. And I am sure the hostess will be thrilled. Nothing makes a party the talk of the town like a good fight." Alex turned to Sabrina. His body was still humming with energy from the confrontation, but concern for Sabrina overrode even that. "It was you I was worried about. I thought you were about to faint back there."

"It was a near thing, I'll tell you. When he said—" She stopped, tears threatening to overcome her voice.

Alex took her hand and squeezed it. "It will be all right. Don't worry."

"How can I not?" Sabrina cried. "Oh, Alex, what if I *am* married to him?"

"All we have is his word for it. I don't trust the man—either of them. You'll notice he said nothing about being married to you until *after* Miss Holcutt mentioned you don't remember anything. Safe enough thing to say then."

"I didn't recognize any of them," Sabrina said softly. "Not even Miss Holcutt."

"You'll notice that neither did she tell you what bosom friends you are until after learning your memory was gone."

"Alex, no! Surely you don't suspect Miss Holcutt."

"She was certainly quick to tell the Dearborns your memory was gone…just as if she were letting them know they would be free to make up anything they wanted."

"No, don't say that. I asked her to call on me tomorrow—she will be able to tell me all about myself." She paused, considering, then shook her head. "No, I cannot believe that she wishes me any harm. I immediately liked Miss Holcutt. I felt comfortable with her. My feelings about the Dearborns were just the opposite."

Alex smiled down into her face, rubbing his thumb over the back of her hand. He intended to reserve judgment on Lilah Holcutt, but there was no need to dampen Sabrina's pleasure at finding a friend. "Very well, I'll give you Miss Holcutt. I had no feeling, really, about her, other than I got the sense she was the one who wrote you that letter you had in your pocket. However, I definitely did not like the Dearborns. Even if he hadn't claimed to be your husband, I wouldn't have liked them."

"Don't you think— Alex, wouldn't I recognize my own husband?"

"One would hope. The fact is, the whole thing could be a tissue of lies. We don't even know if it's true that his father is your guardian."

"Oh, Alex!" Sabrina's hand tightened on his, and her eyes were suddenly swimming with tears. "If he is my guardian, then that means that my parents are gone. I don't even know them, and now they're lost to me."

"Sabrina…" Alex's chest tightened unbearably at the sight of her tears, and he could not keep from reaching out and pulling her into his arms. He laid his cheek against her head and held her, his hand stroking up and down her arm soothingly. "I'm so sorry."

"I knew… Last night I knew he must be dead when you told me the owner of that house had not been back there in years, but I hoped. I really hoped. But now… I'm so alone. I don't even know myself."

She began to sob in earnest. Alex felt helpless; all he could do was hold her. He wished he could take her pain himself; it would be far easier, he thought, than watching her suffer.

"Shh, there now." He kissed her hair and murmured meaningless words of comfort, tightening his arms around her as if he could protect her from her sorrow. When after a moment, her sobs began to quiet, he said, "You're not alone. You have me. You have my family."

Sabrina sniffled and he could feel her smile against his chest.

"They were very kind to gather around us tonight."

"They're my family," Alex said simply. "If I need help, they'll be there. They have taken you under their wing, as well. Even if they had not, they wouldn't countenance unfairness or coercion. I've no doubt when Mother hears about this, she'll be ready to stand guard at the gate."

Sabrina smiled faintly. "I can just imagine the duchess doing that."

"There's nothing she likes like a good fight. Megan's just like her that way. If Theo hadn't married Megan, I believe Mother would have adopted her."

"Mmm. Kyria doesn't seem like much of a pacifist, either."

"Good Lord, no. She's not one who looks for a fight, but if anyone threatens her or hers, she's a tiger."

They rode in silence for a moment. Alex knew that he should unwrap his arms from around Sabrina, should set her aside. Holding her had become more pleasure than comfort. It was wrong of him. Much as he hated to admit it, it was all too possible that she was married to another man. And whatever she felt about that man right now, if and when she recovered her memory, she might very well remember, too, that she loved the bastard.

But he could not let her go, however much he could feel his blood heating, however unwise it was. He wondered how long it would take the carriage to reach the house. Hopefully it would be a very long time. Perhaps they might run into another tangle of traffic.

Sabrina's thoughts were obviously in another place than his, for after a moment she said, "I have put your family in a terrible position. If he is right, if I'm married to him, you would be in trouble for keeping me from him. All your family would. I couldn't bear that."

"Believe me, the Morelands need no help to get into trouble."

She frowned, sitting up and moving away a bit. "I think I should leave."

"What? No!" Alex took both her hands in his. "Listen to me. Don't worry about the Morelands, least of all me. I've gotten into and out of more scrapes than you can imagine. You stay right here at Broughton House. I promise you—whoever the Dearborns are, whatever has happened, whatever *will* happen, I will not let them hurt you. I won't let them take you, and neither will anyone else in my family."

He kissed her lightly on the lips, more promise than passion. "Do you believe me?"

Sabrina smiled up at him. "Yes, I believe you." She nestled against him, his arm sliding naturally around her shoulders. "I'll stay."

Without thought, Alex bent and kissed her again. And this kiss was all passion. Sabrina twined her arms around his neck, pressing her body into his, and for a moment Alex could think of nothing but her mouth and his need. He kissed her deeply, all the desire of the evening flaring up in him again. His hand moved over her, caressing her soft curves, and she let out a quiet moan.

At that sound, all coolness and reason, all thoughts of right and wrong, fled his brain. Alex didn't care that she might be married, didn't care that he was not acting the gentleman. All he could think of was carrying Sabrina away somewhere and making love to her. His hand slipped inside her dress, finding and caressing her breast, the nipple prickling beneath his touch. His mouth moved down her neck, and Sabrina's head fell back, offering her soft throat to him.

Suddenly the cessation of movement and the coachman's voice calling to the team pierced the fog of Alex's desire. The carriage had stopped. He felt the coach shift a little under the weight of the coachman climbing down from his seat. In another moment, one of the footmen would reach them and open the door.

Letting out a groan of sheer frustration, Alex released Sabrina. She simply stared at him for a long moment, her eyes wide, her chest rising and falling rapidly, her mouth so rosy and soft from their kisses that it was all Alex could do not to pull her back to him.

"We're home." His voice came out a croak, and he cleared his throat. "I... Sabrina, I—"

"No," she told him breathlessly, breaking from her trance. She turned away and straightened her dress. "Don't. Please don't say you're sorry." She drew a breath and faced Alex as a footman swung the carriage door open and stepped back. Her eyes were bright, her voice low but fierce as she told him, "Because I'm not. I'm not sorry at all."

Sabrina scrambled out of the carriage and hurried into the house, leaving Alex behind, watching her.

ALEX SET OUT to see Tom Quick first thing the next morning. He had had a difficult time sleeping the night before and had finally given up and gotten dressed when the sun crept through the curtains.

Downstairs, even before the servants had laid out breakfast in the dining room, he cadged a cup of tea and some biscuits from the cook and headed out to find Quick. Now more than ever, he wanted to learn what Tom had found in the city records, and he had no desire to wait for Con's employee to call at Broughton House. When he did not find Tom at the agency, Alex went on to the man's rooms, only a few blocks away. Tom answered the door in his shirtsleeves, hair uncombed, a cup of the strong coffee he favored in his hand.

"Hello, guv," he greeted Alex cheerfully. "You're on the march early this morning. Want a cup of coffee?"

"That tar you brew? No, thank you."

"Come in and sit while I do. I'm no good 'til I've had at least one cup."

"I'm tempted to say you're no good then, but you left me too easy an opening."

"Aye, well, I'm off my game this early," Tom said as he led Alex into his small kitchen. "I'm guessing you want to know what I found out yesterday. I was going to tell you first thing."

"I know. But I was up early, and I want to know now. To whom does that house belong?"

"Sabrina Lilian Blair, minor," Tom said, as if quoting. "But under the guardianship of a Niles Dearborn until she reaches majority."

"Next month." Alex dropped down into the seat across the table from Tom with the ease of long familiarity.

"I wouldn't know about that. It was formerly owned by one Hamilton Blair, who died on… Hang on, I've got the date jotted down." He started to rise.

"Never mind. I don't need the exact date."

"So, figuring you'd want to know about Hamilton Blair, I went to the probate records and looked up his will. He left a small portion and a life estate in Carmoor—that's a house in Somerset somewhere—to his wife, Claudia, and the rest of his estate, which appears to be mostly in funds, to his only daughter, Sabrina Lilian Blair." He cocked an eyebrow. "You don't seem to be terribly surprised by this news."

"I was expecting something like this. We ran into Niles Dearborn last night and he claimed to be her guardian."

"Oh. Problem solved, then." Tom paused. "Isn't it?"

"Dearborn and I don't see eye to eye. He seems less interested in helping Sabrina than in getting her back into his clutches."

"You think he's the bloke that hit her?"

"I think it's probable." Alex set his jaw. "I don't mean to let him do so again."

"'Course not."

"Anything else of value?"

"I looked up the wife, just to make sure, and she died almost four years back. She, too, left everything to her daughter with this Dearborn as guardian of the estate and the girl. Of course, the life estate in the country house went back to Miss Blair." He shrugged. "That was all I had time for before the offices closed. I planned to start looking into Niles Dearborn today, see what was what with him." He looked at Alex. "I'm thinking maybe you still want to do that?"

"I do, indeed. First of all, I want you to see if you can find any record of a marriage, probably within the last few weeks, of Miss Blair and a Peter Dearborn, Niles's son."

Tom let out a whistle. "Good way to keep the money in the family."

"Yes, and time would have been running out for Dearborn, what with her turning twenty-one in three weeks."

"You think he's been embezzling from her money?"

"No idea. The will probably left him some recompense for managing the estate."

"A token sum." Tom lifted a shoulder. "But he had full authority—no one's auditing him. And there's a great deal of leeway in the provision that Miss Blair and her guardian be given 'ample' money to keep her and her household in the style to which she is accustomed."

Alex nodded. "I want to know if they were married. It wouldn't be here in London. Maybe at this Carmoor place, which I'm guessing is near Wells. Or perhaps where Dearborn lives, if you can find that."

"I can."

"If you find that they were indeed married, I want all the details you can get on it, even if you have to travel to the place and question the witnesses."

"Leave London?"

Alex couldn't help but smile at the other man's dismayed expression. "It won't kill you, Tom, I promise."

"Maybe."

"I also want to know everything you can get on Niles Dearborn and his son. What's their financial status? Do they gamble or did they lose money on investments?"

"Your brother's better at that sort of thing than

I am," Tom protested. "They hear me talk and servants and workmen'll open up. Clerks and bankers and moneymen hear me and they freeze up. But Con, now, can charm them into talking like magpies."

"Be that as it may, Con happens to be in Cornwall." Alex sighed. "Lord, I wish he'd get back. This is exactly the sort of thing he thrives on."

"He'll be sorry he missed the excitement, right enough."

"That he will." Alex stood up. "I'll let you know if I find out anything that will help you. Miss Blair's friend is slated to call on her today, and she may be able to shed some light on all this, even if unwittingly."

Tom studied him. "You don't trust this friend?"

Alex shrugged. "Let's just say I'm going to make a point of being there when she talks to Sabrina. I don't know that there's anything wrong with the woman. She may be exactly what she appears, a close friend of Sabrina's who is as in the dark about what's going on as the rest of us. It's just…"

"Just what?"

"Doesn't it seem a bit fortuitous that all three of these people happened to be at the same party last night—Miss Holcutt and both the Dearborns?"

"Weren't you trying to find someone Miss Blair knows?"

"Yes. I realize I'm looking a gift horse in the mouth. It's just… She seems a mite chummy with the Dearborns. She is the one who told Sabrina that Dearborn was her guardian. I fear that she may press Sabrina to go back to her guardian. Even if she is not in league with them, she may think it's more appropriate. She seemed a very proper young lady."

"It's the proper ones you always have to watch out for," Tom said, eyes twinkling.

"So Con tells me." Alex grinned.

He wasn't sure why he was uneasy regarding Miss Holcutt, a problem he pondered on his way home. There had been something about the look in her eyes when she had at first mistaken him for Con—not dislike, exactly. Dismay, perhaps? Wariness? And that telltale glance at him when she asked Sabrina if the story were a jest, as if she suspected him.

Strangest of all, she had almost immediately realized that he was not Con. He and his twin were so alike in looks that everyone outside the family had trouble telling them apart. That would indicate she knew Con well, yet she had been adamant in denying that she and Con were friends, consigning him to acquaintanceship. The only thing he could draw from this contradiction was that she knew Con but disliked him.

It was not a common attitude among young ladies, but Miss Holcutt's cool expression and tight smile, her stiff stance, the very proper, even bland way she dressed, all added up to the sort of woman who would disapprove of the Morelands on general principle. If Con had somehow offended her as well, her feelings might be stronger. In that case, it would be little wonder if Miss Holcutt thought her friend would be better off not living with the Morelands.

There was even the possibility that Miss Holcutt was not really an impartial friend, but an active participant in what had happened to Sabrina. They had only her word that she was Sabrina's friend. Just as with Peter's claim of marriage, it was an easy thing to say when there was no chance of Sabrina knowing it was false. And that look of dismay when she first saw him—perhaps it was not because she thought he was Con but simply because Sabrina had someone there to protect her.

So deep was he in thought about Miss Holcutt that it seemed almost fate when he saw her step out of a carriage in front of Broughton House just as Alex walked up. She was dressed in fashionable but circumspect clothes, as she had been the evening before, her carriage straight, her bright red-gold hair hidden beneath a prim straw bonnet.

"Miss Holcutt." He politely swept off his hat as she turned toward him.

"Lord Moreland."

"Please, call me Alex. There are far too many of us Lord Morelands in the house."

"Very well." Miss Holcutt regarded him shrewdly. He had the feeling she was recording and itemizing all his traits.

"You are here to see Miss Blair, I take it."

"Yes. I know I am excessively early, but Sabrina seemed quite anxious."

"She will be delighted to see you. Please, come in." He accompanied her to the front door.

On the stoop at the top of the steps, she turned to him abruptly, her face set. "I must tell you, sir, that I am not intimidated by your family's title."

"Indeed? Well, that's settled, then." Alex suppressed a smile. He could not help but admire the determined way Lilah Holcutt faced him, and he realized that he hoped his suspicions about this woman would be proved wrong.

"No, it's not," she said firmly. "What I am saying is that I have no intention of allowing you to take advantage of Sabrina."

He looked at her levelly. "That makes two of us, Miss Holcutt. Please, come inside."

CHAPTER FIFTEEN

SABRINA SAT IN the sultan room, trying to recall what she had dreamed the night before. It had frightened her, she was sure of that, but the dream had vanished as soon as she woke up. She thought it had been something other than the nightmare of falling that she had had the first night she'd slept in Broughton House. Indeed, she had not experienced that dream since.

However, the harder she sought to remember the details of last night's nightmare, the further the memory retreated. It was a relief when Alex and Lilah walked into the room. She jumped up and started toward her friend. "Lilah! I'm so glad you came."

"I was fortunate enough to run into Miss Holcutt as I was coming in," Alex told her. "I hope you will not mind if I join you ladies."

"No, of course not." Sabrina smiled at him, then turned to Lilah, who was glancing around the room, doing her best to conceal her astonishment at the lush red room and its tentlike fabric ceiling. "Please, sit down with me and tell me…oh, everything, really." Sabrina tugged her friend down onto the sofa beside her. "I remember nothing."

"It is so odd. What *do* you remember?" Lilah asked.

"I remember nothing before I woke up on a train

in Paddington Station over two weeks ago," Sabrina said. "I had no idea who I was or why I was there."

"But how did you come to be here?" Lilah glanced over at Alex.

"Sabrina came to Con's agency—perhaps you are aware that my brother Con has an investigative agency."

"Yes." From the tightening of her mouth, Sabrina suspected Lilah had little regard for Con's business.

"I happened to be there instead."

"Alex's family took me in," Sabrina said. "It was extremely good of them, for I must have looked very disreputable, what with the bruises on my face and being dressed in men's clothing."

Lilah's jaw dropped. "Bruises! What… But why—"

"I don't know the answer to any of that. But we're inclined to think that I was running away."

"From Mr. Dearborn?" Lilah asked in shocked tones. "Surely not. Why, he's been your guardian for years. You are…were fond of him. I thought."

"I have no idea how I felt about him or what our relationship has been. Please, tell me about the Dearborns. Why is he my guardian? What happened to my parents?"

Lilah looked at her sympathetically. "I'm afraid your father died of apoplexy when we were around twelve or thirteen. He named Mr. Dearborn as your guardian, along with your mother, of course." She paused. "I should start earlier than that. It will be more understandable. You see, the three men were all friends—Niles Dearborn, your father and my father. Indeed, their fathers were friends before them. You and I grew up not far from each other."

"In Wells?"

Lilah looked startled. "Near there. Do you remember that?"

"No, not at all. It was just, um…" Sabrina found herself reluctant to tell this obviously very proper woman that she had broken into a house and discovered the picture.

"It was a clue we came upon," Alex said, coming to her rescue. "We thought it was possible she had come from Wells."

"Niles Dearborn, Peter's father, came to visit my father and yours frequently, and he brought his son, so the three of us were friends. However, Peter was a year older than you and me, and he came only now and then, so he was not as close as you and I were. You and I also went to Miss Angerman's school together."

"We did?"

"Yes, we quite enjoyed it—although you, of course, were more enamored of learning the subject matter than I, I fear." She smiled, and Sabrina was struck again at how much the smile warmed her friend's face. Lilah was an attractive woman, but there was a certain cold symmetry to her features that changed into real beauty when she smiled. "That was when you were older—we were fifteen when we went to the school. It was right before—" She stopped and cast a hesitant glance at Sabrina, then said, "Before your mother passed on."

"My mother is dead, too, then."

"Yes, I'm sorry. She died when you were at school. We were sixteen. It was very hard for you, of course."

"She and I were close?"

"Yes. She was always so sad after your father died.

Both of you loved him dearly. Mr. Blair was a very kind man. He loved to read. You used to say you got your love of books and learning from him."

"It's so strange to have you tell me what I am like, the things I said, what I enjoyed. You know me better than I know myself."

"You know yourself," Alex told her. "It's only the details that have escaped you." He looked at Lilah. "With Mrs. Blair's death, then, Mr. Dearborn was Sabrina's sole guardian?"

Lilah nodded. "Mr. Blair appointed him mostly because of the business affairs, you see, to manage the estate Sabrina inherited and so on, but of course she lived with Mrs. Blair. Peter and his father continued to come to visit frequently, just as they had in the past. He wanted to keep an eye on things and to help Sabrina's mother. She was— Mrs. Blair was always very anxious, very concerned about Sabrina's health."

"I was sickly?" Sabrina asked, startled.

Lilah laughed. "No. You were healthy as a horse. I think it was just that Mrs. Blair was so distraught by your father dying that she was fearful something would happen to you, too. She wanted to keep you close, and, of course, since you were shy, you didn't really mind staying home with your books."

"I'm shy?" Sabrina glanced at Alex, who looked as surprised as she did.

"Well…yes, you don't much like meeting people. You didn't want to come to London and make your debut. And you know how often I've invited you to— well, no, I suppose you don't—but I asked you to come visit me in London many times, and you never would. Sometimes you seemed to want to, but in the end, something always came up."

"Oh, dear, I sound quite dull."

"No, not all! You are very enjoyable company. Why else would I have wanted you to come visit? Or trek to Dorset to see you?"

"Dorset? I thought we lived near Wells."

"No, you haven't lived at Carmoor—that's the name of your estate—in years. After your mother passed on, you went to live with Mr. and Mrs. Dearborn. You were only sixteen, after all. You've lived there ever since."

"So it would appear I am quite close to Mr. Dearborn."

"I always thought so, yes." A small frown formed between her eyes. "Sabrina…"

At that moment voices sounded in the hall, followed by rapid footsteps, and a man rushed into the room. "Alex, what is this Phipps is say—" He stopped short. "Oh." His eyes swept the room, taking in the two women, and his cheeks reddened slightly. "I beg your pardon, ladies." His eyes went wonderingly to Alex.

Sabrina stared at the intruder. The man's hair was wildly tousled, but that was the least of the oddities in his appearance. He wore a loud yellow-and-brown-checked suit and carried an ornate cane. His mustache was waxed into stiff horns ending in upturned curls, a foolish look only intensified by a set of muttonchop sideburns. Sabrina's first thought was that he looked absurd. Her second was the startled realization that underneath the silliness he looked like Alex.

"Hallo, Con," Alex said easily, a grin breaking

across his face, and he went forward to shake the man's hand. "Ladies, this odd character is, alas, my brother Con. Con, allow me to introduce Miss Blair and her friend Miss Holcutt."

"Ladies." Con made a flamboyant bow to them. "I am most honored to make your acquaintance, Miss Blair." With a wary glance at Lilah, he added, "Miss Holcutt and I have already met. Though, of course, I am eager to renew my friendship with you, Miss Holcutt."

"Lord Constantine." Lilah's nod was crisp, her expression cool. "I would not think our acquaintance would rise to the level of friendship."

"Miss Holcutt, you wound me." Con's bright green eyes, so like Alex's when he was bent on mischief, danced, and he placed his hand over his heart in a theatrical gesture.

Lilah raised one eyebrow and said drily, "No doubt."

"Did you just get in?" Alex asked his brother. He turned toward Sabrina and her friend and explained, "Con was on an investigation in Cornwall. A group awaiting the end of the world, apparently with great eagerness."

"Really?" Sabrina looked at Con, intrigued. "Is that the sort of thing you investigate?"

"Whenever I can. Fortunately, there's usually something going on regarding the mystical realm."

"How exciting." She turned toward her friend. "Did you know about his work, Lilah?"

"Yes, I am aware of Lord Constantine's...unusual interests." Lilah's response was less than enthusiastic.

"Miss Holcutt believes my endeavors are..." Con

turned toward Lilah. "What was the word? Ludi-crous?"

"Buffoonish was what I said, I believe. It is bad enough that people believe in such nonsense without someone like you encouraging them in it."

Con grinned, apparently undaunted by Lilah's opinion. He looked down at his coat. "No doubt you don't approve of my attire, either."

"It's perfectly acceptable if one wishes to look like a music-hall performer."

Alex glanced from his brother to Lilah and back, then said lightly, "Well, Con…since we all know the world did not end, is it safe to say his believers' eyes were opened?"

"Of course not. They're determined to be duped. But that wasn't why I left. I, um—" Con shifted, casting a glance at Lilah and Sabrina. "It was noth-ing important, really."

"I see." Alex nodded. "Why don't we go try to wangle a bit of food from Cook? I'm sure you must be hungry after your journey." He turned to Sabrina and Lilah. "If you ladies will excuse us…"

Lilah and Sabrina watched as the twins left the room, and as soon as they were gone, Sabrina turned toward her friend. "You dislike Alex's brother?"

"No, of course not. I barely know the man." At Sa-brina's skeptical look, Lilah sighed. "I'm sorry if I was rude. It's not that I dislike Constantine—actually, I am quite indifferent to him. We've danced a time or two, but that is all. It's difficult to have any real con-versation with the man. He's utterly frivolous. He's a well-known flirt who doesn't mean a word he says. He's certain he can get out of any problem by being charming and good-looking. And the galling thing, of course, is that he *can*—all the girls fawn all over him." Lilah sniffed. "He just…sets my teeth on edge. It's as if he tries to irritate one. He's never serious about anything. He's one of those young men who thinks life is all joking about and playing pranks and carousing. He's forever making a show of himself—I mean, really, look at the way he was dressed. He hasn't the slightest regard for what's appropriate. And these silly investigations—chasing ghosts and legends and otherworldly happenings! It's ridiculous."

It seemed to Sabrina that her friend had a good deal to say about someone she barely knew and was indifferent to, but she decided it was best not to say so. "He doesn't sound much like his twin brother."

"No, I am sure not. I hope you will not think I hold Alexander in disregard. He seems a good man, and he's clearly concerned about you. One could hardly ask for anyone to be more kind or generous than he and his family have been." She paused, the same small lines beginning between her brows.

"But…" Sabrina said, her tone making the word a question. "You seem to have some reservations."

"I don't understand why you were reluctant to go with Mr. Dearborn and Peter last night. You seemed… You seemed frightened. And I get the impression Alexander is quite set against them. Do you really think that you ran away from Mr. Dearborn?"

"I don't know. Perhaps it's just the fact that I don't know anything that frightens me. But you wouldn't say that I am the sort of person to run away on a whim or to create a stir, would you? To dress up in disguise and jump on a train to London?"

"No! Not at all. You've always been shy, as I've said, and, well, even timid, I suppose. And you've never wanted to visit me in London."

"Then it would follow, wouldn't it, that it must have been something quite out of the ordinary for me to have done this?"

"Yes, it would seem so." Lilah's face was troubled.

"I bought two different tickets. I believe it was to make it appear that I might have gone somewhere other than London. I can't help but think I was running away from *something*. And if I was living with the Dearborns, then…"

"Yes, it would seem you were escaping. But are you sure it was from the Dearborns? It's so hard to believe—we've known them all our lives. Could… could someone have abducted you and you escaped from them?"

"Why would anyone abduct me?"

"I don't know. There is the, um, obvious thing, of course." Lilah gave her a significant look.

"Oh." Sabrina felt her cheeks warm up.

"Aside from that," Lilah went on quickly, "I believe you are something of an heiress. You inherited your father's entire estate, after all. I've no idea how much that is, but I believe he had various investments, and there are the two houses, of course, your home and the one here in London."

"Did I live here? In the London house? Could I have been meaning to go live there?"

"I suppose you could have decided to, but as far as I know you never lived here. You grew up at Carmoor. Your father came to London on business and sometimes your mother did as well, but I don't believe she was as fond of the city as your father was. He loved all the libraries and bookstores, of course."

Sabrina nodded. It made her feel better to know that the house that had seemed so unknown to her was, in fact, not a place she should recognize or feel at home in. "Lilah...do you believe that I'm married to Peter Dearborn?"

Lilah was quiet for a moment, then said slowly, "That is what Peter told me last night. We exchanged greetings, and then he said something like I must congratulate him, that you had consented to marry him. I thought he meant you were engaged, but when I asked the date, he said, no, you had already gotten married. He didn't say when exactly."

"Do you think it's true?"

Lilah shifted, looking uncomfortable. "You believe Peter and Mr. Dearborn are lying?"

"I don't know. I don't feel anything for Peter. Well, that's not true—I felt something, but it wasn't a good feeling. I was uneasy when he was there, and I *didn't* want to go with him."

"I suppose he would have seemed a stranger, since you cannot remember him."

"Yes, but so did you, and I liked you. I trusted you. Nor was I frightened by Alex, whom I had never met. Tell me this—were you surprised when Peter told you we were married? Had you thought we were likely to?"

"Yes, I was surprised, a little. It seemed very sudden, and I wondered why you hadn't written me about it. But maybe that was more because I felt a little hurt that you hadn't confided in me. It would not be un-usual, I suppose, for you and Peter to have developed strong feelings for one another, living in the same household as you have for the past four years. Still, I've never seen anything to indicate that you were attracted to him or that you felt anything more for him than I did—the affection of a friend whom one has known for many years. You didn't mention any particular regard for him, even when we were talking about the headmistress's nephew, whom all the girls admired."

"Did we really?" Sabrina giggled.

"Oh, yes." Lilah grinned. "In our defense, he was very good-looking—dark-haired and brooding. In retrospect, I think he was probably just sulking because he didn't like to visit his aunt, but at the time we found him quite Byronic."

"It seems likely that I would have told you if I had developed a *tendre* for Peter—or written you."

"Yes. You wrote me about all sorts of things."

"What things?"

"Oh…you talked about being excited at receiving a book you'd ordered or that you were bored or feeling a bit blue. In your last letter, you wished you could see the ball gowns I'd described. That was why I invited you to visit me. I had mostly given up trying to persuade you to visit, but your letter sounded so…I don't know, restless, maybe even unhappy. I'm not sure—the only thing you specifically mentioned, though, was disliking the new gowns Mrs. Dearborn had bought you."

"Then I *didn't* like that gown I had in my case," Sabrina said triumphantly. "I wondered why I had chosen such a fussy dress."

"Mmm. Mrs. Dearborn does love ruffles and ribbons and bows, I fear. You thought they looked too schoolgirlish—'like a baby' is how I believe you described it. But, of course, you couldn't refuse, for it would hurt her feelings, and she had been so kind to you." Lilah hesitated, then said, "When Peter told me you had agreed to marry him, I worried that perhaps you had done so for the same sort of reason."

"Am I so weak? That I would marry rather than hurt Mrs. Dearborn's feelings?"

"No, not weak, but I know you feel a great sense of obligation toward the Dearborns. And their very kindness often makes it difficult to say no. I am sure you are closer to Peter than I am, having lived in the same household for almost four years now. It would be easy enough to believe that such affection could be love, especially if you dreaded hurting him…well, all of them, really." Sabrina stared at her in consternation, and Lilah looked away. "I'm sorry. I—" She stopped abruptly, her gaze fixed on the window. "Sabrina…"

Sabrina, following her gaze, jumped to her feet. "It's the Dearborns. They've come after me!"

CHAPTER SIXTEEN

"WE AREN'T GOING to the kitchen really, are we?" Con asked as he and Alex started down the hallway.

"No. I got the impression you didn't wish to speak in front of the ladies." Alex turned into the smoking room. "Tell me the real reason you came back."

"I'm not sure, really. I thought you might be having a problem."

"You had a twin moment?"

Con frowned. "Not exactly. It wasn't the way it is when you're in trouble, like the time you were set upon by those ruffians at Oxford."

Alex's eyes lit. "That was quite a mill."

Con grinned back. "It was, wasn't it? But that's not the point. What I'm saying is, my feeling yesterday wasn't like that. It was just a nagging unease. I didn't even realize it was about you until yesterday, and I couldn't get a train past Bath until this morning. I was worried I would be late. Then I get here and find you having tea with Miss Blair and Lilah Holcutt...who is, admittedly, enough to cause one alarm."

Alex chuckled. "I noticed there was no love lost between you and the lovely Miss Holcutt."

"The 'lovely Miss Holcutt' is a prig," Con said flatly. "Surely you must have noticed. Though obviously it's Miss Blair you've your eye on. Who *is* Miss Blair, anyway? Is she the reason for your turmoil?"

"I'm not in any turmoil." Alex flopped down in one of the comfortable chairs in front of the fireplace, and Con settled into the seat across from him. "It's Miss Blair who's in a fix. And, well, I guess that means I'm in a fix, as well. It's the damnedest thing, Con. I *knew* she was in trouble, just the way you and I do. I was sitting there in your office after you left the other day, and I felt this sensation of fear, even panic, and confusion."

"Are you serious?" Con stared. "My God, Alex, what did you... How did you... Did you know who she was? What she looked like?"

"No, nothing like that."

His brother nodded. "I understand. It's simply *there*—inside your chest, really, more than your brain."

"Exactly. I couldn't have known who she was—she didn't even know herself. She'd lost her memory."

Con frowned. "Are you sure she wasn't having you on?"

"I thought the same thing, but it was real." He related their meeting and everything that had happened since then, from Sabrina's bruises and their suspicions, to breaking into the empty house.

"Blast!" Con said feelingly. "I wish I'd been there. What a time to take off to Cornwall."

"You'd have enjoyed it. Yesterday evening we met Miss Holcutt. She is the one who told us everything we know about Sabrina."

"Con! I thought I heard your dulcet tones," said a deep voice from the doorway, and the twins turned to

see their eldest brother. Theo blanched when Con rose
from his chair and turned to face him. "Good Gad,
Con! What the devil are you up to—selling quack
elixirs?" As Con started to answer, Theo waved it
aside. "No. I think I'd rather not know." He came to
stand beside them and propped his elbow on the mantel. "What are you two discussing? The contretemps
last night, I assume."

"What contretemps?" Con asked. "Alex…I thought
you said you weren't in trouble."

"We hadn't really gotten that far," Alex said. "And
I'm not in trouble. Last night we ran into Miss Holcutt at Mrs. Dalhousie's gala—you know how many
people are at those. She recognized Sabrina and told
us that Niles Dearborn was Sabrina's guardian. And
at that moment, Peter Dearborn shows up with his
father saying Peter is married to Sabrina."

"Married! She's married?" Con's eyebrows vaulted
upward.

"*That's* the contretemps," Theo offered.

"The devil of it is that none of us know whether
she's married or not. All we have is Peter Dearborn's
word for it."

"Well, there are times when haste is necessary,"
Con began but stopped short at the flash of fury in
his twin's eyes. "Um, obviously not the case here."

"She doesn't trust him," Alex said forcefully.
"She's frightened of him. If she is married to him, I
don't think it's of her own volition."

"You think he forced her?"

"*Someone* hit her. You didn't see the bruises on
her face." Alex touched his own forehead and cheek,
demonstrating the size of the marks. "It's possible

she was in some sort of accident, but the only bruises were on her face and a few on her arm—the size of fingertips."

"Bloody hell."

"My thoughts, exactly." Alex leaned forward, looking at his brother searchingly. "You know Miss Holcutt. Do you think she could be in league with the Dearborns? It seems very fortuitous that all three of them showed up at the same time. Sabrina trusts her and is certain she's a good friend, but I can't help but wonder…"

Con let out a short bark of laughter. "Miss Holcutt? That woman's incapable of even bending the rules, let alone being involved in something devious. She's bloody beautiful, of course—hard to believe anyone with hair like that could be so prim and proper and stiff as a board, but she is. If these men suggested she join them in a conspiracy, no doubt she would have slapped them."

Theo let out a bark of laughter. "Sounds to me as though you've had some experience in that regard."

"Trust me, I have." Con glowered at the memory. "Once, after we'd danced, I took her out on the terrace. I should have known—it was deuced difficult to persuade her to do even that. When I suggested we stroll through the garden, the woman slapped me! I hadn't even tried to kiss her, but you'd think I'd ripped open her bodice. She said she knew my reputation, knew I was a roue. Which isn't true! You know I'd never seduce an innocent. I wouldn't have laid a finger on her…well, perhaps a finger, or two… But you know what I mean."

"Terrible." Alex smothered a smile. "I'm surprised you survived the embarrassment."

"Oh, shut up." Con gave in and laughed. "Anyway, the long and short of it is that Miss Holcutt is a prissy bore, but she wouldn't lie."

"That is the conclusion I was reaching, as well." He sat back with a sigh.

"So what are you thinking? What are we going to do to protect Miss Blair?" Con asked.

Alex smiled faintly. He had known that whatever was happening, Con would be his ally, but it was nice to hear, anyway. "I'm not sure. If it comes down to it, if Dearborn is her husband and he hit her, I'll sneak her out of the country, where he cannot find her. But—"

"Hopefully it won't come to that," Theo interjected. "You need to set Tom Quick on finding out if there's a record of their marriage."

"I already did. Also the Dearborns' finances." Alex looked at Con. "He says you're better at that sort of thing."

"He's right. I'll—"

He was interrupted by the sound of rapid footsteps in the hall, and a moment later Sabrina burst into the room, Lilah on her heels. "They're here. Mr. Dearborn and Peter are here."

"The devil," Theo said.

Alex stood up, a lethal smile spreading across his face. "Good. I'm looking forward to having another conversation with those two."

"Alex…" Sabrina said with trepidation. "What are you planning to do?"

"Just talk," he said easily. "Theo and Con and I. I'll tell them you're indisposed."

"No. I should be there, too."

"You want to talk to them?" Alex asked.

"Not really," Sabrina admitted. "But I should anyway. It's my life, my future. I'm not going to hide and let you take care of it."

"Of course not. But I want to show these men that they cannot just come here and demand to see you. I won't have them popping in all the time, badgering you and trying to drag you away."

"Tell them she's left," Con suggested. "You've no idea where she went."

"Good idea." Alex glanced at his twin, and identical smiles flashed across their faces. He turned back to Sabrina. "Maybe that will throw them off your trail. Without you and Miss Holcutt there, they may be freer with their story. Once they've set it, we can go about disproving it."

"What if you can't?"

Alex shrugged. "We'll deal with that when the time comes."

"Sir?" The butler paused in the doorway. "There are two men here." He cleared his throat in a way that signified his disapproval of the visitors. "Mr. Niles Dearborn and Mr. Peter Dearborn. They demand to speak to the duke."

"Now, there's a picture," Con murmured.

"And your reply, Phipps?" Alex asked.

"I told them to wait in the entryway while I saw if His Grace would receive them," Phipps said repressively.

"Good man." Theo turned to his brothers. "What do you think?"

"I think it would serve them right to speak with Father," Alex said in an amused tone.

"And the duchess," Con added.

"Lord, yes," Theo agreed. "I believe I'll let Megan know, as well."

"Very well, then. Phipps, let them cool their heels in the entryway for a bit."

"Of course, sir." The butler looked affronted that Alex should think he had to instruct him to dampen the pretensions of their visitors.

"Then go tell Father that they're here to see him. You may have to stress the urgency. Oh, and seat the Dearborns in the formal drawing room."

"Very good, sir." Phipps bowed and left, looking quite pleased with his mission.

"You're putting them in there with the first duke staring down at them?" Con grinned. "That should take the starch out of them—whatever remains after dealing with Phipps, of course."

"That's the idea." Alex turned to Sabrina. "Now, Sabrina, if you and Miss Holcutt—"

"Alex," Sabrina said firmly. "I understand what you want to do, but I want to hear what they say. I have to know what's happening."

"Yes, I know, and I had a thought. That's the reason for putting them in the formal drawing room."

"Ha!" Con said gleefully. "Old Edric's peephole!"

"Old who?" Sabrina asked as Lilah said, "What?"

"Edric Moreland, our great-grandfather. Or was it great-great? Anyway, the one who built this place," Alex explained.

"The person who wanted the sultan's room?" Sabrina asked.

"Exactly. He was a bit of a nutter, and he had this obsession that people talked about him behind his back."

"Which they probably did," Con added, "given that he was a bit of a nutter."

"Edric had a small window put in the room that lies on the other side of the drawing room, with a decorative wooden screen to hide it. He used to sit in the other room and listen to what his guests said when he wasn't around."

"Our grandfather used to converse with callers from behind the screen, I'm told," Theo added. "Because of his fear of getting sick. But no one's used it in years."

"We did," Alex confessed, and Theo laughed.

"Of course you did."

"But the conversation was always so deadly dull, we gave it up," Con added.

"The point is…Sabrina and Miss Holcutt can sit there and see everything that transpires, and the Dearborns will never know you're there," Alex told her.

"Very well." Sabrina nodded, giving in.

"Good. Then, Con, if you will escort the ladies to the viewing room, we can begin the show."

SABRINA FOLLOWED ALEX's twin down the hall, thinking guiltily that she should have insisted on being present at the meeting; no doubt someone like Megan or Kyria would have. But the truth was, she dreaded having to face the Dearborns, that little nasty feeling twisting through her as it had last night, the helpless awareness that she could not remember who they were or whether they were telling her the truth.

Unexpectedly, oddly, she remembered the dream she had tried so hard earlier to recall. Peter Dearborn had been in it. They had been standing together, and she had felt woozy and sick. It was hazy and vague and receding from her mind as suddenly as it had come. Holding on to the memory was like grabbing at fog.

Was this a memory from her past? Had it slipped into her mind when she was asleep? Or had she just dreamed about Peter because she had seen him last night? Whatever the reason, the thought of it brought a sick feeling to her stomach again. She swallowed hard and struggled to pay attention to Con and Lilah, who were walking in front of her and bickering.

Sabrina had the suspicion that bickering was the form of any conversation between Con and Lilah. She wondered if it would always be like this whenever Lilah and Con were with them. She realized, with a shock, that she was thinking of Alex and herself as being together. Having a future.

That was foolish. Beyond foolish. She was grateful when they reached their destination, distracting her from her wayward thoughts.

"This is it," Con said in a low voice. "You'll have to be quiet, for they will be able to hear you as well as you can hear them."

He opened the door onto a small windowless room, dark except for the light filtering in through an intricate wooden screen on the opposite wall. It was easy to be quiet here, for there was a hushed, secretive

quality about the place. Con led them to the screen,
where a narrow wooden chair sat.

Con bent down and peered through the screen.
"Good," he said, still in a soft voice. "Phipps hasn't
put them in here yet. He will soon, though, so…" He
held up his finger to his lips.

"We understand," Lilah assured him.

"Mmm. I just wasn't sure if you were able to re-
frain from talking." He grinned at Lilah's glare and
crossed the room to pick up another chair and set it
down beside the screen.

With a final wink, he left the room, and the two
women sat down to wait. Nerves danced in Sabrina's
stomach. The very silence of the room was oppressive, so that when the door finally opened in the neighboring room, the crack made Sabrina jump. She and
Lilah glanced at each other, then leaned forward to
peer through the screen.

Niles and Peter Dearborn walked into the room
and looked around them. Sabrina froze as Peter's eyes
turned toward her.

CHAPTER SEVENTEEN

SABRINA COULDN'T BREATHE, her heart pounding—she was certain that Peter had seen her. But his gaze slid past the spot where she sat, and he turned, taking in the rest of the room.

"Good God," he said. "Damned gloomy place, isn't it? Look at that old chap above the mantel. He looks like he could eat your liver for lunch."

"Sit down, Peter, and stop fantasizing." Mr. Dearborn dropped into one of the stiff chairs. "No doubt they hope to intimidate us by making us wait."

Peter perched on the sofa at right angles to his father. They waited. Niles Dearborn shifted in his chair. After a moment, Peter got up and began to pace about.

Sabrina watched, her nerves dying down under the weight of her increasing boredom. Peter's nerves, on the other hand, seemed to be growing worse. It was no wonder Alex had put the men in this room; the place fairly reeked of power and privilege long held—it was huge and ornate, furnished in heavy, dark Jacobean furniture. The fireplace was massive, and though she could not clearly see the portrait of "the first duke," which seemed to prey on Peter's nerves, the black walnut paneling on either side of the fireplace was forbidding enough. Intricately carved with all sorts of animals and figures, the paneling was undeniably beautiful, but equally overwhelming.

Peter finally stopped at the mantel, propping his elbow on it in a pose of casual ease. The picture was spoiled, however, by the way he kept shifting and glancing around, running a finger beneath the edge of his ascot.

Sabrina, watching him, felt strangely woozy, her stomach twisting within her. Another remnant of her dream last night crept into her brain. Peter had been acting the same way, nervous and jumpy, his forehead damp with sweat. She closed her eyes, her hand going to her stomach. She could feel the wool of Peter's jacket as, dizzy and disoriented, Sabrina leaned against his arm. Another man was there, too; she could hear him droning on and on, though the words did not penetrate the fog in her brain.

Where were they? Was this scene real, an actual memory? She felt as if her breakfast might come back up at any moment. Lilah put her hand on Sabrina's arm, pressing lightly. Sabrina looked up to see her friend staring at her in concern.

Lilah mouthed, *Are you ill?*

Sabrina shook her head. The vision had faded as quickly as it had appeared, leaving behind only a faint nausea and a lingering uneasiness.

Peter moved from the fireplace to the window, then back again. Stretching his arm out on the mantel, he began to drum his fingers. At last his father snapped, "Peter, do stop that noise."

"Where the devil are they? We've been here twenty minutes at least."

"Yes, well, just possess yourself in—" Mr. Dearborn jumped up as the butler entered the room, followed by the Duke of Broughton.

"His Grace, the Duke of Broughton," Phipps intoned, as if announcing the queen.

The duke glanced about vaguely in his usual way, and Dearborn stepped forward and bowed. "Your Grace."

Broughton peered at him and said mildly, "Hello. Do I know you?"

"My name is Niles Dearborn, Your Grace, and it's an honor to meet you. Pray allow me to introduce my son, Peter Dearborn."

"Yes, very nice, I'm sure." The duke waved toward the chairs. "Do sit. Now, Phipps said this was important. You're here about some artifacts, are you?"

"Artifacts?" Dearborn looked blank, glancing at his son. "I don't understand."

Broughton smiled in a kindly way. "I must warn you that I am interested only in ancient Greco-Roman matters. Not anything more recent or Egyptian—though, of course, that's terribly important as well, just not my area, you see."

The Dearborns gaped at him.

"I don't think they're here about artifacts, Father," Alex said, strolling into the room, followed by Theo, Megan and Con. Surprisingly, even Uncle Bellard shuffled into the room behind them. "I believe they're here to try to take Miss Blair, isn't that right, gentlemen?"

"Miss Blair?" The duke looked confused. "Who—"

"Sabrina, Father," Theo explained.

"Oh, Sabrina! Yes, lovely girl. Now, *she* has a real

appreciation for history." The duke beamed. "Isn't that right, Uncle Bellard?"

"Yes, indeed." The little old man nodded. He glanced around and saw Con. "My boy! When did you get back? I take it the world didn't end, eh?"

"No. It was something of an anticlimax."

Uncle Bellard cackled. "I bet it was. Who are you supposed to be?"

Con said drily, "I have it on good authority that I am a music-hall entertainer."

Sabrina grinned and glanced at her friend. Lilah rolled her eyes, but she couldn't hide the twitch of her lips.

Mr. Dearborn cleared his throat and tried to take charge. "Miss Blair is my ward, sir," he said to the duke.

"Is she, now?" The duke smiled. "How nice. Well, I must get back to my work. Sorry to run, but I have a good deal of cataloging to do."

"But, sir, Miss Blair—"

"Miss Blair isn't here," Alex said firmly.

"That's perfectly all right. I didn't come here to see my ward. I came to talk to the Duke of Broughton. Your Grace, I don't know if you are aware that Miss Blair is married to my son, Peter."

Sabrina thought of her vision a few minutes earlier. What had the other man been saying? A thought teased at the edge of her consciousness, elusive and uncomfortable.

The duke frowned. "My dear fellow, I think you must have that wrong. How can Miss Blair be married?"

"She's no longer Miss Blair, of course," Dearborn said hastily, a faint flush starting on his cheeks. "She's now—"

"But you just said Sabrina was Miss Blair," the duke pointed out mildly. "I confess, I am a trifle confused. Whether Miss Blair is married or not, I don't understand why you wish to speak to me about it. And I really must get back to my work now. Pray excuse me, gentlemen."

"It is your concern, sir, because your son is holding Miss…Mrs. Dearborn here."

"No, no, I'm sure you must have that wrong. I'm sure Miss Blair is quite free to come and go." He turned toward his eldest son. "Theo, perhaps you should talk to these gentlemen."

"I believe this is Alex's concern."

"Is it? Excellent. There, you see, Alex will take care of you." Looking pleased he had discharged his duty, the duke turned toward the door. His gaze fell on his wife as she entered the room, and his face lit up. "Emmeline! My dear. I'm so happy to see you." He walked over to her, beaming.

Behind the screen, Sabrina couldn't keep from smiling fondly. The duke always acted as if he had received a wonderful gift whenever Emmeline appeared, no matter how recently he had seen the duchess—in this case a few hours ago at breakfast.

"Henry," the duchess replied, looping her arm through Broughton's. And if her expression was less surprised than her husband's, her gaze was equally warm when it rested on him. "Alex told me we had guests whom I should meet."

"Oh. I see. Allow me to introduce you to…" He looked toward their visitors. "Mr., um…"

"Dearborn, Your Grace." The man stepped forward and bowed. "And my son, Peter. We are here regarding my son's wife, Sabrina."

"His wife?" The duchess raised her eyebrows expressively. "I didn't realize Sabrina was married."

"We don't know that she is," Alex said quickly. "Unless, of course, you gentlemen have brought some sort of proof?"

"Proof? I give you my word as a gentleman, sir," Dearborn responded indignantly.

"Yes, well…"

"Didn't I tell you about the men who accosted Sabrina at the gala last night, Duchess?" Megan asked.

"We did not—" Dearborn said hotly.

Megan plowed on over him. "Peter Dearborn claimed to be Sabrina's husband. He told us that Sabrina belonged to him."

"Did he, indeed?" The duchess turned her sharp blue gaze on Peter. "You view a wife as chattel, sir? Subject to your whims and orders?"

"I, um, I meant to say that she belongs *with* me," Peter said carefully, obviously having learned his lesson the night before. "Where I can take care of her."

"I would say that Sabrina belongs wherever *she* chooses to be," Emmeline retorted.

"She is my wife."

"But not your slave," the duchess shot back.

"Peter…ma'am…please, let us not exchange hot words that we will all later regret," Mr. Dearborn said in a conciliatory manner. "Please, let's sit down and discuss this civilly."

"I rarely regret my words, hot or otherwise," Emmeline assured him. "However, I am always willing to discuss matters in a civil manner." She swept forward and sat down on the sofa, Henry settling down beside her. Hands folded in her lap, she looked at Mr. Dearborn regally. "Now, then, what do you have to say for yourself?"

"I told your family last night that Sabrina had wandered off after a carriage accident, but that wasn't true."

"Indeed? That seems an unusual way to start your argument."

"I made it up because I was trying to protect Sabrina. I don't know what sort of wild stories she may have told you about us, but I can assure you that Peter and I have Sabrina's welfare at heart."

"Interesting that you should think Sabrina would have told us otherwise," Alex pointed out.

"Of course she would not, if she were feeling herself. But the truth is…she is… Well, she's not in full possession of her faculties."

"She's lost her memory, yes, I know," Emmeline said. "But that hardly makes her unable to make her own decisions."

"No, ma'am, I fear she is not." Mr. Dearborn gazed somberly at the duke and duchess. "She is… What I mean to say is that Sabrina is a bit mad."

Sabrina's jaw dropped, and beside her Lilah gasped, then clapped her hand over her mouth guiltily. The sound of her gasp was covered, however, by the exclamations from the occupants of the other room.

"How dare you!" Alex took a quick step forward, his face so fierce it took Sabrina aback. Con was beside him in an instant, his pugnacious stance making it clear he was not there to restrain his twin but to join him.

"I assure you, sir, that I do not say this lightly." Mr. Dearborn rose to face Alex, his manner grave and dignified. "Sabrina's father was my dearest friend his entire life. For Hamilton's sake, I took on the responsibility of his daughter after his death. It was his express wish, for he knew that she was not able to live on her own."

Sabrina stared, aghast, as the man continued to tell his story.

"Hamilton was one of the brightest minds in the country, but his wife, Claudia, was…odd, I guess you'd say. She was excessively concerned about Sabrina and insisted on keeping Sabrina close to her, yet she allowed the poor child to do whatever she wished, with no guidance at all, really. She was herself somewhat given to the same sort of fits and starts that Sabrina is."

"Fits and starts?" Alex said. "Sabrina is not given to fits and starts—in fact, she's bloody calm about a number of things that would make most people scream."

Dearborn fixed him with his heavy gaze. "Don't you think that in itself is rather peculiar? What sane person would be calm when she could remember nothing, including her name? The truth of the matter is, this is not the first time Sabrina has had one of these episodes. She has done it many times. She does some wild, outrageous thing, then bolts. We have no idea where she's gone or what she's doing."

"So you're saying this isn't the first time you've mislaid her?" Theo asked.

"We didn't mislay her, sir, and I resent your implication. Sabrina is cunning in her madness. She appears to lose all idea of who she is, where she lives, everything. Yet she cleverly does all she can to make it difficult to follow her. She climbed out of her window on the upper floor—it was foolish of me, I see that now, but I could not bear to put bars on her window—and she stole a horse, not to mention a bag full of money. We managed to track her to Newbury, but as I said, she is clever, and she bought a ticket to Bath, just to deceive us. When we could not find her there, we had no idea where to turn, but finally we came here in hopes that she might have fled to Miss Holcutt, who is her friend. It was a shock to us to see Sabrina there last night."

"I am sure it was," Alex agreed grimly. "Especially when you found that she had friends to protect her."

The other man's mouth tightened. "I told you, I have no desire to harm Sabrina. When she is herself, she is a sweet and biddable girl, charming, really."

"As is proper for a woman, no doubt," the duchess added.

Dearborn flushed. "I assure you, madam, that I have done nothing but try to help Sabrina. Peter even married her so that she would have someone to take care of her and protect her the rest of her life."

"My, Peter must be a saintly man, indeed," Alex drawled. "I'm sure it had nothing to do with Sabrina's fortune."

"Did she tell you she was wealthy?" Dearborn shook his head, letting out a sad little chuff of a laugh. "Oh, dear, no, Sabrina has next to nothing. I provide for her. I fear that Sabrina spins all sort of pretty stories about herself. Things that make her life more exciting. Sometimes she is an heiress. Once, I believe she was a spy for the Home Office in France. Sadly, I often figure as the villain in her tales because, you see, I am the person who must tell her no, who must see that she is kept safe. When this episode is over, she won't remember any of whatever she's made up this time, any more than she will remember you, Lord Moreland."

Dearborn gazed at Alex pityingly. Sabrina's stomach clenched. What if the Morelands believed him? What if *Alex* did? Dearborn was so grave, so certain, so reasonable. And Sabrina, not knowing anything of her past, could not even dispute him. Anyone would trust him over some girl telling a mad tale. It was almost enough to make Sabrina question her story herself—what if she *did* do this all the time? She wouldn't know because she couldn't remember anything.

"I know that it is difficult, sir," Mr. Dearborn went on. "Sabrina is a winsome girl—it's easy to feel affection, even pity, for her. But it's clear that she needs help. I promise you that if she stays, one of these days she will have another of her episodes and you won't be able to contain her, and she'll be off again. Let us take her home where she belongs. We'll take good care of her, see that she's well cared for."

"And make certain that she is locked up more securely?" Alex asked in a mild voice.

Fear flooded Sabrina's throat, and she felt about to choke. Did he believe him? Was he about to let this man have her? They were going to lock her up somewhere, tell everyone she was mad.

"Yes, indeed, we will. You see, don't you, that this must be done, that she must be kept from harming herself."

"I *see*," said Alex, "that you are a slick, conniving blackguard who intends to take Sabrina with you by hook or crook. Do you honestly think we are foolish enough to believe your lies? The only harm that might come to Sabrina is from you." Sabrina relaxed, her eyes filling with tears at Alex's defense of her, as he continued. "Of course you'll make certain that she won't escape again. Bars on her window—or maybe a cell in a madhouse, eh? I think the fact of the matter is that Sabrina is about to reach her twenty-first birthday, and you are in a panic at the thought of losing your hold on her money." He took a menacing step forward. "I know her father left her his estate—not only money, but two houses. I've never seen the one in Somerset, but the one here in London would bring a pretty penny."

Dearborn gaped at him. "But how do you know—You said she remembered nothing!"

"She didn't." Alex's smile was thin and lethal. "But almost anything can be found with a little effort. I believe it's time you left the house."

Dearborn's face flushed red. "You impudent—" He swung to face the duke. "Surely you are not going to allow your son to dictate to you."

"Oh, I don't think that he's dictating to me—he was speaking to you, I believe. Now…as I said, I have a good deal of work awaiting me. Good day, Mr., um, Deerfield." He offered his arm to the duchess. "Emmeline, my dear?"

"No." Dearborn stepped between Broughton

and the door, and everyone in the room stiffened, the duke's three sons converging on him. Dearborn stepped back, pasting an unconvincing smile on his face. "Sir, think…what about the scandal? It will be all over the city that your family is keeping a young woman from her husband."

Alex let out a bark of laughter. "Scandal? You think to threaten the Mad Morelands with a scandal? Half the city already thinks we're completely outrageous."

"I don't know, Alex," Megan said, strolling toward Dearborn. "Mr. Dearborn is right. It will make a great scandal—all the newspapers will have a grand time with it. Just think of the story—young bride flees her home and husband immediately after the marriage. Terrified. Bruised and battered. Not even knowing who she was. What could have happened to her? Why did a sweet young newlywed need to escape her husband? Then, of course, there is the noble family, moved by pity to protect her. It would make fascinating copy. Why, I'm tempted to write about it myself." Crossing her arms, she fixed her challenging gaze on Dearborn.

Niles Dearborn's face was now so deep a red he looked as if he might explode. "Everyone's right. You *are* mad as hatters."

"Father…" Peter went to Niles, his voice placatory. "Perhaps we should go."

The young man reached out to take his father's arm, but Dearborn shook him off. "You cannot keep her from me," he thundered at Alex. "I am her legal guardian. Peter is her husband. You have no right.

I'll bring the law down on you. I'll make you return her, and you'll rue—"

"You do that." Alex cut through his enraged monologue. "Be sure and bring the marriage certificate with you. Oh, and you'll probably need a few policemen, as well."

Dearborn was fairly trembling with rage, and his son grabbed his arm, more tightly this time. "Come, Papa."

With a final glare at Alex, Niles turned and, yanking his arm from Peter's grasp, stormed out of the room.

CHAPTER EIGHTEEN

"WHAT A DREADFUL MAN." Sabrina overheard the duchess's pronouncement and turned away from the screen.

Her stomach was churning, and it was all she could do not to burst into tears. Lilah stared at her, eyes wide, face white with shock. For one painful instant Sabrina thought her friend was frightened of her, believing Dearborn's lie that Sabrina was out of her mind.

But then Lilah said in a low voice, "How could he say that? I… We've known him all our lives! Oh, Sabrina." She reached out, taking Sabrina's hand and squeezing it tightly.

The door opened, startling them, and Alex strode into the room, his forehead creased in concern. "Sabrina?"

Lilah jumped to her feet. "They were lies! Everything Mr. Dearborn said. Sabrina has never had 'episodes' or acted daft. I am certain of it—I lived with her at school for three years, and I would have noticed."

"I know." Alex smiled faintly at Lilah's indignant defense of her friend. "That's clear to anyone who has met Sabrina."

"I can't imagine why Mr. Dearborn would act like this. He's always been such a gentleman."

"I'm afraid you mistake gentleman for good man, Miss Holcutt," Con said, strolling into the room after his brother.

Lilah frowned at Con, but after that Sabrina lost track of what the others were doing, for Alex came over to her and took her hands in his. "How are you? I am sorry you heard that. I should have insisted you go up to your room."

"No. I'm glad I heard it. The last thing I want right now is to be ignorant. There's already far too much that I don't know." She smiled up at him. There was such emotion, such warmth in his eyes that she felt as if her heart might crack.

"I'd like very much to kiss you right now," he murmured. She could see the truth of it on his face. "I wish my brother and Miss Holcutt were anywhere but here."

"I... You know we cannot" was all Sabrina could manage in reply. The truly dangerous thing was that she wanted him to do just that. She longed to lay her head against his chest and hear the steady rhythm of his heart beneath her ear, as she had last night in the carriage. She ached to have the strength of his arms around her.

But it was weak and oh, so, wrong of her. Especially now, after what she had just heard and seen— and with the suspicion that was growing in her by the moment. She should tell Alex about the dream she'd had last night.

The words refused to come to her lips. It seemed as if to tell Alex would give them substance. Truth. Instead, she seized upon the other worry that turned her chest to ice. "I should not have come here. I shouldn't have put your family in this position."

"Nonsense. I thought we settled this last night. You're not endangering my family, which is, by the way, quite capable of taking care of itself."

"Yes, I know you are. You are all wonderful, kind people. But don't you see? That makes it even more deplorable for me to bring scandal to your name."

"Pfft." He made a derisive noise. "Scandal is the last thing we worry about. What I said to Dearborn was the truth. Everyone already thinks we're eccentrics at best, lunatics at worst. Dearborn's claims would only be one more tidbit for them to chew on. Besides, he's not going to create a scandal. It holds far more risk for him than it does for us. You could see the fear in his eyes when Megan was telling him what the press would have to say on the matter. He understands how badly your running away would reflect on him, and he doesn't want that. Nor, I suspect, does he want newspapers digging into his affairs."

"But he said he would bring the law down on you. He was horribly angry there at the end. I think he's capable of doing that."

Alex shrugged carelessly. "Maybe. But he won't get anywhere. Trust me, the police aren't coming to haul you out of here without proof."

Sabrina wanted to believe him. It was easy to do so when she was looking at him, so strong, so confident. She wanted to simply let go, hand over her problems to him and let him deal with them for her. Given the way Lilah had described her, Sabrina suspected that was what she would have done in the past. But she could not help but believe that Alex was too confident in his family's name protecting them from any attack. Not even a duke could defy the law.

"I—" Sabrina took a step back. She had to think. "I am rather tired. I should go up to my room and rest a bit."

"Of course." He took her hand and bowed over it, pressing his lips against her skin. It was amazing how such a brief, light touch could send shivers running all through her.

She made herself pull back from him and said, "Lilah? I'm going to my room. Would you walk with me?"

"Of course." Lilah turned with alacrity. Given the irritated set of Con's mouth and the speed with which Lilah walked away, Sabrina suspected that neither of them was displeased at having their conversation interrupted.

"Rough going with Con?" Sabrina murmured, linking her arm with her friend's and leaning in as they walked out of the room.

"That man is so full of flattery."

Sabrina chuckled. "That's a bad thing?"

"It is when it's clear he doesn't mean a word of it. He always has this look in his eyes, as if he's about to laugh at me." She waved her hand as if sweeping something aside. "But let's not waste breath on him. *You* are the one I'm concerned about. Are you all right? I would never have dreamed Mr. Dearborn would say such things about you."

"I suspect it's shaken you more than me, for I have no previous opinion of him."

"It was true—the part about him being your father's good friend. All three of them were—my father and the two of them. It's beyond belief that he should betray your father's trust in this manner."

"I'm terribly worried, Lilah."

"The Morelands will protect you," Lilah said quickly. "Whatever one might say about Constantine, I know he's utterly loyal to his twin. Indeed, I got the impression they are all that way. It's clear that Alex is determined to keep you out of Mr. Dearborn's clutches."

"That's why I'm worried. If he is my guardian, he probably does have the right to demand they let me go. I don't care how old and aristocratic the Morelands are, they can't break the law."

"I'm not really sure this family would care whether it's legal."

"Probably not, but I can't let them get arrested because of me. I can't make Alex face a decision of whether to give me up or bring trouble to his parents."

"But what can you do about it? You don't mean you're thinking of going back to the Dearborns, do you?"

"No! No, I couldn't. I don't know what I could do."

"You could come home with me. Perhaps Mr. Dearborn would be more reluctant to act against my aunt and me, given his friendship with my father."

"I wouldn't want to put you in that position, either."

"You can't just go off on your own!"

"Of course not." Given the shocked look on her friend's face, Sabrina thought it unwise to say anything else.

They had reached the top of the stairs, where a bow window gave a view of the street below. A comfortably plush window seat filled the curve of the window. Sabrina paused there for a moment, gathering her thoughts. Her posture stiffened, and she leaned forward, staring out the window.

"That's odd. There's a man out there in the street."

"Why is it odd?" Lilah turned to follow Sabrina's gaze.

"He's not doing anything, just staring at the front door of this house. If he were here to visit someone in the family, he'd come up to the door, wouldn't you think?"

"He's not dressed like someone who would come to the front door," Lilah pointed out. "More likely a tradesman or someone waiting for one of the maids, perhaps."

"If he were waiting for one of the servants, he wouldn't expect them to come out the front door. He'd be watching the kitchen door at the other end on the side street. He can't even see that door from where he's standing—the house is in the way."

"What are you saying? He's waiting for someone in the family?" Lilah looked at her, her eyes opening wider. "You think he's watching the house, don't you? Spying on the Morelands."

"I think at the least he's watching to see who comes and goes so he can tell Mr. Dearborn."

"The Dearborns hired him?"

"They wouldn't want to loiter on the streets themselves. And I don't think they believed Alex when he said I was no longer in the house."

"They intend to snatch you if you walk out of the house? But that's kidnapping! Surely it's illegal."

"Is it? He *is* my guardian. I fear the law would agree with him."

"How awful. And unfair." Lilah frowned. "But he wouldn't have had time to have gone and hired someone since he left here. It's only been a few minutes."

"I think… I think maybe he brought the man with him. He might have thought that if he showed up, I'd escape out another door, and the man could grab me. Since that didn't happen, maybe he told him to wait and watch, in case I left."

"I don't *understand*," Lilah said. "Why is Mr. Dearborn so intent on your returning? Why is he pretending you married Peter?"

"Maybe he's not pretending." Sabrina sat down on the window seat, tugging her friend down to sit with her. "What if I really am married to Peter?" She reached into her pocket and pulled out the ring she had brought with her, holding it out on her palm. "I meant to ask you about this earlier, but in all the uproar, I forgot. Do you recognize it? Is this something you've seen me wear before?"

Lilah plucked it from Sabrina's palm, holding it closer to the light coming through the window. "No…" She frowned, turning it over in her fingers. "I don't recall ever seeing this. But that's no proof of anything, really."

"It looks very like a wedding ring, and it must be important to me. It's one of the few things I brought with me."

"Yes, it does look like a wedding ring, but it doesn't have to be one. Or perhaps it's a keepsake, like your mother's wedding ring."

"Do you remember my mother wearing it?"

"No, but, really, Sabrina, I can't remember your mother's jewelry. I only visited on occasion, and it's been years. Besides, it could have been your grand-mother's."

"Or it could be the obvious—it's a wedding ring, and I have it because I was wearing it when I escaped."

"Still, it's not proof you are married."

"But it's such a bold lie for Dearborn to tell. What if I had suddenly recalled everything? I'd know it wasn't true."

"Saying you had run mad was a bold thing, too. Any number of people know that you don't have episodes of insanity."

"The Morelands wouldn't. Mr. Dearborn didn't know that you were here or that you had told us about my past. All he needed was for them to believe it long enough to get me out of their grasp and whisk me home, where they could keep me locked up. Besides, being married to Peter is a necessary part of their plan. I don't think he would have left that undone."

"What's their plan?"

"I don't know, but clearly it requires Mr. Dearborn having control over me. I presume he must want control of my money, and that will end in only two more weeks. The only way to ensure that he would keep that power is if I'm married to one of them. No one would question my husband and his father handling my estate."

"But that doesn't necessarily mean you have already had the ceremony. Maybe he just wants to get you alone and convince you to do it. Force you, if he has to."

"Yes, but…" Sabrina drew a breath. "I had a dream last night. It was very hazy. Not just that the dream is now hazy to me—everything was vague and unclear in the nightmare, as well. That was part of the reason it was so frightening. I felt lost and so confused. I was groggy and hot and nauseous. And I was standing with Peter, beside him, even leaning against him."

"It would only be natural to dream about him when you'd just seen him."

"Yes, that's what I told myself. But it nagged at me, and a while ago, as I was looking through that screen at Peter, I felt it all over again. I saw it. I felt those sensations—the heat and dizziness. It was as if I was remembering, not the dream, but the scene itself. I remembered things that I don't think were in my dream."

"Like what?" Lilah's forehead creased with worry.

"There was another man there."

"Mr. Dearborn?"

"No, I—I don't think so. I can't picture him clearly. I know I must really sound mad now! Everything in the scene is very hazy, and I feel…the way I do when I'm sick. Running a fever. Everything is remote and distorted and…wrong somehow. I'm not explaining this well."

"I understand. I've felt that way with a fever, as if nothing is quite real, and you drift in and out of consciousness. Even when I'm not ill, I've had dreams in which I was looking at a person and yet somehow I couldn't make out his features."

"Exactly." Sabrina let out a sigh of relief. "That's the way it is, and I know there's a man there with us, and he keeps talking and talking. I don't know what he was saying, and as you said, I remember it all in just bits and pieces. But he's standing right in front of us and— Oh, Lilah, he's wearing a white collar!"

Lilah stared. "You mean…"

"Like a priest," Sabrina said flatly. "Yes. I think… I'm afraid I'm remembering a wedding ceremony."

CHAPTER NINETEEN

"IT'S BARELY PAST NOON, but I think a drink is in order after that scene," Con told his brother as they returned to the smoking room.

"I agree." Alex crossed the room and pulled the stopper from one of the decanters.

"What do you plan to do now?" Con asked.

"I don't know. You're the one who's a detective. I merely draw blueprints."

"Seems like you've done well enough so far." Con grinned, taking the glass his brother held out to him. "You've started everything in the right direction. I dig into the Dearborns' finances, see whether they've lost a fortune or have a gambling problem. It also wouldn't hurt to learn exactly how much fortune we're talking about Miss Blair inheriting—and whether or not Dearborn has been sneaking money for himself all these years he was her guardian. But all that will tell us is *why* they want Miss Blair back so much. What we really need to find out is whether or not your lady really married that weasel."

"Sabrina's not 'my lady,' but yes, we must make sure she's not married to him—and if she is, figure out how to get her out of it."

"*That*, dear brother, would not be an easy task."

"I know. But I have no intention of sending her back to that lot."

Con regarded him in silence for a moment, then said quietly, "You're in love with her, aren't you?"

Alex shrugged one shoulder. "Love? I barely know her. Indeed, I *don't* know her."

Con snorted. "Don't be daft. You have the look of the Moreland male in love—like you've just been struck between the eyes with a cricket bat."

"Don't start all that Moreland love-at-first-sight lecture again."

"It's worked well enough for all the others. I don't seem to have that ability any more than I can foretell the future or whatever it is you do." A certain wistfulness touched his face before he grinned and went on. "It would certainly be nice to have Anna here. Maybe she could tell us what happened to Miss Blair."

"I don't think she's all-knowing, Con. She just gets flashes of events that are going to occur."

"She knew where those murders happened—she felt it at the scene. Remember?"

"All too clearly. I remember tossing up my accounts."

"It was rather gruesome."

"In any case, *I* am able to feel that sort of thing, too, and it hasn't helped me a bit. Although…I have found that I can do more than I realized. I've been working at it a little since Sabrina arrived, and I'm getting rather good at getting at least some sense of a person who's emotionally connected to an object. I'm able to detect the gender most of the time now, and I can even distinguish in some vague way whether

I'm getting the same person from various objects. It works better the more recent it is."

"You can identify the person?"

"I don't know who they are. I can't describe them. But I can recognize it as the same sensation that was connected to something else."

"I don't know why you were the one to get the talent. Your ability would be much more useful for me. Although…" Con mused. "What would be best is to be able to tell when someone's lying—the way I can tell you are when you say you don't love Miss Blair."

"I didn't say I didn't love her."

"No, you just avoided it. Which, I must add, is another thing you're terribly good at."

"The devil take it, of course I care for her. I *could* care a great deal. It would be the easiest thing in the world to fall in love with Sabrina."

"So what's stopping you?"

"I don't *want* to fall in love with her! It could be disastrous. She doesn't know who she is."

"She does now—Miss Holcutt told her. That's what *she* is good at, knowing everything."

Alex chuckled. "You're rather hard on Miss Holcutt. She's not so bad."

"She's not bad at all. Ever. And *that* is her problem. But we're talking about you and Miss Blair right now. Why does her lack of memory stop you? She's the woman you know now, whatever her past may be. I can't imagine that her lack of lineage would make you hesitate."

Alex made a face. "Of course not. And it's not because I've known her such a short time. I trust my instincts, as we all tend to. I know who she is right now. But what's going to happen when she remembers her past? I want her to recover her memory because it distresses her that she cannot. I want her to look at me then and say, 'Oh, yes, you are exactly the man I want.' But what if she doesn't? She might be a very different person when she comes back to herself."

"You really think she would change that much?" Con cocked a skeptical eyebrow.

"I have to consider the possibility. Don't roll your eyes at me. I'm trying to be practical. To do the right thing. It would be vastly unfair of me to take advantage of her vulnerability. To woo her, knowing that she's grateful to me, to us all, and needs my help, that she can't really weigh me against the other men she knows."

"Well, she knows Peter Dearborn. I think you can safely say she likes you better than him."

"You can be very irritating."

"So I've been told."

"The thing is, what if this claim of marriage isn't a lie? She could be married, and she's not the sort of woman who breaks her vows. If she remembered after we…after she'd committed herself to me, it would cause her a great deal of pain. If she loved me but felt obligated to him, she would be torn. Or maybe he's telling the truth, and she did love him. That's possible—maybe his father is merely obnoxious, but he had nothing to do with their marriage. Or maybe she loved some other man. She's twenty and beautiful. How likely is it that there aren't men lined up, wanting her? Or that she hasn't fallen in love with any of them? Whoever it was, she would feel guilty because she had been unfaithful to him—and guilty for hurting me when she went back to him."

"That's a lot of speculation."

"It's hardly a well-ordered situation."

"You think too much about everyone else's wounded feelings and what they want or deserve. What about you and what you want?"

"I am thinking of me," Alex protested. "Don't you see? How can I give her my heart when I know she may realize she doesn't love me? What happens when this deep Morelandesque love isn't returned?"

Con looked at him for a long moment, then sighed. "I don't know." He finished his drink and set aside his glass. "Makes it even more imperative to find out the truth about her, then, doesn't it? I'm going upstairs now to get out of this idiotic disguise. Come with me and we'll decide what we're going to do once I look normal again."

"Or as normal as you can look." Alex followed him out the door.

"Ha. Any criticism of my looks only reflects badly on yours," Con retorted.

They went up the stairs, amiably exchanging brotherly insults. At the top, they heard the sound of women's voices coming from the small room their mother had taken over as her office. The men exchanged grins.

"Sounds like Mother has taken the girls captive," Alex said. "I guess Sabrina didn't make it to her room to rest."

"The mind boggles at the idea of Mother and Miss Holcutt exchanging ideas."

They turned in that direction, and as they drew

near, they heard the duchess speaking in a tone that brooked no argument. "...the time for extreme action! Women are fully capable of deciding their own destinies."

"Of course they are," Miss Holcutt replied in a cool, precise voice. "But surely a woman can be strong and accomplish much without having to perform outrageous stunts."

"Chaining oneself to the prime minister's railing is not a stunt. It is a very apt symbol of the blatant slavery in which women have been held for centuries. Moreover—"

The twins stepped into the room as Alex said, "Careful, Mother, you'll frighten our guests away."

"Ha! I doubt Miss Holcutt is the sort who will cut and run." The duchess's eyes were sparkling, her color up, and it was clear she was enjoying herself thoroughly.

Apparently so was Miss Holcutt, if high color and bright eyes were any indication, though she sat with the same prim correctness she had downstairs, with her hands folded in her lap. Of Sabrina, there was no sign.

"Where's Sa—Miss Blair?" Alex asked, glancing around the room.

"She's taking a nap. I was leaving her room when I ran into the duchess," Lilah explained.

"Yes, we have had a most invigorating chat. I can't tell you how good it is to have a discussion with someone of the opposing viewpoint who can actually think."

"No doubt."

The duchess came over to her sons, reaching out

to pull Con into an embrace. "I didn't have an opportunity to greet you before, love. How are you? And why are you wearing that horrid disguise? Some case, I take it."

"Yes. The Divine End congregation. They thought they, the righteous group of eighty-one, would be transported straight up while the rest of us would plunge through great cracks in the ground down to the fiery pit. Though why anyone would choose those eighty-one souls to spend eternity with, I cannot imagine."

"Eighty-one? What a peculiar number," Miss Holcutt said, then looked a trifle embarrassed and added, "Not that it's anything but nonsense."

"They decided eighty-one was the sacred number because three times three is nine and nine times nine is eighty-one, so that's the maximum extension of the Trinity. Personally, I thought three times three times three would be the most trinity-invoking, but I suspect their leader wanted the worldly possessions of more than twenty-seven people."

"Well, I do hope you are going to change back, Constantine dearest," the duchess said, patting his arm. "Those checks are dangerous to one's eyesight."

He grinned. "I'm going to change right now. Then I'm off to investigate the Dearborns. Alex, it seems to me that it might be good for you and Miss Blair to go back to her London house, give it another try."

"Oh, no! You mustn't," Lilah protested, and the others turned to her in surprise. "I mean, well, of course you can, but I don't think it would be safe for Sabrina to leave the house, with that man watching it."

"What?" Alex stiffened. "What man? What are you talking about?"

"The man standing across the street, staring at the house. At least, he was there a while ago when Sabrina and I came upstairs."

"Perhaps you should ask Miss Holcutt to work at your agency, Con," his mother said in an amused tone.

"It was Sabrina who noticed him, actually."

"Where?" Alex asked. "Show us where you saw him."

Miss Holcutt swept out of the room, followed by Con and Alex and the curious duchess. She led them to the bow window and its plush window seat. "Oh. He's gone. He was right there by that lamppost." She pointed. "No, wait! There he is. He's farther down the block, by that carriage."

All of them leaned in, peering at the figure beside the carriage.

"Are you sure that's him?" Con asked. "It's a long way away."

"Unless you think there are two men wandering about this street dressed in workman's clothing and wearing green caps." Lilah raised an eyebrow at him.

"Yes, yes, I didn't mean to insult your eyesight," Con responded. "Wait here—keep an eye on him. I'll be back in a tick." Con took off down the hall at a trot.

"Where is he off to?" Lilah asked.

"I'd guess he's looking for his spyglass," Alex replied, studying the carriage. Below them, a maid walked past the house in the opposite direction, and a hackney rattled down the road, but Alex didn't bother to glance at them. "Do you recognize that carriage, Miss Holcutt? Could it be the Dearborns?"

"I don't know, but I would guess that they aren't at their London home often enough to have a carriage here, unless that's how they arrived in London."

"Probably renting it, then." Alex wished Con would hurry up.

"If that is them in the carriage."

"I think it's unlikely that this isn't related to them."

Con returned, spyglass in hand. "Here." He handed the instrument to Lilah. "See if you can tell who is in that carriage."

"Me?" Lilah looked up at him in surprise.

"Yes. You know them better than any of us—you'll be more able to tell if it's one of the Dearborns."

Lilah nodded and held the instrument up to one eye. She jumped as a window loomed before her. "That's so close."

"Yes, it's powerful. Here." Con gently pushed the glass downward toward the carriage. "Just move it slowly. It'll come into view."

"Oh! There he is. Yes, that is definitely the man who was standing across the street. I can't see anyone in the carriage, just an arm on the window. A man's arm, but his face is too far back in the shadows." She watched silently.

Alex wanted to snatch the spyglass away from her and look through it himself, but he refrained. He wasn't sure why he felt so restless. There was nothing the man could do, just sitting there in the carriage.

"He's moving now," Lilah said.

"Who? The carriage?"

"No, the man standing beside it, the one watching the house. He's headed away from here. I think he's leaving."

"What about the man in the carriage?"

Lilah shook her head, then stiffened. "He's leaning forward now, he's looking up at the house." She jumped back, lowering the spyglass. "I'm sorry—he just seemed so close. Yes, that's Mr. Dearborn. I don't know if Peter is with him. I only saw the man on this side."

"Maybe he's going to take over the watch," Con suggested. "A chap loitering about the lamppost was sure to draw attention eventually. A carriage will provide better cover." He glanced at Alex. "Alex? What's the matter?"

"What do you mean?" Alex jammed his hands in his pockets.

"You're nervous as a cat," Con retorted. "You keep glancing around."

"I don't know. Just Dearborn watching the house, I suppose. It's only... Something feels wrong."

"Wrong how?" Con narrowed his eyes at his brother.

"Alex!" The duchess stretched her hand out to touch his arm. "Are you all right? Is it one of your—" She stopped, casting a little glance at Lilah, and continued, "Are you feeling something?"

"It's nothing, Mother." Alex shook his head. Lilah Holcutt was not someone they should be discussing his peculiar abilities in front of.

"About Sabrina?" Con asked intently. "You're sensing—"

"Good God." Alex froze. His chest felt peculiarly... empty. "You're right. It's Sabrina. She's gone."

CHAPTER TWENTY

"WHAT?" LILAH HOLCUTT gaped at him.

Alex whirled and took off down the hall toward Sabrina's bedchamber. "Sabrina!"

The others hurried after him, and Lilah cried out, "Wait. No. Sabrina's sleeping. You can't barge into her bedroom!"

"The hell I can't." Alex flung open the door. He saw, as he had expected, a bed still pristinely made up. He began to curse.

"How did you know…what happened?" Lilah looked around in confusion. "I don't understand."

"Alex can—" Con paused, glancing at Lilah. "He has a connection to Sabrina."

"What do you mean?"

"It doesn't matter," Alex told Lilah tersely, grabbing her arm. "Where is she?"

Lilah stared at him in astonishment. "I don't know. How would I? I thought she was in here asleep!" She winced as his grip tightened.

"Alex…" Con took his twin's wrist. "Ease up. You're hurting her."

"Oh." Alex looked down at his hand in surprise. "I beg your pardon, Miss Holcutt." He released her and stepped back, shoving his hands into his hair, willing himself to think. "Where could they have gotten in—"

"Don't be daft," Con told Alex. "She's probably just gone to…to the library. Or Wellie got loose and she's chasing him."

"Chasing Wellie! Who's that?" Lilah stared at him.

"No, she's not here. She's— I can't…" Alex felt as if he were drowning.

"Oh, for goodness' sake." The duchess walked briskly to the bellpull and yanked it several times. "Let's do something useful."

His mother's unflappable demeanor calmed Alex, and while the panic didn't leave him, he was able to tamp it down to a manageable state. He drew a deep breath, and his brain began to work again.

A maid hurried into the room and stopped abruptly, her face going pale at the sight of the group. "S-sir?" She looked from Alex to the duchess. "Ma'am?"

"Where is she?" Alex barked. The guilty look in the girl's eyes hinted at some secret knowledge, and Alex was convinced of it when she didn't offer any answer, just swallowed and cast a desperate glance toward Con. "Did they pay you off to get inside and take her?"

"No!" The maid gasped. "Who? I never— I never meant… I didn't know it was wrong…" The girl ended on a wail and began to cry.

Alex cursed, fighting the urge to grab the girl by the shoulders and shake her. Con went to the maid, his voice soothing and low. "Of course you didn't mean anything wrong, Milly. We aren't angry." The maid cast an uncertain glance at Alex, but Con took her hand, drawing her attention back to him, as he smiled down into her face. "Just tell us what happened."

"She asked me to. I didn't know it was bad!"

"Sabrina?" Alex stared. "She *asked* you—"

Con shot him a dark look and turned back to the maid. "Now, Milly, what did Miss Blair ask you to do?"

"She wanted my cap and…and one of my dresses."

"The maid!" Alex straightened. "The devil! I didn't even glance at her."

"What? Who?" Lilah and Con said at the same time.

"A maid was walking past the house while we were watching the carriage," the duchess said. "I registered the clothes and didn't really look at her. How terrible of me, to dismiss her because she dressed like a servant." She frowned.

"Let's worry about your social conscience later, Mother," Alex said drily. "Right now, we have to get Sabrina back. Milly, did she say anything else? Where she was going? Why she wanted your clothes?"

The maid shook her head. "No, sir. I didn't ask— it's, well, Broughton House…"

"Where odd things often happen?" Con asked, smiling, and the girl nodded gratefully. "Are you sure that's all Miss Blair said? Nothing else at all?"

"She said, 'Thank you, Milly.' And she give me this." She pulled a silver coin from her pocket, extending it toward him. "I guess you want it back now."

"Keep the coin, Milly," Alex told her. "She meant for you to have it. And I apologize for snapping at you. It wasn't your fault." Alex turned to Lilah, who was staring at him in even more astonishment than the maid.

"You apologized to your maid?"

Con laughed. "As Milly pointed out, things are odd here, Miss Holcutt. We actually have the bizarre belief that servants are people."

Lilah's cheeks reddened. "I didn't… I don't— Of course. But your father is a *duke*."

Con laughed again, and the duchess seized the opportunity to start a lecture on one of her favorite subjects, but Alex cut through them all. "Con, do shut up, and, Mother, please, not now." He gazed intently at Lilah. "Miss Holcutt, did Sabrina say anything, anything at all, about going somewhere? Did she mention any place, even if she didn't say anything about going there?"

"No! I would tell you if I knew. I'm worried, too." She hesitated. "Do you suppose— You don't think it happened again, do you?"

"A recurring episode like Dearborn suggested?" Alex retorted scornfully. "I thought you were her friend."

"I am." Lilah's eyes flashed. "Don't snap at me, Lord Moreland." Con, who had opened his mouth, shut it with a small smile. Lilah went on, "I didn't hide Sabrina nor do I know where she went. Furthermore, I have to point out that she is a grown woman and has a right to leave this house if she chooses. What I'm saying is that perhaps suddenly her memory returned. And when it did, she didn't remember what had happened in this time between. We know nothing about what happened to make her forget everything or what would happen if she recovered her memory. Who's to say it might not happen again?"

Alex drew a deep breath. "You are right. I apologize. Again." He thought it over. "If she found herself in a strange house, she might flee. But why would she bother to disguise herself as a maid? I think she did that to escape the attention of the man watching the house. I think she's fleeing because of the Dearborns. I'm sure she was careful not to tell you she was leaving or where she was going. Sabrina is too clever for that."

"And rather accomplished at escaping," the duchess interjected.

"That, too. But perhaps we can find a clue in what she did say. If you would tell us what she was talking about before you left her…"

"She was very concerned about you and your family and what might happen to you for harboring her. She was afraid she would get you into trouble. She didn't want you to have to make the choice of giving her up or bringing harm to your family."

"Blast it. She said as much to me, too, but I thought I had reassured her."

"I believe she was of the opinion that you might have overestimated your family's ability to do whatever they chose and avoid the consequences."

Alex ground his teeth in frustration. "Anything else?"

"She was… That ring weighed on her mind. She was afraid she might in fact be married to Peter, though I think she was making too much of a dream."

"She dreamed she married him?"

"Not precisely. It sounded quite vague to me, but

it clearly alarmed Sabrina. She wanted the matter settled—she wanted to know the truth."

Alex nodded and started toward the door. Con reached out to stop him. "Wait. What are you doing? Do you know where she went?"

"No, but I have a pretty good idea. She talked earlier of going back to the place where she first boarded the train. I don't think she's trying to run from the Dearborns as much as she's trying to find out what happened when all this began. I'm going after her."

"But what about Mr. Dearborn?" the duchess pointed out. "He's lurking in that carriage. He'll see you leave and follow you. You would lead him straight to Sabrina." She paused, then added, "You'd better put on a disguise. Take Con's wretched suit."

"Wait. I've a better idea." Con's eyes gleamed. "I'll go out the front door pretending to be you. Miss Holcutt can go with me."

"Me? Why?" Lilah goggled.

"You'll pretend to be Miss Blair. You can wear a hat to hide your hair. Remember, they don't know that you are here, so they'll have no reason to think it's you. If they see a woman with Alex, they'll think it's Sabrina. That way, we draw them away from the house and Alex is free to leave."

"Or I could simply go over the back wall." Alex hesitated, considering the idea. His first instinct was to rush off without waiting, but Con's plan had merit. It would take more time than Alex liked, but it would be better to pack a few things to take, anyway. If he couldn't catch up with Sabrina here in London, he wouldn't be far behind her. If the Dearborns were following Con's false trail, Alex could rest easier, knowing the Dearborns weren't pursuing Sabrina.

"Where will you and Miss Holcutt go?" the duchess asked, and Con shrugged.

Unexpectedly it was Lilah who answered. "My house. It's likely that they will come to call on me, because I witnessed the scene at the party, and I can stretch that out to delay them and give Sabrina and Alex a head start. In fact…" She grinned, her eyes suddenly dancing. "I could provide them information that will send them off on the wrong track. For instance, I could let it slip that she's on her way to France, and they might take off for Southampton."

"Bully for you, Miss Holcutt!" Con grinned. "I wouldn't have thought you had it in you." He glanced over at his brother.

Alex nodded. "Very well. That sounds excellent. But I don't want to waste any time leaving, so I'll go over the back wall as soon as I can. I don't imagine the Dearborns have someone watching there."

"What if they do?"

"I'll take a peek first," Alex promised. "In the meantime, you and Miss Holcutt can lead them on a wild-goose chase. But while it would be fun to send them haring off to Southampton, I don't really want to set them searching for Sabrina anywhere. They might decide to try more than one place, particularly if they suspect Miss Holcutt isn't necessarily on their side. I'd rather they believe Miss Blair is here, safe and sound, and all they have to do is be patient and eventually they can snatch her up."

Con nodded. "We can just take a little stroll and come back home." He frowned. "Though if they decide to accost us on our walk, they will discover she's not Miss Blair."

"Stay to well-populated streets," Alex advised. "Hopefully they won't attack you in front of a number of people."

"I'll go with you," Emmeline announced. "I would think they'll be reluctant to set upon a duchess. I'll take my umbrella, of course, just in case they do."

Con left to begin the drastic change in his appearance, and Lilah offered, "If Sabrina left anything of hers here, I could wear it." Lilah entered into the planning, apparently having lost her astonishment over the Morelands' peculiar ways. "Mr. Dearborn would probably recognize the style of it, if not the actual dress. His wife is fond of buying Sabrina the fussiest of clothes." She opened the wardrobe closet. "Perfect."

"Yes, that's what Sabrina brought with her," Alex said. "She hated it."

"It's no wonder," the duchess commented. "Now… I'm sure I must have a hat that will hide much of your face. And a pair of flat shoes to make you shorter. Come along, dear, and let's find one." Emmeline linked her arm through Lilah's and started toward the door.

"Miss Holcutt…" Alex said, and Lilah turned back to him questioningly. "I apologize for my rudeness earlier."

Lilah smiled. "No need. Just bring Sabrina back."

"I will."

The two women started off down the hall, and his mother said, "Do you think a veil would be too suspicious?"

Alex shook his head and muttered, "And she wonders why Con loves disguises."

He wasted no time; Miss Holcutt would be back soon. He wanted to see what he could learn in this room with his talent. He ran his hand along the dresser, then the table beside her bed, picked up a book lying beside the chair and held it for a moment. They all conveyed the sensation that said *Sabrina* to him, but beyond that he felt nothing. Finally, he wrapped his hand around the door handle; it would have been the last thing Sabrina touched, so he hoped for some residue there.

He went utterly still, concentrating on his hand. The sense of her was palpable. And here, at last, he drew a feeling of her emotion. There was fear and eagerness and sorrow, too, and laced through it all was a dominating thread of determination. She was bent on finding out…something. That part was vague, but Alex was even more convinced that Sabrina was backtracking, hunting for the thing that had impelled her to escape.

There was no more to be found; he would only be wasting time here. Telling the maid to pack a few things of Sabrina's—he had seen her case sitting atop the wardrobe, so she must have set off with nothing—Alex hurried to his room and threw his shaving kit and a few necessities into a leather valise. He added a sheaf of bills from his lockbox. It would be enough…as long as Sabrina had remembered the pouch of money. He hoped she made it to Paddington without incident, that no man decided to take advantage of her, seeing she was a woman alone. Would she be able to find the ticket office? The right train? Paddington was so large and confusing, and she—

Oh, the devil, he was acting like an idiot. His mother would box his ears for thinking a grown woman couldn't do anything for herself. He didn't really think Sabrina couldn't handle the trip; obviously she had managed to escape the Dearborns and make it to London on her own, even hurt as she was. It was just that…well, he wanted to do those things for her, to help her and hold her and make sure she was safe, to ward off any fellow loitering about the station who dared to ogle her.

Nor could he help but feel a stab of hurt that she had not trusted him to protect her, that she had felt it necessary to flee. She hadn't even told him she was going! That sentiment was equally silly, he knew. She had done it out of too much concern for him, not a lack of it.

Irritated with himself, Alex buckled his case and left his room, picking up the carpetbag Milly had packed for Sabrina, as well. He trotted down the back stairs and out into the garden, releasing some of his pent-up energy by running along the winding path to the far end of their estate. There a spreading oak towered over the wall, offering a convenient escape route to anyone willing to crawl out onto a limb, drop onto the top of an eight-foot stone wall and climb down the other side—which, of course, he and Con had been willing to do.

He hadn't made the climb in years, and he found it was a more difficult proposition when one was carrying two bags. There was also the problem that the wall did not seem quite as wide as it had to him ten years ago. But the height of the tree made it possible to search the area for anyone watching the back of the estate. He saw no one, so he dropped the two bags on the other side of the wall, then swung down to hang for a steadying moment from the limb. Letting go, he landed in a crouch on the top of the wall, then walked like a man on a tightrope to the spot where he and Con had long ago found the best handholds and toe-holds for climbing down.

The small juts of stone were still there—though they, too, seemed to have shrunk over the years—and he clambered down. Picking up the bags, he hurried down the street, forcing himself not to attract atten-tion by breaking into a run.

Two blocks down, he was lucky enough to spot a hack, and he hailed it. As the hansom rattled up the street, crossing the intersection of the street where Broughton House lay, he looked out the window. There, a block away, were two women and a man, strolling along, talking, with a carriage trailing some distance behind them. His mother, God bless her, was carrying her umbrella propped on her shoulder like a rifle. Even in the midst of his worry, Alex had to smile.

Woe betide the man who tried to grab Miss Hol-cutt while the duchess was there. Alex hadn't seen his mother slam Con's cricket bat into the head of an intruder when the man knocked a ten-year-old Con to the floor; he had been busy at the time running for help. He could imagine it, though; his mother had al-ways been something of a warrior queen.

Traffic was thick and Alex's progress slow. Alex fidgeted on the seat as they crawled toward Paddington, and when they came to a complete halt at a snarl involving a wagon filled with barrels, an omnibus and a carriage drawn by a fine set of grays, Alex abandoned the cab altogether. Jumping down, he tossed the driver the fare and set out at a lope for the train station.

He went straight to the ticket office, glancing around him all the while for a sight of Sabrina. At the ticket office there was a queue, which tried his patience further, but he used the time to crane his neck all around, looking for Sabrina. He suspected everyone around him was beginning to think he was a fugitive fleeing Scotland Yard.

"Next train to Newmarket leaving at two forty, sir," the agent told him cheerfully. "That's three minutes. Platform seven."

"Yes." Alex thrust the bills at the man and grabbed his ticket, then whipped around and picked up the cases.

"'Ere, now, don't you want your change?" the agent called, but Alex had already loped off.

He wove through the other passengers, trotting when the space was open and slowing to a swift walk when it clogged. Ahead he saw the platform, the train still sitting there, steam billowing up from the engine. Then, with a clang and a jerk, it started forward.

"No! Wait!" Alex broke into a run. It would be the height of frustration to have come this close and missed it.

The wheels turned slowly, gradually picking up speed. Waiting passengers turned to stare at him. One man let out an encouraging "Halloo!" Legs pumping, heart pounding, Alex drew tantalizingly close to the rear car. Only a few more feet.

He transferred the handles of both cases to his outside hand and, putting on a last extra burst of speed, he reached for the metal railing. His fingertips touched it. He wrapped his hand around the pole, taking a last desperate leap. His foot landed on the step and swung up. For an instant he teetered there on the edge, the tracks rushing beneath him at a dizzying pace. Then he swung the bags up and over, and the momentum carried him forward onto the platform.

Wrapping his arm around the pole, he leaned against it, catching his breath. He'd made it.

Now…he certainly hoped Sabrina was on this train.

CHAPTER TWENTY-ONE

SABRINA HURRIED DOWN the back staircase, carrying the small sack that held her few necessities. It was easy enough to get through the kitchen and out the door. The servants, used to unusual behavior, barely gave her a glance. She paused in the small alleyway outside the door, surprised at how much it hurt to leave. She had known it would be hard, but she hadn't expected to feel like a vise was closing around her heart. For an instant, she thought of turning around and going back. Staying with Alex.

Stiffening her spine, she started up the walkway. She was doing the right thing, however much it might make her chest ache. Until she knew what had happened, it was folly to be with Alex. Worse than folly, for she was endangering him and his family by doing so.

As she approached the street, she saw that the man who had been watching the house was no longer there. A quick glance the other way told her that he had gone to the next block and stood beside a carriage, and he was talking to someone within. Quickly, she lowered her head and turned the other way.

Her instinct was to run. She hadn't seen anyone in the carriage, but she feared it was Mr. Dearborn to whom the man was reporting. Sabrina had counted on her disguise fooling the watcher, who had never seen her in person and would be relying on a physical description, at most a photograph or drawing of her. But the Dearborns knew her well. They would be much more likely to recognize her if they were careful enough to look beyond the cap and dress of a maid and actually see her.

But to run would guarantee getting their attention, so she forced herself to walk forward briskly, as if she were on an errand, but not so fast she looked as if she were escaping. She kept her eyes on the sidewalk in front of her, shoulders tensed, listening for the sound of running footsteps or the roll of carriage wheels.

Nothing came and she turned at the corner, casting a sideways glance back down the street. The carriage remained where it was, and the man had disappeared. She stopped once she was out of sight, knees trembling, and caught her breath. The side street was deserted, no sign of a hansom cab, so she started walking again, finally finding a busier street.

She tried to hail a cab, but two of them rolled past her without even a pause, and it struck her that her disguise, while quite useful for slipping away from the house unnoticed, was anything but that for getting a vehicle. Dressed as a maid, she was immediately dismissed as a nonpaying customer. She marched on. No chance to change her clothes until she got to the station. What would a maid do if she needed to get to Paddington?

Omnibuses. She had been quite intrigued when she saw one of the long vehicles filled with people the other day; it would be exciting to actually ride in one. But how was she to know which one to take to get to Paddington?

She found a clot of people standing at one corner, obviously waiting for something. She studied them for a moment. There was a young woman about her age, dressed in a practical suit much like the ones Megan wore, and she had the look of someone who knew what she was doing.

"Excuse me, miss." Sabrina walked up to her.

The woman glanced at her in surprise, her eyes swiftly taking in Sabrina's attire. "Are you speaking to me?"

"Yes. I was wondering if this was where one caught an omnibus."

"Yes," the woman said coolly and turned back to look up the street.

Sabrina felt a spurt of resentment. One would think the woman could have shown a bit of graciousness toward a fellow workingwoman despite the fact that Sabrina was dressed like someone lower down the social ladder than she. As much to annoy the woman as because she wanted to know, Sabrina said, speaking to her shoulder, "I was wondering which one to take to get to Paddington Station."

"I'm sure I don't know" was all the other woman said, giving her a dismissive glance.

"I'll show you, sweetheart," a man said beside her. She looked at him. He was sharply dressed, with a diamond pin twinkling in the folds of his ascot, and he smiled at her in a way that was entirely too familiar. "Just come with me, and…"

"Get on with ya, mister." An older woman wedged

her way in between them, scowling at the man. "I know what you're wantin', and it ain't to help a girl."

"Thank you," Sabrina murmured.

"Just up from the country, ain't ya?" The woman shook her head and sighed. "Too pretty by half to be wanderin' about so innocent." She turned to shoot a glare at the man who had spoken to Sabrina, but he had moved away and was studiously ignoring them.

"Yes, I'm new to London." Sabrina knew her manner of speech didn't match her disguise, but there was nothing she could do to change that. If she tried to imitate one of the maids, she felt sure she would make a mistake, and that would be even more suspicious. She lowered her voice and said confidentially, "Since my father passed on, the family's fallen on hard times, so I came to London to make my way."

"Terrible." The woman clucked in sympathy and reached out to pat her arm. "Well, just take this one that's comin'." She nodded toward the omnibus rattling toward them, a block away. "It's not the one I take, or I'd show ya meself. But it's easy enough, just get off when ya see the station."

"Thank you." Sabrina beamed at her.

"Ah, lass." The woman heaved a sigh, shaking her head. "With a smile like that, trouble's sure to find ya."

Sabrina refused to be disheartened by the woman's gloomy appraisal. She turned back, considering her next problem. She had no idea how much it cost to ride the omnibus. She reached into her pocket, surreptitiously poking into the bag of money. It would not do for a maid to pull out a big pouch of coins. Nor did she want to present a gold coin—that was bound to be far too much—and since sovereigns and crowns made up the bulk of her coins, it presented a bit of a challenge. She was rather sure she had seen a shilling in her purse, but she doubted there was anything smaller. Surely a shilling wouldn't be more than a maid would have. The problem was that the gold sovereign and the silver shilling were actually not very far apart in size, and it was hard to tell the difference by touch alone.

It was with some relief that she found a smaller coin, probably a sixpence or threepence, and she lifted it out, sneaking a glance at it in her palm. It was a sixpence, which, as it turned out, was large enough that it earned her a frown from the conductor as he sorted through his pennies and threepence pieces to give her change.

Riding in the omnibus was a rather slow and dull affair, as it stopped often for passengers to get on or off, but Sabrina entertained herself watching all the people and vehicles traveling the streets. She kept a sharp lookout for Paddington and finally saw it a block down on a cross street. Quickly yanking the cord as she had seen others do, she got off when the vehicle came to a stop and walked to the station.

Forewarned by her earlier experience, she went to the privacy of the lavatory to pull out her money pouch and take out the coins she might possibly use. She thought about changing into the clothes in her sack as well, but it was a tight and awkward place to do so, and anyway, she decided, it would probably look less odd for a maid to be buying a ticket for her employer than for a young lady to do it herself.

She just wished she had some idea what it would

cost and how much she should have ready. How was it possible that she could know so little of what anything cost? Was that another problem of her failed memory or evidence of how little she had ever handled anything in her life? She had heard the duchess go on at length about the way young ladies were kept removed from the practicalities of life, everything purchased for them by parents or husbands.

She remembered the ticket office from the day she and Alex had come here, so she found it easily. After a wink from a man toting baggage and a leer from a man dressed much like Con had been this morning, she made it a point to keep her gaze forward and down. But as she stood in line, she couldn't keep from looking all around her, searching for a sight of the Dearborns…or Alex. She saw neither, and while the lack of Dearborns reassured her, her heart grew heavier at the thought of Alex.

It was silly. There was no reason to think he would have followed her. She had done her best to conceal her departure. He probably didn't yet know she wasn't napping in her room. Even when he discovered she was gone, he wouldn't know where she went. And really, why should he follow her? It wasn't as if he could make her return to Broughton House. Her absence would resolve his problem with the Dearborns. He would understand that it was better this way.

There was no reason that thought should make her heart feel so leaden. It was what she wanted. She had wanted to get away from Broughton House. To spare him the difficulty of hiding her from her guardian. To protect him from scandal. She was doing the right thing.

She just wished doing the right thing didn't hurt so much.

After buying the ticket, she made her way to the platform. The train sat there, passengers trickling on board, baggage carriers trundling their carts to the baggage car. She looked around a last time or two and climbed on board.

Her compartment was at the far end of the first-class passengers' car. She closed the door, turned the latch and pulled down the shades on the window. She pulled out the dress she had carried with her in the sack; it would be suspicious for a maid to be traveling in a first-class compartment alone. The frock was crumpled, as was the small, plain bonnet, but they would have to do. Dressing quickly, she tossed her disguise aside and dropped down onto the padded bench seat.

She tried not to think about Alex, but her mind went to him despite her best efforts. She thought of when she had first seen him standing outside the agency door, slim and straight, those bright green eyes focused on her. She felt again that instant tug of attraction, of rightness, the sense that she knew him. An image flickered in her mind and was gone; she tried to call it back but it remained elusively out of reach.

The train jerked beneath her. They were starting. The train began to roll forward, gradually gaining speed. Sabrina thought of raising the window shade to watch London move past them, but she didn't want to watch it slip away from her. Tears pooled in her eyes, and she blinked them away.

She heard the clang of the car's connected door

close, and then the faint sound of knocking and the murmur of voices. It moved down the corridor toward her, growing louder and louder. The conductor was taking up tickets. When the tap sounded at her own door, she rose, unlocked it and pulled it open.

A man stood in the corridor, face flushed, hair in disarray.

"Alex!"

CHAPTER TWENTY-TWO

To Alex's surprise, Sabrina launched herself into his arms. He squeezed her to him, his cheek against the softness of her hair, letting the anxiety drain out of him. Finally recalling that they were standing in a public hallway, he stepped into her compartment, carrying her with him, and closed the door. Only then did he set her down.

"Thank heavens you're here." He smiled down into her face, smoothing one hand over her hair. "I've alarmed every passenger in this car, looking for your compartment." He wasn't going to tell her how scared he'd been, thinking that he had chosen the wrong direction and she was lost to him.

She laughed, and her eyes shone in a way that warmed him. "Perhaps you wouldn't have alarmed them so much if you didn't look like a wild man." She cast a meaningful glance at his hair.

"Yes, well, I wouldn't have looked so much like a wild man if I hadn't had to run to jump on board." He combed his fingers through his hair, bringing it back into some kind of order.

"Did you really?"

He nodded. "The conductor thought I was a madman." He paused, then added candidly, "That occurred to me, as well."

"But why? How did you know where I was? How did you even know I was gone?"

"I can't explain it. I didn't know what it was at first—I just felt uneasy. We were busy watching the Dearborn carriage and their cohort, and I suppose I laid it down to that. But suddenly I realized that the house felt…empty." Alex shrugged. "So we looked for you, and then I questioned the maid you bribed."

"I didn't *bribe* her."

"That's good because she gave you up as soon as I asked. Next time I'd choose another if I were you." He tilted his head, his voice turning serious. "Did you really think I wouldn't follow you?"

"I—" Sabrina paused. "You shouldn't have."

"Why not?" He placed his hands on her upper arms, his eyes intent on hers. "Tell me, Sabrina. Do you really wish I had not? Would you rather I stopped hanging about? Left you alone?"

"Of course I don't," she snapped, turning away from him.

"Why did you leave, Sabrina?" He hadn't intended to ask her, at least not so abruptly, so harshly, but he couldn't stop the words. She turned back sharply, her eyes searching his face, as he rushed on. "Why didn't you tell me before you left? Why did you sneak out of the house as if you were escaping prison? Were you so unhappy there?"

"Of course not. I was happy. Horribly happy." Tears shone in Sabrina's eyes. "I had to leave secretly because that man was watching the house. I knew I must use a disguise. What else was I to do?"

He steeled himself to her tears. "You could have stayed. Did you not trust me to take care of you? Did you think I was too weak to hold off Niles Dearborn? Or was it that you feared I wouldn't protect you when it came down to it? That I would turn you over to him despite everything I said."

"No!" Sabrina cried. "I trust you with my life. But even you can't defy the laws of England. I couldn't let you sacrifice yourself and your family. Don't you see?"

"No," he said flatly. "I don't. All we have to do is stave them off for a couple of weeks until your birthday. Then Dearborn will no longer be your guardian. He won't have any right to control what you do."

"That won't matter if I'm married to his son!"

"You're not. There's no reason to think—"

"But there is." Sabrina's voice caught. "I—I remembered something. That's why I didn't tell you. I couldn't—" Her voice broke and she had to start again. "I couldn't bear to tell you... I think it may be true. I'm afraid I'm married to Peter."

"Why? Miss Holcutt said you had a dream about him, surely that's not enough to—" He stopped, a sharp pain in his chest. "Did you remember something? Are you... Did you realize that you loved him?"

"No!" She looked up at him, her expression so horrified that Alex relaxed. "I don't feel anything when I look at him except fear and dislike." She paused, frowning. "But if I am married to him, I'm legally bound. You can't protect me—no one can."

"I don't give a damn what the law says." Alex's eyes flashed. "I'm not turning you over to either Dearborn unless you want to go back. If it comes down to it, I'll take you out of the country, where he cannot get you. We'll go to America."

Her gaze softened, and she reached out to him. "Oh, Alex…you are very kind. But I can't ask that of you."

"You don't have to ask. That is what's going to happen. I *can* protect you, and I will, no matter what."

Sabrina burst into tears, burying her face in her hands.

"Sabrina…no, don't cry." Alex folded her into his arms, holding her as she sobbed. He stroked her back soothingly, laying soft kisses against her hair, and made comforting noises. When her tears began to quiet, he said, "It'll be all right. If you don't want to leave the country, we shan't. I'll find another way."

She made a little noise, half laugh, half sob, and said, "It's not that. I don't care where I go." She wiped her tears away and looked up at him. Her eyes were soft and glowing, her lashes clinging together wetly, like the points of a star. She was, he thought, the most beautiful woman he had ever seen. She went on, "When I'm with you, I feel as though anything is possible."

"Anything *is* possible."

Sabrina smiled, and he couldn't fathom how a look could stab right through his chest and at the same time fill him with happiness. She rested her palm against his cheek, murmuring his name.

Alex had sworn he was not going to enter these dangerous waters again, was not going to kiss her or caress her or woo her. But at the sight of her, his good intentions melted away, and he bent to kiss her. She made a soft noise of pleasure, and he wrapped his arms around her even more tightly as he kissed her again and again.

The things going through his head were too inchoate to be termed thoughts, but he was intensely aware of how alone they were in the this small, private place, locked away from all eyes, how easy it would be to pull her down with him, to unfasten her garments. His mind was filled with memories of that night in her house in London, of the satin softness of her skin beneath his hand, the plump curve of her breast, the taut hardening of the nipple.

He sat down on the long seat, pulling her into his lap without loosening his embrace around her. She settled into him with a soft sigh that heated his blood. He kissed her cheek, her ear, her throat, his hand roaming slowly over her, exploring the soft hills and plains, until he could not bear to have the impediment of her dress between his touch and her skin.

Deftly unbuttoning the large, decorative buttons of her bodice, Alex slipped his hand inside, caressing her through the thin cloth of her chemise. But soon that was not enough, either, and he tugged loose the bow that fastened her chemise. Then his fingers were on her bare skin, gliding over the supremely soft flesh and curving down to arouse her nipple to further hardness.

He kissed his way down her chest, his lips replacing his teasing fingers, and when he took her nipple into his mouth, she arched up against it with a little moan, sending his own desire skyrocketing. He slid his hand down her leg and up under her skirts. Alex ached to feel that bare skin as well, but just the heat of her against the thin cotton, the hint of what lay beneath the cloth, tantalizingly veiled from his touch, was enough to make him tremble. When his fingers edged between her legs, gliding up to find her, hot and damp, it was all he could do not to strip away the material.

Instead, he stroked her through the cloth, delighting in the way she moved against him, her own fingers sinking into his hair. He wanted more, much more, and he pulled his hand away to fumble at the buttons of her skirt, inconveniently behind her back.

A knock at the door cut through their haze of passion. Alex raised his head, letting out an oath. "The bloody conductor."

Sabrina sat up hastily, pulling her clothes back together, and as another knock sounded sharply, Alex jumped to his feet. Pulling at his clothes and swiping at his mussed hair, he went to the door. God only knew what he must look like. What the ticket taker would think.

He opened the door narrowly, hiding the rest of the room from the man's gaze. "Yes?"

"Ticket, sir?" The man's gaze went curiously over Alex's shoulder to the room beyond.

"Yes, of course. Um…" Alex began to search through his pockets, trying to remember where he'd stuck the blasted ticket, and at the same time did his best to keep the door nearly shut. His blood was still rushing through him like fire. How had the situation devolved into a farce so quickly?

"Here." Sabrina thrust a ticket into his hand.

He held it out to the conductor, who said, "This is just for one, sir." The man's eyes narrowed suspiciously.

With relief, Alex found his ticket and handed it to the man. "Here."

"This is for a different compartment, sir."

"Yes, well, I'm not there." Alex glared at the conductor.

"I see, sir." A sly grin touched the other man's mouth.

"Good day," Alex said and closed the door, turning the latch with a firm click.

Taking a deep breath, he turned back to Sabrina. She was holding her hands against her burning cheeks, her eyes bright. He tried to think of what to say. "I, um…beg your pardon."

She began to giggle. Alex's own mouth twitched, and he let out a long sigh, leaning back against the door. "I *am* sorry, Sabrina. At least he didn't see you."

"I suspect he will be looking for me when we leave." She laughed again and plopped down on the seat. "I'm sorry, too. You were the one who had to face him."

"For you, my dear, I'd dare anything." He grinned, crossing his arms and regarding her. What was he going to do if Sabrina was married? How could he bear to lose her?

"But we can't continue to do this." Sabrina sobered. "It's wrong, not knowing whether… Alex, we simply must find out what happened."

"I know." It was too dangerous to sit down beside her, Alex decided, so he remained by the door. "You could have told me that you feared you were married, you know. You can tell me anything."

"I didn't want it to be true. I thought if I could

just find out it wasn't true, I wouldn't have to even admit it."

"I'm not at all sure it *is* true. If it were, why didn't he bring proof of it with him today?" He paused. "I don't dismiss your dream. We Morelands tend toward dreams of portent. Still, it's not a memory, really. What made you fear it was true?"

"I was standing beside a man, and I felt ill and dizzy. Another man across from us kept talking on and on. I can't remember his face, but he wore a clerical collar. I think— I think I nodded as he talked." She stood up and began to pace around the small area. "Maybe when I saw Peter last night, it triggered that memory."

"Was it Peter you were standing with?"

She hesitated. "I'm not sure, but I think so. I didn't really look at him, but today, when he was in that room, it came over me again. I felt so ill and scared. It keeps returning."

"Have you remembered anything more about the scene?"

She shook her head. "No. And it really doesn't get much clearer." Sabrina hesitated. "Well, a little while ago, something popped into my head and then was gone. It was so quick, I couldn't grasp it. Then you came and I forgot all about it." She sat down, closing her eyes. "I don't think it was connected to that dream. I think— I think it was something about a boy."

"A boy?"

"Yes. A child. I—" She sighed and shook her head. "I can't remember. I don't suppose it would be much help anyway."

"You think it was Peter? Lilah said you knew him when you were children."

"I suppose." She shrugged. "I don't know anything about the boy. It was just…an intense feeling, but I'm not even sure what the feeling was."

"No one has said anything about there being a child," he mused.

"It didn't feel at all like that dream. I doubt it's connected."

"Probably not." Alex sat down. "What's first on your plan?"

"My plan?"

"Yes. For finding out what happened. What you decided to do when you left Broughton House."

"Oh. Yes. That. I don't know that I really had a plan, other than to go to Baddesly Commons and see if anything looked familiar. Perhaps they would sell me a ticket. If that is where I lived, then people would recognize me. Maybe they would know what happened." She straightened her shoulders. "I could go to the church, check their marriage records."

He nodded, feeling no more happy about the idea than Sabrina looked.

"The vicar would remember if he'd married us," she went on, pressing her hand to her stomach. "I dread it, frankly. I'm afraid of what I'll find out."

"I know." Alex reached over and took her hand. "But we'll do it together."

"Yes." Sabrina smiled at him. "That will make it much easier."

There was certainly nothing that stirred Sabrina's memory about the Newbury train station. It took little time for them to walk all around it. When they questioned the ticket agent about whether he had sold a ticket to Sabrina three weeks before, he gave them an odd look but said only that he didn't remember.

"What about a young man who resembles her?" Alex asked, which earned him an even more suspicious glance. "Her brother," Alex added hastily.

"No. Nor her father or mother, either, I 'spect."

They beat a quick retreat, finding a seat out of sight of the ticket agent. Alex glanced at her, and they began to laugh. "I wonder what that man must have thought of us," Sabrina said.

"Hopefully there's not a madhouse close by," he replied. "But I do hope the train to Baddesly Commons comes soon, before he decides to turn us in as suspicious characters."

"It's wrong of me," Sabrina said, "to be pulling you deeper into this, but I am awfully glad you followed me."

He slanted a smiling glance at her. "Two is generally better than one in finding something."

"No, not just because you're an extra set of eyes or because the ticket agent talked to you more freely than he would have to a young woman. It's *you* that makes it better. Just you."

ALEX SAID NOTHING, just looked at her for a long moment, then glanced away, but the expression in his eyes warmed Sabrina down to her toes. She folded her hands in her lap demurely and thought about those moments in the train when Alex had taken her into his arms. She supposed that she should feel guilty and sinful, or at least blush, but the truth was, she had found the whole thing glorious and had been very sorry when the conductor knocked on their door.

She thought about this evening. They would have to spend the night at some inn. They would be alone among strangers. The only thing to keep them separated was their conscience. And Sabrina's conscience wasn't feeling very powerful right now.

The train to Winchester, which would pass Baddesly Commons on its way south, was announced, and Sabrina pulled her thoughts from the irrelevant and highly improper paths to which they'd strayed back to the matter at hand. They boarded and carefully sat at the opposite ends of the padded bench of their compartment, even leaving the door open.

Sabrina leaned her head back against the high seat and closed her eyes. She was tired, and at least she wouldn't be able to think about Alex if she were asleep. That hope proved to be wrong, though, for a dream in which she was hurrying through seemingly endless doors, frantically searching for something, ended up with her gazing out a window with a man standing behind her, one arm hooked around her waist.

Though she could not see him, she knew it was Alex. He stood so close she could feel the warmth of his body all up and down hers. He was murmuring something in her ear, but she couldn't understand it because all she could think of was the desire pulsing through her. He began to kiss her neck, and his hand left her waist to glide up and down her body. There was a growing, insistent ache between her legs. She let out a soft moan, and the noise awakened her.

Sabrina's eyes flew open. She felt warm and positively tingling all through her body. Had she actually made that noise or had it been only in her dream? She glanced at the other end of the bench, where Alex sat, watching her, an answering heat in his eyes. He quickly looked away.

"I, um, I'm going to take a walk along the corridor."

He was gone so long Sabrina thought he must have walked through every car in the train—twice—but she was grateful for the time to bring herself back into composure. After he returned, the air was still fraught with tension, and Sabrina avoided giving Alex more than a brief glance. She was grateful when they reached Baddesly Commons and were able to disembark.

The small station was deserted except for a man sweeping up. But he was happy to give them directions to the inn, which was apparently the only one in the town and was located on the main road, a short walk from the train station.

There was, Sabrina decided, probably nothing that was more than a short walk from the station, for Baddesly Commons turned out to be only a short string of shops along a High Road, all shuttered for the night. Nothing about the place looked familiar to her, which disappointed Sabrina but did not surprise her.

The road was dark, but the inn's lone lamppost acted as a beacon. They walked into the inn yard, and a man came out of the stables beside it.

"Can I help—" he began but stopped as he peered at them in the low light. A beam broke out across his face, and he said, "Why, it's you. Welcome back, miss!"

CHAPTER TWENTY-THREE

SABRINA STIFFENED. "YOU know me?"

"Oh, aye, miss, I'm not likely to forget a girl ridin' in 'fore full light and stabling her horse. Not to worry, your father and brother came along soon enough, and they sent your animal back. Not a good enough mount for ye anyway, I'd say, for ye had good form."

"Um, well…thank you." Sabrina wasn't sure how to respond to the garrulous man's response.

It turned out there was no need to, for he went on. "I 'spect they found ye, eh? They seemed dead worrit about ye."

"Yes, we've spoken to them," Alex said.

"Good. Ain't right for a young lady to be out alone like that."

"She's not," Alex said repressively.

The man nodded wisely. "That's what I thought—elopin', weren't ye? I figured as much with your father in such a pucker."

Sabrina's eyes widened and she started to protest, but a little poke in the back from Alex's finger stopped her.

"Quite right. But Mrs. Mor—" Alex stopped abruptly, then continued, "Mrs. *Moore* is safe now in her husband's protection."

Surreptitiously, Sabrina put her hand into her

pocket and grabbed the ring, slipping it onto her left hand behind her back, all the while smiling madly. Alex took her arm, steering her away.

"Why did you say that?" Sabrina whispered as they approached the inn door. "Now we're in a tangle."

"I had planned to say I was your brother, but the Dearborns already usurped that. I thought yet another brother would seem peculiar. And I didn't want to set every tongue in the place wagging."

"But what about tonight? Do you mean to share a room?"

"I'll get two rooms."

"Newlyweds? Oh, no, *that* won't cause tongues to wag."

As it turned out, the inn was small and had only one room available, the host apologizing profusely that the best rooms had already been taken.

"But we have a private room to dine in," the innkeeper added, beaming. "And there's no roast beef like my Ellie's, if you're feeling peckish."

"Yes." Alex smiled stiffly. "Excellent."

The innkeeper grabbed their bags and showed them up to a small room tucked under the eaves. Its ceiling slanted at a sharp angle up from the low outside wall, leaving only half of the room in which Alex was able to stand without stooping. There was but one window, a single straight chair, a small chest of drawers and a bed, which barely qualified as large enough for two people.

Sabrina glanced around at everything in the room but Alex. The innkeeper, seemingly sensing the tension, said, with a hopeful smile, "It's small, I know, but you'll not find a place cleaner than here, and the bed's soft as a cloud."

"Yes, of course, thank you." Alex hustled the man out of the room, closing the door behind him, and turned back to Sabrina. "I'm dreadfully sorry."

"It's not your fault. I am sure we'll do fine," Sabrina lied firmly.

"I'll sleep in the chair." They both turned to eye the narrow chair with the wicker seat.

"There must be another way."

"Perhaps I could sleep in this private dining room he mentioned," Alex offered next.

"That would *really* set tongues to wagging."

"I'll sleep on the floor here, then." When she grimaced, he went on, "I've slept in worse places, believe me. The time I was kidnapped by that gang of goddess-worshippers, I was stuck in a dark place with only one high window, and the bed had a mattress an inch thick."

Suddenly Sabrina could not breathe. She sat down hard on the small chair, her head swimming.

"Sabrina? What's wrong?" Alex was beside her in an instant, going down on one knee and taking her hand. "What happened? You look like you've seen a ghost."

"I think I have—well, not a ghost. I remembered something. But it's impossible." She raised a hand to her head. "I dreamed that once."

"Dreamed what?"

"A boy on a bed in a little room, with a window high up on a wall. A long time ago. He was bigger than I, older, but he was all alone and scared. I—I think that's what came into my head on the train, the little flash of memory I couldn't recall."

"I don't understand."

"I don't, either. But I… The boy was you. That's why I thought I knew you when I saw you that first day."

"But how could you have dreamed—" Alex shook his head. "No, never mind that, I'm accustomed to things that can't be explained. What happened in this dream?"

"At first the boy was sitting there, leaning against the wall with his knees drawn up and his arms around them, and he was… He was scared, but then he got up and he climbed up to look out the window. It was high, and he put a stool on the bed to stand on it and see out. What?" She stopped as Alex's face turned almost as white as hers.

"Nothing. Go on," he replied hoarsely. "What happened then?"

"I'm trying to remember. Oh, I know, he pulled things out of his pocket and sorted through them—a little penknife and some pebbles or marbles or something and a bit of string."

"Good Lord."

She looked at him gravely. "That happened, didn't it?"

"Yes. Yes. I was trying to find a way to escape."

"That's all I can remember. I think I must have awakened then. But I wanted to help you, to find you, but when I told Papa, he said— Alex! I remember him! I remember my father! I remember the smell of his pipe and him holding me, telling me not to fret." Tears glimmered in her eyes. "I loved him."

She curled her hand into a fist and laid it against her chest. "I *feel* it, how much I loved him. Oh, Alex..."

She went into his arms, and he stood, pulling her up with him. "I'm sorry he's gone."

"No, don't be. I'm not crying because I'm sad." She pulled back, wiping the tears from her cheeks. "I am sorry he's gone, of course, and that I won't see him again, but it's so wonderful to remember him. To know I had a father and to be able to feel that love again. I was beginning to think I wouldn't ever remember my life. But this gives me hope! I don't care that it was only a snippet or that it's a bit blurry around the edges. I have regained a little piece of myself and that's wonderful."

"It is, indeed." He smiled down at her. "I am very glad to see you so happy." His eyes went to her mouth, and he leaned forward slightly, his hands coming up, but he pulled back abruptly and cleared his throat. "I'm very glad," he repeated.

Sabrina decided this was not the time to tell him how much it warmed her to think that the memory connected her to Alex, so she merely nodded. "Well..." She gave a final swipe of the hand across her cheekbone. "I should wash up a bit before supper."

"Yes, of course. I'll just...uh, go down to check on that private dining room. Come down whenever you're ready."

THE POT ROAST made by the innkeeper's wife was every bit as delicious as the man had promised, but Sabrina found she had little hunger for it. She took a few bites of everything, smiling and assuring the woman that the food was excellent, but other than that she ate little, pushing her food about on her plate and sipping her glass of wine. Perhaps it was the excitement and fear, the nerves engendered by her mad flight from London, that made her feel so jumpy, her insides so uncertain.

Or perhaps it was Alex. Sitting here alone with him, enclosed from the rest of the world, she could not keep from thinking about tonight and that small room. The passion between them this afternoon on the train. How would they manage to not give in to their desires in such close quarters? Did she even want to?

Alex was as silent as she. Were his thoughts straying to the same place? She looked at his hands carving the roast and could not help but think of the way those long, expressive fingers had roamed her body a few hours ago.

Sabrina cleared her throat. "Well, now we know I am not from Baddesly Commons."

"That groom can tell us where they returned your horse. We're getting closer."

She nodded. She wasn't sure whether that thought made her feel pleased or scared. Whatever it turned out her past had been, she was certain that she had not been as happy in it as she had been these past weeks. How could she have been when Alex was not part of it?

They lapsed into another awkward silence. Sabrina searched for something else to say. "How did you get out of the house undetected?" She frowned. "They didn't see you, did they?"

"No. What they saw was my mother and I taking a little stroll with you."

"What?"

He smiled. "I went over the back wall, where they had no one watching. In the meantime, Con pulled them off their post by changing his disguise—including the great sacrifice of shaving his mustache—so that he would look like me. Then he went out for a stroll. They were bound to follow him because Miss Holcutt dressed in your old gown, put on a big hat and accompanied him. The duchess tagged along—to make sure the Dearborns wouldn't have the nerve to attack them on the street, she said, but in my opinion, she simply wanted to get in on the fun."

"Lilah?" Sabrina goggled at him. "Lilah pretended to be me?"

"Yes, I was a bit surprised myself."

"I don't remember her, so I can't say for sure, but she didn't seem the sort to disguise herself and play games with pursuers."

"She *is* very…correct. However, I believe her ire was raised. She even offered to go home, change back into herself and tell the Dearborns, when they came looking for you, that you had run off to catch a ship in Southampton. Though I gather the even greater sacrifice was spending twenty minutes with my brother."

"They didn't seem to like each other very much," Sabrina agreed.

"No. Which is a little odd, for Con is in general a more sociable fellow than I, and women usually fall all over themselves trying to get his attention."

"I'm sure they do—he's very handsome."

His eyes lit with humor. "Why, Sabrina, you'll make me blush."

Sabrina, realizing the unintentional compliment

she had given him, felt a telltale blush blooming on her own cheeks, but she said tartly, "It would be silly, wouldn't it, to deny what is so obvious to everyone. Including yourself."

"Sorry. I shouldn't tease you." He reached out to take her hand.

"No, I like it when you tease," she replied honestly, then her eyes widened as she realized the double meaning of her words. Alex went very still. Suddenly the familiar ease that had sprung up between them the past few moments was gone. His skin against her hand flared with heat, and the very air between them seemed to tremble. Whatever thoughts had been in Sabrina's head vanished.

His hand moved on hers, his fingers stroking across hers with a featherlight touch. She felt the whisper of the touch all through her, the simple sensual movement warming her to her core. Alex continued to gaze into her eyes, and she could look away no more than he could.

"I like it, too." His voice was husky.

Though she did not move, everything in her yearned toward him. His mouth softened, his eyes burning into hers. Then, with a low noise of frustration, Alex jerked his hand back and rose to his feet.

"No, I cannot. I will not." Shoving his hands into his pockets, he turned aside and looked at the door rather than her. "You need not worry."

"I'm not worried."

He ignored her words, plowing on. "No doubt you're tired. I'll go for a walk to clear my head. It will give you time to, um, change and…all that. You will probably be asleep when I come up, so I'll say good-night to you now."

With a punctiliously correct bow to her, he strode out of the room. Sabrina sat for a long moment, looking after him. She had meant it when she said she didn't worry; she knew Alex would do whatever it took to protect her honor, even from himself. The question, though, was…did she want him to?

Sabrina picked up her glass and drank the rest of the wine as she mused on the night ahead. She could do as Alex said—get washed and change into her nightgown and be in bed before he returned. She might even fall asleep, or at least pretend to, and that would make the situation less strained. Or she could do something else entirely.

She left the dining room, deep in thought. She thought of Alex and how little time she had known him. She thought of what lay in the future—the possibilities and practicalities, the pain and heartbreak and happiness that danced before her like a mirage. It was hard, she thought, to conceive of the future when she had so little of a past. Her life, as it had been the past several weeks, was in the here and now.

The smart thing, the reasonable thing, was to exercise caution, to feel one's way forward like a man creeping through the dark. How could she know what she felt, who she would be a day from now, a week from now, when she recovered her memory? On the other hand, was she to sacrifice her happiness on the altar of what might be?

She thought of the memory she had had of her father this afternoon. She had not known he was her father because she recognized him physically. It was simply that she knew him—in her heart and soul, her spirit. She had known him in her blood and bones, not with her eyes, not with her mind. It was the feeling that had come back to her, the emotion. That was what was important, wasn't it?

Sabrina trotted up the stairs, her steps growing faster and surer. Skinning out of her clothes, she carefully folded them and set them aside; there was no telling how long she would have to wear them, and she had brought only one other dress. She washed as best she could with only a washbasin and soap and slipped into the nightgown she had brought with her.

She ran her hands down the front of it with a sigh, wishing for something prettier. But the nightgown Alex had put in her bag was equally simple and unadorned. She smiled to see that he had also included a light dressing gown—trust Alex to remember the details. Wrapping the robe around her, she brushed out her hair and sat down to wait.

It seemed forever before she heard Alex's footsteps in the hall outside. She jumped to her feet and faced the door, heart pounding. Alex slipped quietly inside, then turned and saw her. "Sabrina! What are you doing up? I thought you would be, um…" His gaze slid toward the bed, cover turned down invitingly, then quickly away. "Asleep," he finally added. He took a step back, reaching for the door handle. "I'll go back down and—"

"No, wait." Sabrina stopped, embarrassed. Why hadn't she thought this through? Decided what to say? "I…didn't want to go to sleep. I wanted to see you." She moved forward. As he was already at the door, he could not back up any farther.

"Oh. I see." His eyes dropped down to the white V of nightgown that showed between the lapels of her robe, then back up. "Of course. But, thing is, this may not be the best time to talk. Tomorrow morning, perhaps." He felt behind him for the door handle.

"No, not tomorrow morning. It must be now."

"Very well." He paused, one hand on the door, poised to leave. "What is it you want?"

"You," Sabrina replied and shrugged off her dressing gown, letting it drop to the floor.

CHAPTER TWENTY-FOUR

ALEX STARED, HIS MOUTH opening and closing without a word coming out. At last he said hoarsely, "Sabrina… you don't know what you're asking."

"I beg your pardon." She cocked an eyebrow at him. "I most certainly do. I'm not a child."

"No, of course, I didn't mean that." His eyes flickered down her. Sabrina knew that even in the dim light, he could see the outline of her body, the darker circle of her nipples, and it made her blush. If he refused her, she didn't know how she could face him again.

His hand tightened on the door handle, and he said, "I meant, I can't— If I kiss you, if I touch you, I'll only want more. It's easier not to start."

"But I want more, as well."

"Sabrina…" He stretched the word on a groan. "I cannot." He let go of the handle and half turned away, sweeping one hand back through his hair.

"I'm sorry." Sabrina faltered. This wasn't how she had pictured it; in her mind, everything had simply flowed. He would see her dressed for bed, waiting for him, and he would know. He would take her in his arms. She looked down at her discarded robe, wondering how she could gracefully pick it up and put it on again. "Perhaps I have presumed too much. I thought you wanted to…"

"Of course I want you!" Alex insisted, his voice rising. He stopped and drew a breath, visibly reining himself in. "I think I'll go mad sometimes, wanting you. Do you know how much I think of you? How often I remember kissing you, holding you? But I would be the veriest cad to take you to bed tonight. When your memory returns, you may not feel the same. For all we know, you might not even remember me or this night. What if our assumptions are wrong? What if you love that man? You would regret tonight and curse me for having taken advantage of you. The last thing in the world I want is for you to despise me."

Sabrina looked at him for a long moment, then said softly, "I could never despise you." She came closer. "I've thought about this all evening. I've worried about what I would do if my memory returned or I found I'd been married. But I realized, the other things don't matter. This is what I want."

"But—"

"Shh." She laid her forefinger against his lips. "Listen to me. The past doesn't matter. I don't care what the legalities are. If I awoke tomorrow and didn't recognize you, it would make no difference. I know you in here." She laid her hand over her heart. "I remember nothing else in my life, but I remembered that one dream of you. You are who I want. This is what I want. No matter what the future holds, I won't regret tonight."

His eyes darkened, and when he said her name, it was a caress. "Sabrina…" He cupped her face in his hands, his thumbs stroking over her cheeks. "You are so beautiful." He bent and pressed his lips lightly to hers. "When I'm around you, I can't think of anything but you." He kissed her again, more lingeringly this time.

His palms against her cheeks were suddenly searing, and he moved into her. Never breaking their kiss, he let his hands fall to her shoulders and glide down over her arms, setting every nerve there alive. Sabrina kissed him back eagerly, wanting to know, wanting to feel, and he answered by putting his hands to her waist and pulling her tightly against him. She felt his body, so hard, so different from her own, pressing into her.

He kissed her again and again—her lips, her cheeks, her eyes, her throat. His mouth roamed over her skin like a man long starved. Sabrina reveled in the sensations coursing through her—wanting to luxuriate in every sensual moment yet wanting to race forward to the destination that beckoned. Deep within her, heat grew and pulsed. She yearned to be rid of her clothes, ached to feel Alex's hands on her skin. His skin beneath her fingertips.

Alex's needs obviously matched hers, for he pulled back to sweep off his jacket and toss it aside, followed by his ascot and stickpin. Sabrina's fingers went to the buttons of his waistcoat. When she was done, there was still the line of buttons down the front of his shirt—why did men have so many pieces of clothing? she wondered. A waistcoat seemed excessive, especially given the added entanglements of pocket watch, fobs and chain.

But when she had the shirt unbuttoned, her fingers slowed, enticed by the sight of his bare chest, lean and

muscled. She pulled the sides apart and back, expos-
ing more of his skin. She spread her hands out over
his chest. His breath came in and out more rapidly,
but he said nothing, merely watched her, mouth soft-
ening and eyes burning more hotly, as she took her
time exploring him.

The tails of his shirt were still caught in his trousers, and she pulled them up and out. There was another button, and then his cuff links to be undone,
but he waited patiently, unmoving except to suck in
his breath when her fingertips drifted across the soft
skin of his stomach. Sabrina slanted up a questioning glance, but seeing the heat in his gaze, she let
her fingers drift back, slowly circling and teasing
across his flesh.

Gliding her hand back up, she circled each taut
masculine nipple, feeling her own nipples tighten in
response. She knew that Alex, too, saw hers hardening, thrusting against the thin cotton of her nightgown, for he swallowed hard, his eyes fastened on her
chest. Almost lazily, he raised his hand and brushed
his knuckles across her breasts, arousing the sensitive tips through the material.

He cupped her breasts in his hands, watching the
circling of his thumbs around the tight buds of her nipples. A damp warmth blossomed between Sabrina's
legs, and she began to ache, the feeling growing with
every stroke of his thumbs. When he kissed her, taking
her mouth as he caressed her breasts, she shuddered,
desire blazing through her.

His hands left her breasts, but before she could
utter a murmur of discontent, they were gliding over
her stomach and around to her back. His fingertips

trailed down her spine, light as down. He spread out his hands and curved them over her buttocks, lifting her up onto her toes and into his pelvis. She felt every hard inch of him pulsing against her, and the throbbing between her legs grew even more insistent.

One arm hard around her waist to hold her to him, Alex teased his other hand between her legs from behind, startling a surprised noise from her. He lifted his head and smiled down into her eyes, his fingers working the sensitive cleft.

"Too much?" he murmured. "Shall I retreat?" His fingertips glided teasingly back out.

"No." She rested her head against his chest. "Advance."

She felt the huff of his laugh against her ear. "Perhaps I should do both."

He slid over her, back and forth in a light rhythm, until it was all she could do not to squirm and clamp her legs together over his questing fingers.

"Alex?"

"Mmm?" His mouth was busy on her earlobe, the dual attack sending her senses into a frenzy.

"I think…I want more."

"Do you?" There was a faint smugness in his tone that was curiously arousing. "Perhaps this?"

He released her to take her gown in his hands and shove it up until his hands found the bare skin of her thighs. He slid beneath the garment, his hands smoothing in the same pattern over her bare flesh and into the liquid heat of her desire.

"Or would you rather this?" He moved his hand back around, now caressing her stomach and going lower to delve between her legs from the front.

Sabrina let out a soft whimper, each movement of his hand arousing her more.

"Or, no, I think this." He took her gown in his hands and pulled it up and off, revealing her naked body. His eyes glittered, moving over her hungrily.

"Yes," he whispered. "This is definitely better." He caressed her breasts, her stomach, her back, her legs. He took her mouth with his, kissing her deeply, as he stole between her legs again, finding and entering her, stoking the fires of her passion until she thought she must simply shatter.

With a groan, Alex broke away and lifted her in his arms, carrying her to the bed and laying her down on it. Swiftly he divested himself of the rest of his clothes. Sabrina had time for only a brief startled glance at his naked body, and then he was on the bed beside her, his hands and mouth making her forget all else.

Sabrina moved against him, not sure exactly what she wanted but knowing that she needed it desperately. Every sense was heightened, her skin aware of even the soft brush of air against her, her ears filled with the rasp of his breath, her body thrumming with the rush of her own blood through her veins.

She caressed his shoulders and back. Her fingers tangled in his thick hair, silently urging him on. Finally, when she was blazing with heat, her skin trembling, he moved between her legs. His engorged flesh probed at her center. Her breath caught as he moved slowly, insistently, into her. There was a flash of pain, startling her and making her tighten, and in the next instant he was sliding deep inside her, filling her in such a way that she gasped, her fingers digging into his back.

He paused, his breath hard and fast, his face tight, and looked down at her. Sabrina smiled slowly and arched up a little against him in a silent urging. His smile in return was slow and sexual as he began to move within her.

She had never known this, never expected it, never even dreamed of it. Sabrina was certain of that. His movement was an exquisite torment, a slow entice-ment of heat and pleasure. Alex moved in slow, deep strokes, vaulting her desire higher and higher, then easing up to tease her back to the top again.

A strange, wild, exhilarating pleasure took her, pulling her under like a great tide, and then exploding deep within her, rolling outward in wave after wave of pleasure. She cried out in surprise and delight, and for a long moment she was aware of nothing except the dark beauty enveloping her.

She looked up at him, blissfully spent, feeling boneless and malleable as wax, and she saw that his face was still sharp with desire, his eyes burning, his skin slick with sweat. And she realized it wasn't over, that there was something more awaiting her. He began to move again, dropping his head as he pumped his hips, his strokes growing faster and harder. Amaz-ingly, Sabrina felt her body awaken again, the sound and sight and feel of him arousing her once more, shooting her up and up.

This time, though, she knew what awaited her, and she rushed to meet it, caressing his muscle-hardened body, moving her body in an answering rhythm. Again the fire exploded through her, but now when she was swept into ecstasy, Alex rode through it with her, shuddering under his own release, and collapsed into her welcoming arms.

Sabrina was awakened the next morning by Alex stringing kisses down her back. Smiling to herself, she turned over to curl her arms around his neck and pull him down for a long, slow kiss on the mouth.

"There," she said when she pulled back. "That's a proper kiss."

"It is, indeed." He rolled onto his side, propping himself up on his elbow and grinning down at her. As he talked, he trailed his fingers over her flesh in a lazy, meandering path. "One thing we can be certain of now—if you were indeed married, it was unconsummated."

Sabrina blushed at his words, and he bent down to plant a soft kiss on the hollow of her throat. "I love watching you blush."

"Then you should be a happy man," Sabrina replied tartly, "since you so often cause me to do so."

He laughed and said, "What shall we do this morning? Follow your horse back to its original stable? That seems the likeliest way to go."

"Mmm-hmm." Sabrina slid her hand up his arm and onto his shoulder. "Though breakfast might be in order first."

"That, too. Or, perhaps, we might linger here a little while," he went on, his hand gliding lower as he bent to kiss her again.

When at last he lifted his head again, Sabrina replied shakily, "That sounds like a remarkably good idea."

Their lovemaking this morning was slow and soft,

an almost casual exploration of each other's bodies
and desires. They kissed and touched and murmured,
letting their desire grow until at last they came together in another cataclysm of desire, so intense, so
sweet, so powerful that it brought tears to Sabrina's
eyes.

Lying there afterward, holding him, Sabrina knew
that whatever her past held, her future was with this
man. She could not ask Alex to link himself to a
woman without a past; she would not hold him to
anything beyond this moment. But for her the bond
between them would last the rest of her life.

Their morning continued at a slow pace. They
rose and dressed and breakfasted without haste, too
wrapped up in one another to care about time or their
mission. Alex asked the head groom for the name of
the place to which they'd returned the horse Sabrina
had ridden. The man gave him a curious look, but he
did not ask why "Mr. Moore" hadn't simply gotten the
information from his wife, just gave him the name.

They leased a one-horse gig, the only vehicle the
stables offered for hire. It was slow, but it was a pleasant enough day that an open vehicle would do, and
spending more time driving down a country road
with each other had its own appeal.

They traveled west along a narrow lane, clearly
not a well-traveled route, arriving after a few hours
in the village of Cumbrey. It looked to be an even
smaller village than Baddesly Commons, but the main
road, which their own lane intersected, was on a well-
traveled route to Winchester, and for that reason, it
boasted more than one inn.

"The Blind Ox, the head groom said," Alex said

as they turned left and rolled along the wider thoroughfare. "It ought to be easy enough to find an inn with such an unappealing name."

They had almost reached the edge of town and Sabrina was beginning to think they had gone the wrong way when her eyes fell on an old building done in the distinctive black-and-white pattern of the Tudor era. It sagged here and there as if it had partially melted, giving credence to its having been there since the reign of Queen Elizabeth.

Sabrina stiffened. Her stomach roiled, and suddenly her head felt as if it was about to split in two. "Wait! Stop."

Alex pulled up and turned toward her. "What? Did you see a sign?"

"This is it!" Sabrina said, her voice hushed but intense. "I'm certain of it. This is where I escaped."

CHAPTER TWENTY-FIVE

"SABRINA!" ALEX'S EYES WIDENED, and he reached out to take her hand. "You remember it?"

Sabrina did not reply, just clenched his hand tightly. Memories were flooding into her mind, almost swamping her. She climbed down from the gig, Alex right behind her. Instead of going toward the front door of the inn, she started around the side. "The stables." She flicked her hand to the left. "That's where I got the horse. I don't know who it belonged to—it was terrible of me to take it, but I didn't know what else to do. I had to get away as quickly as I could."

"Of course you did."

They reached the back of the inn. She pointed to a small, shedlike extension with a slightly slanted roof that had been built onto the back of the place. "I landed on that." She looked up at the window above it. "I was in that room, and I climbed out." She pressed fingers to her temple. "I... It's fuzzy a little. I was climbing out and I remember falling...yes! He was trying to pull me back in, and he leaned out too far. I tried to pull away, and then suddenly we were falling." She shivered, her face pale.

"Sabrina, you don't have to think about it right

now." Alex's forehead was creased in concern. "We'll sit—you can have something to drink and rest a bit."

"No. I'm fine." The truth was she felt strange and more than a little ill, but it was all roaring through her now, an unstoppable wave sweeping everything before it.

Taking Alex's hand, she rushed through the back door, startling the cook and a scullery maid, and emerged into a corridor. She hurried toward the stairs at the end of the hallway.

"Where are you going? To the room you pointed?" Alex asked.

"Yes, yes." Sabrina came to a halt at the top of the stairs and glanced around uncertainly. "I'm not sure. I don't remember how it looked." She glanced up at the ceiling and it swam before her eyes. "I remember that light fixture."

"Judging from the outside, it should be this way." Alex pointed. "I think." A maid was walking down the hall, carrying a pail and eyeing them curiously. "Excuse me. Miss...can you tell us which room has the window directly over the roof of the kitchen extension?"

She gave him an odd look, but when he dropped a few pence in her hand, she pointed and said, "That one there. The Bombay room."

"Bombay?" Alex raised an eyebrow, and the girl smiled.

"Yes, sir. He's grand, Mr. Hudspeth is. At least there's a chest from India in it. The St. Petersburg room's as Russian as my aunt Sally."

"Is it locked? We'd like to go in and look."

She shrugged. "No. I just cleaned it."

Sabrina was already starting toward the door before the girl finished. She swung open the door but
paused on the threshold, for a moment overcome by
a wave of nausea. She took a half step back, coming
up against Alex. The warmth and strength of him was
reassuring, and she managed to step into the chamber.

"It was here," she murmured, her eyes moving
slowly around the room. "It's all…so vague. I was
dizzy, and nothing made sense, but I knew…I knew
Peter had betrayed me." She paused, feeling again
that stab of pain and loss.

"Betrayed you? How?"

"He… I'm not sure. I just remember feeling it quite
strongly. I woke up on that bed." She closed her eyes,
frowning. "I don't remember coming here or lying
down. I was alone and very confused. I didn't know
where I was or why. What had happened."

"Ease up. Don't try to pull out the memory by
force. Just tell me what you *do* recall."

She nodded and took a breath. "Um, I got up—
well, I rolled off the bed, actually. I was wobbly and…
curiously remote, almost as if I were watching someone else. Nothing seemed quite real." She glanced
at him.

Alex nodded grimly. "I think you'd been drugged."

"Yes, I suppose I had, looking back on it. When
I got to the door, I found that he'd locked me in."
Alex let out an oath, but she ignored it. "Our cases
were over here, and I grabbed mine. I was going
to climb out the window, but somewhere in there I
thought about a disguise. I hadn't time to change—
and frankly, I'm not sure I was clearheaded enough to
have done so right then. So I opened his case and took

some of his clothes. And there was that bag of money. I stole it—I was thinking clearly enough to know I'd need money—and put it with my things. I had to take my dress from my bag to fit in his clothes. I even took his shoes. Not the cap, though, I took that from a hook in the stables. I really was quite larcenous."

"I think you can be excused for it. What did you do then?"

"I heard Peter at the door and I tried to climb out the window, but he grabbed my arm, and we struggled. I was hitting and kicking him, and he slapped me." She glanced at Alex and said lightly, "Don't look so murderous. I don't think that caused all my bruises—a lot of it was the fall."

"Which was his fault, too. I intend to have a talk with Peter Dearborn when we get back."

"A talk?"

"Something more than a talk," he admitted. "But go on. How did you get away?"

"I think he was surprised, actually, by slapping me. I grabbed the water pitcher and bashed him with it. I climbed out the window. I was going to climb down the drainpipe, you see. But he leaned out the window and grabbed me, and I couldn't get away from him. I kept tugging and…he fell. He'd leaned too far out. But he still had a grip on me, so he pulled me down with him." Sabrina went to the window and stood gazing down at the roof below them. "I must have hit the roof and rolled off it. I don't remember any of that."

"Let's go downstairs," Alex suggested, taking Sabrina's elbow and turning her toward the door. "You should sit down and rest, have something to drink, take a few moments to adjust to all this."

Sabrina nodded. The nausea and headache were receding, but she still felt jittery and tumbled up inside. They went downstairs, where Alex quickly arranged for a private parlor and a pitcher of cider. Sabrina was soon ensconced in a comfortable chair by a window, Alex pulling another chair close to her and taking her hand. She looked at him and smiled faintly, squeezing his hand. "I'm all right. Really."

"You looked terribly pale for a moment there."

"I'm not going to faint, I promise. But it's so strange." She frowned, reaching up to rub her temples. "I can hardly remember anything right before I woke up in that room. What I can remember is like my dream, but no more solid than the dream was— just a vague sense of being woozy, almost asleep as I stood there with Peter...wherever it was. And that man talking at me. I was so hot. I felt as if I could hardly breathe."

"He had to have drugged you. I can't wait to get my hands on him."

"Well, I hope never to see him again," Sabrina said flatly.

"Before that, what's the last thing you remember?"

"Being in my room at home."

"Home? You remember where you lived?" Alex's face brightened.

"Yes. Well, it isn't really *my* home. It's the Dearborns' estate in Wiltshire."

"That's excellent. We'll get a map, locate the place, and then we can plot the likeliest course you took from there to here. It will give us some reasonable limits to where this 'wedding' might have taken place."

"Mrs. Jones!" boomed a cheerful voice from the doorway. "Mrs. Jones, how good to see you again." The voice belonged to a man as large as the voice implied—he had a rounded, wide body topped by a rounded, wide face.

"Good heavens. Another name," Sabrina said under her breath. "Little wonder I couldn't remember my own."

Alex turned and stood up, and the other man stopped abruptly. "I—I beg your pardon, sir. I thought…" His gaze went back to Sabrina, and his voiced faltered again, his face growing even more puzzled.

"I am the lady's brother," Alex said quickly. "Mr. Moore."

"Ah, I see, sir," the other man replied, though his face clearly said he did not. He bowed to Alex. "My name is Hudspeth. I am the proprietor here at The Blind Ox. We were honored by Mr. and Mrs. Jones's company a few weeks ago." Turning once again to Sabrina, he went on, "I am pleased to see you have returned, ma'am. Especially after you had to depart so quickly. I was alarmed to hear that you were so ill."

"It was rather touch and go," Alex agreed blandly.

"I knew it must be something dire," the innkeeper said, unable to quell the spark of curiosity in his tone. "When they came in, I told my wife, 'Mrs. Hudspeth,' I said, 'that poor little lass is dead on her feet.'" Looking suddenly alarmed, he added, "Not really dead, you understand. Just pale, you know, and drooping. Mr. Jones had to half carry you up the stairs. So it wasn't a surprise when his father told me Mr. Jones had had to take you to a doctor."

"I'm sorry about, um, taking your horse," Sabrina said.

"Ah." He made a dismissive noise. "It was no matter. An emergency like that—a single horse is faster than a carriage. And, of course, the elder Mr. Jones was kind enough to compensate me and send the animal back when he joined you."

"Do you remember what time she and Mr. Jones arrived here? Do you know where they had been?"

The innkeeper stared at him. "Yes, it was quite late, sir, but surely you—"

"I fear Mrs. Jones remembers almost nothing from that night. She was so ill, you see. The, um, the fever."

"Yes, yes, of course."

"Did they come from the church? Or from another town?" Alex went on hurriedly, "She lost something, you see, and we are trying to find it. An earring. Quite valuable."

"She didn't lose it here," the other man protested. "I'd have told you right off if we'd come upon a fancy earring."

"No, no, we weren't implying that you had anything to do with it. We think perhaps it was lost along the way. So we are trying to retrace their path."

Hudspeth frowned, suspicion growing on his face. "But surely Mr. Jones can tell you that."

"He succumbed to the illness, as well," Alex told him. "Quite laid up—some sort of tropical fever, you know. His father, as well. Perhaps they mentioned to you where they last stopped."

"No, naught like that. They didn't say a word about

it. But their driver, now, he might have said something to the stable lads."

"Yes, of course, thank you. We shall just finish our drinks and be on our way. Sorry to have bothered you." Alex handed the man a silver coin, and the man's face cleared, his suspicion apparently dismissed in the face of cash.

"Yes, sir, thank you, always glad for your custom." The innkeeper bowed out of the room. Alex followed him, firmly closing the door behind the man.

"A tropical fever?" Sabrina asked, her eyes dancing with laughter. "Really, Alex."

"First thing that came into my head. For all he knows, the Dearborns have been in Burma for a year." He grinned. "But I suspect we ought to leave before he has time to wonder why you are jaunting about the countryside looking for a lost earring while your husband is in bed with a terrible fever."

They left their cider on the table and headed toward the stables, where, they found, a groom had seen to their horse. Again, Alex tipped him lavishly before inquiring about the carriage that had arrived three weeks earlier. It took some time and conversation between the stable lads before the head groom was called from the back.

"Mr. Jones? Nay, I can't say I recall the name."

"Three weeks ago, late at night," Alex prodded.

"Oh! Aye, I remember that now. A hired carriage, it was. Horses were dead tired, and the coachman was fair disgusted with them. Not the horses, the people what hired him."

"Why is that?"

"Said they was going to lame his animals the way they was rushing on. They wanted to keep on to Winchester, see, but he told them they could do it on foot, then, for he wasn't forcing his horses."

"They were headed to Winchester?"

"Aye. At least, that's what he said."

"Do you know where they had been before? Perhaps they'd stopped at a church along the way?"

"A church?" The groom looked at him blankly. "Nay, he said naught about stopping or churches. They'd driven from Andover."

"Andover, eh? Thank you." Alex pressed a half crown into his palm. "Do you remember anything else about the carriage or the people? Did the driver say anything about who they were?"

The man tucked the coin in his pocket and took up a pose of deep thinking. "Well…there was a woman asleep in the carriage. The man had to carry her to the inn. Or maybe she was sick." He shrugged. "That's all I remember, sir."

"You've helped a great deal," Alex assured him.

They climbed back into their gig and Alex picked up the reins. But he didn't move forward, turning to look at Sabrina.

"Where now?" Sabrina asked. "Should we check at the church here?"

"No, it sounds as if they only stopped here because the driver insisted. I think we should take the road back to Andover. At least we have a destination now. I imagine that is where we'll find out more." He paused, then added musingly, "Still, that scene you remember could have been at a church anywhere along the way, too."

"We're going to stop at every church from here to Andover?" Sabrina asked. "That will take hours... days."

Alex grinned. "Then we'd best get started."

CHAPTER TWENTY-SIX

THEY STOPPED IN the next village, which was only a few miles away. The church was on the main thoroughfare. It was a small structure made of gray stone with a modest spire, its only unique feature lying in the fact that it did not face the road but lay sideways to it. A vicarage of similar design stood behind the church, and it was there that Alex and Sabrina made their way.

The door was opened by a smiling, dimpled woman who was obviously pleased to receive company. She showed them into the vicar's office. Alex noted that he looked far less pleased to see them than his housekeeper. It was also clear that he did not recognize Sabrina.

Still, Alex asked him about any recent weddings he had performed, this time spinning a story of a fictitious cousin who had eloped.

"Young man, I am not in the habit of marrying any stranger who passes through town," the vicar told him with a disapproving frown. "I don't like this practice of marrying with a special license, and I can tell you that I have not done so anytime in the past year. Indeed, I have not performed a wedding ceremony, even with banns read, for over a month. St. Edward's is a very small parish."

"Would you know if there were any other churches in the area they might have gone to? A vicar who is not averse to marriage by special license...or to strangers?" Alex asked, taking a new tack.

"I should think not." The priest looked horrified. "I imagine your cousin went to Scotland for that."

Thanking the clergyman, Alex and Sabrina left. He looked down at her as they walked to their vehicle, noting the paleness of her face. "You know, I saw an inn as we drove into town. I think we should stay the night here."

"Don't you think we should press on? Drive on to the next village?"

"What I think is that you should rest."

"I'm fine," she said stoutly.

"Well, *I* could use some rest." Alex gave her a wry grin. "Our horse could, as well. Besides, we should get organized instead of continuing in this haphazard manner. We need to look at a map and figure out your route, as we talked about earlier. I'd also welcome something to eat. Breakfast was a very long time ago."

"You're right." Sabrina rubbed her temples. "Perhaps food will help me think better."

He turned the gig around and drove back to the small inn they had passed as they came into town. It was a quaint little building, with only a few rooms, and as there was no tavern attached, it was pleasantly quiet, as well. They were the only guests, and Alex was pleased to find that attached to the bedroom was a small sitting room where they could eat their meals and discuss their plans in privacy.

Sabrina went into the bedroom to freshen up, and

by the time she emerged, tea and cakes had been brought up and set on the small table. She had taken down her hair, and Alex's abdomen tightened at the sight of her loose black curls tumbling down about her face. He could not keep from thinking of the nearby bedroom and the night ahead.

"Ah…" She breathed a sigh of relief as she sank into one of the chairs. "How lovely. I hope you don't mind—I had to unpin my hair. It was making my head hurt."

He smiled faintly. "Mind? No. I love your hair down." He came up to stand behind her and placed his fingers on her temples, rubbing them gently. She let out another soft sigh of pleasure, and that made the desire coil even more tightly in him. He slid his fingers into the thick mass of her hair to massage her scalp, telling himself that it was only to ease her headache. Nothing more—no matter how arousing it was.

Sabrina's head fell back against him, as if too heavy for her neck to hold. His hands slid down to her shoulders, rubbing out the weariness there, as well. He should stop this before he could think of nothing else but taking her to bed, but he could not bring himself to move away just yet. "How do you feel? You look less pale."

"I'm not dizzy or nauseous anymore, and I think my headache is disappearing. But I feel so…adrift."

"Adrift? Why?" The concern her words raised in him made him drop his hands and sit down beside her. "I don't understand."

"I'm not sure I do." She made a self-deprecating little moue and reached out to pour the tea. "When I came to your office, I was desperate to find out who

I was, to settle my mind. But now that I remember it all, I feel even stranger." The words tumbled from her mouth now, as if once begun, she could not stop. "It's as if I'm two different people. When I saw that inn, it wasn't just that I remembered my name and the things that had happened to me. I suddenly *was* me again. The same person I used to be, with all my old feelings and fears and hopes and beliefs." She looked at him inquiringly.

"I understand. I would think that's natural." He kept his face composed, not showing the tendrils of anxiety that were winding through him. Had his fears been right? Had her feelings for him disappeared when she regained her memory?

"But I'm also still the person I've been the last few weeks. And these two people are now struggling to somehow become one." She glanced at him ruefully. "I know I must sound mad."

"No, not at all." He paused for a moment, then said carefully, not looking at her, "Now that you have regained yourself, do you...do you feel differently? Than the way you felt last night?"

She looked at him in surprise. "About you? About us? No, no." She put her hand on his arm. "I meant everything I said last night. That hasn't changed."

Everything in him eased, and he smiled, taking her hand and bringing it up to kiss it.

"What I feel is more... Well, it's as if I were a girl before and now suddenly I'm a woman, but there was no gradual change in between, no growing up. I'm that girl, and at the same time I'm the Sabrina I've been the past several weeks."

"Is there so much difference between the two of you?"

"Lilah was right—I was shy. After Papa died, Mama and I spent all our time together in the country. She knew I didn't like to meet people, that I preferred to sit at home and read. I was like Papa that way—I loved books and learning. She was very protective of me. I imagine most would say she coddled me. And after Mama died and I went to live with the Dearborns, I was happy to be sheltered, away from the world. I didn't want to make my debut. I didn't want to go to London. I was timid."

"Timid? Bashing someone over the head and climbing out a window hardly sound timid."

She smiled self-deprecatingly. "I was rather frantic at the time. Looking back, I'm amazed I did those things. All my life, I've done what everybody wanted. I was obedient and afraid of upsetting anyone. My clothes, for instance. I didn't like my dresses—they're too frilly and flouncy. But I wore what Mrs. Dearborn wanted. I couldn't bear to disappoint her because she was generous, and she wanted so much for me to like them. I felt I would be an absolute ingrate to complain about them. She was very kind to me— they were all kind to me." She paused. "Or at least I thought they were."

"I'm sure they did care for you," Alex said quickly, wanting to banish the sadness in her eyes. "How could they not? But greed overtook them, and it seemed the easy solution—keep you and your money."

"I suppose." She gave him a quick smile that didn't quite reach her eyes. "Anyway, that is the person I was—shy and scared and bookish. But now I look back and think how silly it was to wear clothes I didn't really like. Why was I so scared I would upset other people? Why did I let other people decide everything for me? I wouldn't do that now—at least, I think not. But how do I know? How can I be sure which person I really am?"

"Sabrina, you're the same person inside. There aren't two Sabrinas. There's only the one brave and determined woman I know. You were young—it's not unusual for a young person to be unsure. Ladies are raised to be sweet and compliant and unsure. It's only natural that you felt grateful to the people who had been kind to you. But when you were faced with a dreadful situation, you responded. When you found out the Dearborns weren't the people you thought they were, you didn't crumble. Of course you were scared—who wouldn't be in that situation? But you overcame your fear. You took control of your life. You did that *before* you lost your memory, not after. You didn't change. You simply realized who you were."

Tears glittered in her eyes, and for an instant he feared he'd wounded her, but he realized she was smiling, as well. She leaned forward and kissed him softly. "Thank you."

He cupped her face with his hands, and their kiss lingered. He pulled back reluctantly and turned his attention to the table. "Now, I suppose we'd better eat before I forget everything else."

Her low laugh was like a finger running delicately up his chest, and he wondered how quickly he could get through teatime.

However, before they had finished, a maid brought up the map Alex had requested, and, much as he preferred to spend the rest of the evening in bed with Sabrina, he gave in to duty. Shoving aside the remnants of their repast, he spread the rolled map out on the table, anchoring it all four corners with a sugar pot, creamer and two saucers.

"Now, where exactly is the Dearborns' house in Wiltshire?"

"It's north of Salisbury. It's near the village of Clemstock, though I'm not sure it's on that map. It's quite small. Ah, here." She pointed her finger to a spot on the map. "It's not far from Lower Dunford."

Alex's eyebrows rose. "There are a lot of churches between here and there. I wish I knew why..." He turned to her. "Sabrina, I know it's painful for you, but anything you could remember about that day might help us find the truth about what happened that night. What's the last thing you do remember before you awakened at the inn?"

"When Mr. Dearborn locked me in my room."

CHAPTER TWENTY-SEVEN

"HE LOCKED YOU in your room?" Alex's brows drew together thunderously. "Did he do this frequently? Did he— Did he harm you?"

"No. He never hurt me. He'd never locked me up before this or threatened me. He was always quite pleasant. Even paternal. He didn't need to be. He just manipulated me. Doing all the things they did for me—it was to make me feel obligated. Dependent on them. Even Mrs. Dearborn buying me those girlish dresses—they wanted me to seem young, to feel young and naive. I *was* shy, but I can see now that they encouraged that in me. They could have taken me to London. I didn't have to make my debut or call on many people. I could have just gone to plays and museums and art galleries. Libraries." Her eyes shone. "All the things you took me to see."

"But they didn't encourage you to visit."

"Just the opposite. They never suggested I go when Peter or Mr. Dearborn traveled to London. The only traveling I did was to my own house in Somerset when Mr. Dearborn went to see if it was being managed properly. And even then, I didn't always go with them. It was a given that I would stay with Peter's mother in the country, seeing the same people, doing the same things."

"You were bored."

"Yes. Much as I love books, I wanted to do other things. Over the years, I grew less shy. Lilah's letters about all the things she did…the parties, the dresses, the people, the opera—it all sounded so lively and fun. I wanted to go visit her. Indeed, I would have liked to return to Carmoor to live. But Mr. and Mrs. Dearborn discouraged that. Whenever I wanted to accept one of Lilah's invitations, they would remind me how much I disliked crowds and meeting new people, how I'd never wanted to go to London before. Mr. Dearborn would say how much he feared I would regret it and would want to come back home right away. And I feared he was right, that I would hate it and I would look foolish to have insisted on going."

"So you would give in and not go."

She nodded. "Mrs. Dearborn would worry and fuss, and she has always been so very kind to me. She didn't like London, but she insisted on accompanying me if I went. A young lady couldn't make such a journey on her own, and, anyway, I wouldn't know what to do or where to go. It would have meant burdening her, which I hated to do, when she had been so good to me. I believed they were concerned for me, wanted the best for me. Once or twice I resisted because I wanted so much to see Lilah, to do something different, and those times, he would agree, but then one thing or another happened—some crisis arose on my land and of course he had to go there, and it was unthinkable that I travel to London without his escort. Or it was too cold or hot, and we should wait for better weather. Or Mrs. Dearborn became ill, and we had to delay, until finally the idea just died. I can see now that they purposely made it difficult. That they wanted to keep me there."

"Where Dearborn could control you. He kept you away from your friend, kept you from making new acquaintances, emphasized every fear or concern you had, painted dire consequences if you left there. Played on your kindness and your regard for Mrs. Dearborn."

"I was such a fool," Sabrina said bitterly. "I never questioned anything he did. I never asked to look at his accounting of the money my father left me. Never made a move on my own."

"You weren't a fool. You were young, and you'd lost both your parents. He was your guardian, your father's friend—you'd known him all your life. Of course you trusted him and depended on him. And when you made any attempt to move away from that dependence, he thwarted it. My guess is his main concern was that you might meet someone in London, might fall in love and marry someone other than his son."

"He was always hopeful that Peter and I would make a match of it. So was Mrs. Dearborn. She would talk about how wonderful it would be, how I was a daughter to her, and when Peter and I married, I would be her daughter in fact. She would tell me romantic tales of other couples who had known each other all their lives and gradually grew into loving one another or suddenly realized that they did. I didn't say much to dissuade her, I'm afraid. I didn't want to hurt her feelings. But I knew I would never marry Peter. He was— He was like a brother or a close cousin. Part of my family. I had no desire to marry him."

"What about Peter? Did he pursue you?"

"He was attentive whenever he was home. We talked a great deal. Once or twice he seemed to be working around to a proposal, but I managed to wriggle out of it before any damage was done. He never…" She cast a sideways glance at Alex. "He never said the sort of things you have. Or did the things you have. But he could have just been gentlemanly."

"I'm very glad he's such a gentleman. Such a foolish gentleman." He wanted quite badly to pull her up from her chair and kiss her, but he forced himself to stay focused on the issue at hand. "I'm sure Dearborn was getting worried as your birthday approached. You would come into your estate, and he would no longer have any legal hold on you."

"Yes, he talked more and more about Peter and me marrying. He went from suggesting it or explaining how beneficial and easy it would be to trying to talk me into it. We quarreled a bit about it a time or two. That was another reason why I wanted so much to accept Lilah's invitation to visit her. I *needed* to be away from them. It was so cloying, so suffocating there. I felt quite guilty about it, given all they'd done for me. But, deep down, I yearned to get away from them, to be on my own. Free and independent. I wanted to see things. Do things. Make decisions for myself. Buy the clothes I wanted."

"Of course you did."

"So that afternoon, I told Mr. Dearborn that Lilah had invited me, and I wanted to go. He brought up all the usual arguments, and when he wasn't able to persuade me not to go, he suggested I postpone my visit. He wanted me to think about whether it was really what I wanted to do. I told him I didn't want to wait. We quarreled more than we ever had before. And finally he said I couldn't go. He wouldn't let me. I was furious, and I told him he couldn't stop me, I would go anyway. He said he was my guardian, so he could refuse permission. He knew what was best for me and he had a duty, a responsibility. Then, as if offering me a treat, I suppose, he said that I could go to London with Peter after we were married."

"And you told him you were never going to marry Peter."

"Yes. I had never been so blunt before, but I was terribly angry. I told him I was going to leave when I turned twenty-one and I would move to London if I chose to. We had a bitter quarrel, and at one point he grabbed the letter and it tore. That was why I had only that one torn sheet. He crumpled up the rest of it and threw it in the fireplace. Finally, it all ended with him telling me I was spoiled and silly, and I must go to my room and think about my behavior."

"As if you were ten."

"Yes. I was so incensed that I ran up to my room and slammed the door. I was going to just pack my bags and leave. And then…I heard him turn the key in the lock!"

"What did you do?"

"I was determined not to stay there. I packed my case. I knew I must wait until everyone went to bed before I sneaked out. I planned to climb down—there was a balcony off my room, and at the end of it was a trellis of roses. I'd always been pretty agile at climbing when I was young. I was going to put on my riding gloves to protect myself from the thorns and climb down the trellis, take my horse from the stable and ride away, catch a train to London. The maid brought me supper, and I ate it. I wrapped up the roll and put it in my case to have something to eat later. Then I sat down to wait for everyone else to retire. I began to feel very sleepy."

"He put something in your food."

"I think so."

"Did he say anything about Andover? Or Winchester?"

"No, not that afternoon. I suppose he may have mentioned them in the past, but just in a general way. I don't know why he would have taken me there. Why take me somewhere else at all?"

"Maybe he thought the local vicar would not participate in such a sham."

"True. And I think Mrs. Dearborn might have balked at that. I do think she liked me and enjoyed my company. Besides, the servants would have talked about it. It would have been all over the village."

"Do you remember anything about your journey?"

"I have a very vague memory of being in a coach." She paused, thinking. "Not really a memory of the coach but of that motion, and I woke up a little once. The motion had stopped. I could hear voices outside and there were lights…" She shook her head. "That's all I remember. It's not very helpful, I'm afraid."

"Perhaps you'll remember more. You didn't remember this at first. If you relax and don't try to force yourself, just let your mind drift…"

She closed her eyes. After a moment, she said softly, "I fell."

"From the window?"

"No. Not that kind of falling." Eyes still closed, she went on, "Stumbling and falling. Someone grabbed my arm. I felt weak and dizzy, and everything sort of swirled around me. I think I remember someone shaking me, and I—I might have said something. That man who kept talking wore a white collar, and he's— I can see his face, but it's very vague. He's rather young. He's smiling at me, and I feel as if I'm about to be sick right there in front of him." She opened her eyes and shrugged. "That's all."

"It's all right." Alex took her hand. "Don't worry. You've remembered a good deal more. Would you recognize the man who wore the collar?"

"I'm not sure. Possibly. But I…was unable to focus. That's what's so frightening about those memories. I couldn't make myself look at things. I couldn't concentrate. I couldn't wake up. Oh, Alex." Sabrina jumped to her feet and began to pace, wrapping her arms around herself. "I think I must have married him. That was surely a wedding!"

"No, that wasn't a real marriage. It was clearly without your consent. You were drugged, incapable of making any decision. That makes it a fraud. Coercion." Alex took her arms and peered intently into her face. "Sabrina, listen to me. Do not worry. I swear to you on everything I hold dear, I will not let him have you. You will *not* be his wife—even if I have to make you a widow."

CHAPTER TWENTY-EIGHT

SABRINA STARED AT HIM. "Alex, no! You can't."

"I can. I will. There's nothing I wouldn't do to protect you from that bastard."

Sabrina supposed that such a declaration shouldn't fill her with warmth, but it did. She reached up, cupping his face with her hands. "No. I won't have you taking that burden upon yourself. I won't let you risk the gallows for my sake. But thank you." Tears glittered in her eyes, threatening to spill over. "Thank you for offering."

She went up on tiptoe and kissed his lips. Words of love filled her throat but died unsaid as Alex deepened their kiss. Caught in the wonder of his mouth on hers, his hands gliding over her, she gave up all worry and fear, forgot all pain. There was in this moment only Alex, no other world but in his arms.

When at last he lifted his head, Sabrina pulled away. His arms tightened for an instant, then let go. She took his hand. "Come." Turning to look back at him over her shoulder, her lips curved up in a seductive smile. "I think it's time we went to bed, don't you?"

It was only a few feet to the bed, but the journey there took a long time, for they paused to kiss, to caress, to unfasten a garment and toss it aside. By the time they reached the bed, their clothes were gone, their bodies too heated to feel any evening chill. Sabrina gazed at Alex's long, lean body in appreciation, all former embarrassment falling away. Placing her hand on his chest, she moved it slowly across his skin, tracing the lines of his muscles, the bony ridges of his ribs, following the hard center line of his chest downward.

She kissed his flesh, her tongue circling the hard buttons of his nipples as he had done with her the night before, and her hands roamed farther, skimming down his back and over his buttocks, sliding back around across his thighs. Every small sound he made, every twitch, every flare of heat in his skin, multiplied her own pleasure. She felt the passion surging in him, intensifying her own.

Beloved, she thought, though she dared not say it. Not yet. Not now.

Alex lifted her up and laid her down on the bed, stretching out beside her. He caressed her body with the same loving attention Sabrina had shown to his, and as his hands and lips moved over Sabrina, the heat inside her built to such heights she thought she could not go any higher, feel any more. Yet each time his lovemaking carried her on.

Then, at last, he moved between her legs, coming into her with the same slow power. Sabrina wrapped herself around him, moving with him, and gave herself up to the storm of pleasure. He filled her senses, her mind, her very being, it seemed, and when she reached the peak and shattered, she felt him shudder and fall with her into the sweet ecstasy.

HE AWAKENED IN a dark room, the only light a shaft of tepid sunlight through a high window. And even in the dream, he recognized it as the same place, the same time, the same chill of fear. He tried to turn over and bury his head to make it go away, but he couldn't move, couldn't think, trapped in the undefined dread.

"Alex. Alex!"

His eyes flew open. Sabrina bent over him, shaking his shoulder. He stared at her blankly, lost between worlds. "Oh. Sabrina. I'm sorry." He sat up, rubbing his hands across his face. "Did I wake you?"

"You were dreaming. I woke up and you were thrashing about and mumbling."

He could feel the film of sweat on his skin and the heat of his body beneath it. Why had his body betrayed him, sending the dream to him now, of all times? The last person he wanted to witness his weakness was Sabrina.

"Yes. I had a nightmare."

"About what?"

"Nothing, really, you know, just the sort of crazy thing one dreams. It's over now."

Sabrina's forehead creased in concern. "It didn't seem like nothing." She paused, looking at him, and when he didn't reply, she let out a sigh and flopped over onto her back. "Very well. If you don't wish to tell me…"

The chill in her voice equaled the one of the air touching his damp skin.

"It's not that I don't want to tell you," Alex explained hastily, then stopped, scrabbling for a reasonable excuse, since the fact was that she was exactly correct. "Bloody hell," he muttered.

"I told you about my nightmare," Sabrina pointed out.

"Yes, but…"

"But what?"

"It's not the same."

"Why?" She turned to her side again, batted her eyes at him and said in a saccharine voice, "Because you're a big, strong man, and I'm just a little woman?"

"No!" he said in a groan, pulling at his hair. "Devil take it. You've clearly been around my mother too long. It's because I don't want you to see…that."

"See what?"

"My fear. Over nothing. My…weakness."

"Alex…" She snuggled up to him, laying her head on his chest and wrapping her arm around him. He had to admit, it made him feel inexplicably better about the whole thing. "Having a frightening dream isn't weakness. Everyone has nightmares. I'll warrant even Achilles had nightmares."

"Yes, well, who wouldn't, getting dipped in the River Styx when you were a baby?" She chuckled, and that sound, the vibration of it against his chest, somehow made everything better, too. He let out a sigh. "I have the same nightmare, over and over. I've had it for years. I'm in a dark room. Alone, knowing I'm locked in. Unable to get out."

"Like what happened to you years ago. When I 'saw' you."

He nodded, sliding his hand up and down her arm. "Yes. They started after that."

"That's perfectly understandable."

"Yes. For a child. Not for a grown man. I'm not small, I'm not young. It's not even life-threatening— no monstrous creature chasing me, no falling off a cliff. You'd think one would get over it after a time. I thought I had, but this past year they've started up again."

"The unknown, the invisible, can be scarier than something you can see."

After a moment, he said quietly, "I've never been as brave as Con."

"As brave or as rash?"

Alex laughed. "Obviously didn't take you long to peg my brother."

"It was rather apparent—a steady sort of man wouldn't run about dressed up like a carnival barker, even in disguise."

"He has an odd sense of humor," Alex agreed. He smiled. "I fear I share that—at least to the extent of laughing at what he does."

Sabrina rose up to look him in the face, her arms braced on his chest. "It must have been difficult being a twin—always compared to one another. I suspect that you have qualities Constantine wishes he had."

"He'd love to have some peculiar ability like mine," Alex admitted. "Lord only knows why."

"It's not a crime to be different from your twin in some ways."

"It feels odd. We were always so similar. We acted the same, thought the same—Con was like another part of myself."

"Is he no longer that? Do you not know what he's thinking? Or doing?"

"Oh, most of the time I know. One has only to

look at Con to know he's contemplating mischief."
He paused, then added, "Or when he's sad, though
that doesn't happen often. It's dead easy to read him."

"For you. Not for everyone else." Sabrina leaned
down and kissed his lips. "You don't have to be Con.
And you don't have to be ever brave. Especially when
you aren't conscious." She kissed him again. "Most
especially for me. You know me better than anyone, however short a time you've known me. And
I know you. There's no need to be anything other
than yourself." She smoothed a hand across his chest,
then leaned down to kiss the skin where her hand
had been.

"You are a persuasive woman," Alex said, wrapping his arms around her and rolling over so that she
was beneath him. "And I know an excellent remedy
for nightmares."

She smiled. "Really? And what is that?"

"This." His mouth came down to fasten on hers,
and all thoughts of dreams or fears disappeared.

ALEX AWAKENED THE next morning in an empty bed.
His stomach clenched and he sat up, shoving the covers aside, but then he heard the sound of Sabrina's
voice in the next room, followed by the clatter of
dishes. He eased back down, linking his arms behind
his head, and let himself float for a few moments in
the aura of domesticity.

But the tug of duty, not to mention hunger, pulled
him from his bed to clean up, shave and dress. When
he stepped into the other room, a few minutes later, he
found Sabrina standing at the window, looking out,
humming beneath her breath. Since the day outside

was gray and drizzly and the view she had was of the stables, Alex suspected it wasn't the scene she contemplated that made her so cheerful. She turned and her face lit up, warming him in a most gratifying way.

"I had them bring breakfast." She came forward and went on tiptoe to brush his lips with hers. He pulled her back for a longer kiss.

"I'm not sure I'm hungry," he told her in a low voice.

Sabrina pulled away, laughing and rosy, and took his hand to pull him to the table. "I am. Tea?"

She poured him a cup while Alex began to pile food on his plate. They sat down to eat, talking as they did so. "Are we going to the next town on the road to Andover to visit the church?"

Alex half shrugged. "My guess is that this 'wedding' took place in Andover, as there would be more clergymen to choose from, but I don't see how we can afford to pass them by. Truthfully, I cannot imagine how any minister could have agreed to marry you, special license or not, given the condition you were in. You had to be propped up to even stand, and I can't imagine that you were able to give clear answers."

She nodded. "It would have to be a very havey-cavey sort of churchman."

"Yes, I would think that a large payment would have been involved, if the man was venal enough, or perhaps a bit of blackmail. Or both. I've been thinking. That's why they took such a peculiar route. Look." Drawing on an invisible map on the table, he went on, "They started here, then up to Andover, but then they turn to the southeast."

"Didn't the driver say they were headed for Winchester?"

He nodded. "I have some thoughts on that, too. Do the Dearborns have any connection to Winchester?"

"Not that I know of, but obviously there were a number of things I didn't know about them."

"I can't help but notice that below Winchester is Southampton."

Sabrina's eyes widened. "You think he was going to take me onto a ship?"

"It makes sense—in a very slimy sort of way. We've already posited that he took you away from home so that no one who knew you would see what happened. But where are they to go after that? If they come home, you'll eventually emerge from your fog and tell everyone what happened. If they travel to some other place in England, there's the chance that you'll wake up and call for help—or escape, as you did. But on a ship, he can keep you locked up and drugged and excuse it with sea sickness. Even if you awakened, you'd be on a ship in the middle of the Channel or crossing the ocean—there'd be no escape."

"Until we docked—where I would be alone in a foreign country, among strangers, disoriented, not knowing the language. It would put me at a great disadvantage."

"Exactly."

"But we couldn't have stayed away forever. We'd have to come home sometime. People would wonder where I was."

"True. But Mr. Dearborn could go home, say you two had a whirlwind marriage and sailed off to Europe on your honeymoon. You could be gone several weeks, a month, with no one thinking anything of it. By the time you come back…" Alex had managed to keep his tone even and logical so far, but now he could not hold back the raw fury in him. "By then, you couldn't deny his story without ruining your reputation beyond repair. You would have to reveal that for a month you had been living with a man. You could even…" He cleared his throat. "You could have even been carrying his child."

Sabrina blanched. "You think he would have forced me?"

Alex reached out, resting a hand on her arm. "Given all the rest he did, I don't know why he would have stopped at that. But even if he had enough decency not to, everyone would assume otherwise. If you left him, if you told people, you would have suffered terribly from the scandal. I imagine they hoped that once you saw how your circumstances were, you would give in. Accept it. After all, you had 'til then been compliant with them. You and Peter had affection of some sort for each other."

"Not at that point," Sabrina said flatly. "But yes, I can see that they would believe I was too spineless to kick up a fuss. But if they meant to take me to Southampton, or even just to Winchester, why wouldn't they drive straight there? It would have been much closer."

"Exactly. Andover is so far out of the way that I can only think they went there because they knew a clergyman whom they could rely on to do it. One who could be paid or blackmailed."

Sabrina sat back. "That makes sense. Unfortunately, I don't know who they knew in Andover."

"A vicar of questionable morals would probably not be someone they would have introduced to a young lady."

"I don't think we can be positive it took place in Andover," Sabrina mused. "They would have probably taken that road to get to any town between Andover and here. That's a main thoroughfare."

"Yes. You're right. We can't just head for Andover. We really must stop at each and every one."

They spent the morning in pursuit of their elusive clergyman but met with little success. It was early in the afternoon when they stopped at their third church. The pastor there was a jolly sort and willing to help, and if he found their questions odd, he evinced none of the surprise or suspicion that the first two clergymen had shown.

"Let me see, let me see," he mused, bouncing a little on his toes. "Three weeks ago. Was that the weekend of the fete? No, that was the week before. Ah, I remember! I took a few days after the fete— they can be quite exhausting, you know. We went to the theater in Andover one day that week. I cannot remember if it was the exact date you mentioned. Wonderful performance—a farce, which I prefer to a drama, don't you?"

"But did anyone—" Alex began, but the man had turned and was puttering around at his desk.

"I believe I have a program from the theater. Perhaps it has the date. There we are." With an air of triumph, he pulled out a booklet from a pile and came back around to show them. "Hmm, no, it doesn't seem to have a date." He leafed through the pages and sighed. "That's too bad."

"Wait!" Sabrina snatched the program from the startled man's hands and flipped back a couple of pages.

"Sabrina? What is it?" Alex went to her, alarmed by the sudden pallor of her face.

She pointed to a page containing pen-and-ink drawings of the cast. "This man. That's him. He's the priest."

CHAPTER TWENTY-NINE

"Oh, no, dear," the vicar told her kindly. "That man is an actor, not a clergyman. He was in the play we saw—though I don't believe he was the vicar. That was a shorter man."

"An actor!" Alex exclaimed, grabbing the pamphlet from Sabrina's trembling hands and peering at the drawing. "Of course! Why didn't I think of that?" He let out a low curse.

"Sir!" the vicar said in an appalled voice. "Think where you are. And there's a lady present."

"Oh. Yes. Sorry."

"Terribly sorry," Sabrina told the cleric, giving him a shaky smile. Her stomach was like ice, and her heart pounding. "We are, um... What I meant was, I've seen this man. In a play."

"Then you know the company?" The vicar beamed.

"No, I... It was somewhere else."

"Where is this place?" Alex turned to the reverend, tapping his finger on the cover. "This theater. Where is it in Andover?"

"Why, near the center of town, close to the old market. But why—"

"Thank you," Alex said. The look on his face was so fierce that the other man stopped speaking and took a step back.

"You've been a great help," Sabrina assured the vicar as Alex whisked her out of the room.

Behind her, she heard the man splutter, "But, sir! Wait! My program."

Outside, Sabrina turned to Alex, her eyes glowing. "This means it was a sham, doesn't it? He wasn't a clergyman, just an actor pretending to be one."

"Yes. It makes perfect sense. They had to act quickly once Dearborn locked you in your room. No time to get a special license, and I would imagine it's a difficult task to find a wayward clergyman who would be willing to perform such a ceremony. Far easier to get an actor who would play the part for a fee. He probably even had a handy clerical suit from the troupe's wardrobe."

"Peter or Mr. Dearborn probably knew him and knew he would do it. That's why they diverted their course to Andover."

Alex nodded, taking her hands in his. "The important thing is…you're free, Sabrina. You're no one's wife."

"Oh, Alex!" Sabrina threw herself into his arms, and Alex picked her up and whirled her around, laughing. "I'm so glad! This is wonderful. It's such a relief."

"Now," Alex said, setting her down, his voice and face taking on a grim determination. "We just need to find this bloody actor."

Alex set their horse off at its fastest pace, cursing that it was not faster. As they neared Andover, the traffic increased, but he deftly threaded his way through it. Once in the town, it was easy enough to locate the theater.

The theater doors were locked, but Alex pounded on them like a madman until finally a harassed-looking man opened the door and stuck his head out.

"What the devil do you want? The theater is closed now. Performance is in two hours. No one here but me, and I'm trying to get my job done."

"What I want is that man." Alex held out the theater's program, folded back, and jabbed his finger at the picture of the actor.

"Fairfield?" the man asked.

"Is that his name?"

"Only one I know," the other man replied. "Anderson Fairfield."

"Where is he?"

"In his rooms, I imagine." He pointed down the street. "Three blocks down, top floor."

The man seemed happy enough to give up Fairfield, but Alex tipped him a coin anyway, and then they headed down the street. When they reached the building, he turned to Sabrina. "I want to see him alone."

"Alex! I'm not standing by while you take care of it."

"No, it's not that. I've been thinking how to go about it. I don't want him to recognize you before I question him. Just wait in the hall a bit first, then come in."

She followed him up the stairs, hanging back in the shadows of the dim hallway as Alex knocked peremptorily on the door. When the door opened, revealing the actor, it was all Sabrina could do not to gasp. She had been sure he was the right man, but now, seeing him in person, it shook her.

Alex stepped inside the room, forcing the man to step back. Sabrina crept closer so that she could hear the conversation through the half-open door.

"See here, who are you?" Fairfield protested feebly. "What are you doing barging into my room?"

"I've been told you are the man to see if one wants a certain job done."

"Maybe." The actor's voice was both wary and eager. "What is it you want?"

"Peter Dearborn said you did it for him recently— a false marriage. There's a certain female who's stubbornly insistent on having a ring on her finger." Alex's voice was cool and lightly insinuating. Sabrina thought that he had a great deal more of his brother's flair for deception than he realized.

"It could be arranged." Fairfield's tone turned friendly.

"I want the whole thing, just as you did for Dearborn."

"It's no problem. I have the collar and all. Has to be before or after the performance, of course."

"Of course. You go through the entire ceremony, correct? That's what you did for Peter and the girl last time, isn't it? This one's a canny one—she'd catch any slip."

"Don't worry. I'm perfect."

"Peter drugged her."

"Yes. Apparently she was reluctant, but it's not necessary if she's eager to—"

At that moment there was the smack of a fist meeting skin and bone, followed by a crash. "You worthless bastard!"

Sabrina ran inside and saw Fairfield sprawled on

the floor with Alex looming over him. Alex reached down and gripped his shirtfront tightly, hauling the actor to his feet.

"You helped him!" Alex twisted his fist in the neck of the shirt, tightening it and lifting the man onto his toes. "It's bad enough you stood by while he tried to ruin a young girl's life, but you actively participated in it. You're scum, the lowest of the low."

"Alex, you're choking him," Sabrina cautioned.

"Good." But he let go of the man.

Fairfield staggered back. "What— Why—" His terrified eyes fell on Sabrina. "You!" He backed up until the wall stopped him, his head swiveling between Sabrina and Alex. "I didn't— I didn't do anything. I never touched her."

"I think the fraud you perpetrated was enough. You were an accessory to any crime Peter committed."

"You can't." Fairfield rolled his eyes frantically back to Sabrina. "Miss, you can't let him—you'll have to testify, you know. It'll all come out. The scandal will ruin you."

Alex heaved a sigh. "Yes, you're right. I guess it will just have to be because you stole my watch."

"What? I never!"

"Mmm. Who do you think they'll believe, you or a duke's son?" Alex took a firm grip on Fairfield's arm and started toward the door. "Come along, Fairfield. I'm afraid you won't be performing tonight, since you'll be in jail."

"No! Wait! What do you want? I'll do it."

"I can well believe that." But Alex stopped, studying him consideringly. "I suppose...if you were to write out a full confession, detailing the Dearborns' nasty little fraud and their participation in it…"

"Yes! I'll do it. I'll put in everything. And there was that time when we were at Eton when he—"

"You were at Eton together?"

"Yes." The man shrugged. "That was, needless to say, before my family disowned me. Very well, let me get out a piece of paper, and I'll write it all down."

It was a good while later and Fairfield looked considerably more wilted when he signed the paper and handed it over to Alex, then asked sullenly, "What are you going to do with that?"

"I intend to hold on to it. Consider it a bond on your good behavior in the future. I intend to check in on you from time to time. I'll know if you have taken up such tricks again."

"You can't use it without implicating Dearborn."

"Yes—if I were you, that might make me a little leery about Dearborn's actions," Alex said thoughtfully, and the other man's eyes widened in alarm. "Indeed, you might want to consider moving to a sunnier clime."

Alex folded the paper and tucked it into his pocket, then offered his arm to Sabrina. As they went down the stairs, Sabrina asked, "Do you really think that will stop him from doing anything like this again?"

"I suspect so. Oh, I imagine he'll continue with petty larcenies of some sort or another. But he's not a brave man, and he's smart enough to know that if he were caught in anything else of this nature, this paper would guarantee a long term. If he doesn't flee the country, I'll have Tom look in on him now and then, just to remind him."

"I—I guess we have solved our mystery," Sabrina said somewhat uncertainly as they strolled back down the street to their vehicle. She realized with dismay that her time with Alex must now be over.

"Yes, and you are a free woman," Alex agreed. "All we need to do now is keep you safe from Dearborn for the next little while, and he'll no longer have any legal hold on you. I plan to use this—" he patted his chest, where Fairfield's confession sat in an inside pocket "—to make sure he doesn't try the same trick again after you're of age. You will be able to go wherever you want."

Sabrina looked up at Alex, trying to gauge whether that prospect made him feel as bereft as it did her. The truth was she had no desire to leave Broughton House—or rather, she had no desire to leave Alex. "I… That's wonderful," she said with a distinct lack of enthusiasm.

Was it all over now? Would she move back to her estate? Much as she had always loved her home, that seemed a dismal prospect. For the past several weeks, she had been bent only on discovering her past. She hadn't thought about the future.

"What will we do now?" she asked.

"Take the train back to London," he answered. "I'll have the gig and horse returned to The Blind Ox." He glanced down at her, his eyes warming. "Though I think, given our adventures, we deserve a bit of rest first. We can take the train tomorrow morning." He linked his fingers through hers. "And spend the night here."

"That sounds like a lovely idea." Sabrina smiled.

WHEN THEY RETURNED to Broughton House the following afternoon, Alex and Sabrina were greeted with
cries of delight. "Alex! Sabrina!" his mother greeted
them. "Back so soon? We thought you would be gone
a week at least."

To Alex's surprise, Lilah Holcutt followed the
duchess out of the sultan room and hastened toward
them. "Sabrina! Are you all right? What did you find
out?"

"Yes, come tell us. I'll ring for tea." The duchess
swept them all before her.

Alex began their very expurgated story, then had to
start over again when Con joined them a few minutes
later. Unsurprisingly, Lilah was appalled and irate at
the Dearborns' actions, and the duchess wanted to
take the fight to them.

"I plan to, Mother, never fear," Alex told her with
a smile. He glanced toward Con, who gave him a
barely perceptible nod. "If you'll excuse me, I will
leave Sabrina in your capable hands. Con and I have
something to discuss."

The two brothers headed for their sitting room,
where, after an enthusiastic and noisy greeting from
Wellington, they settled down, drinks in hand.

"I was surprised to see Miss Holcutt here," Alex
began.

Con snorted. "She and the duchess are grand
chums now."

"Mother? And Miss Holcutt? I thought they were
going at it hammer and tongs the other day."

"Yes, but apparently they enjoy it. Lilah stayed the
other day after you scarpered. Mother decided that if
Lilah left as herself right afterward, the Dearborns

might catch on to her impersonation of Miss Blair and deduce that she was no longer here. I expected Miss Holcutt to recoil in horror at the prospect, but amazingly she agreed to stay. I'm beginning to think she intends to take up residence."

"It's only been three days."

"Seems like a month. But I've managed to avoid her presence most of the time. Stayed in the flat above the agency."

Alex laughed. "I never thought to see you so frightened of a woman."

"Are you joking? Mother's always scared me." Con grinned. "Frankly, I'm afraid I'll be driven to say something rude to Miss Holcutt eventually, and then I'll hear it from Mother."

"But haven't the Dearborns given up watching the house? I didn't see anyone lurking around."

"No, they simply got smarter and posted their man at the little park down the street."

"That far? Seems iffy."

"He uses a spyglass." Con tossed back the rest of his drink. "Now...tell me what you didn't want to say in front of Mother."

"Actually, I told her most of it." Alex wasn't about to get into what had happened between him and Sabrina. He realized, with a bit of surprise, that it was the first time he remembered keeping anything from his brother. "But I did skim over the details of the Dearborns' plan. I think Peter meant to rape Sabrina at some point. It's possible he was only counting on the scandal to make her agree to the marriage. But getting her pregnant would have cemented it."

"But the marriage wasn't legal. He wouldn't really be entitled to take over her fortune."

"After a time, when she was resigned to the marriage and the scandal would be too great, I suspect he would have told her that something had gone wrong at the ceremony, and they would have gotten married again, for real this time."

"He's a right bastard."

"He is that," Alex agreed. "But what I want to talk to you about is what you discovered while I was gone."

Con grinned wickedly. "For one thing, our friends the Dearborns have some expensive habits. The son spends a lot of time in London, runs with Cartwell and that lot."

"He would certainly need money, then."

"Exactly. Niles Dearborn's father made a pile of money on some India project he invested in. Risky venture, but they found rubies, and he had a tenfold return. He made a few other good investments with the profit—it set the family up nicely. But Dearborn has his father's love of risky projects, but a good deal less luck with them. He has lost a good bit over the years, and they live lavishly. I'd say he badly needs Miss Blair's inheritance, which, by the by, was substantial."

"She's wealthy?"

"Not as wealthy as she was before Dearborn took over."

"The Dearborns have been embezzling her money," Alex said grimly.

"Not at first. Sabrina's father had his money in good, solid funds—nothing flashy, but steady and reliable. But Dearborn decided to invest her money into his usual sort of thing, and he lost, oh, I'd say a quarter of it. He also reimbursed himself for various expenses, and those seem inordinately high for a girl living in seclusion in the country. Those are certainly questionable, but it's the last two years that caught my attention. There's been a steady reduction in funds, and the reason is unclear. In my opinion, it has the hallmarks of embezzlement. I have to dig more deeply to discover just exactly how he accomplished it."

"Do it. I want to build a solid case against him. Not just Fairfield's confession, but evidence of Dearborn's malfeasance as her trustee, as well."

"You intend to turn him in? It will mean scandal for Miss Blair."

Alex sighed. "I know. My intent was to use it as leverage against him. Tell him that should he attempt to harm Sabrina in any way or even approach her, I'd lay charges against him. I think the threat of his ruin would be enough to stay his hand." He frowned. "But if he has stolen a great deal from her, she should have the opportunity to recoup some of it."

"She might prefer to stay silent and lose the money than reveal what happened. After all, it's not as if she's penniless. Miss Blair has a good estate in Somerset and that house in London—which, I might add, Dearborn is looking to sell. In available cash and monetary investments, she's down by half, I'd say. She won't need money after you marry her, anyway."

"*Marry* her!" Alex stared at his twin. "Who said anything about marrying her?"

Con widened his eyes innocently. "Aren't you? Surely you're going to make an honest woman of her."

CHAPTER THIRTY

ALEX SURGED TO his feet, red tinging the sharp edge of his cheekbones. "The devil! Don't say such a thing. How the hell did you—" He stopped abruptly as a smile spread across his brother's face.

"Know?" Con said, finishing the sentence for him. "I didn't until you jumped up as though I'd stabbed you."

"Damn it, Con…you cannot say something like that."

"For pity's sake—I wouldn't say anything to anyone but you. I'm not a dolt—or mannerless, no matter what Miss Holcutt would say." He frowned. "Surely you don't think you can't trust me."

"No. Of course not." Alex sighed and flopped back down in his chair. "I'm sorry. I'd trust you with anything. It's just that, well, it would ruin her reputation if it got out, if others suspected. Why did you suspect we had, um… Did I say something? Do something?"

"No. It's a reasonable guess to make when a gentleman spends several days jaunting about the country with a woman, unchaperoned. Especially when he's obviously mad for her and she for him."

"I'm not in—" Alex met his twin's flat stare and sighed. "Oh, of course I'm in love with her. There's nothing I want more than to marry her."

"Then why all this coyness?"

"I'm not being coy. But I can't take advantage of her like that."

"I'm not sure I see how proposing to a girl is taking advantage of her."

"She's young and naive."

"Sabrina's almost twenty-one. Most young ladies have been out for three years at that age. You're only four years older. It isn't as if you're robbing the cradle."

"But *she* hasn't been out for three years. She's led a quiet, sheltered life. She has no experience with flirtation, let alone falling in love."

"She seemed to me to be the sort of girl who knows her own mind. I've seen her look at you. She's as mad about you as you are about her."

"I think it's too easy to mistake gratitude for love. She was in a desperate situation, and I helped her. But what happens if suddenly she realizes that it wasn't love?"

"You think she's that fickle?"

"I *think* that I shouldn't seize on the situation. I ought to stand back and let her have some time to come to grips with everything. Her life has been far too chaotic recently for her to make reasonable decisions. She needs to have some peace. She ought to be free to go to parties and dance and flirt."

"Oh, yes, I can tell from your scowl that you really want her to do that."

"It's not a question of what I want. I *must* do the right thing for Sabrina."

"Have you told the young lady herself that you're going to cut her loose?"

"That isn't the way it is at all." Alex's eyes flashed. "Blast it, Con, you know better than that."

"I do. I know that you'll eat your heart out because you want to be honorable and fair. I know that you will always err on the side of generosity, not selfishness. But if you're so concerned with doing the right thing for Miss Blair, why did you sleep with her?"

"I shouldn't have." Alex thrust his hands into his hair. "I know that. I just…could not help myself."

"And why do you think you'll be able to 'help yourself' in the future?"

Alex shot his brother an anguished look. "I don't know. But I must."

Con rolled his eyes. "For pity's sake, Alex. You're going to be the death of me." He stood up and set down his glass. "Do one thing for me, would you? Before you go killing yourself on the altar of duty and honor, you might consider asking Miss Blair if she really wants you to sacrifice her, as well."

He strolled out of the room, leaving Alex staring after him in dismay.

A FEW DAYS LATER, Sabrina was sitting in the library, reading, when Phipps announced the arrival of Miss Holcutt. "Lilah!" Sabrina laid her book aside and went to greet her friend. "Come in. Sit down. Or would you rather go into the sultan room?"

"No, this is a lovely library—and the sultan room is a bit…*red*."

Sabrina chuckled. "It is that. But I like it. It suits the duchess, don't you think?"

"Indeed."

"Excuse me, ladies." They turned toward the sound

of a voice and saw Con rising from a chair across
the room.

"Oh. I'm sorry, I didn't see you," Lilah said.

"Of course you didn't." Con nodded politely toward Sabrina's visitor. "Good day, Miss Holcutt. I
have some business to attend to. Sabrina."

The two women watched him leave. Lilah swung
back to Sabrina. "Well, he certainly sped off as soon
as I showed up."

"I'm sure it wasn't because of you," Sabrina assured her.

"No?" Lilah raised a quizzical eyebrow. "Constantine avoided me assiduously those three days I was
a guest here, as well. He finds me quite prudish, I
believe."

"I'm sure it was no dislike of you that sent him off
just now. He was here only because Alex had to go
to his office to finish some plans for a client, and he
doesn't like to leave me alone—though I don't know
what he thinks is going to happen. I doubt the Dearborns will burst through the front door."

"He just doesn't want to take any chances. I think
it's rather charming."

"Not so charming after three days of being stuck
inside the house."

Lilah laughed. "Are you terribly bored? As I recall, you were fond of sitting in the library reading,
anyway."

Sabrina smiled a little sheepishly. "Yes, I was. And
no, it really has not been bad. It's just that time seems
to be crawling by."

"Will you be safe after your birthday? I don't want
to alarm you, but even though Mr. Dearborn will no

longer have control over your property, he could still try to abduct you and force you to marry Peter."

"I think it's far less likely. He must know that he wouldn't be able to persuade me. I certainly would not take any food or drink from him. Besides, people know about it now—you and the Morelands. They're a formidable group."

"Yes, I've seen." Lilah smiled. "I'd put the duchess up against anyone, and I have little doubt that Alex and the others would quickly come to your rescue."

"Alex thinks that he can use that confession the actor signed to keep the Dearborns in line. He's looking into the things Mr. Dearborn did with my property."

"He thinks Mr. Dearborn was misusing your funds?" Lilah's eyes widened.

"Yes. That's what Con has been investigating. He's bribed a clerk in Mr. Dearborn's agent's office to get a look at his books."

"Really? I thought he only went about investigating bizarre things."

"No, I think he does quite a bit more than that."

"And Alex intends to blackmail Mr. Dearborn?"

"Well…yes, I guess that is what it is. Alex says I will be…" Sabrina heard the little hitch in her voice, and she quelled it. "He says I will be free to go wherever I want. Do as I please, without fear."

Lilah studied her friend, her head tilted a little to the side. "Yet I think that you are not eager to do so."

"Of course, I will be exceedingly happy to not have to worry about Mr. Dearborn. And I will enjoy being able to decide everything for myself and—" She sighed. "But I don't really want to leave Broughton House."

"Broughton House or Alex Moreland?" Lilah asked shrewdly.

"Is it that obvious?"

"Your face lights up when you speak of him."

"Does it?" Sabrina put her hands to her cheeks. "I have, um, grown close to him these last weeks— Oh, bother, why am I trying to hide it? I love him, Lilah."

Her friend smiled. "But surely that's good. I've seen his face, too, and I would dare swear he feels the same way about you."

"I thought so," Sabrina admitted. "But things have been different since we returned."

"In what way?"

"I'm not sure." She could hardly tell the very proper Lilah that Alex had not come to her bedroom since they came back, that the kisses and caresses had disappeared. "We don't talk as much, and we are not together as often. Sometimes it feels…almost awkward around him."

"That's only natural, don't you think? When you were on the trip with him—" Lilah's cheeks colored faintly. "I mean, of course I'm sure nothing wrong transpired between you, but the two of you were alone. Here, with all his family around, it would bound to be less comfortable."

"Yes." Lilah was more right than she knew in that regard. It would be very imprudent for Alex to visit Sabrina's bed or even to kiss her. In this house, someone might come upon them at any moment.

"It's no wonder you've seen him less. He's been out trying to unearth information about Mr. Dearborn."

"You're right." Sabrina paused, then said rapidly,

as if she could not contain it, "But he hasn't said anything about how he feels about me."

"Perhaps he doesn't want to be too forward," Lilah reasoned. "You haven't reached your birthday yet. And such a sudden engagement might cause gossip." When Sabrina raised her eyebrow at that statement, Lilah chuckled. "Yes, all right, gossip scarcely matters to a Moreland. But he might feel concern about you, wouldn't want any gossip to affect your reputation."

"I suppose."

"Or perhaps he wants to move slowly. You haven't known each other long. Maybe he doesn't want to rush his fences, so to speak. Or he might be uncertain how you feel about him."

"No, I wouldn't think that's the problem." A reminiscent smile touched her lips as she thought about her enthusiastic response in his arms.

"I have heard that men are sometimes reluctant to admit they love a woman."

"But he hasn't even said he will miss me when I leave. He hasn't suggested that I stay longer or… well, anything."

Lilah started to speak but broke off as the butler entered the room. "Excuse me, Miss Blair. This message just arrived for you."

"From Alex?" Sabrina reached for it, brightening.

"The boy who delivered it said nothing, but I would venture to say that is not Mr. Alex's hand."

Sabrina's eyes fell to her name across the front of the envelope, and her stomach dropped. Hollowly, she said, "Yes, I see."

"Sabrina? What is it?" Lilah started toward her in concern.

"That's Mr. Dearborn's hand." Sabrina stood up.

"Are you certain?"

"Yes, I've seen it several times."

"Don't open it," Lilah said swiftly. "We must get Con." She turned toward the door.

"Excuse me, Miss Holcutt," Phipps interrupted politely. "But Mr. Constantine left the house a little while ago."

"Oh." She turned back to Sabrina. "We should send for him."

"No." Sabrina managed a fair imitation of a smile. "I'm being silly to be so alarmed by a letter. Thank you, Phipps." She nodded to the butler in dismissal. Then, taking a deep breath, she tore open the envelope. Inside was a folded note and another small object. "No. Oh, no."

"What is it?"

Sabrina didn't answer as she opened the note and quickly scanned it. She felt as if all the air had been sucked out of the room. "I have to go."

"No. Wait. You mustn't leave. You can't put yourself in Dearborn's hands."

"I have to." With trembling fingers, Lilah reached into the envelope and pulled out a gold cuff link. "They have Alex."

CHAPTER THIRTY-ONE

"WHAT!" LILAH STARED at Sabrina. Sabrina responded by simply handing the note to her friend and heading for the door. Lilah hurried after her. "Sabrina, wait. How can you be certain that this is true?" She shook the piece of paper. "He *says* that Alex is with them and advises you to join them—and notice how carefully they skirt around saying they're holding him for ransom—but you don't know that Mr. Dearborn is telling you the truth. This could be a trick to get their hands on you. Alex may be perfectly fine. We should see if we can find him before you do anything rash."

"He's not fine. This is his cuff link." Sabrina held it out, cupped in her palm. "You see? It has the letter *A* on it. He told me Con gave them to him as something of joke, saying that now he couldn't get away with borrowing Con's cuff links." The threat of tears roughened her voice.

"He could have lost one, and the Dearborns picked it up or—" Lilah stopped at Sabrina's derisive look. "Yes, I know it's a weak argument. But it is possible."

"Alex is in trouble, Lilah," Sabrina said flatly. "I know it. I feel it." She jabbed her finger at her chest. "In here."

"You feel it? Sabrina, you're not speaking rationally."

"It's *not* rational," Sabrina insisted. "But it's true, nonetheless. There's some part of me, inside, that… that belongs to Alex, that connects me to him. I don't understand it. I cannot explain it, obviously. But it's always there, and just now, when I read that note, I tried to summon it up. And it was all wrong. It was jumbled and…and spiky, somehow. Almost painful."

"I don't understand any of this."

"I know. I don't really understand it, either. But I'm certain of this—Alex needs me."

Sabrina pushed past Lilah and hurried down the hall. For a moment, Lilah stared after her, astonished, then ran after her. "Sabrina, wait!" She grabbed her arm and pulled Sabrina to a stop. "I have no earthly idea what you're talking about. But I do know this— they're going to demand you marry Peter! You can't possibly marry him."

"If that is what I have to do to save Alex, that's what I'll do." Sabrina felt a certain calm determination settling over her.

It must have showed in her face, for Lilah sagged and said, "If you insist on doing this, at least let me go with you."

"It says I must come alone. I can't risk Alex's life by doing anything other than what Dearborn told me to."

Turning, Sabrina strode to the front door, Lilah trailing after her. A footman sprang to open the door, looking askance at Sabrina. "Miss, your bonnet, your gloves… I'll fetch them."

"Never mind that."

"For pity's sake," Lilah exclaimed. "At least take

a parasol." Grabbing one from the stand by the door, she held it out to Sabrina.

For the first time, a faint smile crossed Sabrina's face. "Very well. Perhaps I can whack someone over the head with it."

She sailed through the front door and down the street to the carriage waiting at the far end.

HE WAS RUNNING. Running and running as he had that time across the roofs of the buildings, his captors behind him. But this time it wasn't roofs over which his feet flew, but cobblestones in narrow, twisting streets. And he was running, not toward freedom, but toward something even more important. It was the most important thing in the world to him, and if he failed, if he lost, everything would end. His head ached, and his mouth was so dry it felt like cotton batting. He could feel his energy flagging. He was sweating, and yet he was cold all over. He stumbled. They would soon be on him.

He could not fail. He could not.

Alex jerked awake. He actually was cold, he realized, and his head was pounding like the devil. Alex sat up, and the world tilted alarmingly. Curling his fingers around the wooden side board of the bed frame, he set his teeth, waiting. After a few moments, the dizziness receded.

Where the devil was he? This was not his room. Not anyplace he'd ever seen. He looked around, careful not to move his head too quickly lest he bring back the vertigo. It was a small room and dimly lit, the only light coming through a small window high in the wall. His stomach lurched.

This was the room of his dream. It wasn't the room from his childhood captivity. It was this damp, cold tiny box of a room, with walls of stone rendered grimy through the years. He was imprisoned. The familiar terror washed through him. But this time it had a reason.

Sabrina was in danger. They had taken her or were about to. Fear paralyzed him, and for an instant the past and present mingled, the ice that had lain in that boy's chest long ago growing now in the man. The dark closed in.

But, by God, he hadn't given in to fear then, and he wasn't going to now. He could get away; he could figure it out. He'd always been able to meet whatever came. Idiotic to think he couldn't do it now. Alex surged to his feet.

He wavered but planted his feet farther apart and let the dizziness subside. He lifted his hand to the back of his head, where the throbbing pain was centered. It hurt like hell to touch it, and something sticky matted his hair. Blood.

The fog in his mind was beginning to lift. What the devil had happened? He closed his eyes, calling up the memory. He had been in his office working. He'd heard a noise and stepped outside into the hall. There had been a street urchin there, grubby and thin, and he'd said, "Help me, mister." Alex had started toward him. Then his head had exploded, and he remembered nothing.

Good heavens, what a complete ass he'd been. He should have known that was a trick. They must have knocked him out and carried him somewhere. That had been noon because he had just begun feeling hungry. A fair amount of time had passed, given that he was much hungrier now. But surely he hadn't been knocked out for several hours. Light was still coming through the window.

So, it was afternoon. And wherever he was could not be too far from his office. It would have been hard carrying an unconscious man, not to mention noticeable, even if they'd wrapped him up in something to conceal him. They could have put him in a vehicle, but in London even that was slow-going, given the traffic. They wouldn't have wanted him waking up in transit, so they would have had a hiding place nearby.

Well…none of that was any help. He turned, taking stock of his prison for the first time. A short, stout door stood on the opposite wall. There was a narrow open slot three-fourths of the way up, no more than an inch or two wide. No doubt it was some sort of spy hole through which one could check on the prisoner.

There was nothing in the room besides the bed and a tray sitting in front of the door. He moved closer. The scarred wooden tray held a cup of water and a bowl of some sort of soup, as well as a slice of coarse brown bread. Alex's stomach rumbled at the sight of the food, and his mouth felt dryer than ever. But he thought of Sabrina's drug-laced soup. He didn't dare eat or drink anything.

It was a basement room; it had the damp chill of belowground, and he could see the wheels of a cart rattle by the high window. He thought of somehow climbing up to the window, but it was too small for him to fit through. Breaking it and yelling for help might be an option.

Perhaps the simplest solution was the best. Walk-

ing over to the door, he began to pound on it and yell.
He was beginning to wonder if no one was there when
finally there was the thud of heavy footsteps coming
down the hall. Alex bent and peered out through the
narrow viewing window. He could see nothing but a
stone wall a few feet opposite him.

The footsteps stopped, and Alex began to pound
and yell again, eliciting a loud "Shut up in there!"

The guard came closer and Alex could at last see
him. "Let me out. Please." And then he spoke words
his egalitarian brain had never thought he would utter.
"Do you know who I am?"

"Aye, I ken who you are," the man said in a thick
Scottish accent. "A murderin', thievin' Sassenach
bastard."

Wonderful. His jailer was an English-hating Scotsman. "I promise you, I have never murdered nor
thieved. And my family owns nothing in Scotland."

"Huh! Ye canna fool me. Yer kin of the Butcher."

"Who?" Alex searched his mind. Clearly he should
have studied Scottish history better. "Oh! Cumberland? You mean Lord Cumberland? We are in no
way related to him, I assure you. Not one drop of
royal blood."

"Well, ye would say that, wouldn't you?"

"Look, I can pay you. More than they are."

"Nae. They said ye'd try that. Ye'll play no tricks
on me. And none of your witchery, either."

"My witchery!"

"Aye, they told me about yer family. I don't hold
with magic."

"Has it occurred to you that perhaps they're
lying?"

"No. Now close your mouth. Yer not gettin' out on my watch."

He lumbered out of sight. Alex pounded on the door in frustration, picturing getting his hands around his guard's neck. It took him a few minutes to pull himself back from his rage and return to reason. There was obviously no hope of being set free.

He thought of and discarded several impractical methods to push something through the spy hole and open the door from the other side. Sitting back down on his bed, he put his elbows on his knees and lowered his head to his hands. He shoved his fingers into his hair, pressing them against his skull, as if he could force the solution into his head.

He could not give in to despair. He had to get to Sabrina. She had been safe in the house when he'd left, but who knows what had happened since then. If Con and the others had gotten word of his abduction, they might have dashed out to find him, leaving Sabrina alone and open to attack.

Or Sabrina herself might leave the house to search for him. It would be foolish of her, but he knew well how much the heart could overwhelm the brain. It was no doubt perfectly wretched of him, but he could not help but feel a certain warmth to think she might care so much.

He wished in vain that he had something more useful in his pockets than money. He should carry his lock-picking tools with him. What could he use to get out? He'd been favored with money, status, strength—but none of it could help him. He wished he did have some of this witchery the guard imagined he did.

Of course, there was his "talent." That seemed useless as well in this situation, but there was that connection with Sabrina. He concentrated on Sabrina, but there was only the faint remnant of that familiar sense of her. He didn't feel the disruption he believed he would if something had happened to her, and that was good.

He thought of the way he and Con communicated effortlessly, sensing each other's thoughts or feelings. Perhaps it was possible to do the same with Sabrina through their "connection." Feeling a bit of a fool, he closed his eyes and focused on Sabrina. Picturing her in his mind, he told her not to leave, not to search for him, to stay safe. He felt nothing in return.

Perhaps the mysterious link he felt with her was not as strong as his lifelong tie to his twin. Or maybe it wasn't well enough established—or, a sobering thought, the link was only on his side. So he reached out mentally to Con and thought at him, telling him to guard Sabrina, to not be fooled into chasing down Alex. But he felt nothing, only that same, steady sense that Con was alive and not in trouble.

It occurred to him that such communication of thought might not be possible unless he was actually with Con. He had never before tried to send Con a mental message when they were apart. In fact, when he thought about it, Alex realized he hadn't ever really *tried* to transmit his thoughts to Con. He had just known what Con was thinking and vice versa. Perhaps it was something that could not be forced. Or it only worked one way—he could receive but not return. Why hadn't he and Con ever thoroughly examined it before? They'd just accepted it the way they did the color of their eyes or the shape of their noses.

Well, it was useless to regret what they hadn't done. He turned his thoughts to his other talent, the ability to sense things from objects. But what good would it do him to touch one of these walls and feel the rage and despair of an earlier prisoner here? It would, if anything, only increase such feelings in himself, which he had just fought to batter into submission. The last thing he wanted was for them to rise up in him, swallowing him.

He closed his eyes, opening himself to ideas, but all that appeared was the memory of the time he and Con and Anna, Theo's wife, had stumbled upon the body. It was long ago, before the dreams had started. He remembered standing on the footbridge, gazing down into the water, watching it swirl and tumble over the bed of rocks. He remembered Anna turning and stepping off the bridge onto the dirt path. She stopped in her tracks, looking suddenly pale. He and Con went to her, Alex reaching out to take her arm, thinking she was about to faint.

The most horrible feeling he'd ever experienced rippled through him, a wave of fury and hatred and bloodlust that had almost felled him on the spot. Alex dropped her arm, and the feelings subsided, but there was still a trace of it in the air. He felt it calling to him, and though he tried to push it away, it had been too strong. He turned and looked.

Anna walked toward the body, and he and Con followed. Alex fought the emotions trying to shove their way into him. But it was impossible. The killer's fury swamped him, fury and insane delight, mingling in a horrific way with the pain and terror of the person who had died. The sight of the blood and the battered head were awful, but it was the flood of feeling that invaded him that sent him fleeing from the body and heaving up everything inside his stomach.

It had been the first time Alex had experienced one of his visions, and it had been terrifying. He had not even touched the body, yet the horror had swarmed into him. He had never spoken of it to anyone. Indeed, he had never even acknowledged it to himself. He remembered only the bloody body, ignoring the rest of it. And when he thought of the start of his ability, he always attributed it to a different trip with Kyria and Rafe.

But now the full memory poured through him. Once again he felt the raw, wild emotion, the awful fear of becoming lost in it, being overtaken. Alex shivered, pale and cold as ice. This was what he feared.

The realization struck him like a blow. It was the power of his ability, the possibility of what it could do to him, that haunted his dreams, both then and now. As his power had grown, he had controlled it, disciplined it, removed it from himself. No wonder the dreams had started up again when Sabrina came into his life. She had slipped beneath his defenses, the link he had with her widening the carefully small channel he had allowed for his talent. She had awakened the dormant power, and its strength loomed again, threatening to shatter his carefully built control.

But he was no longer a boy, bombarded by an unknown force. He was a man, experienced in controlling his power now. He could accept the full scope of his ability without being overwhelmed. He could use it.

And to save Sabrina, he would, no matter what it might do to him. Alex stood up and started toward the door.

CHAPTER THIRTY-TWO

SABRINA'S LEGS TREMBLED as she stepped out of the carriage and walked up to the door, but she controlled her expression. She had to be calm and unafraid if she were to help Alex. She rapped sharply with the brass door knocker.

A footman opened the door to her, and as she stepped through the door, Mr. Dearborn hurried toward her, smiling unctuously. "Sabrina. My dear. I am so happy you came."

"I had no choice," she replied flatly. Did the man actually think she was so stupid she would believe his act?

Dearborn ignored her statement. "Come into the drawing room, my dear." He turned toward the footman. "You may go, Wilson." Dearborn reached out to take Sabrina's arm, but she jerked it away, and he turned the movement into a gesture toward the door. "This way, dear."

She stalked into the room he indicated, and Dearborn closed the door after them. Peter stood at the mantel across the room, reminding her forcibly of the scene she had witnessed at the Morelands' house. The Dearborns didn't know she had heard everything they said. Nor would they be aware that she had recovered her memory. Perhaps she could use that to her advantage.

Peter came forward to greet her, but her glare stopped him in his tracks.

"Would you care for some tea, Sabrina?" Dearborn asked.

"This isn't a social call. Where is Alex?"

"I'm afraid I don't keep track of Moreland's whereabouts, my dear."

"Stop calling me that." Sabrina unclenched her jaw and continued, "Mr. Dearborn, I'm not here to play games. You sent me this." She pulled the cuff link from her pocket and held it up. "The implication is clear. You are holding Alex for ransom. I want to see him."

"Now, Sabrina, child, there's no need to be melodramatic. All we want is for you to return to us. To take your rightful place as Peter's wife. I'm sure your memory will return when you come home."

"There is no need to keep up your pretense of affection for me. I've had more than enough of that the past few years."

"My de— Sabrina," Dearborn said reproachfully. "There was never any pretense. I have loved you like a daughter. Peter loves you, as well. You may not remember your life with us, but you were very happy. Don't let Alexander Moreland poison your mind with wicked tales of us. You and Peter fell in love and married—"

"I have recovered my memory." A dead silence fell after her words.

After a moment, Dearborn said, "Oh, I see." Rallying, he went on, "Then you remember how happy you were with us. How much Mrs. Dearborn loves you. All the things we've done for you. We took you in after your parents died. You love us, Sabrina. It would break my heart to lose you. And poor Regina would be devastated."

"If you regained your memory, then you must re-member our wedding ceremony," Peter said in a ca-joling voice. "Saying your vows…"

"I remember saying my vows before an *actor*!" Sabrina shouted.

Peter blanched. "You've—"

"Yes, I have talked with your friend Anderson Fairfield—if, of course, that is his name. My God, Peter, I never imagined that you were so low."

"I'm not! Damn it, Sabrina, I don't understand what's the matter with you. We've always been close. I would treat you like a queen."

"Would that be before or after you locked me away in Bedlam?" When both of them stared at her in as-tonishment, she went on, "You see, I know all of it. I know what sort of creatures you are. I know you have been stealing from my trust for years. I know that you hoped to continue to control my money by marrying me to Peter. You cannot in a thousand years convince me to do that."

"Are you prepared to say goodbye to any hope of seeing Alexander Moreland again?" Mr. Dearborn's face was hard now, his voice harsh, all show of sym-pathy and love gone. "You *will* marry Peter. We have the special license—you will go to a priest and say your vows."

"I will not."

"Well, that is that, then." Dearborn turned away.

Sabrina kept a firm grip on her emotions. "Do you think you can just kill Alex and get away with it?"

"No, no, we won't kill him. All we have to do is not return."

A chill ran through her, and Sabrina knew it must have shown on her face, for a triumph flared in Dearborn's eyes. She shoved away the thought of Alex locked away somewhere, alone, dying inch by inch each day. All because of her. She hated the shakiness in her voice as she replied, "He's the son of a duke. They will bring the law down on you like a hammer."

"Why?" Dearborn widened his eyes innocently. "We know nothing about Alex Moreland or what happened to him. Why should we? We barely know the man. The only one who is claiming we murdered him is a poor girl who has for years been prone to fits of fear and melancholy." His voice turned wheedling. "Come home, Sabrina. Take your vows. We will do our utmost to locate Moreland, if it will ease your mind."

"I will not agree to anything until you free Alex."

"That's out of the question," Dearborn snapped. "Not until we are certain of you. Marry Peter. Now. Or Alex Moreland will disappear." He paused, eyebrows raised. "Well, Sabrina, what is it to be? His future is in your hands."

ALEX SQUATTED DOWN beside the tray of food and took off the glass and bowl. Clearing his mind of all thought, he gripped the tray firmly between his hands and opened himself to the sensations.

He could feel his captor's presence. He concentrated and it flowed into him—bitterness, stubbornness and fear. Yes, mingled with the antagonism and distrust was a strong thread of fear. It seemed absurd that the man should fear him, so Alex dug more deeply, pulling at the sensations in a way he never had before. And, there, sunk deep inside, was the bedrock on which his fear sat—superstition. Primitive, unreasoning superstition, the kind that set men on witch hunts.

Witchery, the man had said. Dearborn had convinced the man that Alex was capable of working magic. Seeing this dark, stagnant pool of ignorance and fear inside his jailer, Alex guessed that it had not been hard to do. Alex set down the tray and began to pace, thinking. There must be some way to use this knowledge.

A time or two in his life, Alex had wondered if his ability worked both ways. They had been small, insignificant things—he had been reading a book of Theo's, thinking how hungry he was but unwilling to pull himself away from the book, and after a few minutes Theo had stuck his head in the door, asking why Alex hadn't come down for tea. Another time he had talked one of their tutors into allowing them to skip their last hour of studies, and afterward he had wondered if the fact that he was holding the tutor's pencil had helped him convince the man.

He had dismissed them as silly, impossible ideas. But what if it *was* possible to touch another's mind or rouse their feelings from afar by using his talent? And if it were, wouldn't the sort of mind that was ruled by superstition be easier to sway? Alex was frankly desperate enough to try anything.

Picking up the tray again, he clamped both hands

on it and focused. When he felt the faint tingle of the man's presence, the trickle of his emotions into Alex's consciousness, Alex directed his own thoughts back into the channel, swimming upstream. It was difficult and strange, and Alex felt a kind of pressure building in him. Then suddenly he broke through, and his thoughts began to mingle with the other man's. He pushed all his will into the Scotsman, urging him to come to Alex. He could feel the other's resistance, then the gradual lessening as fear opened up a path for him.

Alex imagined himself lying ill on the floor. Who would be held liable for killing a peer of the realm if Alex died? Certainly not Dearborn; no, it'd be the Scotsman who'd go to prison. To the gallows. He felt the alteration in the man's emotions, the sudden uneasiness, and he pushed hard on resentment of Dearborn for putting him in this position.

But still the man dithered, his mind circling. Alex redoubled his efforts. Now he infused his thoughts with the threat of magic. He encouraged and increased the guard's belief that Alex was a sorcerer. Alex could reach through walls with his talents; he could turn himself into air and vanish from the room.

He heard footsteps at the far end of the hall, and Alex jumped to his feet. The man stopped. Cursing himself for letting go of the connection in his excitement, Alex once again clamped his hands around the tray and shot his power back into him. Redoubling the fear, he urged the other man to look in the cell, to reassure himself that Alex was still there and not dying.

Without letting go of the tray, Alex flattened himself against the wall beside the door, out of sight of the narrow spy window. He could hear the man pacing about in the hall, his halting steps toward the door. Finally he was at the door.

"Here! You!" His voice was high and thin, at odds with the bluster in his manner. "Show yerself. More- land!" The man pounded his fist against the wall, then stood there, waiting, breathing heavily.

Open the door, Alex urged. *Open the door and see if he's flown.* The key rattled in the lock, and slowly the door eased open. The guard eased his head cau- tiously around the door. Alex, waiting with hands upraised, smashed the tray into the guard's face. The other man staggered back, letting out a howl and clutching his bleeding nose.

Alex stepped forward and swung again, coming down so hard on the side of the man's head that the wooden tray cracked. The guard hit the wall and bounced off, going to his knees. He wobbled, then collapsed on the floor.

Alex stepped over his body and out the door, pull- ing it shut behind him. The key was still in the lock, and he turned it, then ran for the stairs at the end of the hall. He was alert for someone to pop out of another room or to be waiting for him at the top of the stairs, but there was no one to impede him. He emerged into a warehouse, piled high with crates, and ran down the aisles they created until at last he found the doors and burst out onto the street.

Pausing for a moment to orient himself, he took off at top speed, running to Sabrina.

CHAPTER THIRTY-THREE

DEARBORN'S WORDS SLICED through Sabrina. She thought of Alex, imprisoned somewhere, left to die. It was all her fault. She swallowed the sob that wanted to burst out of her and faced Dearborn. He waited, calm and expectant. He was sure she would crumble. Faced with anger, influenced by his manipulation of her guilt and her debt to them, racked with fear for Alex, Dearborn knew she would back down.

She stiffened her spine. "Then I suppose we are at a standstill."

He snorted. "You're bluffing. You won't leave."

That was true, of course, but she had to make him believe her. There was no hope of saving Alex without learning where he was.

"No?" Sabrina raised a contemptuous eyebrow and started toward the door.

Peter stepped in front of the closed door into the hallway, blocking it. She stopped.

Behind her, Dearborn rasped, "Don't be a fool. You aren't leaving here."

Sabrina tightened her grip on her parasol. Perhaps she really would have to use it as a weapon. She swung back toward Dearborn. "You intend to kidnap me, as well? How many more people will you abduct? Lilah knows where I am. She knows about your plot.

By now, I'm sure the entire Moreland clan knows. They'll soon be knocking down your door. Do you intend to do away with all of them?"

Almost as if planned, a thunderous pounding began on the front door. Dearborn's head snapped in that direction, his face almost comical in its dismay. There was the muffled sound of voices, then a clear "Get out of my bloody way!" followed by a resounding crash.

"Really, Con!" Lilah's voice came through the door. "Did you have to knock him into the vase?"

"Yes." Con's voice was so much like Alex's that it made Sabrina's heart hurt. He flung open the double doors.

Peter had whirled in surprise at the noise in the hall. Con grabbed Peter by the lapels and flung him aside, then charged at Dearborn. Dearborn skittered back, knocking into a table and going down in a heap. Con hauled the older man to his feet, shaking him.

"Where is he? Where the hell is my brother?"

"Con, he can hardly talk with you shaking him like that." Lilah entered the room in Con's wake and hurried over to hug Sabrina.

Tom Quick entered last, going to Con and tugging on his arm. "Here now, sir. You're choking the man."

Con dropped his hands away. "I'd like to. And I will, if he doesn't tell me where Alex is right now."

Dearborn stepped back, straightening his jacket and trying to regain some shred of dignity.

"You're a madman. I have no idea what you're talking about."

"I think I can persuade you to come up with one." Con doubled his fist.

"Mr. Dearborn, for pity's sake." Sabrina joined them. "Have you gone mad? How do you expect to get away with abducting a duke's son? If you have any hope of saving yourself, tell us what you did with Alex."

"What the devil is wrong with you, Sabrina?" Dearborn lashed out in frustration. "Peter is offering you his name. It's your only hope of salvaging any shred of reputation. No decent man would marry you now. It's obvious you went traveling around with Moreland, alone, unchaperoned."

"I was with them," Lilah said.

Dearborn shot her a withering glance. "I would have thought better of you, at least, Lilah. We all know that's a lie. You were at Broughton House pretending to be Sabrina while she was spending time with her lover. That was obvious as soon as we saw the two of them come sailing back in the other day." Dismissing her, he whirled back to address Sabrina, "It wasn't the first time you've been alone with a man, either. You and Peter shared a bedroom the night—"

"You dare to bring that up?" Sabrina cried.

"That doesn't matter," Lilah said. "No one knows about that."

"Oh, but they will," Dearborn said meaningfully. "Your reputation is in shreds, Sabrina. You have to marry Peter."

"I won't."

"You have no other choice. If you think your precious Alex will marry you, you are sadly mistaken.

No doubt you're fine for dallying with, but a duke's son will look much higher for a wife, believe me."

"And that, Dearborn, is where you are mistaken."

EVERYONE IN THE room whirled around to see Alex standing in the doorway, leaning casually against the frame, his arms crossed. There was a trace of a smile on his lips, but it was as cold as his eyes. "You see, I fully intend to marry Miss Blair."

"You! You— You're—" Dearborn spluttered.

"What?" Alex raised an eyebrow. "Did you really think you could contain me there?"

"Alex! Oh, Alex!" Sabrina broke from her momentary paralysis and ran to him, throwing her arms around his waist, and he curled his arms around her.

Con grinned at his twin. "What took you so long?"

"Sorry. I was a bit delayed." Alex returned an identical smile. "Hope I didn't inconvenience you."

"Not a bit," Con said cheerfully. "I was just about to have a conversation with this chap." He glanced contemptuously at Dearborn. "You saved me a scraped knuckle or two. What do you say? Shall Tom and I take him to jail for you?"

"Jail!" Dearborn looked thunderstruck.

"What did you think would happen to you?" Alex set Sabrina aside and stalked toward the man. "You've abused the trust Sabrina's father placed in you and have been bilking his estate for years. You abducted me. Worse, you abducted my future wife. You drugged her. You and your son concocted a scheme to fool her into thinking she had married him. Your cur of a son hit her. She had to run for her life from

the two of you. I don't really want to put you in jail.
I'd like to *kill* you."

Rage contorted Dearborn's face, and he leaped at
Alex. Alex met his rush, looking, Sabrina thought
with some astonishment, pleased. Raising his left arm
to block Dearborn's wild swing, Alex punched him
in the stomach. As Dearborn doubled over, the air
whooshing out of him, Alex hit him with an uppercut
to his chin, and the man went down in a heap.

"Stop! No! He's an old man!" Peter cried, rushing
over to his father and kneeling beside him, propping
him up as Dearborn struggled to breathe.

Alex squatted down and looked into Peter's face,
his eyes blazing. "Listen to me. Listen well. I have
proof of every crime I just listed. Not only Sabrina's
word or mine. I have written evidence of the many
times Dearborn embezzled money from Sabrina's
fund. And your friend Fairfield signed a confession."

"What?" Peter's jaw dropped.

Alex smiled faintly at Peter's alarm. "Nothing
would give me greater pleasure than to toss your father and you in prison and let you rot. But for Sabrina's sake, and that alone—because her father was
Dearborn's friend, because of the affectionate regard
she holds for your mother, because I will not have any
scandal even *touch* Sabrina's good name—I don't intend to press charges against him or you…yet."

Peter looked at him sullenly. "What do you mean,
yet? Do you intend to make us suffer, wondering
when you will ruin us?"

"No, that's the way you and he would think, not I.
I won't reveal any of this as long as you meet my conditions. You take him to your home in the country.

You stay away from me and mine. You say nothing of any of this, and you never, ever come anywhere near Sabrina or attempt to contact her again. Am I clear?"

Peter nodded, clenching his jaw. "I understand."

"I hope you do. Because if I hear of any scandal regarding my future wife, if there is even the slightest bit of gossip about Sabrina, if you ever so much as speak to her again, I will come down on you like the wrath of God. Your name will be ruined, and you and your father will spend the rest of your lives in prison."

Alex held his gaze until Peter dropped his eyes. Alex stood up and turned to the others. "I think we're done here."

ON THE CARRIAGE ride home, Alex regaled them with the story of his capture and imprisonment, and because of Lilah's presence, he carefully omitted all mention of his unusual ability. Con, frowning slightly, said, "Yes, but I don't understand. How did you lure him to open the door?"

"I pretended to be ill." Alex sent his twin a look.

Con's eyebrows flew up and he settled back in his seat, then said, "Ah. I see now."

"What about you?" Alex asked, directing the conversation away from that precarious subject. "How did the three of you wind up there?"

"Sabrina went running to the Dearborns to save you," Lilah began.

"I got a letter from them," Sabrina explained. "Just a note and your cuff link." She held it out to him.

"I wondered where that had gotten to." Alex plucked it from her fingers, his eyes warm on hers.

"So you went to sacrifice yourself to obtain my release."

"Well, I hoped to discover your location from them somehow and rescue you before I had to go that far."

"It was terribly dangerous. I'm sorry you were worried so."

"You'll find Alex manages to extricate himself from the places he keeps getting locked up in." Con grinned at his brother. "At least no jumping across roofs this time, eh?"

"No. I was grateful. I'm no longer as agile as I was at ten."

"But how did you and Con and Mr. Quick come to be there?" Sabrina asked Lilah.

"Did you think I would let you throw yourself into the fire? I sent a note to Con's office, telling him where to go, and then I went after you. Just as I was leaving, Con ran up, shouting that something had happened to Alex."

"I had one of those stabs of twin-ship." Con glanced at Alex. "You know."

"I do. I hoped you might."

"I was in a meeting with the old man's agent, pinning him down on the illegal payments, and suddenly it hit me. I jumped up and took off. No doubt he's convinced I'm quite mad now."

Lilah continued the story. "I told Con where Sabrina had gone, and we jumped in a hack. Tom had gotten my note, and since Con was not there, he came himself. He got there while Con was arguing with the footman at the door." She turned toward Con. "I still think you could have gained entrance without resorting to violence."

"It wouldn't have been nearly as satisfying," Con retorted.

Sabrina jumped in to forestall an argument, saying, "Here we are. Oh, look, Megan and Theo are hailing a hack." She paused, then added, "Um, Theo is carrying a gun."

Alex stuck his head out the window to flag down the couple. "No need! Stay there."

"How do they know where to go?" Lilah asked, staring in some astonishment.

"No doubt Phipps told them," Con said lightly. "Nothing happens in that house that Phipps doesn't know."

It took some time to explain everything that had happened to the gathered members of the household. Leaving Con to describe the final scene, Alex slipped from the room, drawing Sabrina away with him. He led her down the hall and into the secluded room where she and Lilah had listened in on the Dearborns' conversation. There he did what he had been longing to do from the moment he'd entered the Dearborns' house. He pulled Sabrina to him and kissed her, then simply held her tightly.

"I was so scared when I got back here and Phipps told me where you had gone. I hoped Con would reach you in time, but I was scared you would jump into something dreadful to save me." He pulled back and gave her a stern look. "Don't ever do that again. Promise me. Con's right. I'm like a cat. I'll always manage to find a way out."

Sabrina chuckled, but he could hear the tears in her voice. "I can't promise that." She tightened her arms around him for a moment, then sighed and said, "Oh, Alex…what a coil this is. You must know I will not hold you to your announcement of marrying me."

Alex went cold inside and his arms fell away. "Of course. I'm sorry. I didn't intend to obligate you."

She nodded, stepping back and wiping away a tear.

Alex forced himself to go on. "I—I know that you are young, and it would be foolish to commit yourself. You need time to gauge your feelings. To have fun, meet other men and…" He could not manage to get anything else out.

"Meet other men? Why would I want to do that?"

"Well, you know…because you have a choice now. You can decide what you want to do freely, no longer under pressure from Dearborn. And away from the excitement and emotion of this moment, as well." He smiled at her faintly, though his heart ached at releasing her. "But I must warn you, Sabrina, I won't give up. I mean to court you, to win your heart."

Sabrina stared. "Win my heart! What are you talking about? You have already done that."

Alex gazed back at her, nonplussed. "But you just said you didn't want to marry me simply because I told Dearborn I was going to."

"Well, of course I don't want to marry you because you said that!" she responded, putting her hands on her hips. "Who would want to marry for such a reason? I don't want to…to use your sense of duty and obligation to trap you into a marriage you don't want."

"Don't want! Sabrina—"

She rushed on over his words, pacing about. "I realize you cannot marry me. My name, my lineage, is not at all what one expects for a duke's son, and even if you've scared the Dearborns into not revealing any of this, it wouldn't be surprising if something leaked out. There have been many people who have seen us together—think of all the people at that party who witnessed the scene with the Dearborns. Not to mention servants and innkeepers and—" She swept her hands out in a vague gesture of inclusion.

"Sabrina, stop." Alex grabbed her hands in his and pulled her to a halt. "Listen to me. None of that matters to me. You must know that. I'm a Moreland. I have never been conventional, and I never shall. I don't care about your name or lineage, and I doubt very much you could make my family more scandalous than they already are."

"But you said—"

"I said I don't want to force you or maneuver you into marrying me because of what I said—or because of anything else. It's not my choice—it's yours. I don't have a choice—I love you."

She stood stock-still, gazing at him in surprise. "What?"

"I love you." He looked at her quizzically. "Surely you must know that."

"But you never said anything. You said I would be free to leave—and you didn't even say you would be sorry to see me go!"

"I couldn't take advantage of you, tie you to me when you were caught up in the emotion of the moment. Because you were grateful."

"I'm not! I mean, well, of course I am grateful for all your help, but that isn't why I love you!"

Alex's heart seemed to roll at her words, and he had to fight for cool rationality. "You're young—you have no experience with the world. You don't know—"

"If you tell me I don't know what I want, I shall scream." Sabrina jerked her hands from his. "I don't care if I won't be twenty-one for another week. It doesn't matter that I've lived a quiet life. I know perfectly well what I want. And what I want is *you*!" She crossed her arms and glared at him.

Alex began to laugh, then reached out and pulled her to him. "I think perhaps we are being extremely silly."

Sabrina resisted for a moment, trying to keep up her glare, but she gave in and began to laugh, going into his arms. "You never told me."

"You never told me," he countered.

"How could I tell you my feelings when I didn't know if you returned them?"

"Then let me make myself clear," Alex said in a determined tone. "I love you. I loved you the moment I saw you. I have never felt with any woman what I feel for you. Without you I will never be whole again."

"Oh, Alex." Sabrina took his hands in hers, gazing up at him with eyes filled with love. "Don't you see? We are already joined, you and I. When you were gone, you were still in here." She laid her hand over her heart. "You will always be here. And I refuse to wait a few years just to suit appearances. You may be unwilling to push me, but I am not so delicate. Alexander Moreland, will you marry me?"

"Spoken like a true Moreland female." Laughing, Alex picked up Sabrina and swung her around in a joyous circle. "Of course I will marry you." He set her down and looked into her eyes. "I love you more than words can say…though I assure you I will say them all anyway."

"And I love you."

"Well, then…" His eyes gleamed devilishly. "I think it's time we stopped talking. Don't you?"

* * * * *

LET'S TALK
Romance

For exclusive extracts, competitions
and special offers, find us online:

f facebook.com/millsandboon

⊙ @millsandboonuk

𝕏 @millsandboon

Or get in touch on 0844 844 1351*

For all the latest titles coming soon, visit
millsandboon.co.uk/nextmonth